PRAISE FOR LAUR~

"Laura L. Zimmerman's YA fantasy *Keen* enthralled me from beginning to end. This present day Faerie story featuring a baffled teenage banshee and her unlikely high school friends has heart, lots of twists and turns, and a great message about using one's gifts for good. *Keen* would be the perfect next read for fans of Holly Black's Folk of the Air series and Maggie Stiefvater's *Lament*."

~Carrie Anne Noble, award-winning and bestselling author of *The Mermaid's Sister*

"A powerful story of an outcast discovering the beauty of her own voice, filled with memorable characters and vivid twists, Laura L. Zimmerman's spellbinding debut *Keen* will echo in your memory long after you've turned the last page like the eerie final note of a banshee's song."

~Kara Swanson, award-winning author of *The Girl Who Could See*

"I haven't devoured a book this quickly in a long time! Its unique premise, relatable characters, rising stakes, swoony romance, and engaging narrative style make *Keen* a perfect stay-up-all-night kind of read, complete with a beautiful message of healing and self-worth. Laura L. Zimmerman has launched herself right to the top of my list of favorite paranormal fantasy authors!"

~Laurie Lucking, award-winning author of *Common*

"A fantastic debut! Zimmerman draws the reader into the multifaceted world of *Keen*, where nothing is as it seems. I loved the characters and found myself fully invested all the way to the last beautiful page. I can't wait for the sequel!"

~J.M. Hackman, award-winning author of *Spark*

"The lure of the banshee's song is irresistible in life (and death), and it's no different in *Keen*. I was pulled into the story from the first line to the last. Laura Zimmerman's debut novel is intriguing, engaging, and hard to put down. I can't wait to see more from her!"

~Pam Halter, award-winning author of *Fairyeater* and the Willoughby and Friends Series

"A modern twist of mythical Irish folklore, *Keen* packs a fast-paced punch along with well-developed characters. I couldn't put it down!"

~Missy Kalicicki, co-author of the Sinners Series

"The modern faerie tale I've been waiting for! *Keen* grips you from the first page and pulls you into a story you won't want to leave—rife with magic, teaming with incredible characters, and filled with the promise of hope in a dark world."

~Ashley Townsend, author of the Rising Shadows Trilogy

"*Keen* weaves such a fantastical mystery, in a sense that your nose will remained glued to the page until you've pulled back every layer and uncovered every hidden clue. Nothing is ever simple for a banshee living through high school."

~Desiree Williams, author of *Illusionary* and *Sun and Moon*

"A banshee tale? So here for it! *Keen* is a powerful story of friendship, love, loyalty, and sacrifice where snappy dialogue and evocative prose paint a vivid backdrop for delightful and dangerous hints of faerie. Snag your copy ASAP!"

~Gillian Bronte Adams, author of the Songkeeper Chronicles

"A captivating story that will enchant you from the very first page. In *Keen*, Laura L. Zimmerman balances the fantastic and the everyday to give us a world that feels both profoundly relatable and strikingly beautiful. *Keen* deftly navigates its themes of belonging, vulnerability, and love, giving readers a page-turning adventure that will keep them reading late into the night."

~Catherine Jones Payne, author of the Broken Tides Series

"Fans of clean YA paranormal romance will be swept away by this brooding debut from Laura L. Zimmerman. A small-town twist on centuries-old Irish lore, a journey of self-discovery, and a healthy side of teen angst—what's not to love?"

~Lindsay A. Franklin, award-winning author of *The Story Peddler*

Keen

BANSHEE SONG SERIES
◄ BOOK ONE ►

ALSO BY LAURA L. ZIMMERMAN

Now Available:

Keen

Banshee Song Series, Book One

Coming Soon:

Lament

Banshee Song Series, Book Two

Silence

Banshee Song Series, Book Three

Keen

BANSHEE SONG SERIES
◄ BOOK ONE ►

LAURA L. ZIMMERMAN

Love2ReadLove2Write Publishing, LLC
Indianapolis, Indiana

Published by Love2ReadLove2Write Publishing, LLC

Indianapolis, Indiana

www.love2readlove2writepublishing.com

Library of Congress Cataloging-in-Publication Data is on file at the Library of Congress, Washington, DC.

ISBN-13: 978-1-943788-40-8 (Ebook edition)

ISBN-13: 978-1-943788-39-2 (Paperback edition)

Library of Congress Control Number: 2019943542 (Paperback edition)

This is a work of fiction. Names, characters, incidents, and dialogues are products of the author's imagination and are not to be construed as real. Any resemblance to actual events or persons, living or dead, is entirely coincidental.

Cover Design by Sara Helwe (www.sara-helwe.com)

For Tim
Thank you for nineteen years of listening to my songs
and keeping my cloak in place.
I wouldn't have found my way without you.

1

CAOINE

I AM CURSED and I am blessed. I am the harbinger of death and I am sent to protect.

I am also late for my first day of school.

The bell rings as the last few stragglers race across the hall to their classrooms. I clench my class schedule and swear inside my head. Why didn't I take the guidance counselor up on her offer to give me a tour of the school yesterday?

I've changed schools sixteen times in twelve years, but nothing about this has become normal.

I brush aside my platinum-white hair so I can see which direction I need to go, then let my long tendrils fall back in place. Better to hide, for now. My odd-colored eyes and pasty skin will scare away most of the students by midday anyway.

No need to rush it.

I stand alone in the middle of the hallway, close my eyes, beg for just an inch of peace to splash across my chest, to center my head before I dive into the lion's den. *The new girl in school has arrived.* No big deal, right?

Sweat gathers along my upper lip, but I swipe it away before I continue searching for my class. I've done this far too many times. I already know how this day will end. My legs go shaky, and I glance at the room numbers once more.

As it turns out, I only have to walk past two more rooms before I find the one I'm looking for. I look at my now-crumpled schedule. *Senior-level British Literature.* Right.

Five seconds pass as I listen to the drone of the teacher inside. Another five pass. *Just get this over with.* With a swallow and a hiccup, I yank on the door, wait for the inevitable crash of a million stares meant only for me. The teacher stops talking. My cheeks light on fire.

I duck my head and cross the front of the room, my schedule held before me like a surrendering flag.

He smiles. "You must be the new student. Mrs. Harding told me to expect you." He glances at my schedule and frowns.

"It's pronounced *Cane*," I say, but not loud enough for any in the class to hear. The fewer people who know me, the better. For their sakes and mine.

His smile broadens, but I'm careful not to look directly into his eyes. No doubt my appearance has already thrown him, though at least he doesn't flinch like most do. But my eyes — they're another story.

Remember the rule, Caoine. Never let anyone see your eyes.

"Well, Miss Roberts, it's a pleasure to have you in my class. We're only two weeks into the school year, so you shouldn't have a problem catching up. Take a seat and we'll continue."

Again, I don't bother to look up. I've learned through the years there's always a seat somewhere in the back of the room. In every classroom, in every school in America.

I snake my way through the desks and ignore the weight of the eyes that follow me. I know what has the students transfixed, unable to tear their gazes away. My skin, so white it's almost unnatural, the same shade as my long curtain of hair. I've received the same response from every person throughout my life. But I will never grow used to it.

A single seat waits for me, close to the exit. My heart skips a beat with relief. At least my escape will be quick. The teacher continues with *A Midsummer Night's Dream*. Surprise, surprise. British Literature always = Shakespeare. Another thing that never changes from one high school to another.

I slide into my chair and get busy stuffing my backpack away and pulling my books onto my desk. Another three seconds, and the final stares will return to the front of the room and away from me.

Three, two, one . . .

The girl beside me doesn't look away.

Stop staring! I can see her in my peripheral. *Turn away, girl, leave me alone.*

Her black Doc Martens tap the floor, as if she has a song in her head.

I flip open my textbook and search for the page the teacher is salivating over. Doc Marten girl still watches me. I press my lips together. *Maybe I'm not the only freak in this school. What is with her?* She shifts in her seat, and neon-colored chunky plastic bracelets clank together. *Does she even know what year it is?*

Still, she doesn't look away. I huff in frustration. She's forcing me to do something I don't want to do, something I never do on my first day of school.

I look over my other shoulder, check out the floor beside me. There's zero reason she should still be entertained by me. When I look forward again, I still feel her eyes worming their way beneath every layer of my skin. *Fine.*

Slowly, so slowly, I lift my gaze to hers, and wait.

Wait.

Wait.

Await the disgusted cringe that is sure to follow.

But instead . . .

She smiles. I gasp.

Then I blink.

No flinch? No hesitation whatsoever?

"Hi," she whispers. "I'm Aubree."

I don't answer. Why isn't she scared out of her mind? My eyes aren't normal. She should be wincing away.

Her smile deepens, and my belly does something weird. It warms, fills with something. Hope? She certainly isn't like any other high school girl I've met over the last few years.

She's got gray eyes and silver hair with pink tips that flows over her shoulders and down her back. She literally reminds me of a K-Pop star. Even though she's sitting, it's obvious she's tall. Like really tall. She holds out a hand for me to shake, her fingers long and slender. I gawk at it.

When I don't shake it, she continues to smile and waves it away, turning her attention back to the teacher, whatever his name is. I bite my lip and glance at Aubree out of the corner of my eye. She's still smiling. I furrow my brow.

In a world of extroverts, I'm the introverted snob no one understands. And I've been fine with that. I've had almost eighteen years to be fine with that. My chest tightens. Maybe Aubree might be different? Might not see me the way everyone else does?

I swallow and pretend to listen to the teacher, even though I have no clue what he's saying. It's not like I haven't heard this all before. My gaze shifts back to Aubree. She's doodling now in a journal. I tilt my head an inch. *Is that Princess Leia?*

Spit lodges in the back of my throat, and I choke. I attempt to hide my cough but not as hard as I try to hide my face as the class turns my direction.

That same fire returns to my cheeks. *Fantastic. Way to draw all the attention, Caoine.* I lick my lips. Tap my notebook.

But I can't keep my eyes from wandering back to Aubree's work of art. I squint. Right next to Leia is Darth Vader with a smaller rendition of Han Solo to the right of it. Star Wars. Aubree is a geek.

My eyes accidentally meet hers. She lifts her journal so I can see, her brows raised in question, as if she's asking if I want to see better.

4

I suck in a breath and look the opposite way. *Awesome, Caoine.* The idea is *not* to gain interest from fellow classmates just yet.

Forty minutes later, the bell rings, and instinct forces my head down to avoid gazes. I move fast, hoping to speed away before anyone else gets the bright idea to be friends with the new girl. Or worse, to begin endless questions about my appearance.

But Aubree is faster. As I slip out the door, she's right beside me.

"So what's your name?"

I watch her, unafraid to let my unusual eyes do their best to scare her. Again, she doesn't flinch. Instead she glances at the dumb schedule that's still in my hand for some reason, like it's my baby blanket I just can't let go of.

"Cao — Coi — Ceyoiay — " Her efforts look painful.

"You say it like sugar *cane*," I finally say.

"Oh." She smacks her forehead. "Wow! Butchered that one."

Her reaction is sincere. Kind. It brings a ghost of a smile to my lips, something that hasn't happened in a long time.

"It's okay." I clear my throat and attempt to talk a little louder, over the din of the surrounding students. "Everyone always does."

"Well, *Caoine* — did I say it right?"

I nod.

She grins. "Well, it's nice to meet you. Where are you headed next?"

I hold out my schedule. She frowns. "Bummer. We don't have any more classes together."

I blink. Why would she want to have another class with me?

I search her eyes. My above-average height usually puts me at eye level with most girls, but Aubree towers over me. Her ultra-lean physique reflects a cross between a basketball player and a supermodel. *What on earth do her parents feed her?*

"Well, what about lunch?" She raises her eyebrows. "Got plans?"

"No." I never do. And I like it that way.

"You do now." Her eyes sparkle as she adds a little skip to her step.

I look at my feet.

"You're sitting with me."

My head buzzes and my heart races in the opposite direction. I've never sat with anyone before.

I nod. Then freeze. *Wait. Did I just agree to something?*

She squeals. "Sweet!" She wags her brows. "Hey, I've gotta get going so I'm not late for my next class. See you later!"

She's gone. My body deflates in relief, even as a newfound struggle presents itself. I won't be meeting her for lunch. Today or ever. Lunchrooms and I haven't ever gotten along, not with their packed bodies and whispered gossip. And I don't anticipate getting along with one now.

I lope down the hall, maybe in the direction of my next class, maybe not, when a scream splits the air in two. The space around me convulses as students crash against me, pushing, clawing into the room to my right. Against my will, my feet take me with the wave of people as it crests and deposits me front and center in a room I've never seen.

My palms go sweaty, and I can't stop the pounding inside my ears, the constant beat that tells me I shouldn't be here. *I don't want to be here.*

Because I know what I'll find.

An elderly teacher lies facedown, unconscious. *Lifeless.*

A student bends over him, her face twisting. "He's dead."

My head spins. I already knew.

Goose pimples pop up along my arms, and a chill tickles the back of my neck. A pulse begins deep in my throat. A tick. A vibration I've come to understand all too well.

No. This can't be happening! This *shouldn't* be happening.

I dry heave and bend at the waist as I run from the room, punching and kicking and forcing my way through the crowd, away from the innocent.

Away from those I might hurt.

My head fills with lead, my chest about to burst. The world around me swims, warning that my song will explode from me no matter how hard I try to stop it.

If only I can get outside. *Maybe I won't hurt anyone else if I make it outside.*

Tears swim in my eyes, and I try in vain to swallow back my curse. But there's no stopping it.

There is never any stopping my curse.

As I step out a side door, my jaw falls open, and I scream unlike any human should be able to. Earsplitting, gut-wrenching—enough to convince any and all around me that the apocalypse has finally descended.

Somewhere behind me, glass breaks as I fall to my knees and grab my head. A headache the size of a school bus slams into my temples, and the light of day fades as voices float toward me, someone touching my arms, my shoulders.

I don't understand why my scream came so late, why the man died *before* the call came predicting his time on earth was at an end.

The man is dead because of me. He's dead because the banshee finally sang his song. He's dead, and once again, it's my fault.

2

CAOINE

THE SCENTS of Mexican food and stale beer crawls its way under my skin the minute I step through the door.

"Dad?" I yell to nowhere in particular.

His new job isn't supposed to start until tomorrow, but it's possible he's out on a beer run. He pops his head out of the kitchen.

Guess that answers that question.

"You're home early," he says, his words more accusation than statement.

I flinch, heat flooding my face. His brown eyes soften.

I sigh and toss my backpack onto the sofa, joining him in the kitchen. It's far too small for most people's taste, but it's exactly the right size for our compact house.

If only we could stay here.

The cabinets are clearly vintage, and the rooster wallpaper trim suggests the place hasn't been updated since the 1970s. But it's home. For now. Three empty beer bottles line the back wall of the sink, but it doesn't look like he's started his drinking for the day. Yet.

I slide onto a countertop and watch as he slices tomatoes. "Afternoon snack?"

He nods, a brown curl falling across his eye. "Nachos. Want some?" He glances over his shoulder at me. "I'll leave the meat off."

I shake my head, and my stomach flips upside down and back around. Nothing about this day has given me any semblance of an appetite.

"So you gonna tell me why you're home, or do I need to call the school?"

I roll my eyes. He'd never call the school. My life is strange enough as it is. He'd never betray me like that.

"There was—an incident." I swallow and hold my breath.

My dad stops chopping long enough to make the silence uncomfortable. Heat snakes along my neck and up my cheeks. Do I tell him the truth?

"A teacher died." I still don't breathe.

He looks up, brows pulled together. "At the school? During school hours?"

I can feel the insinuation beneath every word.

I press my lips together and nod.

My dad tosses down the knife and leans against the counter. "Spill."

Spices from frying meat press against my temples, force a lump into the back of my throat. I know what has him panicked. He's afraid we'll have to move. Again.

"The guy was old. It was a heart attack. Nothing out of the ordinary."

My dad visibly relaxes. "And?"

Should I tell him about my scream? About the way my banshee curse betrayed me and decided to come out in broad daylight? Which it has never, ever done before, not to mention while I was without my cloak I always wear when my banshee side comes out to play.

My gaze flicks to the beer bottles. "No. That's all. Grief counselors are at the school today and tomorrow for any students who want to talk about it." My palms sweat as my lie burrows deep inside my chest, plants its roots like thorns around my heart. Begins to grow.

A few seconds pass before my dad nods. "Good. As long as no one suspects . . ."

"It's fine," I say, my voice a little too cutting. "Our secret is safe."

Liar.

It's not at all safe. I completely passed out and had to be revived by one of the teachers. Not to mention the four windows I broke.

Oh right, the administration had an explanation for that. *A mild tremor must have come along just after the teacher collapsed.* Since earthquakes are *so* totally normal around here.

I sigh. At least no one mentioned the crazy inhuman scream I'd given minutes after the teacher died. Although I'm positive half the student body swung by my spot on the ground to check out the new freak girl who can shriek like a witch. *To see the monster I am.*

All those eyes boring into me, digging under layer after layer of my skin, beneath muscle and bone. Tearing into my soul and ripping holes that can never be stitched back together.

Anger boils in my belly, and I clench my teeth. "Can I be homeschooled?"

My dad jumps, then his expression settles into annoyance. He turns back to chopping veggies. "No. We've had this discussion a million times, Cay. That would be impossible. I have to work all day. There would be no one to teach you."

"But there are so many good online schools now—"

"I said drop it."

I glance away as his voice turns sharp. Razor sharp.

"It's good for you to be social. You need friends in your life. School has never killed anyone."

I snort at the irony of his statement. He doesn't join in my laughter. "But Dad, you don't get it—"

"I absolutely get it." He throws a look over his shoulder

that stops me short. "You're a teenager. Teenagers hate school. I'm sorry. You've got to go."

Except my hatred of school has nothing to do with school itself. I close my eyes and try to breathe. I only see more images of kids staring at me, judging me for the way I look, the way I sound, the way I—

I hate them. I hate them all. And I hate that my dad won't listen to me, refuses to hear me. If only he knew . . . if only I could tell him how my curse backfired today. How it threw me under the bus with a vengeance. How it came out far too late but far too early, all at the same time, totally mixed up and upside down and inside out and *absolutely wrong.*

If only I could tell him how I feel, how I hate every single stinking bottle of beer that has littered our lives, and how I can't stand that his life is miserable because of me.

Because of me.

Because of me.

All of this is my fault. Every single beer he drinks is blame I cannot dodge. Every. Single. One.

"Are we clear?" He crooks an eyebrow.

"Yes," I whisper, jumping from my perch and running to hide in my room.

It's clear I'm alone in this, just as I've always been. I'm the only girl my age with a curse. The only girl with darkness inside her, a darkness reflected with every song I sing, even though I so badly want to be light. The light I can never be.

I'm the only girl my age who kills people, even if she doesn't want to.

3

THE UNSEELIE PRINCE

SHE IS BEAUTIFUL. Skin as pale as a china doll, with pearl-white hair that radiates light as if she were light itself. Which she can be, if she only allows herself the chance. *Something I cannot allow.*

Both of her eyes are so pale they're almost white, one with a silver tint, the other, green. They hold depth, pain. But also so much more.

Hope. For the future, if she discovers herself to be light.

I tense, yet I dare not tear my eyes away from her.

She's built like a waif, her arms just a bit too thin, her hip bones jutting through her jeans in an unnatural way. Built just the way all faeries appear, the ones who haven't learned to glamour themselves, of course.

I walk beside the lockers in silence, track her down the hall at a distance. Her gaze flickers toward each classroom door. It's only her second day of school. Her first had been far more eventful than she'd planned, something I had a hand in . . . regrettably. Pain pierces my sternum.

It almost broke my heart to lead her on like that, to confirm her suspicions that she is the cause of death, the bringer of evil wherever she goes. It's right there in her name. She believes

Caoine means only to lament, to cry. But it's so much more. *It's always been so much more.*

Gentle. Beauty. Fair.

Good.

Yet she must never see herself as these things.

As she stops before a room, a boy moving a bit too fast bumps into her, a careless apology thrown over his shoulder as he races away. Her eyes avert to the floor. A curtain of hair covers her face like a veil on a wedding day. She squeezes her books to her chest a little tighter as she disappears within herself.

As she disappears.

Disappears.

I lean against a locker, my pulse racing inside my inhuman veins. Forehead tilted against hard metal, I swallow, accept the burning sensation the iron pulses into my skin. *So beautiful.* How can she not know what an amazing creature she is?

I raise my head, pull away from the pain.

So beautiful. Yet I cannot tell her. I can't even allow her to know of the light within her, of the good she can do. She believes she is defined by her role in the faerie kingdom, sees nothing beyond what she was groomed to do. The dark side of it, anyway.

I grind my teeth, run my fingers along the cold steel beside me, yearning for the sting once more. Father will never allow me to tell her, no matter how much I beg. In fact, I need her to believe the lies of whom she is to make the magic of my spell that much stronger. No matter how much it hurts me to hurt her, I must do what my king has sent me to do.

To save him. *To save my people.*

The bell rings, and her head whips up, her focus once again on that cursed door before her. Why won't she go in? What is she so afraid of?

I sigh, my gaze on those impossibly long legs, that lithe frame I will never know the privilege of holding. Father would flip if he knew I even had these thoughts. That I'd become so very weak. A stone sinks to the pit of my stomach.

People. That's what she's afraid of. People finding out about her gift, of the way she calls those destined to die to a better place. To a place of peace.

Her greatest fear is for her classmates to learn that she's a banshee, that she roams the streets at night, waiting to sing her song to the one for whom it's meant.

To give them comfort.

To show them love.

Love.

The hair on my arms and along the back of my neck stand on end.

She walks into the classroom, gone from sight, her closeness now only a memory. I close my eyes and clench my fists.

We would make the perfect couple, if circumstances were different.

If I hadn't been sent here to destroy her confidence and make her believe her gift is the cause of all death—death that comes from me alone.

I open my eyes, lift my chin, and straighten. I've been sent here to do a job. It's what I was born to do, and it's what I will do, despite my feelings. There was never a chance for a prince like me to lead a normal faerie life anyway. To ever know love.

The halls are empty as I spin on my heel and head to whatever class is able to hold my attention for more than five minutes. I've sat through every high school class in a half-dozen schools already.

Caoine is just a dream for me. But dreams are fleeting, not real. A false representation of the world. My reality is so much more. And it's time I started living it.

It's time to bend Caoine to *my* will. To that of my father's.

To break her. To use her.

Caoine Roberts must become the banshee I need her to be so I can finish the work my father sent me here to do.

4

CAOINE

THE MORNING IS GONE. My second day of school, and I wish it were over already. Grief counselors roam the halls, beckoning to any student who needs to talk about the events of the previous day.

I wish I could talk to one, but I could never tell them the truth. The real reason I jail myself inside a silent prison, fear, my only companion. Instead I duck my head and skitter down hallways between classes.

If only I could accept that the teacher's death had been an accident. Or anything besides premeditated. Can death be considered premeditated if someone knows about it before it happens but doesn't *want* it to happen? Except I didn't know this time. My curse failed me.

If only death didn't follow me everywhere I go.

But that's not what has me so on edge today.

I swallow back the bile that creeps up my throat and stare at the hummus and rye sandwich my dad so lovingly packed for me that morning. I sit beneath a stairwell in the east side of the senior wing. All the other kids in my class are in the lunchroom, on the west side. Where I should be.

Except, I can't be there. Not now.

I flip the note between my fingers, the one I found shoved in the slats of my locker just hours ago.

I know who you are.

My stomach clenches, and I squeeze my eyes closed.

It's a joke. It has to be a joke. No one knows me here, couldn't know anything about me. Couldn't know what I am. Not yet.

But—what if they did?

I crumple the small green square in my fist, push the vision of the even block lettering from my mind. *It's totally a joke, Caoine. There's just no way anyone can know.*

Still, I've hidden myself. As far from humanity as one can get while in a high school of thousands. Sigh. I shove the note in my pocket and focus on my sandwich.

I just needed a moment to clear my head, to wrap my brain around the fact that this will never end. That no matter how much I try, I can never stop death from following me everywhere I go.

My eyes sting, and I blink away the wet that gathers in the corners. I slump against the cold tile of the wall, my legs crossed Indian style. Dust bunnies that have probably lived here for years sway back and forth in the dark corner. As long as I don't move, no one will find me here. That is, as long as I don't gag on the musty odor that tells me something may have died here at some point.

The notepad balanced on one knee contains nine words. *Like the night split in two, my scream penetrates*— What? What comes next? I tap my pen against my lip as I think, the words dancing on the outskirts of my mind.

The one constant that hasn't changed between schools is the only outlet that keeps me sane—poetry. As long as I have my words, I won't need to be admitted to a mental hospital.

I massage my temples. Or maybe that would be better. Maybe people would stop dying.

"Hey. You okay?"

I jump and squint against the bright light of the hallway.

Guess my hiding spot isn't so secret.

I nod but don't move. Worn jeans and brand-name sneakers greet my gaze. My eyes stay glued to the floor. The boy is bent low, squatted as close to the overhang as he can manage without crawling beneath the stairwell with me.

"Do you need help or something?"

His voice is gentle, a pleasant tenor that makes my belly flip.

"No." I clear my throat. More explanation is needed. "Just having lunch." I wave my sandwich in the air and tuck my head so I can stare at my knees. My notepad falls gently to the ground.

He chuckles, and I fight to keep my toes from curling in embarrassment. My behavior always elicits this reaction.

"You're eating lunch under the stairs?"

"I'm fine." Anger stirs in my gut, and my voice is forceful now, impatient with his judgment.

He huffs, and I sense that he scratches the back of his neck. "You can eat with me, you know. I mean, I know it sucks being the new girl and all, but there's no need to torture yourself."

I freeze. How does he know I'm the new girl? Oh wait. He probably heard my ultra-weird scream yesterday. But why does he care?

"I'm fine," I say again. *Go away. I don't need your pity.*

What follows is silence. Awkward and never-ending.

He shifts his position but stays low. "Okay. But know that you can always join me tomorrow, if you want . . . Caoine."

I gasp. He knows my name? How does he know my name?

On instinct I raise my gaze to his . . .

. . . and my heart almost stops.

Every molecule in my body protests, chastises me for the mistake I've just made. *He. Will. Freak.* He won't understand what he sees.

But he doesn't freak. Not exactly. When our eyes lock, he

looks surprised, definitely unprepared. But not horrified or disgusted. He doesn't pull back or distance himself from me like most people do.

Instead, he leans forward. I hold my breath.

His eyes search mine, as if inspecting them, yearning to uncover the mystery behind them. "Your eyes," he whispers.

I stay quiet. What's he thinking? That they belong on a demon?

"They're the most beautiful eyes I've ever seen." His face mimics his message, his mouth parted just minutely. Awe tinges the way he looks at me.

My heart stutters. This isn't normal. No one thinks my eyes are beautiful. No one. Not even me.

"I'm Oliver." He holds out a hand.

And, for whatever reason, I extend mine to shake his. I look down at our linked hands. His skin is a dark brown, a sharp contrast to mine, which is far too pale. His hand is soft except for the tips of his fingers, which are rough, calloused. I glance back to his eyes, a muted brown with specks of gray hidden in a circle around the pupil. His lips are full, parted. Beneath them I can see a single tooth, turned, out of place. He closes his lips to grin as he takes his hand back and scratches it along his close-cropped hair.

"It's, uh, nice to meet you." His grin broadens.

My chest heaves as I concentrate on breathing, my muscles still frozen in place. He's not here to mock me? To mercilessly make fun of the way I look?

He pushes back and stands a few feet beyond the stairwell. "Maybe I'll see you tomorrow, then?"

I blink and lift my chin, wishing my lips would move, would say something—*anything*.

Why isn't he being mean to me?

One corner of his mouth tilts up. Then he turns and falls in step with another boy, a redhead who's been standing to the side. Muffled conversation fills the hall and dissipates as they fade away.

My heart slams against my ribcage, and I squeeze my fists, pull my knees against my chest.

What just happened? And why isn't he afraid of me?

It takes the rest of the lunch period to gather my confidence, to regain enough composure to face the rest of the school day. I throw my lunch away uneaten and slink to my next class before the bell rings, ready for the day to be over.

Ready to melt into the shadows of my new school.

Maybe tomorrow will be different. Maybe tomorrow no one will notice my existence. It'll be easier that way.

5

CAOINE

Two hours later, I'm hiding in the back of my final class of the day. I've almost memorized the map of the school and have become proficient at being the first student in each of my classes. It's easier to check in with teachers before anyone else arrives so the question about my name won't result in a long-winded discussion.

By the time the majority of the class files in for last period, I'm tucked away in the corner with my gaze focused on my lap, a long row of windows to my left and endless desks to my right. The room looks like every other in the building. Square, white, and cramped enough I have the constant threat of vomit in the back of my throat.

"Hey! Missed you at lunch," a chipper voice says.

I suck in a breath and dare to allow my line of vision to focus above waist level. My pulse does a tap dance inside my veins. Aubree has taken the seat beside mine, her long, thin legs crossed beneath the slit that goes up her maxi skirt. Black, strappy, high-healed sandals are on her feet. A stark-white peasant blouse would make it look like she was an ultra-trendy waiter if it weren't for the thick fuchsia belt around her waist and canary-yellow bangles along her wrists. Her hair is still silver but with azure tips this time, large silver hoop earrings dangling behind it. Every single finger holds a ring larger than life.

Goose pimples sprout along my arms as my brain races to find an excuse.

"I think Caoine needed a little down time over lunch." Oliver throws me a grin as he slides into the seat in front of mine. His friend with the red hair snags the seat in front of Aubree.

And my heart leaps out of my chest and decides to leave the building. I squeeze my eyes shut to make all the spots go away. Why are these people being so nice to me?

"Yeah, not everyone can be an extrovert on steroids, Aubree." Oliver's redheaded friend laughs and playfully kicks her foot.

"Ha ha, I'm not dumb, Eric." Aubree sticks her tongue out at him, her heavily mascaraed eyes scowling. "I just didn't know one needed to be *extroverted* to do things like *eat*."

I curl into myself another inch and pretend not to hear their conversation.

Oliver leans closer. "Hey, it's no big deal. The school's big, I get it. At least you know you'll have a couple of friends when you do decide to go."

"Yep!" Aubree literally bounces in her seat. "Take all the time you need, girl. I totally get it."

For whatever reason, my lips actually move and say, "Thanks."

My gaze barely raises to look at Oliver, who still wears that grin I don't deserve. I look to Aubree, who's being just as kind, but then I accidentally glance at Eric.

His reaction is exactly what I expect. Shock, followed by a cringe, then a false recovery where he tries to pretend he isn't mortified by my appearance. But then he does something different. He tilts his head and gives me a smile, all while he raises his eyebrows.

As if he knows. Like he knows who I am.

What I am.

My eyes lock with his, and I swallow. His smile deepens, and he gives me a slight nod.

My blood vessels clench tight, and I see those spots again. *He knows.* How can he know? No one has ever figured it out this soon before.

I glance around to find a few other students staring my way. A girl in the front row is turned sideways, her azure gaze heavy on mine. She wears a scowl. Her long, thin nose slopes downward, her full lips puckered. Long auburn curls tumble over her shoulders, and she sits straight, like she's a ballerina waiting to take her spot on stage. Despite her beauty, she looks as if she might devour me at any minute. I gulp and duck my head.

But then the teacher is talking, and Eric and Oliver have to turn around and Aubree no longer looks at me and somewhere along the way my heart decides to rejoin my body and pounds a thousand miles per hour to make sure I'm aware it's there.

The weight of everyone's stare is gone, and no one even looks my way anymore. Which should be a relief. But it only makes me feel empty.

Why do I feel so empty?

My cheeks warm as my gaze settles on the back of Eric's bright-red head. How could he possibly know what I am? There's just no way.

Seconds turn into minutes, but the class crawls by so much slower than any other class I've been in. Should I leave? Should I run home and tell my dad that someone at school found out? That we need to move again already?

The bell signals the end of school, and I don't bother to say goodbye to any of them. I don't have time. All I can think about is barreling home to my dad, confessing how badly I messed up. How I should've been honest with him yesterday, told him about that stupid scream I just couldn't keep inside no matter how hard I tried.

How my life has once more ruined his in every way possible.

I sprint from the room. Aubree and Oliver call after me, but I run. My locker is by the exit, which helps calm my nerves a little. The fluorescent lights are blinding, and I squint as I push against bodies, duck amidst high fives and end-of-the-day chatter. I dare to lift my eyes to see the numbers along the lockers but allow my hair to immediately cover my face as soon as I get my bearings.

1051.

I glide against the lockers, press my body as tight to the metal as I can and still twirl the heavy lock. The lock falls to the side, and I fumble with the books I need to take home. My sack of pencils drops to the ground, and I curse myself as I navigate bending down without getting knocked in the head by the mass of students that jostle around me.

As soon as I regain my composure, a figure blocks the commotion.

"Hey," Eric says, one shoulder leaning against the lockers.

I recoil but manage to keep my books in my arms. My eyes are trained on the middle of his chest, which is easy, since he's so very tall and so very thin. I watch the white skin of his neck as his Adam's apple bobs with a chuckle.

"You're fast," he says.

I don't move.

"So, um . . ." He adjusts his position on the locker so he's even closer to me. "I just wanted you to know that I *know*."

My gaze races to connect with his, and my belly drops to the floor. His smile is broad but sincere. How can he be so flippant about the fact that he knows what he knows? This is crazy!

"It's written all over your face, actually."

I look away. It is? Could others possibly know what I am? Heat barrels through my chest like a pack of wild wolves.

"I mean, I'm sure Oliver didn't pick up on it, but I did."

My eyes travel back to his. Oliver? What does he have to do with this?

"It's easy to see you're crushing on him. I could sense it the minute he sat next to you in class."

Eric thinks I'm crushing on Oliver? Saliva rushes back into my parched mouth, the band around my chest loosening half an inch.

"No worries." Eric gives me a wink. "Your secret's safe with me. I won't tell. Just thought I'd give you the heads-up so maybe you can try a little harder at keeping those emotions in check." He socks me in the arm like we're old friends.

I still don't move, but at least I can breathe again.

"Hey, I'll see you around, Caoine." He pushes away from the lockers. "You've got a strange name for a girl, you know that?" Eric laughs and heads down the hall.

Bodies continue to move around me, a whirlwind I can't stop nor want to stop. Students with lives and cares and all things that scream life pass me by while I stand frozen in place.

Eric doesn't know. I was wrong. I'm safe. For now.

I'm safe until someone finds out my secret. And then, my dad and I will move again. To keep them safe. From me.

To keep them safe from my curse.

6

CAOINE

I COME home to an empty house. My dad has gotten a job working construction, which means he'll be late. So I have no choice but to make myself supper and wait.

I'm always waiting.

Waiting for my curse to surface, waiting for the kids at school to hate me even more than they already do. Waiting for my dad to die of the alcoholism I've caused.

My stomach flips, and I let my spoon fall. The dining room light is still out, simply because I never bothered to turn it on. There's something therapeutic about sitting in the dark.

The door clicks as he walks in, covered in grime and stink and exhaustion. "Hey, hon." He takes off his hat and tosses it on the counter, scrubbing a hand through his curly brown tangles. Then he yawns.

I answer his greeting by gesturing to a reheated plate of pasta Alfredo across from me.

His grin is tight. "Thanks. How was school? I got a call about that history teacher who died yesterday."

"Yeah." I flex my jaw and avoid his gaze. *Please say they didn't mention my fainting spell.*

But before he sits down, his arms are around me and he's

pulling me into a hug. Which is totally awkward, since I'm sitting. "Hey, it's not your fault," he whispers. "Just remember that."

Okay, so I guess they didn't mention the passing-out thing. A lump forms in my throat, and I push away from him.

He pulls back and looks into my eyes. His, a medium brown, are such a contrast to my freak-of-nature eye color. "It sounds like he died of natural causes."

Should I mention he just said it wasn't my fault when we both know it absolutely was?

"We'll save the next one, right?" he says.

I swallow against stiff muscles. "Sure." Right. Because so far we'd saved so many people from my curse.

Exactly zero.

He kisses my forehead before he grabs his plate. "Things will be different here, Caoine. I can feel it. This is a new town, new possibilities."

I nod and force the doubt from my face. "I'm going to work on homework." Which isn't really true, since I finished the little I had already.

"All right, sweetheart." His smile is weary, strained.

I leave him to his thoughts—and the beer that will eventually take my place—and retreat to my room. Even though it's close to eight, I won't be going to bed anytime in the next few hours. Neither will he. My curse won't allow it. The ritual has always demanded we stay up past the witching hour.

My new room is still filled with boxes, distant and unwelcoming. But I don't feel like unpacking. Not now, anyway. I lie down on my bed and close my eyes, breathe, push images from the past two days out of my head. The teacher's face. Aubree's smile. The way Oliver doesn't flinch when he looks at me. Slowly, my body relaxes, falls into a rhythm of peace and tranquility. The buzzer on my alarm goes off. It's ten o'clock.

The curse always awakes sometime after ten, always at night—other than the freak show that happened yesterday. It usually awakes before midnight, although my curse has been known to stir past then. But for the most part it's kind to us, my dad and me. It allows us at least a few hours of sleep at night.

I don't know how much time passes. Five minutes? Thirty? Then I feel it. The urgency. A fire that burns deep inside my belly, that demands attention. Heat radiates to every limb, makes my head spin, sets my skin aflame. My fingers and toes buzz until I'm nauseated. This is it.

In one swift motion, I glide from my bed, slip my feet into shoes, and snatch my silver cape that hangs in my closet. It reaches my ankles and shines in the moonlight that filters through my window. The September night air is cool, but the chill won't penetrate my cloak. I pull the hood over my head, prepare my mind for my evening walk.

Ten seconds later, I rap my knuckles on Dad's door, alerting him, before I head downstairs and wait by the door.

Waiting. Always waiting.

I sense Dad behind me as he struggles into his shoes. He must have fallen asleep. Guilt stabs my heart.

It comes, the trance. The fire from my belly creeps up my torso, envelopes my neck, my face, my head. I clench my hands as pain tears across my upper body, leaves me gasping, arms trembling. I keep my eyes closed so Dad doesn't need to watch my transformation, how my irises turn pitch black, like the creature I am inside.

I'm gone, no longer Caoine but an evil that can't be described. I am no longer me. Yet I float above, watching, as I walk out the door, down the street, through the shadows of the night. Dad follows wordlessly. Like always.

I don't walk far this time, three blocks. I stop, the air around me in a swirl, echoing and screaming to my soul, begging me to stop the madness. But I can't. My curse won't allow me to stop. I can never stop.

My mouth opens, and the song tumbles along the wind,

carries to its victim, damns another life to an eternity away from earth. The music embodies every cell of my body, takes over any amount of self-control. Colors flash before my eyes, the vibration of nature in my ears, the finality of life balanced on my tongue. My cheeks are wet. Yet I sing.

The song is melancholy. A lament that would move even the most hardened of hearts. To the average hearer it is beauty, pleasure to be heard. A soft lullaby that helps them drift into slumber. The Gaelic words make no sense to me, never have. But they will to the person they're meant for. Their victim. The one who has only hours to live.

I sing for two minutes, cross into three. My body trembles, caves under the pressure. My trance breaks, and I collapse. My head aches. All I see are spots. The ground isn't solid beneath me any longer, like quicksand that wants to swallow me whole. To take me to another reality.

A bubble feels like it floats along the top of my spinal cord, moves slowly toward my neck. I'm blind. The noise of nature wounds like a freight train ready to slam into my head.

Then the pain hits.

It sharpens, a knife slicing across my forehead, along the base of my skull, literally inside my teeth. My head pulses like the beat of a drum. I can't focus, the world around me scatters into fragments of a puzzle with all the wrong pieces. Lights flash and dance even though my eyes are closed. Nausea invades me, an overwhelming feeling of sadness. I moan in agony.

Dad holds me, removes my hood, pushes hair from my face. "Shh. It's okay. It's done now. I'm here."

The buzzing returns to my hands and feet, nausea back in my stomach, my spirit one with my body once again. I struggle to my feet.

We're standing in the middle of a playground, at the end of a street in the next development over. My heart sinks, and my beautiful wail from a minute before turns into real weeping.

My dad swipes at my tears, pulls me in to the warmth of his body. "It's okay, baby. Next time."

"I'm sorry," I say. Because I really am. I'm sorry for the victim and for the family and for the way I've failed them. "I tried to withstand it this time. The pain."

"I know, sweetheart. You can't control your gift."

My gift. The sick in my stomach lurches to my mouth.

"Next time," he says.

"How do you know? Why are you so sure I need to leave my hood in place? What's so special about my cloak?"

He sighs, strokes my hair. "I've been through it a thousand times, sweetheart. Your cloak has to be the clue. It's got to be the key to how your gift works."

I swallow to shove back the way I want to gag on that word. *Gift.*

"Next time you'll be able to leave the hood in place, to make sense of the images. We'll save them next time."

And my heart breaks like shards of glass because I know he believes it. I stifle a shiver and allow him to guide me home, to return me to the safety of our house.

I hang my cloak in my closet and slip into my pj's, my bed never close enough to swallow me once my banshee song is complete. I lie in bed and cry angry, hot tears for the person whose life I've just doomed. Pathetic mourning tears, wishing I could take it back. That I could take back every scream I've ever given throughout the years. From every family I've allowed my keening to envelop in tragedy.

Grieving pain for the monster I am.

7

CAOINE

THE PAPER IS CRUMPLED and torn. I pull the note from the depths of my backpack as I stand next to my locker, door open. My heart slams against my chest in a steady cadence of fear and dread. I blow at a stray piece of hair that's fallen across my brow as I flatten the green stationary against a book, my eyes adjusting to the neat, box-like script scrawled across it. Familiar handwriting. My stomach drops to my feet.

Late night?

Two small words. My world caves in from all sides, forms pressure along my temples, inside my chest, across my belly. My legs shake, and there is no air.

No air.

No air.

Why can't I breathe? I read the words again. *What does it mean?* Again. *How could they know?* Again.

"Where have you been hiding all day?"

I flinch and drop my book, along with the note, into my locker. Aubree stands over me, a silly grin on her face.

Tell her. You should tell her. No. I can't mix her up in something that's nothing. This is just a prank from a bloodthirsty student who wants to bully me. Right?

My fingers fumble along the zipper of my pack, and I end up dropping that, too. I blink away the streaks of light that invade my vision, and my gaze darts to every person within a ten-foot radius.

Who gave me that note?

"Caoine?"

I jump again, clutching the locker door like a lifeline. *Aubree.* She's here, talking to me. I focus on my toes and concentrate on breathing.

Breathe, breathe. There's no one here. It's just a prank. No one can possibly know. Not yet.

I swallow and look at her. Her silver hair is pulled into two messy buns on the sides of her head, and she's sporting thick-framed glasses. She's covered her sequined tank with a layered jacket made of a strange fabric that looks like it stepped right out of the 1970s. Her army pants are covered in patches and buttons, and her shoes are cute Oriental slippers. With bells. Somehow the entire ensemble flows together, a flawless extension of Aubree's personality.

I look around at my fellow students once more, searching for the mysterious note giver. No one even looks in my direction.

"I missed you," she says.

I blink at her. *Oh right.* That whole avoidance thing. I pick up my book and add it to the pile in my backpack so I won't have to come back later.

"You can really disappear when you want, huh?" Her gaze is sympathetic, and my heart trips over itself.

Yeah. My people are really good at hiding. Instead I say, "I've been around. It's lunchtime so—"

"Yes, I know. That's why I'm here. To take you to lunch." She nudges some random dude standing behind her, but he just grunts a greeting, his gaze attached to the old-school handheld Nintendo in his hands.

Every muscle in my body tenses. I have a poem in my head

that's floating around, restless, eager to bleed onto my trusty notebook pages. Not to mention I now have a strange stalker to find as well. "But I —"

"I, whatever, girl. Come on. You're coming with me." She slips one arm around my shoulders and guides me in a direction I've never been before. Random dude just follows.

I pout. Drat.

Other students slink around us, but none look our way. Which is odd, since normally I'm the freak of nature everyone stares at. But no one appears particularly interested in the unusually tall Asian-American girl and the Albino chick with strange eyes or the also unusually tall Asian-American guy following close behind. Everyone seems . . . normal. I duck my head as she drags me through the halls.

Once we entered the cafeteria, my nerves go all jittery. I can't help but look around in disdain. These people. Ugh. They are so everything I'm not, as they often like to remind me. At least in other schools they've gone out of their way to remind me of this. I assume this one will be no different. My belly bubbles with anger as I think of the year to come. The humiliation and pain that most assuredly awaits me once the taunting begins and they find my weakness.

I spy the most remote table in the corner, break from Aubree's grasp, and beeline to it. I'd rather be alone. Life is always much easier alone.

They've hit the lunch line and are back in minutes. She giggles at something random dude has said and settles beside me, her tray of food overflowing with fries and chocolate cake. He sits across from her, empty-handed. Why did he even bother to go through the line? A waft of fried goodness slaps me from across the table and mixes with other scents like B.O. and aftershave. I pull out my brown paper sack and find my celery and carrot sticks.

"So, Caoine. Meet Seamus. Seamus, meet Caoine." Her voice is a little singsongy as she points to random dude.

I allow my gaze to drift up a few inches but make sure not to make direct eye contact with him. He apparently doesn't care. He's sort of slumped in his chair, one arm slung over the back, entirely bored by the situation, although in a very non-snobbish sort of way. It's more like he really doesn't care about anyone or anything, but he doesn't care that he doesn't care and he's not concerned about making himself look like he doesn't care.

The whole scene makes my head hurt.

The one thing that registers is that he's taller than Aubree, possibly thinner than Aubree, and definitely just as stunningly beautiful as Aubree, in a male way. His hair is natural brown, longish and jagged, hanging over his eyes and across one cheekbone. His style screams trendy but somehow looks rumpled enough that there's absolutely no way he's made an effort at being trendy. A single mole above the right side of his mouth draws my attention, and I fight not to stare.

"Hey," he mutters as he checks out a table beside us filled with jocks.

I nod in his direction—even though there's no way he saw the motion—and take a bite of my carrot. He says nothing more, which is good. I wouldn't be able to hear him anyway. The place is loud—so loud. Voices echo off dingy white tables and scuffed tiled floors. I can feel the crowd of students as they pack inside the place, even though I refuse to turn and look. I'd rather face the wall. There's a shout and a holler before some girl squeals, then a table to my right breaks out in laughter.

"Are you—?" I begin to ask Aubree.

"Nope. Totally not related," she says.

I blink, shocked that she read my mind. How did she know I was going to ask if they were siblings?

"Seamus and I have absolutely no relation. And although it does smack slightly racist that most everyone here assumes the two tall Asian-Americans must be related, I'm used to it, so no hard feelings." She shrugs.

Heat radiates up my neck. *Great job, Caoine. Way to be judgy.*

She shrugs. "Really. It's no big deal." She lifts her crazy-elegant chin in a way that looks far too regal and looks around the cafeteria. "Ooh, look. There're Oliver and Eric."

And I choke on my carrot stick.

She stands and waves them over as I hack up one of my lungs. Not more people! I hate people. My belly grips in panic, and my head spins in multiple circles. I dare a glance in the direction she's waving and see the two boys seated at a table of all guys, most of whom look athletic. I close my eyes and slump in my seat. Did she really have to draw the attention of an entire table of *guys*?

I assume the two have picked up their lunches and are on their way over since Aubree is suddenly bouncing in her seat and there's a deep-voiced, repeated "hoot" coming from the other table. Why are the guys chanting like that? Guys are weird.

"Hey," Oliver says as he glides into the seat across from me.

His crooked grin makes my palms sweat, and I find myself daring to grin back at him. Sort of. I'm quite positive it looks more like a grimace, but it's all I've got so I go with it. My chin stays neatly tucked where it always is as my toes tingle. My face is crazy hot. What is wrong with me?

"Ladies," Eric says. He plops on the other side of Oliver with a tray twice as full of food as Aubree's. "Good to see you both have such fine taste in lunchtime company. Delighted to provide my services." He looks right at me. "Caoine, looking beautiful today."

My cheeks warm, and I duck my head. *Is he making fun of me?*

"You know, you have quite exotic eyes. Interested in going out sometime so I can study them a little closer?" I dare to glance up, only to be met by a saucy wink.

Oliver punches his friend's arm. "Shut it, Eric. Not cool to tease the new girl."

Eric fakes an expression of shock. "Who said I'm not serious?" Then he takes a big bite of his hamburger and bobs his head, looking around the lunchroom like this happens every day.

Seamus snorts.

Aubree bites her lip and eyes him. "I'm trying to help Caoine *not* look like she's in a constant state of deer-in-the-headlights. I agree with Oliver. Shut it."

I almost crack a smirk at the last part but then whip around and stare at her, my mouth hanging open. What had she said about deer and headlights?

"What?" She shrugs. "It's true. You need to loosen up, girl."

I scowl as I turn back to my lunch. Why had I let her talk me into eating in the lunchroom?

"What's up with the rabbit food, anyway?" Eric shoves a handful of fries in his mouth as he nods toward my veggie pile.

"I'm . . . a vegetarian." I take another bite of my celery and want to sink through the floor.

The whole vegetarian thing is only partly true. The nature of my existence requires I be so. My dad discovered I puked every time he fed me meat when I was a toddler. Apparently, being *less-than-human* meant I had to miss out on the finer things in life. Like bacon. Sigh.

"Cool!" Aubree gushes. "I am too! We can be twinsies."

I blink at her. Yes, other than the fact we look nothing alike and one of us is an extrovert while the other would rather walk across hot coals than be here right now.

"Gross," Eric says. "Keep your leafy greens. I'll take the good stuff!" He holds his burger in the air as if it's a burnt offering before he tears into it again.

Oliver shakes his head. "Idiot." Then he turns to me. "I

think it's cool, you being all one with nature and stuff. Very zen."

I press my lips together. If only he knew how very un-zen I am. Like bringer of death, un-zen. I fish through my sack for my baggie of grapes. Seamus finally makes a move on Aubree's french fries. She doesn't bother to stop him, which I think is super nice. I would hate sharing my fries. They're seriously my most favorite food ever.

"Attention, students." Principal Perry's voice breaks through the overhead intercom. The din of noise in the cafeteria drops to a respectable level. "A reminder that the science department storage rooms are off-limits to all students. Several items have gone missing, and I'd like to remind you that some of those chemicals are hazardous and should be handled by an adult professional. Please refrain from exploring the science department for your enjoyment or for any practical jokes you might have your mind set on. Thank you."

Eric raises his brows. "Someone's in trouble." He cackles like he's just told the funniest joke ever. "So what are we really doing here?" His question is directed at Aubree.

"We're prepping Caoine for survival at West Lincoln High."

"We are?" Oliver asks.

You are? My eyes grow wide, and I stop chewing.

"How so?" Eric asks.

Aubree squints and surveys the room. "Well, for starters, see that table over there? The one right beside the girls' bathroom?" I venture a glance. "Yeah. Don't ever talk to any of them. Like, ever. Or you might be sucked into their world of lip gloss and makeup tutorials on YouTube, never to return." She curls a lip. "It's a thing."

Seamus snorts again and steals more fries from Aubree.

She shakes her head as if people have actually perished from such circumstances. Oliver and Eric laugh.

I secretly spy out the table in question and see what she

means. Each girl holds the proverbial "mean girl" vibe, not a hair out of place and dressed in haute couture. Every single one of the five holds a small mirror and is fixing their hair or eyeliner. It's like a scene out of one of those slasher movies, right before the popular girls get axed.

"What about Anthony Marino?" Eric says as he gives an exaggerated shiver.

I follow his line of sight to a spot two tables over. A guy bigger than The Rock sits like a lump, a look filled with so much hate I'm fairly certain Lucifer would ask permission before he dared sit with the guy. He has multiple trays of food before him, and it appears he's going to eat them all. His neck is bigger than my waist, and I cringe at the thought of just how many inches his biceps might be.

"He's not well liked . . . by *choice*." Eric take another bite of his burger and talks around his meal. "His life consists of weightlifting and being mean. I sometimes wonder if he hasn't killed his own family and eaten them."

Oliver smacks the back of his head.

Eric whines. "What? I'm just saying . . ."

"It's true," Seamus mutters.

"Okay, but let's take a more positive note, shall we?" Oliver takes his time as he scans the crowd.

I find my gaze is content to rest on him. For some reason I can't stop looking at the way those gray flecks reflect against the brown of his eyes. Almost . . . hypnotic.

Aubree looks between me and Oliver. Then she does it again. She throws me a smirk. My stomach clenches.

"So, Oliver . . ." she says.

I swallow, take a deep breath.

"You and Caoine wanna meet up with Seamus and me after school? Maybe go to the diner?"

I freeze. Luckily, Eric is distracted by a table of girls to our right, and I don't think anyone else around us heard.

"I've got soccer practice," Oliver says. His gaze shifts to the guys at the table he came from, but they're involved in their own conversation.

Aubree sighs dramatically. "It's going to be fun. You'll be missing out."

I want to puke. I know exactly what she's doing, and it's *so* not funny. Not even a little.

"What if you came quick during a break?" she pushes.

I curl my hands into fists beneath the table, digging my nails into my palms.

"Breaks?" Oliver says with a furrowed brow. "You think we get breaks?"

"What're we talking about?" Eric wags his brows, suddenly intent on our conversation.

I cringe.

Aubree flashes a grin. "Oh, I was just inviting Oliver to the diner with us after school today."

His shoulders visibly droop. "Let me guess. I'm not invited to the party?"

"Not when you're back heel stinks so bad," Oliver quips.

I jolt, shocked by his insensitivity.

Eric's jaw drops. "What? I kick just fine—"

Oliver shakes his head. "Not from what Coach says."

His friend slumps in his seat, fuming, but it appears to be all in fun. Weird. I don't get boys.

Oliver rolls his eyes and turns to Aubree. "I can't miss practice. Sorry." He glances at me. "I really wish I could."

"Yeah, not when he's captain of the team." Eric shakes a fry in our direction, then pops it in his mouth, clearly recovered from his temper tantrum already.

"You're captain of the soccer team?" I ask Oliver. *Wait. Did I just speak? Out loud?* My face goes hot, and I attempt to melt into the floor.

He looks at me, a gentle smile in place. "Yeah. Do you like soccer?"

I lick my lips. "I don't know. I've never seen a game before." Or any sporting event, for that matter.

"It's okay if you don't like it," Eric says. "Neither does Oliver." Oliver whips around, his gaze hard on Eric. "What? It's true." Eric turns to me. "He only plays because his parents make him. Cause they want him to get a soccer scholarship to college."

I raise my brows.

Oliver gives Eric a look that can kill, then turns to me. "My older brother played, too. He had, uh —" He clears his throat. "He'd gotten a soccer scholarship. So I guess my parents think I'll be able to, too."

"That's cool," I say.

But for whatever reason, everyone at the table avoids Oliver's gaze, their looks no longer happy or jovial. Like there's an elephant in the room, and I'm the only one who can't see the beast.

Aubree shifts in her seat. "So back to our original conversation . . ."

Eric snorts. "Which was?"

She narrows her gaze at him. "We're trying to steer Caoine toward safe people she should be friends with. And those she should avoid, of course." She looks around the cafeteria. "There." She points to a table to our left. "Amanda, Brady, Kirk, Emma, and Tyler. They make up the Debate Team. They're all super nice."

"Yeah. If you want to be bored to death." Eric waves the suggestion away. "Now, if you want real friends, you need to find a good old-fashioned sports team. Like the soccer team." He motions to himself with a large grin. "The table we were just with? Those are my brohan." He holds his hands up like he's waiting for applause.

Oliver stifles a laugh. "Brohan?"

Eric scowls. "What? They're your brohan, too."

Aubree shakes her head.

Oliver just sighs. "It's true." He looks at me, and my blood vessels constrict like they've forgotten how to work. "We are part of a certain *brotherhood*. I'm not sure I'd classify it in quite the same way as Eric, but yeah, the guys on the soccer team are cool."

"The real question is" — Eric points a finger in my direction — "what about you? What's your story?"

Seamus finally looks right at me and sits up in his chair a few inches.

My cheeks go flaming hot. Again. "My story?" I fix my gaze on my lunch and realize I've forgotten to eat.

"Sure," Aubree says. "Where are you from? Why'd you move here? Blah, blah, blah."

"Oh, um . . ." What can I say? I've literally never had any friends to ask me such questions. I swallow. "Um, well, I'm sort of from all over. We move a lot."

"Military family?" Oliver asks.

I shake my head. "My dad works construction."

"Oh man, I'll bet your mom hates packing so much," Aubree says.

My gaze falls into old habits and settles in my lap. "Oh, uh . . . my mom died" — *In childbirth*. Ugh. Don't say it. Don't tell them how you killed your mother and are responsible for your single dad — "when I was little. It's just my dad and me."

Aubree's gaze crumbles. "I'm so sorry. No wonder you move a lot. Your dad probably needs to go where the work is, and it's easier if there's only two of you."

"Yeah, something like that." If she only knew it has nothing to do with my dad and everything to do with me. The freak daughter.

"Well, I'm glad there's construction to be done here in Lincoln County," Oliver says. "Otherwise, we never would've met you."

I try to smile, but it falls short. All I can manage is a nod as

I glance away. I dig my fingers into my palms and count the minutes until lunch is over.

No one in Lincoln County should be happy I've arrived. Not really. It's the reason I've been friend-less for so long.

A banshee is never welcome for long.

8

CAOINE

A VICE CLENCHES tight around my ribcage, and my lungs fail to work. Aubree has brought me to the local diner for an after-school milkshake.

And apparently everyone else in school has decided to come, too.

It isn't my first choice in post-school activity, but when she invited me during last period, I had zero excuses to give her. My dad works late, she knows that now, and there's only so much homework a brand-new student can do on day two of a new institution. Against my better judgment, I agreed.

I can see now it was a big mistake. Huge.

"I see a table in the corner," Seamus says. With the poise of a ballet dancer, he dodges a waitress with a tray in one hand and coffee pot in the other.

My feet stay planted.

Aubree tilts her head. "Come on, Caoine. You'll be fine. It's not so bad. You can do the corner, right?"

I press my lips together and avoid her gaze.

The joint is beyond packed. Every table is stuffed with bodies, most booths beyond capacity with extra chairs pulled up to the ends. The establishment is likely used to this kind of business, but all I see is a fire hazard. The black and white checkered floor and turquoise booths and chairs give a retro feel. Pop music spills from a jukebox in the far corner, and the servers actually do that thing where they call the orders back to the cooks behind the kitchen window in diner language. It's something right out of a movie.

And I hate it.

I fidget with my bracelet as Aubree rolls her eyes and grabs my arm. The two of us duck between bodies and slip behind other groups of teens to join Seamus in the last open booth. The oversized menu makes a nice hiding spot for me while Aubree and Seamus whisper across the table.

I will not look up. I will not look up. I will not look up.

I look up. And my belly falls to my feet. Ugh. The place has to hold at least sixty people, maybe even seventy-five. Everyone talks at once. How can anyone hear when everyone's talking at once?

"What're you getting?" Aubree asks me.

I swallow, glance down, look back to her. Without shutting my menu, I say, "Milkshake. Chocolate. With whipped cream and a cherry."

"Ooh. A decisive girl. I like it." Seamus gives me a wink but goes back to perusing his menu.

Aubree reaches up and tries to pull mine down, but I resist. She guffaws. "Caoine." Her tone has a *very* motherly lilt to it. "Get over yourself and join the world, please."

My shoulders slump. Easy for her to say. The world is an easy place for people like her.

"Look," she says. "I think we've made it obvious, but Seamus and I aren't going to bite."

I stare at her.

"So?"

I continue to stare.

She sighs. "So what's the problem, Caoine? I mean, I get that you're shy, but locking yourself away from humanity won't do you any good. Can you at least pretend everyone else doesn't exist? Like, block them out or something?"

Sure. It's easy to block everyone around me. Especially when one of them could be the next person to die. Because of *me.*

Seamus leans forward. "I think what my cohort is so *ineloquently* trying to say is, maybe things aren't as bad as they seem. Maybe you're making it worse by focusing on the fact there are so many people here and you hate being around people."

I bite my lip. *Truth. Am I that easy to read?*

One side of his mouth lifts into a grin. "I'm right, aren't I? You hate people. But that doesn't mean you need to hate every moment of every day. Act like no one else is here, like it's just the three of us. You'd feel more comfortable if it were just us three, right?"

I nod.

"Cool." He sits back, puts both hands behind his head like he's just solved the mystery of time travel. "So it's just us, then. Having a nice . . . quiet . . . after-school snack. No problem."

Right. I suck in a waft of greasy air and close my eyes. *It's just the three of us. No big deal. Nothing bad is going to happen for just getting a shake, right?*

The jukebox switches to the next song, and a popular tune apparently everyone on earth—besides myself—knows comes on. All the tables around us immediately break into chorus. My eyes fly open. I glare at Aubree.

Seriously my worst nightmare.

She and Seamus laugh. "It might take some practice," she says.

I force myself to relax as the waitress comes over to take our order. Seamus sticks with coffee, black—and weird—and Aubree joins me with a milkshake and a round of cheese fries for the table. She immediately takes my menu away and hands it to the waitress so I have nothing to slink behind.

Traitor.

"So, Caoine, you going to tell us why you're really here?" She lifts one eyebrow and puckers her lips.

My heart stutters over itself, and I squeeze my knees together.

Seamus laughs. Again. "Dang, Caoine. You really need to work on getting a poker face. Do you realize every emotion you feel is reflected on your face? Relax. Bree's question isn't some sinister plot to unearth all your dark secrets. We honestly don't know anything about you. But we could tell you weren't being totally honest with us at lunch today, either. We just want to know what's what."

What's what? I give a heavy exhale and center my thoughts. What's what. *Okay, I can give them something.* "Well . . . we do move a lot, that's true."

"We didn't doubt that," Seamus says, but Aubree elbows him.

"And my dad does work construction but . . ." *Breathe, Caoine. Breathe.* "That's not really the reason we move."

"Yeah, got that," Seamus says.

Aubree glares at him like she might rip his heart out through his throat, then softens her gaze as it returns to me. "What the idiot is so *ineloquently* saying is, we get that there's more to your story. No one moves because of construction. Every town needs construction, not just ours. And it's obvious you're an introvert for a reason." She twists her mouth as she looks for her next words. "But we want you to know we're safe. As friends, I mean. We get there's more going on in your life than maybe you're comfortable saying right now, but if you ever want to talk, we're here for you. No matter what you need to talk about. K?"

I look at her. Really look at her. And I can tell. She means what she's saying. She *is* safe. I might actually have a friend for the first time in my life.

After a minute, I glance at Seamus. "What she said," he says with a nod.

And I giggle. For the first time in I can't remember how long, I actually giggle.

Aubree smiles bigger than an air balloon, which only makes my heart swell with a new sensation, something I've never felt in my entire life.

Friendship? Yes. For the first time ever, this feels like something *real*.

The waitress delivers our food and drinks while Aubree and Seamus banter about something they've apparently been fighting over for years. Over the next few minutes, my brain actually blocks those around me—the noise, the music. Even the crazy-strong scent of cooked meat that usually turns my stomach. For a single moment, my life is almost perfect, a normal teenager in a normal town with normal problems. With normal friends.

But nothing about me is normal. I should know this by now.

Cold washes down the back of my neck. Pain pushes against my abdomen; a rock the size of my fist lodges in my throat. I blink, my fingers tight around my frosted milkshake mug.

It's here. It's coming. Right now.

My vision goes black for a split second, and I remind myself to exhale.

"Caoine? Are you all right?" Aubree's hand reaches for mine, but I pull away, stumble from the booth.

"I . . . I—" My vision is black again. This one is coming fast.

I need to run, now!

Suddenly every single body in the claustrophobic restaurant presses against me at the same time. I can't move, can't breathe. I push, shove. Despite a squeal and an angry voice that says "Hey!" I push through the crowd.

"Caoine!" Aubree yells.

But I don't stop. I don't turn. All my energy is focused on the scream, on stopping the inevitable from happening in this incredibly public place. *Without my cloak.* I need my cloak.

Why is this happening during the day? For the second time this week?

Knives stab my legs, slice across my back as I slam into the door that refuses to cooperate. It finally opens. Blessed fresh air melts into my skin, welcomes my retreat. I gasp, blink.

No, no, no, no. This can't be happening. I shudder, prepare for the oncoming song that will cause more damage than this world will ever need.

And then it's gone. Like someone's flipped a switch or something. The feeling is gone.

An apparition.

The ghost that haunts my dreams.

It leaves me. I stand there breathing and staring and wishing I could fly into the sky, away from the eyes that watch me through the diner window. Away from everything and everyone and every possible moment in the future that will remind people I'm a freak. But the moment isn't over. It can never be that easy when it comes to my curse. In the end, the curse always wins.

Through the thin glass window of the diner door, a waitress screams, and I wish once more to fly away, never to return.

Her words are exactly what I expect.

"He's dead! Someone call 911! The cook is dead!"

9

CAOINE

THE THREE OF us are silent as we walk to Aubree's canary-yellow VW Jetta. The parking lot is full of emergency vehicles, flashing lights, and officers in uniform. Most of the customers cleared out long before the police arrived, but we stayed.

Why did I feel the need to stay again?

A gurney with a white sheet haphazardly thrown over a body is rolled out and wheeled toward an ambulance. The man is overweight, apron stained with grease, sweat marks beneath his underarms. The waitress has already given her statement, her voice loud and hysterical. She said he was diabetic, that he'd shown symptoms of shock just moments before he fell. Which would make perfect sense under normal circumstances. But nothing about me is normal, and nothing that happens around me is ever normal, either.

That symbol, the same one I saw on the blackboard the day the teacher died, it was there. In the diner. I hadn't noticed it on my sprint out of the place, but images raced into my mind as soon as I calmed enough. There, on the silver counter where the cook put the orders. In a pile of salt. Happenstance for passersby, but not to my practiced eye.

I see things. Things that aren't coincidence.

A symbol had been drawn in that pile of salt, the same one left near the first body. The one I hadn't noticed until I saw it a second time. But what does that mean? Who did it, if it wasn't a simple case of insulin and sugar imbalance?

"So do you have them often?" Seamus asks.

I jump, jerk my gaze away from the gurney, back to my new friends.

"The panic attacks." He frowns.

Right. Because that's what I told them I had. A panic attack from the number of people in the diner.

"Um, sometimes, yeah." My line of sight shifts back to the ambulance, the gurney now safe inside.

"Weird that it happened right before that waitress screamed." Seamus shoves his hands in his pockets.

My nerves rattle inside my flesh.

"Lucky is what it is." Aubree's looking at me like a mother hen again. "It might've been worse if you'd been inside when everything happened. Everyone went berserk. Like, crazy nuts."

I swallow and nod. Yes, I saw the chaos. The chaos I created. My ears buzz as my gaze settles across the lot on the beat-up Chevy truck, blue, with rust along the bumper.

Just like the one I'd seen the night before, two driveways down. One of the many houses that could've held the answer to my midnight cry.

The house that *had* held the answer to my cry.

A chill runs down my spine despite the humid afternoon sun that still hangs above. Seamus falls into the backseat, and I settle next to Aubree, wordlessly. In a daze.

We make it three blocks before Seamus breaks the silence. "That doesn't normally happen." His voice is constricted, apologetic. "Someone dying in the diner, I mean." He looks at his lap like he's searching for more words.

Aubree grips the steering wheel, her knuckles white, and I think I see her chin quiver. I duck my gaze.

This. This is why I don't go out in public. It's bad enough my nights are plagued with death, but to have to face it during the day as well? I blink back tears of anger and regret while the world blurs by outside the car window. I don't realize my fists have squeezed so hard, not until a sting flashes across my palms and I open them to see red, my nails aching, skin raw.

What am I doing? I have no business making friends with these people. Not while I'm cursed. Not while even being near me is a danger to them.

"Why did you run out when you did, Caoine?" Aubree whispers. Her jaw works side to side, her gaze locked on the road.

I glance at her out of my peripheral. "What?" My voice is soft, almost inaudible. My heart pounds inside my chest.

She waits for a beat. Then, "Seamus already told you. We can see it on your face. You're different somehow . . . special . . ." I cringe and she stops. Swallows.

I need to get out of the car. I need to be as far from them as possible.

"You ran out like you knew what was going to happen." This, from Seamus. "Why did you run out right then?"

Cold spills across my shoulders, down my back, settles in my belly. *This needs to end. Now.* I've been reckless. I can't let our friendship go any further.

"What is it, Caoine? Did you know him? The man who died?"

I shake my head. Wordless answers are safest.

"But you recognized his car?" Aubree asks.

The world around me spins, and I close my eyes, inhale synthetic pineapple, courtesy of the scented filter hanging from her mirror. I grip the door handle.

"I saw your double take at the blue truck," Seamus says. "Was it his?"

I nod. Why do I nod? I just admitted I knew he would die!

"But you didn't know him?"

Again, I shake my head. Will they believe me?

We ride in quiet another few minutes before Aubree speaks. "Like we said, Caoine. We know there's more to you than you might want us to know —"

My body jerks to life. "Um, can you just drop me off here?"

I begin to pull on the handle like I'm going to open the door while we're cruising at forty-five.

Aubree gasps, and Seamus grabs the back of my seat.

"But don't you —?" The car swerves as Aubree struggles to slow the car and pulls to a stop on the side of the road.

I yank on the handle and shove against the door. "Actually, I need some air."

"Caoine, wait —" She leans across the seat, her cheeks pink.

"Really, I'll be fine. I've gotta go. The walk will do me good." I lean back in to grab my backpack. It's better to make a clean break before I get too attached.

"But Caoine . . ." Seamus looks confused. "We —"

"Honestly guys, can't you take a hint?" I stand straight and sharp, my posture reflecting the same tone as my voice. "I said I want to walk. Really. You don't need to babysit me. I can handle myself." My gut flips as I rip into the only friends I've ever had.

"Can we at least —?"

"Seriously, guys. Can't you just leave me alone?"

Hurt flashes across Aubree's face.

My hands quiver, right along with the rest of my insides. "I told you before I didn't want to go to that stupid diner, but I went along to be polite. But to be honest, I'm just not interested in hanging with you guys. Thanks for the effort and all." Then I slam the door.

A mountain-sized lump forms in my throat, and I purposely walk the opposite direction so they can't follow. In fact, I don't walk, I run. With tears in my eyes and regret in my heart, I run from the first friends I've ever had. I run and run and run.

If only it were as easy to run from my curse.

10

CAOINE

I CLOSE my eyes and breathe, slowly in, then slowly out. A synthetic clean scent tingles my senses. The janitor must've mopped recently. I glance around my cubicle under the stairwell. It feels bigger now, not quite as cramped as day one. My chest is no longer burdened by the mass of people that accompany me to classes, that invade my insides and refuse to allow me to relax. Now it's laden with more significant problems.

Like the fact I put my very first friends right in the line of fire. What was I thinking? There's a reason I never make friends, and this is exactly it. When people get close to me, they die. I have no choice. I need to make sure Aubree and Seamus stay far away, that they don't attempt anything regarding friendship with me.

For now, my goal must be to figure out what's going on with my curse. Why it's suddenly coming to life smack dab in the middle of the day. What those strange symbols mean, if anything. And most of all, now more than ever, I must find a way to *stop* my curse, to defy the laws of nature and find that "off" button that will turn me into a normal teenage girl. My brain is stuffed. Crowded with cotton balls of thoughts no teenager should ever need to worry about.

I shake my head. No. Not now. Now is not the time to solve the mysteries of the world. My pad of paper and favorite pen sit on my lap. I came here to write, not to think about the suck that is my life.

Words that floated through my mind seconds before disappear altogether, and I scrunch my forehead. The prose on my tongue fails to make it to my hands. Where did it go? The poem refused to leave my head earlier, followed me all through the previous period, yet it's totally gone now. I toss my pad to the side and snag my lunch bag. Never mind. The worries of the world have chased away all the words trapped inside me anyway. Maybe after I eat . . .

My hummus, avocado, and bean sprout on pumpernickel calls to me, and I smile. Food always makes things better. At least, that's what my dad says.

"What are you so giddy about?"

I jump as Oliver plops down beside me, a brown bag similar to mine in hand. His grin is lopsided, hiding that mangled tooth he always appears worried about, even though it's become my favorite part of him.

On instinct I avert my eyes. "Just having some alone time." *Go away. It's safer.*

His face falls. "Oh. Do you want me to leave?"

My heart skips at the idea. *Yes.* "No." I bite my lip at how forceful I sound. "Erm, no. You can stay. I don't mind."

Although, I absolutely should. He needs to stay away from me.

I lift my eyes to his. "What do you have for lunch?" My breath hitches in my throat. Even that single question of extroversion has tired me out.

He slips a plastic-wrapped sandwich from his bag with an evil grin. "Sorry, animal lovers of the world. It's turkey and ham on the menu today."

I laugh and marvel at how easy it is to do. How dangerous

it is. "It's okay. I'm not, like, offended or anything. I just . . . never mind. I just don't eat meat."

His brow pulls together, and his hands stop midair on the way to his mouth. "Don't hold back. You can tell me. I won't judge."

"It's nothing. Stupid, really. The reason I don't eat meat is because my stomach couldn't handle it as a child. It actually has nothing to do with animals or eating healthy or all those other reasons people become vegetarians."

"Interesting." He chews deliberately, like he's trying to solve a problem. "So your body rejected meat as a kid. Have you tried eating it since?"

I cringe. "No. My top pet peeve is puking. I'd honestly rather not eat meat than to suffer from vomiting uncontrollably. Besides, it's no sacrifice for me, really, since I've never had it anyway. I'm not mourning what I'm missing or anything."

"So what're you working on?" Oliver nods toward my abandoned pad of paper.

My heart pounds. *Turn him away, Caoine. Make him go away.* "Oh, nothing. It's just a poem . . . or something resembling a poem. I had it all worked out an hour ago, but now that I'm free to write it down, most of the ending has run away. I'll work on it later."

Before I can stop him, he picks it up, his brown eyes skittering across the pad. I freeze. No one has ever read my work before. Not even my dad.

"*'Fear floods my core, washes away my guilty sin, replaces it with longing, confusion, expectation, frustration, swirls between my veins and calls out to my deepest desires. Wash away shame, wash away wickedness. Come no more to haunt me, for the nightmares of my past are here to choke me, drown me, to never let me forget.'* Whoa." He slumps in his spot and stares at the lined paper.

My belly squeezes tight, and I lose my appetite. "It's just a first draft."

Oliver is silent for a moment, and my back drips with sweat. My gaze drifts over his long nose, his strong jaw. His lips twitch, and my pulse jumps right along with it. "This is good, Caoine. Really good. Have you ever thought of joining the school paper?"

I blink. "The school newspaper? No way. I don't think I write the way they want—"

He shakes his head. "If you can write something this good in a few minutes, you can definitely write an article and get your name in print. Believe me. I've read some of the stuff published here. It sounds like a first grader wrote it."

My jaw clenches as I search for an excuse why I shouldn't do it.

He tilts his head. "Don't you want to be published? At the very least it will look good on your transcript when you apply to college."

College. Is that even a possibility for someone like me?

"At least let me help you out." He pulls out his cell and scrolls.

Jealousy tastes sour in my belly. I want a cell phone, but I can't have one. Yet another thing my dad has forbidden in his effort to make me *safe.* Something about not being tracked or some nonsense. But who would want to track me? Who could he possibly be afraid of?

"I've got a—" He freezes, licks his lips. "Well . . . she's a—" He huffs a breath. "I mean, she was—" He looks at me. "We dated last year. But it's been over for a while, totally no big deal." He shifts in his spot. "I'm not sure why I'm even telling you all this . . . not that it matters. I mean, we're friends now, so I'm sure she'll help you out."

I focus on the center of his chest and pretend the things he said have no meaning to me. Why should I care if he dated some other girl? Or whether they're still together? He isn't my friend. In fact, he needs to leave right now.

His eyes tumble across my face in a way that leaves me

thirsty. Why am I so uncomfortable? Haven't I always wanted a boy who wouldn't stop looking at me like he wants to say more but is afraid of screwing something up? I sink my teeth into my sandwich and raid my lunch bag for more food, even though I'm not anywhere close to hungry anymore.

No. I shouldn't want this.

He goes back to texting. "There. Her name's Jessica. I asked if any positions on the newspaper are still open." He scratches the back of his neck. "I think there are. I feel like I saw a flyer hanging around one of the classrooms asking for interested seniors to apply. I'll let you know what she says."

"Cool." I nod.

Nothing about putting my writing out there is cool, but somehow I know it's what I need to say. To stop the awkward.

"So Seamus tells me you all had an exciting time at the diner yesterday?" Oliver crumples his empty baggie and pulls a bag of chips from his sack.

"Yeah." Exciting is one way to put it. "Um, it was . . . quite a welcome to town."

Oliver leans forward. "Are you okay? I mean, Seamus said you saw the body and everything."

"Totally," I lie. I'll never get used to seeing death. "It's not like I knew the guy." I only predicted his death.

He nods, but his gaze won't leave my face, like it's connected with an invisible string. I chew my last few bites and lick my lips before I finally allow my gaze to succumb to his.

"You have beautiful eyes. Has anyone ever told you that?"

No. They haven't. I've been called "demon freak," "spawn of Satan," "one-eyed witch," but never beautiful. I shake my head.

One hand lifts, like he might touch my face, but he stops just inches away. "The way one is so clear silver, like the lining of a cloud as the sun reflects on the other side. Almost white. And the other, such an interesting green. Incandescent. Almost as clear as the other but with that dark ring around the outside."

"It's a genetic mutation." I look at my lap.

"Heterochromia."

I suck in a breath. "Yes. How did you know?"

"I looked it up . . . after I met you the first time. I was curious."

"Oh." I bite my cheek. He thought about me outside school? He shouldn't think of me outside school. He shouldn't think of me at all.

Oliver's jaw flexes, and he presses his lips together, like he wants to say something but is fighting it. "Look, I've got to go. Would you—I mean, do you think we could ever, ya know, hang out sometime?"

Hang out? I blink at him, my blood racing through my veins. "I—sure. I guess." Why did I say that? I'm supposed to be driving people away, not drawing them closer!

He grins, breathes. "Cool. I'll see you later then?"

"Yeah." I sit frozen as he scuttles from under the stairway and disappears down the hall.

It's not until he's gone that I notice he's left his cell phone. I notice because it buzzes, a return text from the girl he messaged just minutes before.

As the screen shines bright beneath the stairs, I pick it up and glance at the screen on instinct.

My stomach clenches, and my body goes rigid. The text is clearly meant for his eyes only, an unfortunate fact since I've already comprehended the words.

Caoine? She's that new freak everyone's talking about, right? Sorry, O. I don't think I've got any spots for her. The paper isn't that desperate for writers. LOL.

I drop the phone and sprint from my hiding spot. I don't want to read what else she has to say. But really, who am I kidding? I have no business getting close to any of the students at West Lincoln High. Even some ex-girlfriend I've never met.

11

CAOINE

I AWAKE FULLY CLOTHED. The sun peaks around the edge of my curtains, and the now-familiar aroma of new paint greets me, along with the sight of a billion boxes left untouched in my bedroom. My dad insisted on allowing me to make my space "mine," which included a fresh layer of paint, new shag rugs, and a weird lava lamp on my dresser. I stopped short of adding a stick-on constellation system on the ceiling. Clearly I'm too busy announcing death to worry about finishing decorating. Or unpacking.

My jeans cut into my skin, and I'm suddenly aware of how itchy my shirt is. How did I sleep in the thing? I sit up and blink. Wait. I slept in my clothes.

The night is gone. Yet I didn't sing my song. The banshee inside me never woke up or led me to an unknown destination to lament the ending of a life. My insides droop when they should be rejoicing, the obvious question a niggle in my gut.

Why not?

Not that every day must be filled with death, but in an average-sized town, there's at least someone who dies in a hospital or nursing home. My dad has always been good about moving us to a small town where I can walk to most corners easily. But no one is destined to die today? How can this be?

I sigh. This has never happened before.

With a stretch and a twist, I rub my face. My body revels in a full night's uninterrupted sleep. It seriously isn't sure how to respond to such luxury. But then I'm up and showered and getting ready for a completely empty Saturday. I've never slept in, even in summer. It feels like such a waste when there are so many things to do in a day.

Before I sneak out of the house, I pop my head in my dad's room. He's out like a light, same outfit as yesterday, too. He'll be just as surprised to find we haven't gone on a midnight excursion. I quietly pull the door shut and leave a note on the kitchen counter.

Morning has officially broken free by the time I'm walking to the library, a slight breeze in my hair and the early scent of autumn swirling in the early light. A strange sense of hope blossoms in my belly. Like this might actually be a good day. I shove my hands in my pockets, give a little skip. A smile threatens to come out. This is ridiculous.

The air is a bit too chilly, and a shiver settles along my spine. I regret not grabbing a sweatshirt, but it's too late now. The library will be nice and toasty, and I'm fairly positive I'll be the only patron in the place since I'm practically opening the joint.

Sure enough, the librarian does nothing to hide his shock when I walk through the door. "May I help you?"

He's tall with neatly combed hair and glasses. So cliché for a librarian, yet perfectly at home in his native habitat. He offers what I'm sure he believes is a friendly smile, but what really comes across is annoyance. I know this because, as a fellow introvert, I've been guilty of exactly the same expression.

I clear my throat. "Um, yeah. I'm looking for information

on symbols." *Along with how my banshee curse works and how I can stop it. Got anything on that?*

I keep my gaze slightly downturned since I can tell he's already caught sight of my unusual eyes.

He shifts on his feet. "Of course. Right this way."

Then he leads me to the back of the nonfiction section, down rows of forgotten books, and past piles of dusty collections. With the dawn of the internet, it seems like fewer people use the library. Except for something like this. Not everything can be found on the internet after all. For whatever reason, my gut tells me this is a library type of find.

"This section will have basic information on the historical significance of symbols, and once you hit this spot, it divides the books by specific country or people group." He points to a row that's eye level with me. Probably something too high for the average girl, but not me. "Is there something specific you're researching?"

I hesitate. Do I tell him? I mean, it's not like this information is secret. But considering the symbol has popped up two times—and beside two dead bodies—it feels like I should keep quiet. Then again, I am here for answers . . .

With a swallow, I hold out the scrap of paper on which I've made a crude drawing of the symbol. It looks like the Awen, the Celtic symbol for Divining Illumination. The circle has three vertical lines, the middle one straight, the other two slightly angled out at the bottom. A dot sits at the top of each line, and each one has a distinct break right in the middle. There's a faint overlay of another common Celtic symbol, the Triple Spiral, but with only two legs of the spiral instead of three. Each leg hangs over the far sides of the lines.

Somehow, the artist of both the chalkboard drawing and the salt drawing had a certain flare, a Celtic way of making the thing look elegant. Mine just looks like scribbles.

The librarian gasps and looks between me and the paper. "Where did you see this?"

Ice creeps along my veins, and I choose my words carefully. "I saw it at school." This is true. "I was curious to know its meaning." This is also true. No need to discuss dead bodies.

The man shakes his head and raises his eyebrows. "I've got to tell you, it's highly unusual you're here to discuss this symbol."

"Why?"

"Well, first of all, it's a symbol of slavery. Prior to the eleventh century, Celtic slave owners would brand their slaves with this symbol as a sign of property. One might also find this symbol displayed over the door of a slave house, where slaves were bought and sold. It was common practice to use symbols in place of words, since much of the population couldn't read. By using a symbol, it left no question what that merchant sold or a person represented."

"Oh." *Slavery?* I fiddled with the edge of my shirt. Why had I been expecting something different?

"It's highly unusual you ran across this specific sign."

"Is it a secret or something?"

He shakes his head. "Not necessarily. But it isn't widely known. There are lots of Celtic symbols that have become synonymous with the culture. When most people think of Celtic signs, a few come to mind right away. This is not one of them."

"So only someone who knows a lot about Celtic history would know what this means?"

The librarian shrugs. "I'm not even sure that's possible." He crosses his arms. "See, I'm studying for my PhD in Celtic Anthropology right now. Everything I'm learning has been my life work." He pauses. "The odd thing is . . . I've only run across this specific symbol in the past year. And I've studied this culture for years."

Another few seconds pass, and sweat pops along my brow as he narrows his gaze at me.

"It's interesting you would find this at school, when it's

something so sacred . . . so heavily buried beneath a history of an entire people group. Don't you think?"

I swallow again. I can tell by the way he looks at me that he wants more of an explanation. He totally doesn't buy my lie. "Yeah, I guess."

"Stranger still, that of all the librarians you should talk to this morning, it would be me, the one person in the entire town —possibly the entire east coast—who knows what this symbol means."

My lungs refuse to work, and I lick my lips. His gaze penetrates my skin, digs beneath it with claws and teeth. Why do I feel guilty? Guilt follows me every day of my life. Why do I feel bad about something I didn't do? Don't even know?

"Thank you for your time." Without cracking open any of the books he's shown me, I spin and waltz from his presence.

I have all the information I need. There's no reason to stick around and face the Salem Witch Trials. Apparently, I've stumbled onto something far more sinister.

12

CAOINE

SLAVERY.

Really, slavery? That's what the symbol means?

I turn the crude drawing over and over between my fingers, my head propped up on my pillow as I lie belly down on my bed. Sunday afternoons in my house consist of football and beer for my dad and boredom for me. I groan and flop onto my back to stare at the ceiling.

I've been over it a thousand times in my head. The symbol is really old, Celtic, and has something to do with slavery. Awesome. Can my life get any more vague?

The sun is just beginning to set as I scrounge up the courage to face the unpleasant conversation I've been avoiding. If I can't figure out why my gift is going wonky—which I strongly suspect has to do with the symbol—then my next project is to solve the mystery of how to stop my curse. Not that I haven't tried. My motivation just wasn't quite as prominent as it is now. What with half the student body and everyone at the diner thinking I'm a freakoid. At least my scream fizzled out once I got outside the restaurant. I grimace. Yet one more mystery to solve. My curse has never—*never*—stopped once the song called to me. I need answers.

The TV hums softly from the living room as I descend the stairs. All the lights are off save for the lamp beside the recliner where my dad watches his game. The temperature drops a few degrees, and I rub my arms as I glance at the darkened fireplace. It's only beginning to get cold outside, not quite time for an evening fire to warm up the place.

"Hey kiddo," my dad says as I fall onto the couch and grab a pillow.

"Who's ahead?" I nod toward the screen.

He frowns. "Patriots. But it's still early. Maybe the Panthers can turn things around." He takes a swig of his beer and focuses on the TV.

Uniformed men run across emerald grass until a whistle blows and some guy in black and white makes a call that angers my dad. The players run to stand in a huddle, and familiar music carries us into the next commercial break. Which is fine by me, since I don't even know what colors each team wears.

"What's up?" My dad mutes the TV, his brown eyes tired.

My heart sinks. Should I even be asking him this?

Yes. I need answers. And I have a feeling this kind of talk will never get easier.

"Can I ask you something?" I squeeze the pillow a little tighter.

"Shoot."

"I was just wondering . . . I mean, I wanted to ask about . . . my—my curse. About the night I was born." Every molecule of oxygen suddenly disappears from the room, and flames crawl across my face.

He shifts in his chair, and he won't make eye contact. "We've talked about this, Caoine. I've told you everything I know about that night."

What he means to say is, he's told me everything about the night my mom died. *About my mom dying.*

I clench my jaw to stop the tremble in my chin. "Yeah, I

know. It's just . . ." Just what? It's gone completely bonkers now, and I need to know why? "I—I . . ." The pillow unexpectedly becomes much more interesting, and I focus my gaze there to hide the tears that swim in my eyes. "I'm just wondering if *she* said anything—I mean, if *you know who* did? About my curse? Like, if *she* gave any timeframe for how long I might have it?"

My dad sighs and sits forward in his chair, elbows on his knees and beer still in hand. "This is about school, isn't it?"

I look up in shock. Does he know about my scream that first day? Did the school tell him?

"I knew this day would come." He sounds resigned. "You're getting older, and you want deeper friendships. You want to date, is that it?"

"What? No, I—"

"Look, I get it. I've been waiting for this conversation for a while. Being—the way you are—it's hard on you. I get that, Caoine." His gaze is soft now. "But it was part of the deal, sweetheart. The only reason you're alive is because of who you are. We can't change that. No one can."

"But did you ask her? Did she say anything about a way out? Like another bargain—"

He shakes his head. "No, hon. Don't even let your brain go there. There's no way out. We know this. It's the price we had to pay to keep you alive."

He means the price *I* had to pay. He's not the one predicting death on a nightly basis.

"Yeah but . . . I'm not talking about getting rid of the curse altogether. What I mean is, is there a way to control it? Like maybe stop it sometimes when it comes? A delay—"

"Caoine, really. You need to stop. This isn't healthy. There's no controlling what you do. I'm trying to find a way to use your gift for good, but this kind of thing takes time."

"But couldn't we—?"

"That's enough!"

His voice booms louder than I expect, and I flinch.

"I don't know how many times we need to go through this. You're *gifted*, Caoine. You're lucky. You could've died that night but she—*she* saved you. She gave you life. You should be *grateful*, that's what. I mean, I don't understand why you're so discontent all the time. Don't you see? Can't you see how lucky you are? You're alive, and you have the chance to help people—"

"Help them how, Dad?" I'm on my feet as I throw the pillow on the couch, my voice as loud as his. "I haven't helped a single person in seventeen years of this *blessed* life!"

"That's only because you resist me, Caoine." Now he's standing, too. "Every time I try to help you . . . try to coach you to find a way to use your gift for good, you push me away. You just won't listen!"

"And neither do you, Dad! Did you ever stop to ask yourself if I *wanted* to be saved that night? If I wanted to live?"

He sucks in a breath.

"Why didn't you just let me die with Mom? We could've been together, in the afterlife. Why did you make me stay here in this living hell? Under this *curse*?"

He flinches as if I've physically slapped him. "Being with me is a living hell?" His voice is so soft, I almost don't catch his words.

"No, that's not what I meant—"

"It's what you said, though. It's what you think, deep down inside, isn't it?"

"No, Dad. You're the only thing that does make me happy—"

He pushes past me, headed toward the kitchen. "Don't bother, Caoine. I know what you meant. I didn't realize my presence was such a burden to you. I'll try to stay out of your way from now on."

"Dad, no."

But it's too late. He's around the corner, and the conversa-,

tion is over. From the kitchen I hear the clink of another bottle and the fizz as he opens his next beer. Somehow I know he's going to drink more than his usual dozen tonight. I drove him to it.

Hot tears fall down my face as I ascend the stairs. Not only do I have zero answers about the symbol, I still have no way of stopping my curse and have managed to alienate the one person in my life who knows the truth. The one person I love more than anything else in this world.

I turned away the only friends I had at school, and now I pushed away my only family member, too. My life can't get any worse.

13

CAOINE

I STIFLE a yawn and attempt to focus on the front of the room. Why I'm so tired, I have no clue. Another night of uninterrupted sleep should have done my body some good. So why am I more tired than when I go for my midnight walks? Just how broken is my curse?

The class laughs in unison at something the teacher says, and I jump. Aubree looks at me, her brow pulled tight, but I look away. It's been the hardest trying to ignore her all day. I glance at Seamus, who wears a blasé expression and appears to be in a world all his own.

I tense. Wait.

Then do a double take. Had I just seen . . . ? I squint in his direction without trying to look like I'm squinting.

No. Seamus looks perfectly normal. For a second I thought his ears were pointed, but this is clearly a trick of the eye, brought on by my lack of sleep. Or too much sleep. Or whatever.

The bell rings, and the entire class bolts like the room is on fire. The end of the day will do that to high school students.

Aubree obviously tries to wait for me, but I take my time loading my backpack, and Seamus loudly clears his throat for her to catch up with him. *Good*. At least one of them figured things out. It's literally like nails on a chalkboard trying to get rid of those two. She finally relents and follows her friend out of the room without a word in my direction. My heart pounds unnecessarily hard, and my vision goes fuzzy.

"Caoine?" Oliver says from behind me.

I whip around to find we're the last two students in the classroom. How quaint.

One hand is in his pocket, the other hooked through his backpack strap over his shoulder. I lick my lips and swallow. *Just, wow*. We shouldn't be here like this. Not with how very much I can ruin his life.

"I've been meaning to talk to you, but I, um, couldn't get you alone."

I glance around for help but decide to head toward the door instead. Maybe I'll find a distraction that will pull me away from him?

Oliver ducks his chin to avert his gaze as we saunter down the hall. "Is now a good time to talk?"

Something in my belly flips on its side, and warmth tiptoes up my neck. My eyes dart from person to person, locker to locker. *Please, someone, get me out of here!* "Erm, sure?"

He clears his throat. "Yeah, uh, I wanted to tell you that I talked to Jess. The girl who runs the school paper? She said she'd love to have you join the staff."

I almost trip over my own feet. "She did?" *Because it didn't sound like it in that text you got a few days ago.* He's totally lying to me. How sweet.

"Yep. She said you can swing by after school tomorrow." He pauses. "Which sort of leads me to my next question." He scratches the back of his neck. "I was wondering if you were still up for going out sometime?"

Oh that. Well, see . . . I'm sort of trying to cut off communication with all humanity at the moment . . .

Blood pulses through my veins faster than any freight train

in history. My palms go slick with sweat, and I fumble to keep my books against my chest. "Of course. I said I would." Wait, what? Why did I just say that? I'm supposed to be pushing people away, not inviting them in!

"Well, that's something I wanted to talk about. With you working on the paper and me on the soccer team, it might make things hard. I also work at my parents' grocery store on the weekends. So I was thinking . . . well, this might sound weird . . . but maybe you could come to one of my games? Watch me play? And then we could grab ice cream afterward or something."

I hesitate, confused. *Say no, Caoine. Just say no. He'll only end up getting hurt.*

"I-I know it's not an official date," he says. "Not where I can take you to a movie or where I'll look even remotely nice or anything, but . . ." He hitches his pack higher. "I thought it might be a way to get to know each other until I can take a night off work."

Heat blossoms in my chest, and I can't help but smile. He's apologizing the date isn't *official* enough? Meanwhile, I'm trying to figure out a way to get out of it. If only he could read my mind and end this torture. "Of course. Ice cream in a sweaty soccer uniform sounds great." *No, it doesn't, you idiot.*

He visibly relaxes. "Sweet." His shoulders drop a little as his breathing steadies, his lips hinting at a smile. "I've got one today, if you want to—I mean, I know it's short notice—"

I open my mouth to speak but freeze. Today? I'm definitely not prepared for a date today. My legs turn to jelly, and my ears buzz. Then again, it would be nice not to arrive to an empty home, waiting for my dad to show up hours later.

"Sure," I hear myself say before it registers I've agreed. I flinch.

Now he really does smile, complete with that snaggled tooth and pink along his dark cheeks. "Cool. I've got to go, actually. Coach will be expecting me to warm up the team. But the game starts in half an hour. See you there?"

I nod and cling my books closer to my chest. Did I just bounce on my toes? More importantly, have I become delusional?

"And then we'll do ice cream afterward?" he asks.

Once more, I nod, then stop at my locker. He jumps up and down a few times in victory and gives a quick war cry before he turns and runs down the hall, laughing aloud.

I sigh, lean against the cold metal, close my eyes. There's zero chance I can keep the gigantic grin from my face.

As much as I know I should've said no—that it would be best for him and me if I just avoided him—I can't help but revel in paradise for a short while.

"I've got a date," I whisper to no one in particular. *I've got a date.*

For the first time in my life, I've got a real date.

14

CAOINE

I'M CAUGHT.

What I thought would be a simple task of sneaking off to watch Oliver's soccer game all by myself turned into something So. Much. More. I flex my fingers and attempt to put another inch between Aubree and me.

She followed me to the field. Apparently even Seamus couldn't talk her out of being my friend. I settled myself on the back row of bleachers, but she and her buddy plopped on either side—effectively trapping me.

"You saw a dead body," she said. "You're scared, I get it. But please don't push us away. Not when you don't know anyone else, Caoine."

Seamus wholeheartedly agreed—all the while checking out the spectators beside us. He was clearly *not* the poster boy for focus. I had no choice. I was stuck here with Tweedle Dee and Tweedle Distracted. *Joy.*

"Tell me again why we had to sit in the front row?" I say with a frown. Aubree immediately forced me from my comfy seat as soon as I relented.

The sun reflects off the cold metal stands, which is easy since they're only half full. I squint toward the field.

Aubree chuckles. "You want to see your man, don't you?"

I cringe and glance around to be sure no one around us heard. Other than Seamus, of course. "I told you, he's not *my man*. Will you stop referring to him as *my man?*" The obvious question I was forced to answer as soon as she'd gotten her claws in me was why I was even there. Which, of course, led into an interrogation of the entire conversation I had with Oliver.

I sigh far too dramatically.

She pins me with a look. "Girl, that boy hasn't taken his eyes off you since you walked through our school building. *And* he asked you out. *And* he made it clear this is sort of, kind of a mini-date. He's totally *your* man."

I roll my eyes, but she only laughs. Seamus doesn't notice, still enthralled by a conversation between the boys directly beside us.

The referee blows his whistle for the players to take position, and my heart leaps to my throat. I know absolutely zero about soccer. Why am I so nervous for Oliver? I won't know if he's winning or losing anyway. Another blow of the whistle, and the players run toward one another like freight trains. I bite my lip and press into the hard bench beneath me. That poor ball.

"You can open your eyes, silly. This isn't a violent game," Aubree says. "Now rugby, that's a violent game."

"Well, I'll just have to pray Oliver never goes out for the rugby team, then." I bite my lip. Tell me again why I care so much?

Thirty seconds later, my belly rumbles. My interest wanders to the concession stand at the far end of the field. I didn't eat lunch. Again. Surprise, surprise.

"Come with me to get something to eat?" I ask. Because suddenly I don't want to be alone. It's a strange sensation, like I've swallowed a jar of heated worms that squiggle inside me.

Is this why girls always ask each other to go to the bathroom together?

Aubree's jaw drops. "You can't leave, Caoine. Oliver is watching you."

"How can he be watching me? He's playing in the game." I frown. *Confusion!*

She leans back with a grin. "Oh, he's watching. Every time they stop, he looks this way."

"Really? Oh." My shoulders slump. I just want something to eat.

"I'll get something for you." Seamus sounds bored and a little put out at the same time.

I fight the urge to ask him why he's even here. "Cool. Here's some money—" I dig around in my backpack, but he waves me off and walks away.

"Get me Twizzlers!" Aubree yells after him.

"Oh shoot. I should've told him I want french fries," I grumble.

"And french fries!" she screams just before he's out of earshot.

He does that wave thing again, and I suspect we'll get whatever he can afford and safely transport back to the bleachers.

I relax a notch and try to insert myself back into the game, all while avoiding Aubree's gaze. She's been watching me like a hawk ever since I gave in and spoke to her. Like she thinks I might jump up and run away at any moment. *I'm a banshee, not a fugitive.* Too bad she can't know that.

A boy I think I recognize from math class pushes his way past a group to our right and cuts in front of us, his head bowed, dark circles under his eyes. He rubs his nose like he's got a cold and slumps into a seat at the end of our row. Aubree shoots him a curious look, but I ignore him.

The ref whistles again and play stops.

"Ooh, your man is looking over here." Aubree slaps my leg with too much excitement.

Oliver throws a hand up to wave at me before he takes position again, but I forget to smile until he's already run away. I kick myself. *Ugh. Would it hurt to smile more, Caoine?* Although, I probably shouldn't be encouraging the guy . . .

Another whistle blow makes my heart do that leapy thing again. It's weird. I have no clue what's going on, yet I'm totally hooked once the action starts.

"You'll have to tell me how tomorrow goes, with Jessica and the school paper? I can't wait to see the look on her face when she finds out you and Oliver are together."

"A date. He asked me on a *date*. We aren't *together*." I disregard her sneaky smile. "And why would she care? Oliver said they dated a while ago."

Aubree snorts. "Yeah, maybe they *started* dating a while back, but they only broke up at the end of last year. And it was in no way amicable. Everyone knows it was Oliver who did the breaking up. If Jessica had her way, they'd still be together. She only puts on a good show so he won't hate her and will still talk to her."

"Oh." I pause. "They were together for . . . years?"

She nods. A little balloon that surrounds my heart deflates and sucks all the energy from inside me.

"But Oliver and I aren't really together," I say. "I mean, we haven't even gone on our date yet —"

"Doesn't matter. He's clearly taken an interest, and the fact he's already talking to the new girl has to mean something. She'll see right through it, I guarantee you. Besides, the only reason she's letting you on the school paper is so she can spy on Oliver and make sure you aren't getting serious. That's my guess, anyway."

My belly flips inside out, and a funny taste creeps into my mouth. *Ew.* Could she be right about this?

Before I can say my next words, a girl five seats down

screams and jumps up. I freeze, my fingers curled around the bitter metal of the bleacher. Ice-cold tingles creep across the back of my neck. Pressure builds in my chest, presses against my bones, eats away at my muscles. I'm being squeezed and sucked and shoved into an imaginary box I just can't escape.

Aubree is on her feet, straining to see, but everyone around us is crowding, gawking, mouths covered and eyes wide.

A stone lodges in my throat, won't allow me to breathe, threatens to spill my secret.

The boy with dark eye circles has fallen on the ground, his body in convulsions. Mouth parted, a dribble of drool slinks from the corner. Another student shoots into action, drops to her knees, and cradles the boy's head in her lap. She's yelling for others to keep their distance and for someone to call 911. The boy's friend, who has done nothing but scream until this point, is now silent, mouth ajar.

All this I see from my seated position, between spaces of bodies and shouts of teachers. My gaze lifts to the field, the one that is motionless now. The game has stopped, most of the players standing still, in shock, confused. Oliver walks forward, eyes on me, then back on the boy.

I'm going to puke. No, that's not right.

I'm going to *sing*.

My song is begging to be released. Black spots roll across my vision like that forgotten soccer ball. I grab my backpack and dig to the bottom.

More screams follow and someone says, "He's not moving! What's going on?" Then a shout: "He's dead!" followed by a plethora of shouts.

I pull out my textbooks and toss them on the bleacher, then my glossy new notebook. Where is it?

People are leaving, slipping out the side gate before the police arrive. Others won't move, won't make way for the paramedics as they yell for us to give them space. Why does everyone gawk like their staring can bring this boy back to life?

My hands tremble, my esophagus closes. There is nothing left of me, nothing of Caoine. *Only of the song.* I rip into my bag like a wild animal chasing its prey.

The paramedics work on the boy, pumping his heart, urging his blood to flow.

Ba-dum, ba-dum, ba-dum.

The song pounds inside my head.

La-dum, la-dum, la-dum.

I gag as tears stream down my face. *My cloak!* It's gone. It's not here. Did I leave it in my locker?

My body goes rigid, and I bend at the waist, fighting against a thousand horses that charge from inside my chest, race to be set free. Sweat coats my back and underarms.

"Caoine?" Aubree's eyes go wide.

I run. Before I lose control, before I remind these people of what a freak I really am, I run to find a safe place for my banshee curse. I leave my pack and my new friends and the boy I want to date. And I run.

Right by that bleacher. Right by the boy on the ground. Past the paramedics and the gawking students and the panicked teachers. I flee to find that special spot far away where I can scream so loud everyone will think I'm simply a wild animal.

But not before my eyes see what they're meant to see.

On the seat where the boy sat is a mark. Drawn in Sharpie, a permanent mark to mark a permanent death.

That symbol, the one I've become familiar with, the one no one should know anything about.

Etched into the spot where the dead boy sat is the mysterious symbol for *slavery.*

15

CAOINE

HOPELESS.

My life is hopeless.

Aubree isn't going to let me out of the friendship club, and I *know* I don't want to let Oliver out, either.

But I'm dangerous.

For them, for everyone at school. Everyone I touch.

There's only one thing I can do. I need to force my body into submission.

Attempting to learn anything at the library was a complete bust, and my dad just might snap if I keep pushing him so . . . this is it. I'm going to tame my curse. Even if it kills me.

Rope rubs my already-raw skin along my wrists and ankles, although my right hand is definitely the loosest. Tying myself to the bed was harder than I thought it would be.

The sun has set, the corner lamp casting a faint yellow glow across my too-empty bedroom, along my quilted comforter. The shades are pulled, but I can still see a glimmer of moonlight through my window. My door is shut to deter my dad from finding me in such a state.

He'll think I'm nuts, but whatever. I don't care anymore. Maybe somehow, someway, literally roping my curse into submission will break it. Or . . . what? If I don't do my job, will it bring *her* back? Will *she* come find out why I haven't done what I agreed to do? I wouldn't mind if she did. At least then I could ask her to break the curse, or at least to teach me how to control it so I'm not a danger to others.

I breathe in, close my eyes, relax against my sheets. A faint scent of new paint still hangs in the air. Images from earlier in the day still float through my head. The devastated look on Oliver's face as I ran away from him, abandoning our date. The mass of students and faculty that gathered around the dead body, the one belonging to my classmate.

The one who shouldn't have died.

I don't know why I know this, but I do. I can feel it deep in my bones. Just like my song. It vibrates and whispers and tells me things I shouldn't know. Like I'm its secret keeper even though I never signed up for the job.

Settle, Caoine. I force myself not to think on such things. Instead I concentrate on my curse. How to breathe. Happy times I can center myself around once the urge to scream comes on. That's what they always tell people to do in the movies, right? Happy thoughts. I need to think happy thoughts.

But my body isn't happy nor is it prepared five minutes later when the song decides to wind its melody into my gut, rushing through my veins, wrapping tightly around the vessels of my heart. It slams into me with enough force to derail the mightiest train. I arch my back in pain, squeeze my eyes shut tighter. Breathing, breathing, breathing . . .

It wells up, a knot in my throat, a promise that it will win.

No! Not this time.

I sigh, push against the numbness in my fingers and toes. Focus on that one memory, the one of my dad and me, at the beach, his hand entwined between my five-year-old fingers. I hadn't had the urge to sing in weeks, the longest stretch since my curse revealed itself. He truly believed I'd been freed from it. That *she* chose to set me free. The trip was celebratory. A way for us to reconnect as father and daughter. To rejoice at the end of a painful era. That night I had another visit from my curse. His hope was dashed, just as mine has been over and over and over again throughout the years.

But that day. That one day on the beach. The perfectly serene afternoon we spent together, believing my life would be right. Could be whole again. What I so badly wanted.

After that, the song came on much more often. By the time I hit middle school, it fell into its pattern of visiting every night, never a reprieve or a rest.

Until now.

Fire pulses though my blood, agonizing heat flaring inside each muscle. I groan deep in my throat but clench my teeth. I can't allow my lips to part, can't allow that song to have a millimeter of space to be set free. I must be strong. I need to fight this.

Waves crash against my ankles while seagulls cry overhead. My dad smiles at me, happy for the first time in forever.

My belly is an inferno, every appendage of my body trembling uncontrollably.

I dig my toes into the sand, watch the white foam gather around my feet before it's pulled back into the abyss of sea.

Cramps spread across my belly unlike any I've experienced, spasms tearing the muscles of my legs apart.

My dad finds a shell, the kind you can lift to your ear to hear the ocean roar inside.

A blaze of embers settles in my lower back, and I arch against the ropes, misery my only companion.

Sand castles tower above me, each one my dad builds a little taller than the last, big enough for me to pretend I can live in one forever.

My throat is tormented, lacerated with the aria that begs to be set free, throbbing with dissonance.

How many minutes has it been? I can't hold it back much

longer. When will it end? When will the agony of my curse lift and set me free?

A noise, high-pitched, animalistic, calls from somewhere near. The refrain is pathetic, a testament to something sinking, falling, dying. It squeals, shrieks, hurts my ears. I can't cover them because I'm tied up.

Why am I tied up?

I can't remember anymore. I just need that shrill cry to stop, for the animal to be put out of its suffering.

Then there's banging, something slams shut. Or maybe it's open, I can't tell because my eyes have sealed together, melted beneath the heat of the fire that rages inside me.

Yelling. Someone yells at me, screams my name, hollers like there's a fire nearby. But I know this. The fire is inside me.

Then hands, cool, cool hands. On mine, along my body, tugging at my feet. I'm free and I can open my eyes. And I know . . . that noise is me. That wail is coming from me. It's my banshee cry, never contained, never thwarted.

Always set free.

My song is set free because I can never be.

Silken fabric slides across my skin, and the turbulence of my lullaby turns into just that. A midnight ballad, soft and sweet. My voice changes into what it always sounds like when I wear my cloak.

I sit on the edge of my bed, and I sing. With my dad's arms wrapped around my shoulders and hot pulsing tears flooding my cheeks, I sing. Because that's what I was born to do.

The curse isn't something I have, it's *who I am.*

I know this now.

There is no stopping who I am. I am a banshee. And I must sing my song.

16

CAOINE

JESSICA, as it turns out, is the same girl I saw on my second day of school. The one who wanted to crush me under the weight of her stare. The one who currently looks as if she's ready to sharpen her knives and flay me open like a carp. I cringe and look at my lap.

Her office smells like waffles and perfume. Cheap perfume.

The office isn't really an office, anyway. It's more of a corner, carved from the small classroom allotted to the school newspaper. Mostly, it's too tight a space for the handful of people here—along with Jessica's attitude.

I sit on the other side of her desk, which is clearly not just her desk. Another club must utilize this space. There are a few knickknacks—a miniature stuffed unicorn, a bottle of strawberry glitter body spray, a picture of Jessica and a boy that mysteriously looks like Oliver—all on one end of the desk. That side is unusually tidy, while the remainder is overrun with papers and old food wrappers.

A shoulder-high partition separates it from the tables that fill the rest of the room. Old newspaper copies line the wall, some framed, some not. There are also posters of B-rated movies and cult classics from when my dad was born that hang at obscure angles by duct tape. The foam sword propped against the wall in the far corner and half of a medieval costume makes me think someone around here likes LARPing.

My guess is that the film club meets here also. I stifle a snort.

Jessica looks up in distaste from where she sits. My heart falls a notch. Her azure eyes practically sparkle, and those pouty full lips would make any guy drool. Of course everything is covered with a thick layer of makeup, but most girls at this school feel the need to cover up their natural state. Still, her covet-worthy eyes make me want to crawl beneath my table and melt into the floor. I've seen how her gaze lingers on my own, the slight downward tip of her lips as she squints at them. My eyes repulse her, just like they repulse everyone else. I twist the ring on my finger and find solace in my lap.

"So you want to write for the school paper?" Her tone is bored as she holds a flimsy bit of paper out for me to take.

It's the sample piece of writing I gave her just moments before. I take it and fold it neatly, dropping it into my backpack.

"You know we don't print anything like this, right? The school paper doesn't do poetry." She flips her auburn hair over her shoulder and looks down her nose at me.

Well, maybe they should. "I know. But I've never written anything like what you want for the paper."

She rolls her eyes. "It's not like it's hard. Any idiot can put together enough words to write an article."

One of the girls who works at a nearby table looks up from what she's doing, pushes her glasses back up her nose, and frowns in our direction. Her skin is almost as pasty as mine. Jessica doesn't notice her attention.

Instead she leans toward me. "Look, we really don't need anyone else on the school paper."

Then why do you have flyers hanging around, asking for people to apply? My fingers curl into the wood of the chair, and I stop my nostrils from flaring like they so badly want to.

She flips her hair again. "I'm only doing this because Oliver said you really need to find something to help you fit in around here."

A stab of pain shoots through my belly, and I scream internally for my body not to betray me. There's no way he would say that. Right?

"To be honest, I'm not sure you're a good fit here." She leans back. "Your writing is crazy flowery, way too much feeling—"

"It's poetry—"

Her perfect eyes flash. "I'm just saying I don't even know if you can write well enough to make it here at the paper."

Nice. Because any idiot can put together enough words to write an article? Just *not* me.

"But I'm willing to give you a chance." Those ridiculously glossed lips pucker. "Why don't you start by writing an article about that kid who bit it at the soccer game yesterday?"

I gasp, and the other girl shoots Jessica a glare, along with a boy at the next table over. My brain tumbles in on itself, hardly able to comprehend that she could speak so callously about a fellow student. Especially one who's *dead*.

"You were there, right?" Her lips press together as if I've chosen to dress in refuse from the dumpster. "Oliver said you saw the whole thing."

I swallow. "Yes."

"Good. Write an article about it and have it ready by first bell tomorrow. If it's any good, I'll let you join the team. If not . . ." Her gaze drifts to my backpack where my poem rests. "Well, maybe the yearbook staff will let you add one of your little rhymes to the back of the book or something."

Blood rushes so fast to my cheeks, my head feels like it was hit by a two-by-four. I grip the stupid chair even harder.

Jessica stands, which, again, does nothing for my confidence. She's super petite and adorable, with a great body, of course. Exactly what every girl in high school would ever want. Not my ridiculous 5'9" frame with feet the size of a male basketball player. I duck my head and follow her.

"Just in case I actually like what you write, I'll introduce you to the team." She motions to the tables and the four other people gathered around them. "That's Catherine." The girl with the glasses looks up with a smile. "She doesn't go by anything fun like Cat or Catie, so don't even try it."

The smile on Catherine's face falls. I gulp and look away. At least I'm not the only target.

"That's Adam." She points to a boy, a towhead, with a mass of freckles across every inch of his skin. He glances our way but gets back to work on his layout ASAP.

"Over in the corner are Quill and Pen. No, those aren't their real names. No, they won't answer to anything else." She huffs like it's a majorly big deal and crosses her arms.

Seated on opposite ends of a desk in the far corner are a girl and boy, both with soft brown skin. Neither looks up from their laptops. The girl's hair is in a long braid down her back, and the boy's is shaved close on the sides with a mop of curls on top. I don't need Jessica to tell me they're siblings. My heart does a little skip. It's endearing to know writing means so much to them, like it's a family thing. I look back to Catherine to find her smiling at me again.

I swallow and lift my chin an inch higher. I think I can actually like it here, minus the Jessica factor, of course. Everyone else appears nice enough. And they enjoy writing. With as many cartwheels as my belly has done over the past ten minutes, I'm a little excited about the prospect of getting involved in something school related. I've never ever done anything like this before. Maybe Oliver's suggestion that I check this out hadn't been such a silly idea after all.

"By the way," Jessica says as she walks over to inspect what Adam's doing. "We produce a paper every week, so you'll have to be quick about writing your articles. Mr. Henley doesn't like it if we don't make deadline. Says if we want to compete in the professional world of writing, we need to learn to meet deadlines." She smirks. "I plan on celebrating this weekend, once this one's gone to print." She saunters back to her desk and plops back in place. "I've got plans with Oliver on Saturday. What about you?"

For the third time since I've met her, I feel like someone has punched me in the gut. She has a date with Oliver? I thought he said he had to work?

I make sure my face doesn't flinch. I refuse to allow my chin to dip lower than it already has as I lock eyes with her. What will I be doing on Saturday? "I'll be writing for the school paper. Of course."

She smiles, but it's nowhere near genuine.

Writing for the school paper is apparently all I've got to look forward to. A sick sensation flips in my belly as I walk over to see if I can help Catherine. That's the only action that might actually save my pride.

17

CAOINE

THE LEATHERY SCENT of coffee swirls around me. I try not to gag.

Coming to the coffee shop was Aubree's idea. Since I finally accepted the fact she and Seamus are indeed going to be my friends—that there's no way of avoiding them for the entire year—I agreed to hang with them after school. The regular diner thing is a no-go, obviously. There's just no way I'm going back to a place where I saw a guy die. So as soon as the last bell of the day rang, we headed here to celebrate our Tuesday freedom with fellow coffee drinkers.

Or, in my case, anything *not* coffee. My idea of a beverage includes tea or possibly a fruit-flavored lemonade, but definitely not the bitter taste of the black stuff. Yuck.

"Gee, Caoine. Why don't you tell us how you really feel?" Seamus says, a cocky grin in place.

My shoulders drop. I really need to work on not showing my emotions all the time.

"Ooh, there's a spot over there," Aubree says.

She delicately balances her double shot cappuccino with extra foam while I clumsily spill my blackberry iced tea, unsweetened. Because I'm me. Seamus carries nothing. He "prefers to people watch." His words, not mine.

We grab a cluster of three armchairs in the corner, far enough away from the counter to be semi-private. The walls are covered in fairytale murals, and I notice for the first time that each area of the shop has a specific theme. We are, apparently, in the Tarzan section of this story world, complete with leopard-skin rug beneath our feet and fun plush vines hanging from the ceiling. I squint against the dim lighting and see a section of books to my back. My fingers itch to sneak over and take a peak, but I know this would be rude.

Having friends is exhausting.

We're only seated for thirty seconds when a mother and her toddler bounce by. The mother sets her coffee on a nearby table as she digs in her diaper bag for a ringing cell phone, while her son picks at something on the floor. Emotion stirs in my heart, makes me miss my dad for some odd reason.

Then the mood changes.

Everything slips into slow motion, like I'm watching a movie. Like I'm watching something happen I can't possibly stop. The little boy reaches for his mother's coffee, wraps his tiny fingers around the curved handle, tries to yank it away. But the cup follows, his legs and torso right in the path of searing hot liquid.

Before I can blink, Aubree is on her feet, next to the child, one hand beneath the cup and settling it back in place with all the grace she carries in droves but I can never seem to find. Only a few drops of the drink have even gone over the edge, splashed neatly and innocently on the hardwood floor.

The mother gasps, eyes wide. "Thank you."

"No problem," Aubree says. One hand cradles the little boy. "Are you okay?"

He nods enthusiastically. The mother and Aubree exchange a few more words before the small family leaves for another table and Aubree rejoins our party.

"Whoa," I say. "That was seriously close. You have amaz-ingly fast reflexes."

"*Amazingly* fast," Seamus teases from his seat.

Aubree sticks out her tongue. "Yes. I know. My mom always said I was an aberration—with all the love in the world, of course. I take it as a compliment. At least I can use my superpowers for good." Once more she scowls at Seamus.

I roll my eyes and grab my backpack in search of my jour-nal. Sudden inspiration for a new poem has clobbered me over the head. This one strangely having to do with coffee. Weird but whatever. A writer's got to write.

My fingers brush against something paper, neatly folded, tucked deep within the pages of my journal. Ice spills down my spine, across my shoulders, tendrils digging into my throat and constricting my airways. I wrap my hand around it and swiftly yank it into my lap, my journal and backpack all but forgotten. Slowly I open my palm, my gaze registering the familiar paper, that same box-like scrawl.

A train pounds against my temples, dangles black spots in front of my vision. *No. Not another one.* But I don't stop my curiosity, don't hesitate to look inside.

You can't hide the truth.

I gasp. Seamus chuckles at something Aubree says. I jump, clench the note in my fist, pray it will disappear. Burn to ashes. Melt into the ether and be no more.

How does this person know me? Who is he?

Seamus laughs again. He changes the subject to something he and Aubree did last year in gym class.

I need to look normal, to hide the terror that pulses inside my veins. There's no way I can tell them about the note. I'd never be able to explain it without giving away too much. Like the fact I'm less than human. My head buzzes. *Breathe.* I pick up my tea. Take a sip.

"So how did your meeting with Jerksica go?" he asks.

I choke on my drink and end up coughing like a chain smoker.

Aubree shakes her head. "Be nice, Shay."

He frowns. "What? You dislike her as much as I do."

"Yeah, but you never know when the walls have ears. We don't need to get on her bad side."

My stomach drops. Oh great. There's a bad side to Jessica? I set my tea aside and open my backpack. "Actually," I begin as dig. "You can help me with my first assignment." I casually drop the offending scrap of paper to the bottom. I'll deal with it later.

"Assignment?" Seamus lifts his brows. "So you got the job. Impressive."

"Well, not really." I curl my upper lip. "It's supposed to be a trial article, but I have a feeling she'll take whatever I write. She sounds far too eager to please Oliver, and he wants me on the paper." My blood boils inside my veins, and I clench my teeth.

I told myself I wouldn't think about him anymore. It's clear his request for a date was false, and I need to move on. Simmering on it will just make me bitter. Like coffee. I press my lips together in disgust.

Aubree tilts her head. "What's that supposed to mean?"

Oh great. Emotions written all over my face. *Again.*

I sigh. "Just something she said . . ." *Way to be vague, Caoine.* I clear my throat. "She, uh, sort of mentioned she has a date with Oliver this weekend. Even though he told me we can't go out because he has to work."

Seamus narrows his eyes and grunts.

Aubree appears guarded too. "What exactly did she say? *Exactly?*"

I bite my lip. "Well, she said she's got plans with him on Saturday."

"She didn't say what those plans were?" Aubree looks unconvinced.

"Well, no . . ." I look between them.

She harrumphs and gives Seamus a nod. He returns her sentiments with approval. "They work together."

"Huh?" I do a double take.

Aubree huffs in frustration, but I know it's not because of me. "Oliver and Jessica work at the same grocery store. That's what she meant. Her 'plans' include stocking shelves and ringing up customers. She and Oliver aren't *together* anymore."

My belly spins in a circle. "They aren't?"

"Nope. Not even a little."

"Oh." Now I feel stupid.

"Relax," Aubree says. "Oliver likes you. I can tell." She smiles, and my insides warm.

Wait, why am I so happy? I still haven't decided whether dating Oliver is wise. I'm still very much a danger to anyone who gets close to me. Still, is it possible my new friends just cheered me up? Because I definitely feel a lot better. I chew my lip to keep from beaming, but it's hard not to smile. Having friends is seriously rewarding.

"So what's your assignment?" Aubree asks.

"Oh." My smile droops. "I have to cover the *thing* that happened yesterday. You know, at the game? I mean, how am I supposed to be objective when the guy next to us keeled over from an overdose? And how can I make it sound like a balanced story when so many students are grieving?"

Aubree grinds her teeth. "That turkey. She did it on purpose. She's trying to trap you. In the hopes you write something insensitive that will make everyone hate you."

"Like I said, Jerksica." Seamus runs a hand through his multi-colored hair.

Aubree smacks him, then turns back to me, her head dipped to the side. She narrows her gaze as she forms her next words.

"What?" I say.

"Well . . . I was wondering. What was that symbol you were drawing in your notebook this morning in class?"

My stomach plummets to my feet. Oh crap. "Erm . . ."

"I saw it on the bench yesterday, where the kid who, uh, *died* was sitting."

Right. Of course she did. Crap, crap, crap. I duck my head and glare at my lap. Like it might hold an answer. Or maybe a door to a rabbit hole.

"Come on, Caoine. You can tell us. We're your friends, right?"

"Well . . . I just saw it somewhere." Horrible liar. Horrible.

She raises one brow. "Do you know what it means?"

"I—" Totally. Yes. "Maybe?"

"Seriously, Caoine." Seamus points at me. "Face. Open book. Just spill. We know that you know."

I hiccup. "I—I think it's an ancient symbol for—"

"Slavery?" Aubree says.

My jaw drops. "How did you—?"

"Girl, you *so* made friends with the right people."

Seamus laughs but goes back to his people watching. A table of middle-aged women holds his interest.

"I don't understand. I went to the library. The guy there, he said he was the only one who knew what that symbol meant."

Aubree nods. "He probably is, for this tiny town. But my dad, he was—" She clears her throat, and her skin pales. "Well, he was a bit of a history buff. Like crazy serious. He spent a lot of time learning stuff, especially Celtic symbols."

"Oh." I grab a lock of white-blonde hair and begin to twist. This information could've saved me an uncomfortable trip to the library.

"You're right that no one else around here knows its meaning. Which is weird it was on the bench by that boy, right?" She pauses, licks her lips. "Where else did you say you saw it?"

I hesitate. "I'm not sure you want to know."

"Try me." Aubree has her *I'm not screwing around* face on.

"It was drawn in a pile of salt by that cook who died at the diner." Dare I tell her about the teacher, too?

Her face falls, and she glances quickly at Seamus. "Look, there's something you need to know. Something about that symbol. There's a reason not many people know its meaning. It's because historically, it was never used in conjunction with actual slavery of the Celtic people."

"It wasn't?" Did the guy at the library lie?

She shakes her head. "Nope. It was a bit more . . . obscure. It wasn't used in the way plantation slaves would've used the term slavery, like back during the Civil War. It's got more of a . . . negative connotation."

"Negative?"

"Yes. Like, those who call themselves slaves use the symbol to denote they seek *revenge*."

"Revenge." I say this as a statement, not a question, as it sinks deep into my brain, seeping and settling into place. Revenge. Revenge. *Revenge*.

The room is suddenly hot, and I can't catch my breath.

"And, there's another thing." Once more, she glances at Seamus. He sets his jaw. "This symbol wasn't used in relation to Celtic *humans*." Pause. "It was only used within the Realm of Faerie."

18

CAOINE

IT'S around ten that night when the wave of dread slides down my spine, pools at the base of my neck, and won't leave me alone. I open my eyes, hop from my bed, and slip my feet into my shoes, my cloak wrapped tightly around my shoulders. My source of comfort and grace. Dad already stands in the hallway.

The trance envelopes me like strong arms in an impossible hug. Allowing it to take hold brings pleasure, a deep wanting that disgusts me, even though I can't stop it.

We find the location in a matter of seconds, but I know this is wrong. I can't measure the passing of time while in my trance, barely notice things around me. I may have walked five minutes or thirty. I will only know this once I wake.

The house is dark. It's a two-story cape cod with a small front porch and a silver BMW sitting in the drive. The grass is freshly mowed, the bite of its clippings stinging my nostrils. The night air is crisp, coats my lungs with ice and metal. A tickle skitters across my neck. My mouth opens, and the song begins, strange words I will never understand. Dad isn't far behind me. I know this because every time I bring my song, it's like an out-of-body experience, like I'm floating above, looking down on a scene that doesn't belong to me.

But it does. It always does.

My heart races, and heat builds in my belly, climbs through my chest, claws toward my neck. The end is near. All sensation leaves my feet and hands, and the headache will wash over me like an unexpected wave crashing in the ocean. A curtain on the second floor parts, a vision of a pale face glancing out. The person can't see me. I'm standing beneath the shadows of a tree. But he or she understands me. I know this. The victim whose death I predict can always understand the ancient words I sing.

The song ends. My legs go weak. Dad catches me before I fall, like always, pulling my hood from my head. Blessed freedom from the pain that stabs my brain.

I breathe, close my eyes. Breathe. Breathe. He whispers in my ear, and peace spreads across my core like melted snow. It's time to go home.

But as I stand, a new sensation overwhelms me. Or rather, a familiar sensation. This almost never happens. Almost. But sometimes it does, and it's clear it's happening now.

Without warning, another flood of euphoria liquefies my core. The trance is upon me again, and that same tickle teases the back of my neck.

This time I walk only a few feet, to the house beside the one at which I just sang. My brain tells me I should be confused, but the curse won't allow me to think. *Just sing.*

The song always takes precedence.

Seconds pass, minutes. I hope not more than a few. Poor Dad has been given double duty tonight. Will he be awake for work in the morning? I sway on my feet, but my song doesn't falter. Dad places a hand on my back to steady me.

Again, pressure fills my head, makes the dark night go darker before I regain my vision. I have even less energy than before. I sit on the ground, my balance still dependent on Dad.

Two deaths. That's what will happen sometime over the next few days. My heart is heavy, and I fight back tears. Fill my lungs. Focus. Listen.

Night air catches my parched throat, and I gag.

Again? Not again. *Yes, again.*

A third wave swells from my feet to my head, lifts me up, forces my feet to move. *Like a slave.* Pain stings the backs of my eyes, and my chest feels as if it might explode. Another song? Always. Always the song.

My hands tremble, and the sensation of my curse no longer feels pleasant. It feels heavy. Like lead has weighed my limbs and my core, every bone in my body a burden, a price to be paid. When will this agony end?

Again, I don't walk far, only one house over. This one looks similar to the other two but holds a white Cadillac SUV out front. I whimper as the first notes of melody trickle from my mouth. They spread along the ground, weaving through grass and earth, enter the house, plague this poor family who deserves nothing of my gift. My curse.

This time I'm beyond exhausted. I collapse to my knees as soon as the stupor releases me. Dad is by my side, holds me in his arms. I hear myself pant and cringe in pain when the visions come. The visions that always come when I leave the cape on for too long. He abruptly yanks the hood from my head, and I sigh, sink deeper into his arms.

"Three?" I say, ashamed. Devastated.

He says nothing. Just holds me tight.

After a minute, my breathing returns to normal, mostly. My muscles have stopped their spasms. They'll be sore tomorrow.

"Come on," he whispers as he pulls me to my feet.

"Three," is all I can say.

He nods.

"Have I ever—?"

"No. You've never sung more than twice in a night. Not

that I can remember." He stiffens, keeps one arm around my waist to steady me.

"Then why—?"

"I don't know, sweetheart. I just don't know."

I glance up and see the worry in his eyes, the way his brows pull together. My curse has imploded.

Days skipped with no song. Far too many songs sung in one night. Screams shared during daylight after the victim has already crossed into their afterworld.

Why is it I'm always around to see the deaths I've predicted? This has never happened in the past. Not even once.

"Everything will be all right, Caoine. We'll figure this out."

Will we? How can he know when he's never been able to turn my curse into a gift as he's so often promised? How can he, when he knows so little about who I am, what I do? So unwilling to help me find a cure?

I swallow as a thought occurs to me. There's one person I can confide in. Or people, if I counted Seamus. Aubree knows things, things others might not. Didn't they both come right out and tell me I could trust them? Could tell them anything? Maybe this is something worth talking about.

Aubree knows about Celtic symbols and ancient beliefs of a people who don't even exist. At the end of the conversation in the coffee shop, she'd told me how the symbol—that sign I keep seeing everywhere—is connected to the mythological world of Faerie. She told the tale as if it were a bedtime story.

I can tell she didn't believe her own words, was telling me simply because that was what she'd learned from her father before he passed. So how can I confide in her without telling her about my curse, without admitting I'm anything *other*? Not human?

How can I convince her I'm not actually crazy when she spoke so casually of the land of Faerie, like it was a fairytale?

And how can I convince her I'm a faerie myself?

19

CAOINE

MOLECULES INSIDE MY SKIN VIBRATE, threaten to come undone. Sweat gathers between each of my fingers, at the crease of my neck, at the base of my spine. I close my eyes. This should be a happy occasion, right? I open them and stare at the image in my bedroom mirror.

Pale hair falls straight around my face, like a veil of rain. White rain. My brows and eyelashes are so light they're almost nonexistent as they disappear into the smooth translucence of my face. Pasty, thin lips draw no attention at all. The only things that are noticeable are my eyes. *Always my eyes.* A liquid silver so faded it would seem the color was an afterthought. The other a dull green, just as eager to blend into the whites of my eyes.

A thick lump forms in my throat. Why had I agreed to this date again?

The doorbell rings, and all my muscles jump inside my skin. I lick my lips, smooth the front of the new fitted top I bought just for tonight. I had nothing in my closet but jeans, so that's how I finished the ensemble. *Please Oliver, don't take me anywhere that requires a dress.*

"Caoine!" my dad calls from downstairs.

His voice might sound normal to others, but to me it's laced with his first few beers. By the time I get home, he'll be asleep in his stupor.

I inhale, release it. Repeat. *This is it. My first real date. With a boy. A boy I like.* Fear paralyzes my legs, and I can't move. Why can't I move?

"Caoine! You don't have all night!"

Yes, I know this. It's already past six, and I made it perfectly clear that I *had* to be home by ten sharp. My curse always awakes soon after, and I'm not taking any chances. Thankfully Oliver just thinks I have an overprotective dad.

Muffled conversation drifts up the stairs, and I assume Oliver is getting the "dad talk." There's no time to waste. I fidget with my shirt as I descend the stairs, my gaze anywhere but on Oliver. Will I even survive the night? Can I actually *do* this? I don't know how to be a normal teenager. *Nothing about this is okay.* My insides freeze.

The stairs creak beneath my feet, and I fight a gag from the odor of ramen noodles that hangs in the air from supper. Oliver gasps. I have no choice but to glance up. His eyes are on me, his jaw slightly ajar. *Oh crap. Do I have food on my face?*

"You look beautiful," he says.

My gaze shifts to my dad before it returns to Oliver, then the floor. Do I? I have zero idea how. I look exactly like I do every day.

"Have her back by ten, then?" my dad says.

I swallow. I should've thanked Oliver for the compliment. But now it would be awkward. *Way to start the date, Caoine.*

"Absolutely." Oliver's hand skims my lower back.

I shiver, wipe my hands on my jeans, refocus. I can totally do this.

"I'll be fine, Dad." There's a little too much edge to my tone.

We make eye contact so I can drive the point home. Yes, my curse is scary. Yes, I need my dad by my side when it awakes. And yes, I really do want to go out with Oliver tonight.

My dad's lips form a thin line, but he gives a curt nod before we step out the door. Convincing him this was a possibility took everything in my arsenal two days ago. That was when Oliver officially asked me out. He switched shifts and cleared his schedule just for me. Since our last impromptu date ended with a dead dude at a soccer game and all. A shiver runs down my spine as an image of the guy flits through my mind.

"Any thoughts on where you'd like to go?" Oliver casually snags my hand in his as we walk toward his car. His fingertips are rough against my skin, a contrast to how soft his palms are. *I should ask him about that.*

My heart bounces around inside my chest, and words clog my throat.

But he smiles and squeezes my hand. "No worries. I've got an idea."

He walks me to the passenger side and opens then closes my door. I scream internally at myself to say something, but of course, nothing comes out. Nothing. Somehow I know this gesture is rare, something most guys don't do anymore. His chivalry sends energy along my arms, down each fingertip.

The sun has almost set, and the sky grows darker by the minute as we wind through back roads and across country paths overgrown with dying corn stalks. Still, I have nothing to say. I try not to concentrate on his driving skills, but I'm distracted by how cautious he is. Like he knows he holds precious cargo or something. Totally something my dad would say, not me. But still . . . the blood in my veins pounds a little faster. Could he really like me?

Fifteen minutes later, we pull off the main road onto a stone-filled path. Long stalks of vegetation line the way, and I sense there's water nearby. We round a bend to a clearing that opens onto a large lake. Moonlight reflects on the water, and it's bright enough to light up the area around us. Docks line the edge every fifty feet, and we're not the only ones who have come out on a Saturday night. Every single dock has at least one car parked beside it, and some of the piers hold whole groups of teenagers.

"This is a popular hangout," Oliver says.

I look at him for the first time, and my heart skips over a million rocks.

"There aren't too many places you can go for a free date, so a lot of us like to come here. Even in the fall when it's too cold to swim. I mean, some still get in the water, even though it's freaking freezing, but that's more just to show off."

I smile and he relaxes. Is he nervous?

He keeps driving until we're around the opposite side of the lake, to an empty dock. We park, and he turns off the car. He doesn't move to get out, though. My heart leaps to my throat. *Is he expecting something? Oh my gosh, he's expecting something.* I hadn't even considered this!

But instead, he talks. "Look, I like you a lot, Caoine." His gaze is on his hands, in his lap. "I really do. I knew before I asked you out that you're shy, that there are things you don't want to talk about. But I just want you to know, I'll never hurt you, okay?" He looks at me now, a strange source of affection in the lines of his dark face. "I know this must be hard for you, going out with some guy you barely know when you're not settled here yet. But—" He blows out a breath and gives a soft chuckle. "To be honest, I sort of didn't want to wait. I was afraid if I did, someone else would beat me to it."

I blink. He thought another guy would ask me out? Clearly he has no idea about guys and me. How very uninterested they tend to be.

He reaches over and takes my hand again. "I'm not trying to pressure you, promise. I just wanted you to know. You can be yourself. Around me, at least. Don't be afraid. I like you."

The car is running out of air, and I need to get outside

before I choke on nothingness. I nod and relax my grip. Was I just squeezing his hand? Ugh.

Oliver laughs, and I sit frozen, reviewing his words. Marveling at the fact that he assumes any other guy on this earth might actually want to take me on a date. Then he's at my door, opens it. He's happy to take my hand again as I climb out of the car. All the blood in my body races toward my heart. This chivalry thing could be easy to get used to.

We walk to the end of the dock, a brisk chill on the night air. Moisture clings to my skin, a faint scent of moss hanging above my head. Voices skitter across the water, laughter, a shout. It's too dim to see anything, so I just follow his lead.

We go straight to the end of the wooden planks before he plops down right on the edge and yanks my hand to pull me beside him. Our legs dangle over the edge, but the water is too far below to reach. I exhale, slow and steady. He's right. Everything about this is relaxing. Welcoming. This is a perfect first date.

His thumb runs along my palm, but his gaze is on the water. It gently laps against the wooden poles that support the dock, a strong odor of fish and earth mingling in the air. We sit in silence as my eyes adjust to the light. Most of the docks hold a single couple, just like us. Many are seated or lying on their bellies while they talk. A few are clearly making out. I try not to stare. Why would anyone want to be so public about kissing? My chest tightens as I glance at Oliver.

A burst of laughter draws my attention to a dock that holds at least ten or twelve teens. This would be a fun place to have a party, if I'm ever invited to one.

"So tell me about Caoine. The real one." He smiles. "Not just the one you want to show at school."

I bite my lip. My mind goes blank for a split second, then, "I've moved almost as many times as I am old."

He raises his eyebrows with a whistle. "Now that's what

I'm talking about. Do tell, Ms. Roberts. I'm dying to know the many towns that have shaped who you are."

And for whatever reason, everything I've ever felt, ever thought—every part of me—suddenly spills free. Like a dam ready to break, it flows without any barriers, and all I feel is . . . relief. Freedom.

Belonging.

I talk so long, I think I might run out of words. And I marvel at the way he's gotten me to open up, at the way he listens. *Really* listens. Like I'm the last person on earth, and all he wants to do is listen to me forever.

When I finally stop, neither of us tries to get the conversation going again. An unspoken agreement that what's been said is good and right, but silence is just as right. That sometimes just *being* is better. Even on a date. I look at the night sky and take in a lungful of chilly autumn air. My hand is still in his.

"This place is sort of my refuge," Oliver finally says.

I look at him in surprise. That isn't what I expected him to say. At all.

His face is somber, his gaze still in another place. "A few years back, my family went through a—uh—a tough time. I couldn't drive yet, but I had a bike." Pause. "I came here every day for two years straight. Couldn't keep myself away. It was sort of like therapy, ya know?" He licks his lips. "Although, I did see a therapist, too." He swallows.

"What happened? If you don't mind my asking."

He shakes his head. "No. Not at all." He clears his throat. "About five years ago my brother—he was in an accident. He . . . died."

Pain lances my chest. "I'm so sorry."

"It's okay. It really is. I mean . . . sure, I'd like to have my brother back. He was . . . amazing. Super popular, star soccer player, crazy smart. He was headed to some big-name college. All my parents' hopes and dreams were on his shoulders. Then one night, it was all gone." Oliver shrugs. "My brother had a car accident, and that was that."

"Whoa. I . . . I can't imagine." I blink back tears for a boy I've never met.

He turns just slightly, his free hand now picking at strands of my hair, his gaze on my lips, my neck, my eyes. "I didn't tell you that to depress you, Caoine. I told you because . . . we all have skeletons in our closet. We're all wounded, broken in some way. But that doesn't make us any less. Those fractures, they make us stronger. They make us special." He hesitates, leans closer. "I don't know what happened to you, but I'd really like to get to know you. If you'll let me."

Could I tell him? Is it possible he could actually accept that I'm a freak?

I lick my lips, lean toward him another few inches. He responds, the hand that had been playing with my hair now firmly in place at the base of my neck. His gaze is on my lips now. Only my lips. We are inches apart, and my heart wants to beat outside of my chest, to meld with his. To consume all the good parts of him that make me feel happy and relaxed and wanted. I feel his breath on my lips.

Then I stop. Everything stops.

And I get the urge to scream.

20

CAOINE

TIME STANDS STILL. My throat feels full, like it's ready to explode. I go lightheaded, grip the dock with my free hand, but still sway.

"What time is it?" I whisper, terrified to allow myself to believe this is happening.

"Eight-thirty." He pulls back. He knows something's wrong. "Should I take you home?"

"I—I—" My fingers squeeze his, and I beg my body not to betray me, to keep the curse hidden just a few minutes longer. Strike that. My curse needs to stay under control for at least half an hour longer.

But it's too late. It wants to be set free, must be set free. There's no way to stop it. Lead weighs down my belly as my feet act in obedience. I come to a full stand, turn, and face the dock to our right. I don't want to do this, but I can't stop it. The song is near, the victim, closer.

"Caoine?" Oliver is wary but on his feet.

My heart clenches at the hesitation in his voice.

I dig my nails into my palms but know it will do no good. My curse is about to be released for all to hear. The real curse.

The real me.

My cloak is at home, safe and sound in my closet. That trusty piece of fabric that is my protector. Why hadn't I brought it? As off-kilter as my curse has been lately, why on earth would I think I could leave it home? Without it, my curse won't sound like the eerie lament that floats along the night air. It will tumble from me, raw and ragged.

Tears sting the backs of my eyes, and I gag on the words I am desperate to say to Oliver. *Run. Leave now. What is about to happen will not be pleasant. It will change the way you view me. Forever. And I could never handle that. Not even a little.*

Had it only been moments before I'd actually considered telling the boy the truth behind who I am? This isn't how I'd planned it.

This isn't how it's supposed to go.

Something inside me shatters. My mouth opens, and an inhuman wail blazes forth. A screech that can break glass, a fracture of sound that causes those around to cover their ears. I stand outside myself and watch as my body convulses with a panicked shriek, as Oliver stands back, hands over his ears, horror on his face. As every eye of every person on every dock stops breathing, stops all motion, to turn their attention on the lunatic with the impossible voice.

I scream.

And I die inside one more notch. Because that's what happens when I predict a death, I die right along with them.

My hands and feet go numb as my body shakes uncontrollably. The world around me spins, and I try to catch the dock as it races toward my face, but I'm too late. Pain pierces my cheek as the ground catches my fall. Agony pulses behind my eye, along my temple. Have I broken something?

Oliver is by my side. The night goes black, but I feel arms around me, warmth against my side, whispers in my ear. I strain to see through hazy vision. Oliver looks down at me, concern painted across his features. Compassion. Confusion.

His arms are the ones holding me. I try to shake my head,

but I can't. This doesn't make sense. He hasn't run away, hasn't abandoned me the way he should. Doesn't he realize I'm a monster?

"Caoine," he says. "Are you all right? Are you hurt?"

He thinks I might be hurt? No! I'm not the one hurt. I'm the one who *does* the hurting. The killing.

Bile lunges up my throat, but I manage to keep that a secret, too. I place a hand on my cheek that throbs in misery.

"Caoine," he whispers again.

Then another sound, another scream. This one human. From a girl. Splashing replaces silence, and more voices raise an alarm. I struggle to hear what they're saying, to push past the words Oliver is saying to me, even though I'd rather bask in his comfort.

Someone is drowning. A boy is dying just feet away, and it was me who told his secret. Tears fall freely down my face, across my bruised skin. Still, Oliver's arms hold me tight.

A siren sounds in the distance, and my blood runs cold.

They're coming for me! They know what I've done. I can no longer hide it.

I tense.

"Hang in there, Caoine. Don't give up on me, girl." Oliver yanks me into his arms, my legs dangling as he stands with all the ease of a dancer. I slip my hands around his neck and hold on.

In seconds, he has me off the dock, inside his car. He starts the engine and roars us around the opposite side of the lake, far away from the flashing lights.

They haven't come for me. Of course not. I blink, although one eye is swollen halfway shut. I stare. They've come for the boy. The one who died tonight.

The one whose death I predicted. Who died because of me.

Things go black again, and my head lolls to the side of the headrest, ready for sleep to kidnap me. But it doesn't. Sleep evades the pull, and it can't come because Oliver is talking to me, waking me, forcing me to come back to the person I was before the scream.

"Caoine. Wake up. We're here." His hand on my shoulder is gentle. "Open your eyes. We're not at the lake anymore. It's safe now."

I do as he says. He's right. He's brought us to a side street, parked in front of a darkened house. Somewhere other. Where we can talk. I breathe, sigh. He holds an arm toward me, and I willingly sink into his embrace. Peaceful and safe.

Oliver didn't leave me. He's here to hold me in my despair. He's chosen me. He's chosen to be with a monster.

As my eyes close and I drift into slumber, I can't decide if I'm happy or sad for him.

21

CAOINE

HE HOLDS me for what feels like hours as I drift in and out of consciousness, the cold edge of the leather seat beneath my body. The next time I look at the car dash, the clock reads nine forty-seven. Has so much happened in such a short time?

The warmth inside the car fades as the cool night air sneaks into the holes around us. I shiver and pull back from Oliver's embrace, even though my body fights to stay. A scent of English lavender clings to him. I want to get lost in it. Instead, I lift my sore eyes. One still won't open all the way.

"Thank you," is all I'm able to croak.

He nods but doesn't take his arms from around my waist, like he's afraid I'll run away or something. "You ready to talk?"

No. *Never.* I clench my jaw and square my shoulders. There's no way out of this. He's seen what I can do—in its fullest capacity. He won't walk away without explanation.

I swallow. "I was born this way."

His full lips remain still.

My head spins as I think of where to begin. This whole thing started before I was born. But do I start there and confuse him more, or do I tell him the truth of who I am first? Of the monster inside me?

I close my eyes. "I'm what you would call a banshee." He doesn't make a sound—no gasp or display of shock—so I go on. "There's a more formal name, something foreign and confusing. But the only way to describe what I am is to say: I'm not—entirely human."

There. I said it. I open my eyes. His gaze is glued to my face, but there's no disgust. It's almost a look of awe. His hands are still where they were before my confession. In fact, I think he pulls me closer. How is this possible?

I pull in a shaky breath. "I guess I should just tell you the whole story." Another sigh. "Before I was born, when my mom was still pregnant with me, my parents were visited by a faerie." I look down. "Yes, I know. This sounds unbelievable. But it's true—"

"I believe you," Oliver says.

My gaze shoots to his. "You do?"

"Definitely."

I glance at his dark fingers entwined in mine and relax just a notch.

"This faerie, she contacted them in secret. Her job was to prepare them for the death of their child, to help them bear the despair of loss. Faeries each have a job, and that was hers. Except—" I lick my lips. "Except . . . she couldn't do it. She couldn't bear to watch another child die. So she made them a deal. If they committed my life to the Realm of Faerie, then I'd be allowed to live. They'd still get to keep me; I'd grow up just like any other child. But I would be part faerie. One sacrifice for another. They agreed."

Oliver rubs my back absentmindedly, and I have to refocus.

"I'm part faerie, part human. Neither one nor the other." Pause. "Along with this deal came a job, as a banshee, a.k.a. Harbinger of Death." I shrug. "I announce death before it comes. There's no way I can stop it. I am"—I bite my lip—"*darkness*."

He frowns. "That boy. You knew he was going to die?"

I shake my head adamantly. "No. I didn't know it would be him. Or when, even. When the curse awakes, I become subject to its will. I must announce at that moment where it wants me to announce. But I never know who will die, or in what way. My song can come days before the death or minutes, like it did tonight. I never know. I just . . . do."

He crinkles his brow. "A song?"

My chest deflates. Yeah, I guess that shriek didn't sound like much of a song to him. "Well, it usually is. At first my dad had no idea what being a banshee would mean for me, he was just happy I was alive. But after I was born, I—" Emotion floods my throat, and I blink back tears. "After I was born, my cry wasn't normal. It was that *thing* you just heard. Loud and wailing and totally not human." I gather the courage to say the next words. "A few minutes after my first cry, my mom died from complications from childbirth."

An anvil-sized weight drops inside my chest, and I feel like I might puke. Unconsciously, I crush Oliver's fingers between mine. I flinch and release them, but he grabs my hand again.

"And?" he says.

"And . . . my dad knew the truth. By bargaining for the life of his daughter, he'd given up his wife. My birth meant my mom's death." My chest constricts further. "I literally killed my mom. And I literally kill people around me, too."

Oliver shakes his head. "That's not true." His furrowed brow displays a gentle anger. "And deep down I think you know that. Being a messenger of what's to come is *not* the same thing as killing someone."

I frown but let him go on.

"And did the faerie say it was either your life or your mom's?"

I shake my head.

"Then you can't know what the terms were, Caoine. Maybe she was going to die anyway, and that's why the faerie offered the deal? Besides, your parents did what they could to save your life. Don't you think your mom would've chosen to give hers for yours?"

I never considered this before. I bite the inside of my lip and nibble it raw. "Doesn't matter. What's done is done. She's gone and I—I have the job of death." My laugh sounds hollow. Cynical.

He nudges me. "I want to hear the rest. I know there's more."

"Oh sure, you want to hear all the drama." I roll my eyes, but he gives me a soft grin. I pull in a shaky breath. "No one else died until I was two, when our dog got sick. Real sick. Just before he died, I let out that crazy scream. It freaked my dad out, because he'd sort of forgotten what the faerie said about me.

"When I was five, my grandmother died in her sleep. That night I woke up screaming . . . *that cry* again.

"My dad remembered the faerie had left me a cloak. It's silver and heavy with yards of material, but it's also magical. Faerie magic. The next time I was about to scream, he made me wear it. Instead of a scream, a beautiful lament came out. Seriously, even as a little girl, the song was crazy dazzling. Not trying to brag, but when I'm under my curse, I've got some pipes."

Oliver stifles a chuckle, and I sort of half grin.

"Seriously! I can't sing a note otherwise. I'm tone deaf or something. But with that cloak, I sound like I could go on one of those competition shows. I'm convinced I would get a record deal."

He tilts his head and fiddles with the loose strands of my alabaster hair. My body responds by settling into his embrace.

"So that's my story. It's what I do. Ever since I can remember, I've woken up almost every night, put on my cape, and walked around town, announcing the death of some poor soul. My dad always follows along, since when I'm in my trance, I have no control over my body. He's terrified I'll walk into a pool or something. And there's the fact I'm always depleted of energy as soon as the lament is done. He's there to carry me home if I don't have the strength." I turn in Oliver's arms. "But I guess you had that duty tonight." I swallow against the toad that's taken residence in my throat. "Thanks for that."

He grins, which makes my brain have a nuclear meltdown. He still isn't running from me in absolute terror?

"I didn't mind that so much, actually." Heat from his fingers curves along my jaw.

I nuzzle my head against his shoulder. "Yeah, well, thanks. I honestly have no idea why it happened so early tonight. It usually doesn't rear its ugly head before ten." Then again, the last week has been one heaping plate of unusual.

Oliver nods, then smacks his head. "Oh. That's why you and your dad were so firm with your curfew. I thought he was seriously protective or something."

"No." I roll my eyes. "That curfew was all me. I was terrified something like this might happen, and, well . . . it did. Which sort of blows my mind, since you're like, still here and everything." I look up at him. "Why are you still here, anyway?"

"What?"

"You're here. Why? You should be halfway to Yuma by now, shouldn't you?"

He frowns. "You think the most beautiful, kind girl in school is going to scare me away with one little quirk?"

I raise my brows. "A quirk? I'm the harbinger of death. How is that a quirk?"

He shrugs. "Well, like I said . . . skeletons. We've all got 'em."

I laugh—actually laugh!—and he joins me. Is this even possible? Is this guy really still into me, and is it possible I might be just as into him?

"There is one thing you didn't explain though," he says after a beat.

"Yeah?"

"Well, you keep calling what you do a curse. Why?"

"Why? Why not? That's what it is, isn't it? I literally announce death. How much more depressing of a job can I have? My dad calls it a gift, but only because that's what the faerie called it. But I don't see how it could be even close to a gift, if you ask me. I mean, a gift would be a good thing, right? It should help people, not kill them."

"Well, you said when you have on your cloak, it sounds like a beautiful song, right?"

I nod.

"Do the people who are about to die ever hear the song?"

"I think some do. It's hard because I've rarely known who was about to die. And I haven't always been within earshot. But from the way the faerie explained it, if they hear it, only they understand my words."

"Understand? You don't sing in English?"

My cheeks go hot. "No. I'm not entirely sure what language it is—maybe Faerie? It sounds sort of Gaelic. I've never been able to understand what I sing. But the faerie said the person for whom the song was intended would understand exactly what I say."

"Okay, so, just before a person dies, you sing them an alluring, exquisite song of indescribable beauty—"

"Hey now, I wouldn't go that far."

He puts one finger on my lips to shut me up. "You sing them an unearthly song to soothe their soul. And maybe—just maybe—those words you don't understand say things they need to hear, to help them enter the afterlife." Oliver lets his finger run along my jaw. "Don't you think that's a gift? To be the person to soothe one's soul before they leave this earth forever?"

"I—" My mouth falls open. How has this guy just turned the most negative thing in my life into something positive?

"I'm right, aren't I?" His smile is triumphant.

I stare at him, dumbfounded.

"I think it's a gift."

"Really?" I focus on not falling over.

"Definitely. There's no way I could feel this way about a girl who was cursed."

He presses his forehead against mine, eyes closed, his breath soft against my skin. Heat creeps along my neck and across my chest and down each limb of my body. And I relax. For the first time in my life, I allow myself to believe that maybe I've been wrong all these years. Maybe what I have isn't a curse.

Maybe I'm not the monster I always thought I was. If only the man in my arms would stick around every day to remind me of this.

22

CAOINE

OLIVER LIKES ME. He knows I'm strange and He. Still. Likes. Me!

My heart speeds inside my chest as memories of our date crush against the walls of my mind. The morning sun is bright and already warming the crisp autumn air. Still, I pull my backpack a little tighter to stop the goose pimples from invading my arms.

Something is burning far away, and I remember camping trips with my dad: s'mores over a fire, the yummy scent of waking up in a stuffy tent. It's like all the best memories I've ever had decided to invade my personal space this morning. And for the first time in forever, I don't mind.

My daily walk to school is relaxing. Lovely. Lovely? Yes, lovely. I bite my lip and stifle a laugh at the idea that I might actually skip. Really.

The two-block walk consists of passing a barking dog —*Good morning, sweet pit*—smiling at the old lady next door— actually smiling!—and not crinkling my nose as the garbage truck spreads its stink all over town—*Thank you for taking our garbage, Garbage Men!* I'm on the path to the front door of school in a blink.

"Caoine!"

I jump in place. And then replace my silly grin with the biggest smile ever.

Is this smile real? And is it possible I'm not avoiding eye contact with every single person around me? Yes. It totally is.

Oliver and Eric lean against Oliver's decade-old, scratched and beaten, royal-blue Toyota Camry. From the way Oliver looks at me, I know he's the one who called to me. And the fact Eric appears to be trying to busy himself—pathetically, I might add—while his best friend oogles my bare legs.

I'll admit, I did it. I finally wore the mini-skirt Aubree has been trying to get me to wear. And it's clear Oliver doesn't mind one bit. Although the chill running up my thighs doesn't help matters much. But who cares?

"Hey." I'm breathless as I lean against the car right next to him.

He closes the space between us and slips one hand around my waist. I freeze and attempt to step back, but he's already got his other hand lost somewhere in my hair, his gaze locked on mine. No words are spoken. The moment is beyond perfect. I hold my breath for a full thirty seconds until he pulls back. My knees go weak, and I lean against his side.

"Well, guess your date went well," Eric deadpans from behind Oliver.

I blink. *Yeah. Guess so.* And I guess maybe I don't need to ask the question I've been harboring all weekend—how exactly does Oliver feel about me? A crazy voice in the back of my head has been trying to convince me the whole thing was a dream, or maybe he only used me to prove to his friends he could get with the new girl. Either way, I wasn't positive he'd even talk to me today.

But apparently all those things were definitely in my head.

"You could say that," Oliver says, answering his friend. But his acorn-hued eyes don't leave mine. "How are you?" His voice is lower now, just above a whisper.

"Better now." I stop myself from bouncing on my toes. "You?"

"Better now." He gives me that snaggletooth smile, and every artery in my body wants to explode from the rush of blood crashing through it. "Any chance you'd want to come watch soccer practice today? So maybe we can grab a coffee — or, erm, *tea* — after?"

One side of my mouth curls into a grin. I love the fact he actually listened when I said how much I hate coffee, something every other teenager on earth seems to love in abundance. I nod but then frown.

"What?"

"I forgot. I'm all social and crap now."

"Social and crap?" Eric echoes from beside us, his red hair like brilliant flames in the reflection of the sun.

I glance at him, more out of pity since I forgot he was even there. "I joined the school paper. I'm tied up there until at least four thirty."

"After?" Oliver says.

"Oh sure. Ditch your buddy." Eric shakes his head. "Don't worry about me. I'll be fine. I'll find my own ride home. Maybe I'll play in traffic for a while, try not to get arrested — "

Oliver rolls his eyes and glances over his shoulder. "Just because you bum a ride home with me every day doesn't mean we have a standing date, dude. Find your own way home."

Eric puts a hand over his chest in mock hurt. "You wound me, man. Seriously. Cold. Whatever happened to the bros before — erm, I mean — pals before gals thing?" His gaze skitters toward me but settles back on his friend.

He mumbles something else under his breath and leans against the car, only to pull away with a scowl on his face, the look directed at me. I raise a brow at him. Really? Is my display of affection truly that gross to him? Eric gives a mock huff of irritation and pulls his phone from his pocket to start texting.

"Hey now," Oliver warns his friend before he returns his attention to me. "How 'bout it?"

I slide my hands up his arms, and little chills that have nothing to do with the weather zip along my belly. "My dad doesn't get home until late. As long as I have time to get home and get supper going, I'm sure he'll be fine with it."

Totally not true. My dad flipped when he found out my curse came out early the night of our date. But there was nothing either of us could do about it, so he finally let the issue drop. Not before he warned me to keep my dates closer to home next time.

"Cool. Meet me by the soccer field?"

I begin to nod but am cut off by Eric's dramatics. A string of expletives falls from his mouth as he stares at his phone. "Whoa. No way, that's nuts!"

"What's up?" Oliver asks, but Eric's already shoving the phone in his face. Because, *Eric.*

"Check it out. Some dude went psycho this morning. Blew away both his buddies before the police had to mow him down."

"Wait, what?" I practically tackle Oliver to look over his shoulder. My stomach is by my knees, and my heart is in my throat.

Oliver's good mood is out the window, too, as the three of us watch the police video circulating online.

"*. . . unclear what the motivation could have been early this morning, when a man in his mid-forties unexpectedly confronted a neighbor on his front lawn. When the argument escalated, the man pulled a gun and threatened the victim. It is believed another neighbor tried to intervene to defuse the situation. Within minutes, both neighbors were shot by the gunman, who then turned the gun on any who challenged him. Several minutes later, police were forced to open fire when the man attempted to shoot an officer.*" The news reporter bows her head with a solemn look on her face. "*It's a somber mood here in Penny*

Hills this morning, Jan. More details to come later on this tragic development of three dead in a local community."

I recognize the house behind the reporter, and I think I'm going to be sick. My heart pounds so hard I think it wants to escape. Sort of the way I want to. Right now. I concentrate on breathing, and my fingers dig into Oliver's arm, my teeth clenched. His gaze is on mine, and I can see the questions in his eyes. *Are you all right? Did you know this would happen? This isn't your fault. Relax.*

"Wow. That's crazy." Eric is oblivious to the fact I'm currently having a panic attack. "Some guy takes out two of his neighbors, then bites it? What a way to start a Monday."

"Shut it, Eric," Oliver says. His full attention is on me, and I can tell he wants to take me away, to get me in the car alone before I explode. Melt down. Unravel into a million different things, none of them sane.

But he doesn't have time. Before he can ask me anything, I'm running.

Running. Running. *Running.*

Running from him and away from here and toward the only person who might have some answers. I need to find Aubree, to see if she can make sense of this latest slew of deaths. She's the only one I can trust.

I know this because she knew about the symbol, the one that means slavery but doesn't mean what we think it means. The symbol I saw on the phone, in the video. Carved into the tree behind the reporter.

The same tree I stood beneath on the night I sang my lament.

23

CAOINE

I SLAM through the front doors of the school. My insides are like a volcano about to erupt, on fire and unpredictable as I race down the halls. Pins and needles prick my fingers, and I have to blink away spots. *It's going to be okay. I just need to find Aubree. Then everything will be okay.* Why am I so certain of this? My throat closes as I round the corner to her locker.

She stands by her locker, her plum-hued hair crimped and styled in a high ponytail like she's stepped right out of the 1980s. Her fire engine-red glasses match her slim-fitting dress, patent leather heels a perfect match to her hair.

"Aubree!" I yell far too loudly.

She looks up in surprise. A dozen glances from those around us make my face heat. Even Seamus stirs as he leans lazily against the lockers beside her.

Her brown eyes connect with mine. "What happened?"

She's obviously worried, and immediately a pang of guilt hits me. A week ago I was trying to get rid of her, to separate myself from any sort of friendship. Now I can't figure out what I'd do without her.

I lean close to both of them. Her locker still sways open.

Students are all around us, but I hope the thin piece of metal will give us a little privacy.

"There's been another death," I say.

"Yeah?"

My eyes dart side to side. "Three, actually." Seamus whistles under his breath, but I ignore him. "I saw it on the news. A double murder, and the shooter was taken out by police."

"Okaaay," she draws out. I can tell she's trying to make the connection between my frantic demeanor and some random dude kicking the bucket.

"And . . ." I blow out a breath. "And that symbol was carved into a tree, behind where the reporter was standing."

Her mouth falls open. "You mean, the one you saw at the diner when that cook died?"

I nod.

"The one near the body of that kid who bit it at the soccer game? That symbol?" Seamus echoes, even though he totally doesn't need to.

"What symbol?" Oliver says from behind me.

I freeze. I didn't mean to run away from him. Of course he'd follow me.

"Ya know, the symbol," Seamus says. Like that explains anything.

Aubree rolls her eyes, then gives me a serious look.

Crud. This is so not how it's supposed to go. It's sweet Oliver has taken the news about my banshee-ness so casually, but this is entirely different. This is the third time that symbol has appeared near a death I've predicted. There's no way this can be anything other than *bad*. Oliver needs to be far from this. Nowhere near my curse or the symbols or anything to do with me.

I scrub my hands over my face.

"Caoine?" Oliver says with more patience than I deserve.

Our date. It was so nice. How can I turn him away now?

"You want to go somewhere private to talk?" Aubree offers in a whisper, even though Oliver can totally hear.

"Just—no," I huff. Again, I rub my eyes with the palms of my hands and wish this whole thing away.

What do I do? I can't turn Oliver away, but dragging him further into this is such a bad idea.

I clench my teeth and bang my fists against my legs. "It's fine. He's cool. He—knows things." I pause, lock eyes with him. Oliver knows the truth behind who I am, but Aubree and Seamus *don't*. "He can keep a secret."

Something flickers behind his gaze, but he doesn't break eye contact. Like a silent pledge to stay true or something.

If only I could be sure I wasn't slowly killing him by allowing him into this strange club of death.

"Okay," Aubree says, though she doesn't sound convinced in the slightest.

Oliver steps closer to me, his hands on my shoulders to stop my fidgeting. "What symbol?"

"The one Caoine keeps seeing next to all the dead bodies she finds," Seamus says.

I glare at Seamus. "Not helping."

"What?" His defense is weak, and he immediately gets distracted by a group of guys walking down the hall.

"You've seen people die? More than just that kid from the soccer game?" Oliver looks hurt I didn't tell him. Still, he laces his fingers through mine.

Ugh. Why am I telling him this? This is dangerous!

Aubree's eyes widen at Oliver's affection, and Seamus smirks. I want to kick him but refrain.

"That's not important right now," Aubree says. "We need to figure out why that symbol keeps appearing. And is there a connection to Caoine? It seems like too much of a coincidence that it keeps appearing near you."

My grip tightens around Oliver's. I know exactly how I'm

connected. I'm the harbinger of death. And he knows it too. He squeezes my hand.

"And what this has to do with the whole faerie slavery thing," Seamus tags on.

Now Aubree glares at her friend.

"Slavery?" Oliver asks. "Whoa. What am I missing here?"

The first bell rings, and we jump collectively.

"We don't have time for that now." Aubree looks right at me. "Can we meet after school? To talk?"

I hesitate, my gaze on Oliver's.

"I've got practice," he says. "Will you be all right alone? Without me?"

"What do you mean will she be all right alone? She'll be with us." Seamus looks truly hurt. Aubree smacks him upside the head. "Ouch!"

I ignore him. "I'll be fine," I whisper to Oliver. I'm still not positive this is a good idea. But I've already told him my biggest secret in the universe.

He dips his head an inch lower. "I'll catch up with you right after?"

"Yeah," I breathe. Warmth rolls off his body, and I suddenly wish we were alone.

Aubree bobs her head like it's a plan. Seamus just looks bored.

"Three o'clock," Aubree says. "Don't be late."

She gives me a quick hug, then runs to class. Seamus throws a wink at what could be anyone in our general vicinity, then lopes after her.

Oliver pulls me close, both my hands in his. "I'm sorry I gave up our date."

"I'm sorry I ran away."

He exhales. "We'll figure this out, Caoine. You won't have to face it alone."

Warm liquid bubbles in my core and spreads to every part

of my body. "Thank you." I can't think of any other words to say. I should be telling him to leave me alone. To go away. Forever. Before my banshee song calls to him.

He steps closer, wraps his arms around my waist, presses his forehead to mine. "I'm here for you."

Then he places his lips on my forehead for a split second. Then he, too, disappears. I'm alone in the hallway, frozen in place. Confusion wraps around my body like a set of tentacles. How did I get involved in this whole crazy thing, and why are these people still by my side?

I pause, close my eyes, breathe. *I can't. I just can't right now.* Fully aware the bell could ring at any second, I race to my locker and twist the numbers until they blur and smear in black and white like paint on canvas.

Slam! My locker opens. *This is ridiculous.* I grab books I don't need and toss them in my locker. *Why is this happening? And why now, in this town?* I snag books for first and second period and slide them inside my pack. *Everything about my life has gone haywire, and I can't think of a single thing to do to get things under control.* I zip my bag halfway closed, but then my eyes settle on a scrap of color. A flash of green, a square just large enough to hold a message.

My body goes still. I pull it out with a shaky hand. It's a note. Another love note from my favorite stalker. I pull in a breath, hold it for a second, release it as I unfold the paper.

Sing for me.

My world comes crashing down.

The bell rings. I'm late. But I don't care. There are more important things to worry about right now. Like how I plan to survive the rest of the day when all I want to do is sob and scream and beg the world to swallow me whole. Tears sting my cheeks as I squeeze my eyes shut, crumble the note in my hand. I rest my forehead against the cold steel of the locker and wish I could disappear forever.

Why is he doing this to me? Who can he be?

The hallway empties, and I'm left standing alone. Just as I've always been.

Alone and afraid. Of myself. Of the world. But now, most of all, afraid of a person I don't even know.

24

CAOINE

"My article is on the front page?" My jaw reaches for the floor where I stand.

Jessica flares her nose like a pile of trash is nearby. "Well, it is the biggest news the school has seen in years. I mean, come on, a student died. It's not like that old fuddy-duddy teacher who bit it a few weeks back." She crosses her arms. "And it was well written. I like the angle you took—interviewing his friends and making it more of a memorial than a straight-fact article."

I hold back a sarcastic retort. Was there really any other angle?

Then I almost gag. Wait a second. Jessica put my article— the new girl she so obviously despises—on the front page? I have to find the catch. No way her favors are free.

We're standing in the middle of chaos, inside the confines of the school newspaper workspace. It goes to print in four days, and Jessica just threw the rest of the team for a loop, cutting two major series and inserting a brand-new column. Needless to say, I'm the only one on speaking terms with the girl right now. And that's not saying much.

"Okay. Cool." I try to sound like this is no big deal, but this is totally a big deal.

This is Jessica we're talking about. And she definitely still hates me. There must be strings attached.

"Go over the edits I've made, cut two hundred words, and you should be good." She flips her auburn hair as she heads to her desk but stops midstride. "Oh, and get it done today, please. I've got a new assignment for you. Something I want to run this week."

"Oh?" Another article so soon? I guess I'm officially part of the team. My blood pulses inside my veins, and I try to appear nonchalant.

"Yeah. I want you to do an article on all those missing pets."

I attempt to hide my frown. "Missing pets?"

She rolls her eyes. "Don't you ever watch the news? Missing pets. It's been happening for weeks now. Domestic animals are going missing. There's got to be a billion missing pet posters all over town, Caoine. Seriously. Get with it."

I can only blink at her, at the way she can be so crazy blunt without caring to keep even a single friend in this world.

"Also, you might want to focus more on your duties to the paper." She pins me with a razor-sharp look, and I flinch. "I mean, I know you're still trying to make friends and all, but you might want to keep your distance from some."

"Who?" I frown. Where is this coming from?

"Oliver, for one."

Oh crud. She found out about the date.

"To be honest, I'm surprised he's even given you as much attention as he has."

"Excuse me?" Again, all I can do is blink.

"For being such a flirt, I mean." She gives a breathy giggle like she hasn't purposely meant to hurt me. "You know he's a total player, don't you?"

"I—no." I glance to the side and shift my weight.

She tosses her hair over her shoulder and lifts her chin a few inches. "He's had a tough time coming out of—well, an extended relationship." She purses her lips with a smug smile.

I really want to roll my eyes, since everyone in the universe knows *she* was his last girlfriend.

"He's fallen into a habit of playing the field. I'm fairly certain he's taken every girl out in the senior class at least once."

"Oliver?" My throat constricts, and heat fills my chest.

"Sorry to be the one to tell you, sister. Anyway, just be sure none of your—extra-curricular activities—stand in the way of your obligation to the *Red and Black*, okay?"

Jessica stalks away and leaves me frozen in place. She wants me to buy the idea that Oliver is a player? Is this a threat or a poor attempt at control?

And what's with the missing pets? She gives me *this* after I just wrote a front-page spot? My ribcage clenches an inch tighter, and I huff.

"Ignore her." Catherine smiles as she approaches, her dark curls framing her face. She straightens her shoulders, and I notice she's just about the same height as me, which is impressive since I'm five-foot-nine. She pushes her glasses up her nose. "She's cranky because she missed seeing Oliver this weekend."

Catherine's translucent skin isn't quite as pale as mine. I marvel at the fact I don't look as ghostly while standing beside her. She slides into the seat closest to me.

"Oh?" I lean against the table for support and blink away the shock on my face.

Oliver changed shifts to go on a date with me. My heart pounds a little harder. He missed a shift at work that would've been with her. That's what made her crazy angry. I glance in her direction as she berates one of the siblings—Pen or Quill?

"Everyone else can see it but her," Catherine continues. "Things are over between them. She just won't accept it. She has this nutty idea that the more time she spends with him at work, the higher the chances are of getting him back." She opens her laptop. "In my opinion, he just got wise."

"Huh." I swallow. "So what she said about him—"

"Like I said, ignore her. None of it's true. Oliver's a great guy. She just can't stand that he's even looked at someone else." She gives me a reassuring smile, but I stay rigid.

Does everyone in this school know everyone else's business?

"You can call me Cat, by the way." She purses her lips and glances at Jessica. "I don't like it when she calls me that because there's always this condemnation behind it. Then again, I guess she sounds that way for everything."

She softly giggles, but I stay stiff. It's so weird to be liked more than someone else. Usually, I'm the social outcast everyone avoids like the plague.

"So you're officially part of the team?"

I jump, then relax. Catherine is still wearing a genuine smile. "I guess." I hadn't had any official welcome to the group, other than Jessica's semi-introduction the week before. The morning I handed her my article, she glanced at it, then barked for me not to be late to any of the meetings.

"Do you know what department you'll be working in?"

I bite my lip. "She never assigned me one. Is that bad?"

Catherine tries to hide her cringe. Unsuccessfully. "Well, you might be in danger of getting all the crap articles."

"Like missing pets?" I ask, eyebrows raised.

She laughs. "Um, yeah. Sorry about that. Hopefully next week you'll get something better."

"Yeah." I roll my eyes. It hits me that Catherine hasn't gawked at the way I look. In fact, none of the students on the paper have done a double take. I fight a grin. "What are you working on?"

"Well I *was* working on a two-part series about the music department and how it's changed over the years. Part one focused on the history of the program prior to the twenty-first century. But Jessica nixed part two, so I guess no one will ever find out what happened after the rap music phase."

My eyes go wide, and she laughs.

"I'm kidding! I didn't mention rap music. But she did cut my series." She pouts, then brightens just as quickly. "So I'm gearing up for Halloween. We've only got a few more publications before the big day, and I suggested a series to *spook* the students and faculty." Catherine wiggles her fingers and lowers her voice on the word "spook." It's quite endearing.

"That's a fun idea. Maybe I should think of something to suggest. That way I won't be writing about non-school-related stuff."

She twists her mouth. "You can try, but don't get your hopes up. You never know what you're gonna get with that girl."

We both sigh and glance at Jessica as she sits at her desk and scowls. Her phone is in her hand, and I practically see steam puff from her ears as she looks my way. My skin crawls. Great. Why do I have the feeling my time at the school paper is about to get infinitely worse?

"Gotta get started on that article," I say before I skitter away.

At least I have one friend at the paper. One more friend to add to my growing list of people I'm close to. My belly sinks. This isn't a good thing for any of them, though. People around me keep dying.

My only question is, what can I do to stop it?

25

CAOINE

THREE O'CLOCK CAN'T COME SOON ENOUGH. I'm waiting patiently on the edge of the soccer field, watching Oliver kick around a soccer ball. Where are Aubree and Seamus? Why does this whole thing have me so freaked out?

"Hi-ho Silver!" a male voice calls from behind.

I spin to see Aubree smack Seamus across the chest. "Shut up, idiot."

"What? Her hair looks silver in the sunlight. What'd I do?"

I self consciously run my hand through it. Aubree shoots him a look.

"What?" he repeats.

"Ready?" Aubree asks me, ignoring her cohort altogether.

He snorts and watches the team practice.

"Where are we headed?" I can't help but glance around. The feeling of a thousand prying eyes digs into my brain.

"Follow me." She takes off toward the patch of woods behind the school.

Seamus shrugs, and we follow silently along the edge of the field and past the set of trees that marks the boundary of a small forest, which eventually leads into a bigger one. The school is in the outermost part of town—the last place before hitting no-man's land.

We walk for five minutes, maybe ten. Eventually the path through the trees is lost, and we're stepping over clumps of fallen logs and overgrown plants. A cave pops out from behind a set of trees. My lungs fight against the heavy scent of moss and earth that only grows stronger the deeper we walk.

Aubree's definitely not looking where she's going, but somehow she doesn't stumble over a thing in that crazy, perfectly poised, ballerina way. *How does she do that?* I scramble to grab a branch before I nosedive into foliage.

"I figured this was a good place to talk," she says. "It's out of the way, and there's no place for anyone to hide." She finds a large rock near the entrance of the cave and plops down.

Seamus explores the exterior of the cave. I find a tree to lean against until I figure out how badly it scrapes my back and give up to sit on the rock with Aubree.

"Okay. So what's this about?" My fingers press against the hard surface of the granite, the chill of the stone like a block of ice beneath my tailbone.

Aubree sighs and glances at Seamus, but he's still inspecting the cave. She frowns then steals herself. "This is some pretty heavy stuff, so I'm just going to come right out and say it, K?"

My heart bumps over a few rocks but sort of stays steady.

Then Aubree does the last thing on earth I expect her to do. She looks me right in the eye and says, "Caoine. We know what you are."

I almost gag, but somehow don't, and then realize I'm slipping off the rock.

Aubree steadies me with one hand.

"What do you mean?" My voice is way too high-pitched. "I mean—"

She sighs and rolls her eyes. "Save it, Caoine. We know."

"But . . . but—" There is zero chance she's talking about my banshee-ness. Because, duh. How could she know?

"You're a banshee," she says.

Oh. Um . . .

"You're part faerie," she continues.

I catch my jaw before it hits the earth.

"Faeries can always sense when another's around, even if they've glamoured themselves to hide from humans. It takes a very powerful faerie to glamour themselves against other fairies. But glamouring is something I'm guessing you have no clue how to do, since it's obvious you're also struggling with your gift."

"Faeries—wait, I don't under—"

"We're faeries, Caoine." Seamus smirks. "What's not to understand?"

"You—but . . . you . . . you can't be! This doesn't make any sense. It's impossible."

Aubree tilts her head. "You're a banshee, yet you find it hard to believe other faeries exist?"

"No—yes. I mean—" I run my free hand through my hair. "I don't get it. Why are you here? In high school? Why aren't you off doing important faerie things?"

She narrows her gaze. "You don't think what you do is important? Just because you're among humans?"

My mouth opens, then closes. "That doesn't matter. Why are you here?"

She smiles. "I'm the daughter of the Seelie queen, Queen Failenn. Well, *one* of her daughters, anyway. Seamus and I have been sent on a special mission."

I blink, a thousand different questions swirling inside my head. "But . . . but you don't look different from humans."

Seamus snorts and shakes his head.

Aubree glowers at him, but her look softens for me. "We're glamoured, hon. It's quite common, actually. We can make ourselves look however we want. Even appear to be the opposite gender."

She reaches up and pulls her long plum-colored hair away from her ears. At first they appear normal, rounded and curved in just the right places. Then they elongate, become pointy at the top and narrower at the bottom. I blink, and they return to normal.

"Whoa," I whisper.

"You don't even want to know what color Seamus's skin actually is." She giggles.

"Besides," Seamus says. "Don't we seem kind of tall for the average teenager?"

I pause. He's absolutely right. Aubree herself borderlines six feet, and Seamus is definitely three or four inches taller. Everything about their structure suggests there's more to them than meets the eye.

"So . . . what? You're at West Lincoln on business or something? Why are you here?"

"Well, we think it might have something to do with *you*, actually." Aubree's brows pull together, and her smile falls.

"Me? How?"

"We don't know for sure," Seamus says. "But we don't think it's coincidence we ended up in a school with a banshee. Something's at play here."

I freeze. "You think it has something to do with those symbols?"

Aubree nods. "*Everything*, actually. We were sent here six months ago because of a number of unusual deaths. My mom thinks it might be linked to the Unseelie Court, but she's not sure. To be safe, she asked us to check it out."

"The Unseelie Court?" I really need to do actual research about my heritage.

Seamus huffs a breath. "I forgot you've been raised by humans. The Faerie Realm is split into two worlds—the Unseelie and the Seelie Courts. The Seelie Court represents all the good in the world. Summer and spring. Growth, new possibilities. The Unseelie Court is reflective of winter or fall. Death, things dying. All things negative. Where the Summer faeries might like to play a few tricks on humans—"

"Just practical jokes," Aubree cuts in.

"—the Winter faeries take it to a whole new level."

"Enough to actually kill?" I swallow.

"Definitely," Aubree says.

My blood starts pumping like a jackrabbit. "Okay, so you two are Summer faeries? And the Queen of the Seelie Court sent you here to stop whatever sinister plan the Unseelie Court has going on?"

"In a nutshell," Seamus says. "That is, if it's really them. We haven't confirmed it yet."

"Okay, so what's with the symbols?"

"That's why I'm thinking my mother is right. This has to be related to the Unseelie Court." Aubree pauses and gathers her words. "See, the Winter faeries have always felt slighted that the Faerie Realm and the human world are separated. They enjoy causing strife and chaos among humans and think it's wrong they're cut off from a place of pleasure."

"Wait, cut off? What do you mean?" I nibble my lip as I try to keep up.

"The Veils," Aubree says. "There are Veils, or openings, to the Faerie Realms. But only in a few locations around the world and only accessible at certain times of the year."

"And by specific faeries." Seamus crosses his arms.

She nods. "It's what keeps our worlds apart. Otherwise the human world would be crawling with the Fair Folk all the time."

"A few years ago, Queen Failenn created the Laws of Necessity," Seamus says. "It means the fae must have special permission to enter the human world. The Winter fae are super touchy about the whole thing. They call themselves *slaves* to their own world. It means more than just *slave*, though. It's sinister in intent. It means they will *no longer* be slaves to another's will. Remember what we told you in the coffee shop? Its full meaning includes revenge."

"Revenge." *Right*. I'd forgotten that part.

I can't move, the cold stone beneath me an anchor I never wished to carry.

"Yes." Aubree looks right at me. "I skipped fifth period today to dig a little into what these recent deaths could mean."

"And?" I ask, even though I don't want to hear the answer.

"I think an Unseelie faerie is killing people in a pattern, to enact a special kind of magic."

"What kind of pattern?" My breathing is shallow, and I hate myself for asking.

Her gray eyes grow dark. "Whoever's killing people is doing so according to the Seven Deadly Sins."

26

CAOINE

"The Seven Deadly Sins?" I hop down from the rock and glance around. "Are you sure it's safe to talk here? What if someone followed us?"

"We're fine," Aubree says. "I put a silent spell around the perimeter of the trees."

I blink like I've been slapped.

She grins. "No one can hear us, Caoine. And get used to the fact Seamus and I can do fae-ish things. Like spells, enchantments, that sort of thing."

"Whoa." I breathe purposefully as I sit back down.

"To answer your original question, the Seven Deadly Sins are behaviors that, historically, are thought to give birth to all other immoralities. We think they're being used for something. Some faerie powers can be made stronger if certain rules are followed."

"Like a magic spell?"

Her smile is sad. "Seamus and I think this could be one of those times."

"Okay." I attempt to process all the crazy she just spit in my direction. "Okay." Breathe. "Okay." Swallow. "So they've been killed according to the Seven Deadly Sins? What exactly does that mean?"

"It means each of the victims fits a specific profile." Seamus's usually playful manner is gone. "Mr. Linyard's wife had been telling him for years to exercise. But he wouldn't do it. She claims he did nothing when he came home at night but sit in front of the TV until he fell asleep."

"He was *slothful*?" I ask.

He nods.

It's a stretch, but I keep my mouth shut and stay seated.

"The cook at the restaurant," Seamus continues. "He died from insulin shock from complications with diabetes. Again, doctors warned him to lay off the sugar and watch his blood levels or he'd bite it. According to his family, he wouldn't listen, ate whatever he wanted."

"Gluttony," I whisper.

Aubree drops her gaze and nods.

"What about the boy at the soccer game?"

"Sadness." Aubree twiddles with a piece of hair and avoids my gaze, as if she wishes she were wrong.

"Sadness?" I frown. "That's not one of the deadly sins."

"The early church originally had eight," Seamus says. "Josh—the kid who died—was clinically depressed. His way of dealing with things was drugs, but the root of his death was his extreme melancholy—one of the original deadly sins."

"All right." I hold up a hand. "Three deaths, all with that . . . symbol. All possibly related to a deadly sin." I lick my lips. "What about this morning? I mean, how do two homicides and a lunatic fit the list?"

"Lust. Wrath." Aubree holds up two fingers. "Before today I had an inkling something like this was happening, but the triple murders threw me. I had to do some serious digging, because most of this stuff isn't public, but I got my answer. One neighbor had an affair, the other got mad."

I shake my head. "What about the other neighbor? The gunman shot *two* neighbors."

Aubree sighs, her shoulders slumped. "Wrong place, wrong time. He was trying to break up the fight."

I scrub my hands through my hair and close my eyes. Why? Why did I sing three times at those houses? Why did I predict a death that didn't need to happen? A gag sticks in my throat, but I push it away. "I'm sorry. I feel like we've taken a rabbit trail here. What exactly does any of this have to do with Unseelie faeries and evil magic?"

"We don't know yet." Seamus scratches a hand through his colorful hair. "But we think an Unseelie faerie—most likely a prince—is using dark magic to do something big. And these recent deaths are only a small part of it."

"Wait, why did you just refer to the Unseelie faerie as a boy? Couldn't it be a girl? And why the heck would he be a prince? A prince of *what*?"

Aubree presses her lips flat. "Raghnall, the Unseelie king, only keeps boys. Any girls birthed by the queen are immediately killed. Only the Seelie Realm has both princes and princesses.

"We think it must be someone in the royal bloodline because they have the strongest magic—strong enough to pull off something like this—and because they have clearance to cross the Veils. Like I said, not just any faerie can come to this world."

All girls born to the king are killed? How morbid. "But why here? Why would you be looking for some sinister homicidal maniac here in a small-town high school? I mean, he could be anyone, anywhere within a twenty-mile radius."

"Easy." Aubree shrugs. "All fae look young—like teenagers. We never age. Where better for him to hide than a high school? Especially if his mission could take a year or more?"

"You *look* young . . . wait, aren't you my age?"

Seamus smirks. "Nope. That old lady is one hundred twenty-one."

"One hundred twenty," Aubree corrects. "Don't make me older than I really am." She looks at me. "Although, I'm not even the old one, really."

She rolls her eyes as Seamus proudly puts his hands behind his head in victory. "I'm about to celebrate the big two-oh-oh." He gives a ridiculous smile.

"You're two *hundred* years old?" My jaw goes slack.

"Yep." More gloating commences.

I refrain from stating the obvious: *There's no way Seamus acts anything like an adult.*

"Fine," I say. "So we're trying to find the Unseelie prince in a high school with over a thousand students. How do we go about that?"

"Glad you asked!" Aubree rifles through her backpack with a little too much vigor. "Here." She hands me a small container of what looks like ground-up oregano.

I blink at her.

"It's crushed foxglove."

As if this explains anything. I stay silent and stare.

"Foxglove. It's poisonous to the Fair Folk?"

She says this as if it's natural we humans should know this information.

She rolls her eyes. "Humans are so silly sometimes. They've had it wrong for centuries, you know. Somewhere along the way things got all confused and humans believed foxglove actually *attracts* faeries. That's why people plant it in their gardens—to attract fae. And why faeries are traditionally drawn wearing a foxglove flower. But it's just nonsense." She shakes her head. "It's totally poisonous to us. We can't come within five feet of the stuff...if it's out in the open."

I glance down at the bottle. "But you just gave me some."

"Well, yeah. But Seamus and I were careful when we cultivated that mixture. As long as it's contained, you should be fine."

"Me? *I* should be fine?"

"Yeah, you," Seamus says. "You're part faerie, Caoine."

"Oh great." My sarcasm isn't even close to being subtle.

"This is how we're narrowing down the pool of boys at school." Aubree pulls a list from her bag. "For the last few months, we've systematically been ruling out who the Unseelie prince could be. Even if he's glamoured, no way could he withstand foxglove."

"But I thought you said faeries can glamour themselves as the opposite gender?"

Seamus huffs and shakes his head.

Aubree frowns. "Yes, that's true. But it takes a lot more effort to hold that kind of glamour. The more the faerie changes their appearance, the more magic it takes *not* to let the glamour fail. We're hoping the prince is saving his energy and won't be glamoured as a girl."

"What if you're wrong?" I ask.

"We'll start testing the girls next, then." Seamus shrugs like it's no big deal.

"Here, look. This is what we've got so far." Aubree flips the list so I can see a long list of boys' names. A few dozen have red lines through them.

"Um, that's not very many you've crossed off." I glower at the tattered paper.

She slumps. "Yeah. We haven't gotten far. But with your help, we should be able to double our efforts and figure this thing out in time."

"In time? For what?"

"Well, in time to save the Faerie Realms. And maybe humanity, too, depending on what the Unseelie prince has in mind."

I don't bother to hide my horror. *Is she serious? The entire fate of humankind rests on my freaking shoulders? A banshee that succeeds only at killing people?* "So we're supposed to use this herby-looking stuff to figure out who this guy is? Who may or may not be disguised as a girl? Where do we even begin looking? Is there a look about an Unseelie faerie? Like red hair verses blond or something?" My heart is pounding so hard, it's in danger of blasting a hole right through my chest.

"Sorry." Aubree winces. "Nope. If a fae is glamoured, they look just like any other human."

I shake my head and sigh. "Okay, so what? We look for really angry guys or something? 'Cause that doesn't sound so easy." Anthony Marino immediately comes to mind.

"Wait, why angry?" Seamus asks.

"Because they're evil?" I shrug. "Shouldn't that be like, a major clue? Find the most unpleasant guy in school and dump a pile of this stuff on his head? Voilà. Unseelie prince found."

Seamus laughs. "Well, that might be the case. But don't underestimate the fae. We can be quite the tricksters when we want."

"Fine." I huff far too loudly, since it's obvious Seamus can't be serious for even a single minute. "How long do we have to find him?"

"Easy." Aubree stops me with a single look. "We've got three deadly sins left. We've got to find him before the last person dies."

27

CAOINE

I SKIRT the edge of the soccer field as we retreat from our hidden coven, my gaze glued to the ground, Aubree and Seamus close by my side. Maybe Oliver won't see me?

My brain is muddled. Filled with a million thoughts, not one of them clear. Aubree's voice echoes inside my head, words of faeries and sins and a strange new threat named the Unseelie prince. A flare of pain cuts behind my temples, and I wince. I need to think. I need a solid hour to think things through.

"Caoine!" Oliver yells over the din of shouts and blowing whistles.

His teammates continue their drill, but he breaks away from the pack.

Strike that. *I need an entire day to think things through.*

My heart sags. Oliver. I almost forgot about him, despite the fact he's always on my mind.

I freeze. Aubree gives me an apologetic glance. How pathetic must I look?

"Catch you later?" she asks.

My head nods, the action involuntary. *No! Don't leave me!*

But she and Seamus are already a dozen feet away.

"Hey." Oliver grins as he runs over. Sweat pours down the sides of his face, and he wipes his forehead with the corner of his shirt.

I swallow. The sky is overcast, the light waning far earlier than necessary. A storm is coming. I attempt to avoid his gaze, but my eyes keep darting to his, making things so much more awkward than they need to be.

"Caoine?" His grin is gone.

He senses something's wrong. And there is something wrong. So many somethings wrong. How on earth can I put into words the conversation I just had? And do I even want to?

Wouldn't it be best to cut Oliver loose right now? Clearly this whole Unseelie prince thing is complicated. So, so complicated. Just a few days ago, I'd been worried for Oliver's safety in regards to my banshee song. But this? This takes things to a whole new level. He's no longer in danger from just me, but from a faerie I may or may not know but who probably totally knows Oliver and very well may kill him to get to me.

How can I do that to Oliver? The one guy I really, really like?

"Um, I think I'm just going to walk home, if that's okay." I bend to look around him as if the other players might be calling his name.

He glances over his shoulder but sees he's not wanted. His brow pulls tight. "Everything okay?"

"Yeah, totally. Of course. I just—" Just what? "Should probably get home to my dad. Make dinner and stuff?" The last part sounds more like a question.

His face falls. "Oh, yeah. No after-practice ice cream, then?"

I shrug and shake my head.

He sighs. "That's cool. I mean, but wait, didn't you say your dad was working late?"

Busted. I bite the inside of my lip. Yes. He's totally working late. "Um, yeah, maybe. But I just don't want him to have to wait for supper and all." *Lame, Caoine. Way lame.*

My insides cringe, and a wave of guilt washes from my head to my toes. I need to cut this guy loose. I'm expecting far too much from him, and it's so not fair. At all. Poor guy never signed up for the crazy-train, but somehow he hopped on for the full ride.

Well, not anymore.

His gaze flits from mine to the side. The base of his neck pulses faster than normal, and those stupid tears prick the backs of my eyes. Ugh!

"You sure?" His voice is flat.

"Totally. I've got stuff to do. I'll, um, see you tomorrow." Can he hear the doubt in my voice?

Without a glance back, I slip away and trot toward the sidewalk that will lead me home. Which is probably the kindest thing I've done all day for the guy. It was one thing when he knew I was a banshee and I had my little freak-out over the triple homicide. But now—we're talking secret evil faeries that are killing students and teachers.

My throat closes, and I squeeze my eyes against those ridiculous tears, just as the first drops of rain splash across my arms, my neck—sink into my inhuman skin. My heart plunges to my stomach. My walk home is miserable and welcoming. Everything I hate and everything I need. The cool rain drips across my skin, melts away the awful thoughts of what I've just done to the only boy I've ever crushed on. The truth of my supernatural life and the things I battle. It feels like a few seconds and an eternity before I'm standing on my front porch.

The front door swings open with far too much force when I press it. With a shaky huff, I slam it, close my eyes, and lean against it. That was seriously the Worst. Thing. Ever. And it hadn't even been a real breakup. I mean, were we even really dating? Hot tears bite at my eyes. It doesn't matter. It's over.

"Caoine? That you, honey?"

I jump as my dad calls from the kitchen. What's he doing home?

I take a few seconds to wipe my eyes and settle my nerves before tossing my pack by my feet.

"Yeah, Dad. Had some stuff to do after school, so I'm later than usual." I walk into the kitchen and am immediately slapped in the face with the scent of oregano and garlic. The conversation with Aubree and Seamus floods my mind, and I consider the packet of foxglove stashed in my bag.

My dad stands at the stove, a silly polka dot apron slung over his neck and both hands hidden inside oven mitts. One hand holds an oblong pan; the other holds a bamboo spoon as he stirs what appears to be baked ziti.

"You're home early?" I don't mean for it to sound like a question, but it does.

My dad presses his lips together and avoids my gaze as he puts the baking dish back into the oven.

Oh great. Here it comes.

"Yeah, about that . . ." He pauses too long. "I, uh . . ."

"Did you lose your job?" My voice is soft, much more gentle than I think he's expecting. I stand beside him, all my worries of boyfriends and bad faeries gone from my mind.

An empty beer bottle sits on the back of the stove. He nods but still doesn't make eye contact. I place a hand on his back and let my head settle on his shoulder.

I know how it happened, even though he doesn't say a word. He's always been a heavy drinker, even when I was a little girl. And for the most part, others can't tell when he's drunk—other than me. He's honestly the most functional alcoholic I've ever known.

But there are always those *sometimes*.

Every once in a while, one of his employers will get wind of his drinking, or maybe he'll screw up royally at work and won't be able to hide the fact he's already put a few beers away before he's even clocked in. This is nothing new for either of us, although his pride never gets used to it.

We don't mention it again the rest of the night. Instead I push aside all things faeries and boyfriends and launch into a discussion about my new job at the paper. We talk about ideas for upcoming articles, which at least helps get my confidence in order. He doesn't ask about Oliver, and I don't ask when he's going job hunting. We ignore all elephants in the room. Neither of us mentions the fact the men who died that morning lived in the same houses where I sang just a few nights before. Nor do we talk about when my curse might trigger again.

We both know the answer to that one already.

My curse never stops. It will keep on killing until there's no one left to die.

My only hope is to cut things off with Oliver so at least one person I care about will be safe.

28

CAOINE

I WAIT for Aubree between the rickety bike rack that not a soul uses and the ancient set of steps that lead into school. Or should I say, *I hide.*

The first bell won't ring for another sixteen minutes, but I don't want to miss Aubree. My plan is to stay invisible for the rest of the school year. That can work, right? I mean, yeah, I gave Oliver the cold shoulder yesterday, but what if he doesn't take the hint? What if he comes looking for me, thinking we're still an item or something? I need things to be over so I don't have to face him.

And I need to see Aubree.

Other than the fact I sang my banshee song twice last night —something not normal—I also didn't sleep a wink. The Unseelie prince plagued me, visions of wrath and slothfulness and anger filling my mind.

The sun peaks from behind a cloud but does nothing to warm the early morning air. Autumn has officially arrived, and I forgot my hoodie. Not that it would match my cute overalls and shoulder-less top, but I don't care right now. I'm cold. I snake my hands around my waist and squeeze another inch.

A head of light-pink hair invades my sight, and I contain a sigh of relief. Aubree!

Today she has on a black fitted tank dress that flares at the waist and hangs over pink fishnet stockings. A black leather jacket is thrown over one arm, and she balances on black chunky boots that look like far more work than it's worth. Her look is complete with a black beanie askew on her head and barely any makeup, save for ultra-mascaraed eyes and light-pink lips. Wow. How this girl can rock every single outfit is beyond me.

I smack my forehead and laugh to myself. *Wait. Of course she's stunning in everything. She's a faerie! Life makes so much more sense.*

"Hey," I whisper-yell as I grab her lace-gloved hand and pull her up the steps.

I glance at every student within a mile to be sure none of them is Oliver. My heart skips in disappointment and relief when I don't see him.

"Whoa." Her tall frame gracefully glides up the stairs until we're safely tucked in a corner by our lockers. "Where's the fire, halfling?"

"Halfling?" I attempt to sound as wounded as possible.

She laughs. "Hey, I call it like I see it, girl. And right now I see a girl who's half human and half—"

"Shh!" I jump a little closer to shut her up. "Yeah, I got it. You don't need to blow my cover to the entire student body."

She leans against the wall and drops her pack at her feet. "No worries. There aren't any human ears around to hear our convo. I'd know."

I tilt my head. "Yeah, but are there any fae ears you can't detect?"

She curls one lip yet still looks gorgeous. "Point taken. What's up?"

I open my mouth to jump in but pause. "Wait. Where's Seamus?"

"He went home."

"Home, you mean . . . ?" I make flappy motions with my hands like wings.

Her blank look tells me my joke fell short. "Yes, Caoine. He went back to the Seelie Realm. And no, he didn't fly."

"Is it that easy? To just *go*, I mean? I sort of got the idea it's more complicated than that."

She shrugs. "Well, yes. For the average fae. Those Veils are guarded very carefully. Not just any fae are allowed in or out, especially from the Unseelie Realm. My mother put laws in place long ago forbidding any Unseelie from leaving without clearance from her. It's a bit easier for the Seelie."

I wince. "Hence the reason the prince calls himself a slave?"

"One of many reasons." She rolls her eyes. "But Seamus is on special mission from Queen Failenn. So am I. He can travel back and forth as much as he likes. For now."

"So—what? He went back to visit mommy and daddy or something?"

Aubree shakes her head at my idiocy. "No, Caoine. His parents aren't even alive anymore. The mission? He went back to check on a few things at the Seelie Library."

My jaw goes slack. "You guys have a library?"

"Um, humans have libraries. Why wouldn't we?"

"Well yeah . . . I just—I mean, I—"

"He'll be back in a few days. Don't worry about Seamus. He's a big boy. He can take care of himself." She runs a hand through her pink hair and glances at the rush of students that suddenly appears around us. "What's got you so uptight?"

I twist my hands. "Well, I was thinking about the, ya know, *sins* last night. The ones connected to—"

"Got it." She nods.

"Right." I lick my lips. "So I was thinking. It might not be that at all. It could be a total coincidence. Like maybe we're reading too much into things—"

Aubree sighs and steps another inch closer. "We're not wrong, Caoine. In fact, it's the reason Seamus went back this morning. To find a book. We're hoping to uncover which spell the prince is trying to enact so we can stop it before it happens."

"But how can you be sure? I mean, what if all these deaths are perfectly normal?"

She lays a hand on my shoulder. "Sweetheart, we're sure."

"There's no chance these are just random deaths?" I frown.

She narrows her gaze at me. "You don't know, do you?"

"Know what?"

"About you. About the way things work?"

"Um, hello? I just found out yesterday I'm not the only fae at this school. I know practically nothing."

Aubree blows a stray piece of hair from her eye, her look sympathetic. "We know for sure this is part of a bigger plan because of the deaths. And because *you're* here."

I inhale to ask more questions, but she cuts me off.

"A normal town doesn't have this many deaths, Caoine. Not by a long shot. This place? They've had an increase in deaths by more than tenfold over the last year. Which is when we think the prince arrived."

I blink and try to digest her words.

She squeezes my arm. "Caoine, you're a banshee. You're only ever called to a place like this when something supernatural is going on. When more people die than normal."

"That's not true. My dad, he's the one—"

"He may think he's picking the towns, but really, it's fae magic, sweetie. You've never actually had control over where you went. You go where you're needed."

"But—but—" This can't be true. I'm cursed. I'm an evil that darkens each town I go to. Spots cloud my vision, and I clench my eyes shut. "That can't be true. I'm cursed. I kill people."

Aubree gasps. "Is that what you think? Caoine, no. You

have a gift. You help people cross to the other side. Without you, humans would face a far worse fate than just losing their life."

"But—" I pull in a ragged breath, push it back out.

There's no way. I'm not good. *I can't be good.* I've always been bad, always been cursed. I can't control my curse, and when it comes out, innocent people die.

She steps even closer, her face right by my ear so no one else can possibly hear. "You have a purpose, Caoine. You can help us catch the Unseelie prince. You can even tell us who's going to die before it happens so we can solve the puzzle."

Aubree leans back and looks me right in the eye.

"Don't give up on us now, girl. We need you. We need you to save the world."

29

THE UNSEELIE PRINCE

SHE KNOWS TOO MUCH.

Caoine has discovered far too much about my plan. About the way the fae work.

About herself.

She needs to doubt. I need her to doubt.

The last few students straggle into school, and the sun warms my back. I almost feel guilty, having the ability to glamour myself. Even from Aubree. I'm stronger than she is. Able to hide myself from other Fair Folk, something that takes quite a bit of talent. Their entire conversation happened a matter of feet from me. Yet they never knew it.

I scratch a hand through my mangled hair and shift my backpack higher on my shoulder. I should get to class, although I can use a little faerie persuasion on my teacher if I'm late. Again. That never gets old.

A breeze kicks up, and I turn my face toward it, allow it to flow over my skin, into my pores. Dig deep into my soul. I don't mind the cold so much. In fact, I welcome it. Being a Winter faerie has its perks. One reason I came back out to revel in the chill as I mull over their talk.

I sigh, and my heart sinks just an inch. It's time I step up my game. I need to do something about Caoine and all her investigating. The girl is flawless, beautiful. We would make a perfect pair. If only she'd let it happen.

If only she would stop sticking her nose where it doesn't belong.

Aubree's words run through my mind, and I clench my fists. Caoine can't believe her banshee song is a gift. *She can't know there's another way.*

It's a curse. Her curse. I need her to believe this.

A curse I need to use.

One last bell rings, and I climb the steps. The time has come for me to intervene. Caoine needs to know her darkness. It must come from inside her. From her own mind.

It's time I convince Caoine there is no other way out.

30

CAOINE'S DREAM

It's time for me to sing.

I stand in the dimly lit wing of backstage . . . somewhere. I'm surrounded by curtains and cold air that should send chills across my skin, but it doesn't. No one else is here.

Noise draws my attention through the crack in the curtain. I squint to see. The auditorium is filled. Every single seat filled, a few extra people waiting along the back.

My heart races like I've run a mile. I'm here to sing, and these people have come to listen.

Wait, I'm here to sing?

I clench my fists, look down at my body. I'm dressed in a fancy sequined dress, my hair pulled off my neck into some sort of up-do.

This can't be right. I have a terrible voice. Why would anyone want to hear me sing?

But my feet move of their own accord. Seconds later, I stand center stage, the lights blinding, roasting, unrelenting. Still, I can see the audience clearly. They all face my direction, but they aren't looking at me.

They can't.

Every soul in the room is blindfolded.

I swallow. This might make it easier. At least they can't see the pathetic girl with the train wreck of a voice. I open my mouth.

And I sing.

Not just any song. The most beautiful song I've ever heard. Far better than any singer on the radio or contestant on those competition shows. I'm singing and I'm good. No, I'm great. Fantastic.

My pulse slows just a bit as I relax. The song is familiar, even though I can't remember where I know it from.

Then, a change.

A few of the people in the front row take off their blindfolds. My body tenses, but the song doesn't end. In fact, it only grows stronger, more urgent.

And I see. I can see exactly who has taken off their blindfolds. My friends. I see them. Aubree. Seamus. Catherine. Eric. My dad.

Oliver.

My stomach tightens, but my song continues.

Then my words become real. As they spill from my mouth, they take on a physical presence, become whole. Each syllable turns into smoke, an essence that swirls among itself, then skates away. It floats.

Floats. Down into the audience.

The smoke slithers and winds its way toward my friends, the ones without masks. And it attacks them.

I can't stop singing as my song invades their mouths, penetrates their souls. Their eyes are wide as my words envelope them, coat their skin like sticky honey that just won't let go.

I want to run. To jump from the stage. To beg my song to leave them alone. Go away! Don't hurt my friends!

But it won't. It just continues to assault and violate, smothering its victims.

The rest of the audience takes off their blindfolds. They stop and stare. Watch as my song murders the ones I care about.

They see me. Why must they see me? I can't let them see.

One by one, each of my friends falls to the ground, their bodies lifeless. Their last breaths gone from their empty shells.

And then my song finally ceases. My curse has finished the job it set out to do.

Everyone I know is dead.

31

CAOINE

My LOCKER JAMS for the third time as I stifle a yawn. Everything about this morning has been a disaster. Probably because of the crazy nightmare I had, but who's counting? I yawn again. Oh right. *Me, apparently.*

It's bad enough I have an entire day of avoiding Oliver—again—but knowing I also have to basically become a ninja adds to all the stress of all the things. At least I can skip the one class I have with Oliver until things settle down. The ninja thing will take a little extra work.

The plan is simple. I blended the ground foxglove with some lotion. This—much harder than I thought it would be, since some of the foxglove got on my skin and burned like the freaking dickens—is step one to narrowing down the pool of guys at our school that may or may not—or definitely may—be murderous faeries. Yay.

"Deep in thought?" a female voice says behind me.

I slowly turn, careful to keep my eyes cast low, in case it's a newbie classmate who hasn't been exposed to my mutant-ness yet.

It's Jessica.

I grit my teeth and clench my fingers around the lock that

still hasn't budged. Seriously not what I need to deal with today.

She's dressed like Spencer Hastings from *Pretty Little Liars* Season One but with that red hair—that tauntingly dangerous red hair—flowing neatly down her shoulders and across her chest. Button-down oxford under a white and blue striped sweater vest, a tidily ironed navy pencil skirt, and no-nonsense dark-blue flats. Her eyeliner is heavier than usual.

"Can I help you with something?" I stifle my internal groan that I've just bitten back at my sort-of-boss. Not cool if I want to keep my job.

"You just looked like you were struggling to get your books. I figured it might have something to do with that far-off look in your eyes."

"What are you talking about?" I avoid rolling my eyes.

She tilts her head with a demure look. "Oh nothing. Just thought maybe you were distracted by your new *friend*." Jessica smirks and glances around to see who can hear our conversation.

I shake my head. "You've lost me."

"Seamus, silly. It's so obvious you two have something going on."

My heart skips two beats, and my palms go sweaty. *Fantastic*. Now the whole school thinks I'm dating my only guy friend. *Maybe she doesn't know as much about Oliver and me as I thought. Maybe I'll escape her wrath.*

"We're just friends." Is this true? My voice sounds high-pitched even to my own ears.

"Right." She flips her hair over her shoulder.

Someone bumps into me as they hustle by, and I refrain from yelling an obscenity. I blink at her. If she hasn't heard too much about Oliver and me being together, then she probably hasn't heard that we aren't so much together anymore, either. Or has she? Is this just an elaborate ploy to drive us further apart, now that she sees a crack in our relationship?

"I've got other interests, to be honest."

Her smile falters.

Um. What am I doing? Do I really want her to think Oliver and I are still together? Especially when there's not much chance, even after I figure out how to demolish my curse?

A boy with shaggy blond hair steps to the locker beside mine, and I flinch. "Gotta go, Jess." She hates being called *Jess* by anyone other than Oliver. "Nice talking to you."

"Right." Her smirk is back, along with that annoying hair flip.

There's just no reading that girl. Maybe she really is igno-rant to what's going on around her. She waltzes away without another glance.

Nice.

I look at the boy beside me and get working on my lock again. I wanted extra time at my locker to wait for the boy, Ben. His locker, number 1052, is right next to mine. But getting into my locker is obviously something the universe doesn't have planned for me today. I growl under my breath and try for the fourth time. The jumble of steel and bolts finally flies open, the familiar scent of old socks an unwelcome greeting.

I shove my afternoon class books inside and rummage through my pack for the squeeze tube of lotion. As soon as I shut my locker, I turn to see Ben is packed and ready to leave. Blah. I hoped to have another minute to brace myself. But no. Universe is still against me. Stupid universe.

With a gulp, I crack open the lid of the tube and . . . freeze dead in my tracks. He's wearing long sleeves. And jeans. And all sorts of other clothing that covers lots and lots of skin. Lots of it. I hadn't considered it's now early October and the weather in this part of the country forces people to bundle up. *How's this going to work again?*

"You okay?" Ben has stopped sifting through his books and is now glaring at me.

Awesome.

"Um, I—" My cheeks heat and I scramble. "I like your shirt."

He gets a weird look on his face and leans back minutely. "Thanks?" It totally sounds like a question.

Great. And now he thinks I'm flirting with him.

"I mean, it looks just like my dad's." *Okay, not helping, Caoine.*

His gaze shifts to the other students around us and then back to me. "Okay. Well, nice talking to you."

"Yeah." I duck my head and skitter between the throng of bodies that crowds the hall, then into the safety of my classroom.

Well, that couldn't have gone any worse. Now I've got some dude thinking I'm all into him and stuff. And with my breakup with Oliver, that will only add to his suspicions. That is, if he knows Oliver. Or me. Or even cares.

I slink to the back of the room and find an empty seat near the window. So much for that plan. And Ben wasn't even my intended target. I still have yet to locate and corner one angry Anthony Marino.

Except maybe I'm in luck. A quick glance to my right provides a full view of legs. Manly, hairy ones.

The guy next to me—Derek or Damien or something—clearly missed the memo that cool weather has arrived. He's decked out in shorts and a T-shirt. Ensemble complete with flip flops.

My heart stumbles. Score! With a quick inhale, I settle my backpack next to my feet and sit an inch lower in my seat. The tube is still clutched in my hand, and I knead it for a few seconds as I conjure the courage to pounce. I stifle a small smile when I see he's actually making this easy on me. His whole upper body is turned toward the girl to his right, leaving his legs sprawled in my direction at an odd angle. One squeeze is all it'll take . . .

Splat. A solid four-inch line of white cream drips from his knee to his shin.

I jump as he jumps.

"Hey!" His face is an ugly shade of red.

"Sorry," I whimper. "I was just getting some lotion. Must've squeezed too hard."

"Gross." His nose is wrinkled, and he wipes at the gelatinous muck spreading into his leg hair.

Ew. Gross is right.

The girl beside him giggles. "Oh come on, Derek. It's just lotion. Get over it."

He coughs and scowls. "Yeah, but it stinks." He sniffs his fingers. "What is this stuff? It smells like crap."

Heat creeps up my neck. "Oh, sorry. I think it's scented with rosewater."

Or is it something else? I watch his reaction closely as he rubs the lotion between his hands.

"Oh, come on." The guy in front of him laughs. He leans down and swipes some of the cream off Derek's leg and pats it between his hands, then on his cheeks. "It smells divine, D. Really, you should bathe in the stuff. It would do wonders for that stink you've got going on."

With a chortle, the guy ducks just as Derek swipes at his head, the only one of the group not amused by my "mishap."

"I'm really sorry," I say again, even though I'm totally not.

My insides quiver with excitement that I've actually pulled off my first mission. This whole debacle—as embarrassing as it is—has answered not one, but two questions.

As sly as my inner-ninja will allow me to be, I slide my folder from my pack and glance at the list of boys Aubree gave me. I find Derek's name and cross it off, then rack my brain for the name of the other guy, before I find that one and cross it off, too.

The teacher takes her spot at the front of the room and starts her lecture. I attempt to hide the smile that's dying to come out but totally fail. Two down, a thousand to go. The smile slips. Okay, maybe this is a small victory. We still have a ton of work to do.

My only worry: Will we be able to do it in time? I sigh and push against the tightness in my chest. And will it be before I have to confront Oliver, or will I have to spin another web of lies?

Because no matter how many guys I have to toss foxglove on, that's the one guy in school I don't want to face.

32

CAOINE

By lunchtime I've crossed one more name off my list. I was lucky enough in third period to get close to Sammy Chester-field. I dropped a small finger full of foxglove down the back of his shirt as I passed. With a wince, of course, since the stuff pinched like I'd been stung by a hive of bees.

I was *unlucky* enough that one of Sammy's friends saw me do it and blasted me with a round of questions. It resulted in some pretty nasty looks and having to find a secluded seat in another corner of the room. Not that I minded much. At least it's confirmation one more classmate isn't the Unseelie prince.

By the end of last period, I'm sorting textbooks in the closet in the back of the room. The teacher promised it would only be fifteen minutes of work, which is exactly the amount of time I need to kill. Oliver will be done hanging around the halls waiting to find me, and I'm fine facing the wrath of Jessica by arriving late to the paper. She's far too uptight anyway.

Dust bunnies tickle my nose, and I stifle a sneeze as I slide another text in place on the overcrowded shelf. Does anyone even use these ancient things anymore? The poor light from the bare bulb overhead doesn't help my vision. The concrete walls suck in all surrounding noise and create a weird sort of soundless vacuum. More than once I glance up to be sure the door is still open. Nothing screams horror movie like hearing that door click shut and knowing no one's left in the classroom to open it if it locks.

My heart skips five beats, and I shove the next book in place with too much force. There are only about a dozen left to shelve, then I'll take my chances with Oliver.

"What're you hiding from?"

I swallow my squeal and spin to face the feminine voice.

Catherine stands with her arms crossed, one shoulder leaning against the closet's doorjamb. A friendly smirk hangs in place, and the tension in my neck relaxes.

"Oh, um, yeah. I mean, I'm—just helping Mrs. Hanby. Figured I could be a few minutes late for paper duty."

She lifts one eyebrow. "Brave." I swallow, and she laughs. "I like it. Anyone willing to defy Jessica and her status as queen is okay in my book. Besides, what's she going to do? Replace us? She barely has enough students willing to keep the paper afloat."

"Really?"

"Yeah. Heard Principle Perry threaten to cut the program if she couldn't get the paper out on time. But I'm not convinced he'll actually cut it. I think he's just throwing his weight around."

"Oh. Okay." I fiddle with the spine of the book I'm holding before I realize I could still be working.

"Here." She steps inside. "Let me help you. She can't crucify you if we're both late, right?"

Her smile is genuine and kind, and I can't help but return it.

"Find anything out about those missing pets?" She pushes her glasses up her nose before she grabs the next book, but she doesn't look in my direction.

"Oh, not really. I mean, they're *missing*. That's all. I didn't think there was much story there, anyway. But I tried to make it as harrowing as possible, for Jessica's sake."

Catherine giggles. "Of course." She pauses. "It's good you can make something so boring interesting. Wait till you hear what you're covering this week."

I cringe. "Do I want to know?"

She crinkles her upper lip. "Well, it's slightly less interesting than missing pets, if you can believe that."

Sigh. "Hit me. Nothing can make this day much worse. Or this week, really."

She pauses, her book midair. "I'm sorry. Do you . . . want to talk about it?"

With a wave, I shake her off. "No, no. Go on." The last thing I need is to drag one more person into the world of faeries and death. And dismissed boyfriends.

"Well . . ." She drags in a long breath. "It's the school drama."

"Excuse me?"

"The school play? Jessica wants Mrs. Pearson interviewed for the upcoming opening night. Practically no one in this school ever goes to see those things. None of the other staff are even remotely interested in doing the interview so . . ." She cringes as she attempts to smile.

"Jeez." I shake my head. "Well, maybe it's not so bad. I mean, at least it's *dramatic*, right?" I nudge her with my elbow. "Get it? Dramatic? 'Cause it's the drama department?" I flash her a lame smile.

She rolls her eyes. "Seriously?"

I shrug. "Still . . . it might be better than writing about pets. I mean, at least it's a straightforward interview. Maybe I can insert a few tidbits of juicy gossip about her." I wag my brows, and Catherine laughs. "Sort of like writing our very own soap opera but based on real events."

"Whatever floats your boat, Caoine. I'm sticking with my

Halloween series. It'll be a perfect intro to the Halloween dance at the end of the month."

"Dance?" I push the final text into place, then place my hands on my hips.

"Yeah. It's sort of a school tradition. The senior class always has their own dance for Halloween, no underclassmen invited. Sort of like our rite of passage for getting to graduate in seven months."

"Wow. That's cool. It actually sounds like . . . fun." I clear my throat and avoid her gaze.

This is the truth. I've never attended any dances at any of the schools I've gone to. With friends like Aubree, Seamus, and Catherine, this just might be my chance to experience high school. Like, real high school.

Minus Oliver, that is. My stomach clenches, and I hide my frown.

"Better get started, though. The Halloween dance is a date-only dance. Anyone who goes stag gets pranks pulled on them." She laughs and misses the fact I haven't followed her out of the closet.

Fantastic. Not only did I just break up with the only sort-of boyfriend I've ever had, now I have less than thirty days to find another, or face the cruelty of teens on the most sinister night of the year. I sigh and join her as we exit the classroom.

"By the way" — she digs into her backpack — "the paper finally made its appearance. Care to see your debut front-page article about that student who, uh, died?"

My heart plummets to my feet. Oh jeez. Here it is. Something with my name on it. Something that sets me apart from every other student in the school. How much attention will I draw with this thing? I nibble my lip and hesitate to take the newspaper.

"Go on. Take it." She waves the black-and-white paper like it's a piece of candy. "It's a good article. I'm proud of you." Her smile is genuine.

I sigh and grab the thin paper from her hands, unfolding it slowly, like it's a present I want to savor. My heart rate speeds in an uneven cadence. Is this what it feels like to have notoriety in high school? For other kids to know who I am? A warm feeling spreads across my shoulders. It's not such a bad feeling, really. My gaze lands on the front page.

My jaw drops. "What—?" I have no words.

Catherine's brown eyes go wide, and she straightens. "What? Is something wrong?"

"Well, yes . . . but it's no big deal. I guess." I refrain from rolling my eyes.

She leans next to me and looks at the words that cover the *Red and Black*. "What's wrong with it? I thought it was a good article."

I nod as I skim the piece. "Yeah, I guess so. It's just, that's totally not the headline I came up with. I mean, *Student Dies*? That's so—"

"Blunt?" She raises her eyebrows.

"Uncaring. I mean, it's true, but mine was something like, *School Mourns Loss of Beloved Sophomore*, or something like that."

She frowns. "Maybe she cut it down to save words?"

I shrug halfheartedly. "Maybe. But this isn't the picture I chose, either. The one I picked showed him with a group of his friends. This one . . ." I crinkle my nose. "This one is so boring."

Catherine gives me a sympathetic look. "It's a nice picture, though. His formal shot from the yearbook. No one will know it's not the one you chose."

"Yeah, but my first paragraph has been completely switched with what I had somewhere in the middle, detailing the exact moments of his death. The article doesn't go back and cover his early personal life or extracurriculars until much later. Like Jessica wanted to start this thing like a tension-filled fiction novel or something. Is this normal for the editor to make this many changes without notifying the writer?"

She takes a breath to refute it but stops. Then goes sullen. "No, actually. I mean, yeah, Jessica likes her changes, but she always has the writer sign off, to cover her butt if Principal Perry comes back screaming. She doesn't like to take blame if she can avoid it." Catherine gives a weak smile.

"So what you're saying is, Jessica sabotaged my article?"

"Pretty much, yeah."

My shoulders slump. Great. I no longer have the boyfriend, but somehow, I still have to face the wrath of his ex.

33

CAOINE

"THEY NEVER PUT enough foam on top." Aubree frowns at her cappuccino.

The faerie plops into the same cushy seat she hijacked the previous time she, Seamus, and I stopped at the coffee shop. Goose pimples cover my skin. In fact, the last time we were in these seats, my world was infinitely smaller.

"You not going to get anything?" she asks.

I swallow and avoid her gaze. "Nah. Not thirsty." And not enough money. Until my dad finds a job, there's no way his little banshee can play with her friends.

Three days. That's how much time has passed since I made the stupidest decision of my high school life—albeit, the right one. In that span of time, I've focused on nothing but crossing guys off the possible Unseelie prince list and writing mindless articles for the school paper. But Oliver is never far from my mind.

I force my face to soften so Seamus will stop staring. He got back a few hours ago from Faerie-Neverland, and it's obvious he's dying to ask what my problem is. I've proudly not shared the information.

"So where do we stand with our manhunt?" I ask. A strong

waft of coffee smacks me in the face, and I blink to push away the nausea. I really need to ask Aubree to meet somewhere else.

"Don't you mean, faerie hunt?" Seamus smirks.

"Keep it down, you two. Too many ears." Aubree purses her lips and glances around at the three other patrons, all glued to their phones.

"Really, Bree?" Seamus rolls his eyes and leans back in his armchair.

"Okay." Aubree ignores her friend and pulls her notes from her backpack. "Caoine has been doing some kick-butt work." Her cheeks practically glow. "Seriously, girl. Do you even go to class anymore? How on earth did you knock out—" She glances at her paper. "Forty-three guys in three days?"

Seamus whistles. I duck my head at the unwanted attention.

"Yeah." I shrug. "There may have been an opening to make smoothies for the entire football team at practice yesterday."

"Nice." Seamus practically beams with approval.

"Not even one of them flinched. Which was sort of a bummer, since the chances I'd cornered the dude were pretty high, with the amount of testosterone in the room and all. But at least we know it's none of them."

"Right." Aubree makes some notes on her paper with far too large of a grin. "Clearly Seamus and I need to be taking notes from your playbook, Caoine. That was seriously genius."

The three of us sit in silence for a moment—Aubree, as she jots down her notes, Seamus, as he people watches.

Me, as I push thoughts of Oliver from my mind.

Aubree puts the end of her pen between her lips as she thinks. "I'm surprised you're even here with us, Cay."

"What's that mean?"

"I mean, Oliver." She shrugs. "He doesn't have practice today, right? I figured you might be out with him."

My chest squeezes tight. Really? Was this girl inside my

mind or something? Or do I just think of him far too often? I clear my throat. "Erm, he had other things."

She narrows her eyes. "Is he studying or something?"

"Um, I don't know." I wish I did, but I don't.

"After the grade he got on that last lit test, he probably is—"

"Wait, what? Did he get a bad grade or something?" *Shut it, Caoine.* Why do I even care?

She shrugs. "Well, not bad for most people. I think it was, like, a ninety-two or something. But it pulled his average for the class below four-point-oh, which isn't acceptable by his parents' standards." She pauses, watches my reaction. "You know this, right? I mean, it's common knowledge the boy needs to be valedictorian or his butt is toast. His parents expect it. His brother was, uh, going to be valedictorian. So they expect him to also. He's even set to go to Brown U, the same school his brother was going to." She hesitates.

No. I didn't know this. And somehow finding it out from someone other than him feels yucky. Like I've been a crappy friend and an even worse person for dropping him like a hot potato. I feel about an inch tall.

We sit in silence for a minute.

Finally, I clear my throat. "So, um . . . any idea when we might expect this whatever-tragic-thing-Mr.-Unseelie-son has for us? I mean, in case you haven't noticed, there hasn't been a death related to the 'sins' in over a week." My hands do air quotes before I can stop myself. Blast.

Luckily, Seamus doesn't laugh.

Aubree twists her lips as she thinks. "Yeah. I did notice that. No clue why, though."

"Yeah, but . . . I mean, my curse—uh, *gift*. Is there something wrong, you think?" I bite my lip to hide my cringe. The faeries have made it clear not to refer to what I do as anything negative. It's apparently like, derogatory, or something.

She sighs. "I wouldn't say that. I'm sure everything's just

fine with you. It's just . . . well, for some reason, our Winter friend hasn't shown himself over the past few days. All the more reason to prepare. Something's coming, and it's coming fast."

"You can say that again," Seamus says, his gaze on the guy in the corner who's bobbing his head to music.

"Why?" I sit up in my chair.

"Why what?" Aubree tilts her head.

I glance between the two of them. "Why are you so sure? That this *something* is coming soon? I mean, from what it sounds like, there have been strange deaths for almost a year now. Couldn't the Unseelie prince just be taking his time?"

"We don't think so."

"Definitely not," Seamus says, his attention now on me. "He's going to make his move soon, and it's going to be the big one."

"But—"

"Halloween?" Seamus leans forward in his seat, elbows on his knees. "It's only a few weeks away. If the Unseelie prince is going to reveal himself, it'll definitely be that night."

"What?" I crinkle my nose. "Sorry to sound negative, but isn't that sort of cliché? I mean, Halloween? That's, like, so obvious."

"Well, obvious or not, there's truth to the legend." Aubree lowers her voice. "Honestly, Caoine. The Eve of Samhain, or All Hallows Eve, is the real deal. Various people groups have known for centuries that's the one night of the year the Veil between the spirit and the physical worlds grows thin."

"The night when faeries run free to play tricks and cause havoc," Seamus says.

A chill trickles across my skin. "It's true? All that mumbo-jumbo I learned as a kid?"

She nods. "Most of it, yeah. Probably."

"It's more than that, though." Seamus steeples his fingers like he's a teacher with great wisdom. "The Veil between the spirit world and physical world doesn't just have to do with spirits. It's also the one night of the year when the Veils between the lands of Faerie and the human world are thin enough for either faerie or human to slip through. It's much easier for faeries to get out—"

"And much easier for humans to be kidnapped into the Faerie Realm." Aubree nails me with a look.

I freeze. "Kidnapped?"

"Yep." Seamus nods. "Haven't you heard the stories of all the people who disappear on Halloween night? It has nothing to do with ghosts or any of that superstitious stuff. It's the *Fair Folk*. They're the ones playing tricks. They're the ones who take the humans."

"Winter faeries, of course," Aubree says matter-of-factly. "Summer faeries play tricks, but we don't mean humans any harm. If anything, we try to help."

"Well, that figures." I roll my eyes.

"What?" Aubree's brow is pulled tight.

"Of course the stupid prince would unleash his evil plan on Halloween. It's my birthday." I sulk like a small child. *Is it too much to ask to actually have a birthday where I can have a little fun now that I have friends?*

Aubree smiles. "It is? Happy birthday!"

"Wicked." Seamus smirks. "Cool night to have a birthday."

"Apparently not." I'm not feeling the same joy Aubree is at the moment. "Okay, birthdays aside. You guys think this Unseelie prince—whoever he is—is going to make his big move on Halloween night? Because the Veils to the Summer and Winter Realms will be thin? What's he doing?"

Aubree shoots Seamus a look, shifts in her seat. "Yeah, still working on that, actually."

She glances around us before reaching into her bag and pulling out a big, fat, ancient book. She plops it on the coffee table hard enough to send dust flying. I raise an eyebrow.

"This is what Seamus went to Faerie for. For a set of books."

"A set?" I hate to point out the obvious.

Her mouth turns down at the corners. "He only found one, *the Book of Discernment*. The librarian is fairly certain the other one—*the Book of Judgment*—is *not* in the Summer Realm."

"You have—"

Seamus rolls his eyes. "You have librarians, we have librarians. Can we stay on topic here?"

Says the boy who's never on topic. I press my lips together to hide my insult.

"We still have no clue what exactly this guy is up to, only that it's important." Aubree points to the book. "We've got a lot of work ahead of us, sifting through this monstrosity for clues." Her look is sour as she stares down at the thing. "But we do think we've figured out one piece of the puzzle."

"And that is?"

"Our town—this school. The reason the Unseelie prince chose this exact location to play with faerie magic, we think it's because this place is *the place*. The one place on this continent where the two Veils come together."

"Huh?"

"The Veils to Summer and Winter," Seamus says. "The Seelie and Unseelie Realms? They're spread out throughout the world, most of them hundreds of miles apart from one another. Except here. In this town. This is the one place they converge. On this side of the hemisphere, anyway.

"The one spot where a Veil to the Summer Kingdom and a Veil to the Winter Kingdom exist side by side."

Aubree's eyes find mine. "This is the only place on earth where a faerie can slip from the Seelie to the Unseelie Court within seconds, without being seen." She pauses, makes eye contact with Seamus, who only looks away. "The Unseelie prince came here to start a war with the Seelie Court. We're sure of it."

34

CAOINE

I PULL IN A SHAKY BREATH. *A war between the Faerie Realms? What can possibly go wrong with that?* I bite back my sarcasm and press my fingers to my temples instead. "Awesome. Look, I've had enough of faeries and evil sorcerer princes bent on revenge. I'll catch you tomorrow?" My backpack is already slung across my shoulders, and I stand.

Aubree does a double take and blinks in confusion. "Okaaay. Did we say something wrong?"

No. Everything about my life is just like it always is. I'm a scary monster and apparently scary monsters follow me around. I run a hand through my hair and glance toward the window. Toward freedom. "I'm fine." Lie. "Or, I'll be fine. It's just—"

"Just?" Aubree's gaze softens.

Just that I don't want to be caught inside this vortex of crazy, and the one person on earth I actually want to talk to— the only person who might understand some of the fear that has taken residence inside my core and sprouted into a million little tendrils—is the only person I can't talk to right now.

Playing the martyr truly sucks sometimes.

"Nothing." I sigh. "I'll be fine. My brain is just overloaded, and I need to detox before I can handle any more information. Have fun getting caffeinated."

"If you say so." Aubree looks hurt.

I hesitate. *She'll get over it.*

"See you in the A.M." Seamus slumps in his chair and closes his eyes. How that kid can be so chill at the most inappropriate times is beyond me.

I give him an awkward nod and wave to Aubree before slipping out of the coffee shop. Chilly air creeps under my shirt and burrows beneath my skin. I shiver. *I hate winter.*

With a huff, I stop and balance my backpack on my knee, digging to the bottom for my sweatshirt that's buried beneath every schoolbook in the universe. It starts to come loose but then catches on my spiral notebook. I stifle a squeak and pray I didn't just poke a hole clean through my brand-new hoodie. Finally it breaks free, and I almost drop my pack as I unwind it and fight to find the bottom so I can slip it over my head.

A piece of paper slips from its folds.

My heart stops. The faded scrap of green has become the most dreaded sight of the century. *How on earth does this guy find ways to slip these things inside my backpack?* I don't hesitate to pick it up and tear into it to see what monstrosity the Unseelie prince is teasing me with this time.

But this one is different. It's not the normal small square just big enough for a few words of torment. This one is a full-fledged sonnet. Paragraphs spill across the page, bleed onto the back.

He's written me a letter.

The Unseelie prince wants to talk.

I swallow as my insides turn to ice. *What can the boy possibly want to say to me? More of his childish insults?*

My first instinct is to run back into the coffee shop, to shove the offensive missive in Aubree's face, and beg for her help.

Except I haven't told her.

Like an idiot, I've chosen to walk this road alone. Would she understand if I showed her? Why I didn't say anything?

I glance over my shoulder. The street is unusually deserted for this time of day. I've got no one to help me.

I'm alone.

Seconds pass. I close my eyes, take a breath. Then I hold up the letter, neat block writing coming into focus.

Dearest Caoine,

By now you've learned of my plan. How do I know this? Well, I don't, for sure, but you're smart. If you haven't figured out all the details yet, you will soon. I know you will.

You and I aren't that different, after all. We have a connection. Sometimes I even think I can read your mind.

We both lost a parent at birth, we're the misfits within our own race, we've been raised without the knowledge of our true power. For you, this power is still a mystery.

We're both lonely. Misunderstood. But I understand you, Caoine. I know you. I feel your pain, your longing.

We are soul mates. Two parts of a whole, meant to be one. We can be one, Caoine, if you'll just let me show you.

I've said enough for now. Soon you'll learn who you are, will know who you can become, if given the chance. You have no idea the potential within you, Caoine. But I do.

I do.

Until next time,

Your Prince

P.S. Watch your step. Don't go telling anyone about my love notes, or they might meet an untimely end.

A horn honks and I jump, squeeze the paper in my fist. I'm still alone on the sidewalk, even though it feels as if time is standing still, like I'm the only person alive on earth. My eyes skitter across the words again.

He knows me.

Tears prick the backs of my eyes. I can't tell Aubree any of this. Or Seamus. *The two people on earth who might actually understand what I'm going through, and I can't even tell them?* I crush the paper in my fists and contain the scream that begs to rip from my throat.

Each of his previous notes made this clear, but this one is different. Intimate. He *knows* me. Knows my past, my present. Could he know my future? My stomach flips, and my head spins.

Soul mates.

Why would he think we're soul mates? I don't do crazy, nor do I ever plan on doing crazy.

Exhaust wafts my way, and I gag, sway on my feet. *He's so sure.* The Unseelie prince is so sure we're connected in some way. But why? All I've ever known is this life, stuck here on earth, stuck between two worlds, ushering humans into the afterlife. I've never even visited either of the Faerie Realms.

I shove the paper inside my pack and yank my sweatshirt over my head, all while I blink away tears. Why? *Why is he doing this to me?*

You have no idea the potential within you. How can he know this?

A gust of wind almost knocks me off my feet as I bend and grab my pack, then jog toward my house. To hide in my room.

To hide from the prying eyes of a boy I don't know, but who clearly knows all about me.

35

CAOINE

I SPLASH water on my face and inspect myself in the mirror. The fluorescent lights of the girls' bathroom casts eerie shadows under my eyes, along the ridge of my cheekbones. I look hollow. Maybe I'm dead.

But I'm not, of course. I only *predict* death. It would never come for me. No matter how much I beg it to.

The sink is cold beneath my fingers. I wrap them tight around the edge, lean just an inch closer to my reflection. My white-blonde hair falls around my shoulders, and I can't see where it ends and my face begins. I'm so white. Like death. My silver and green eyes are like a beacon calling to me from the grave —

"Inspecting a zit?"

The voice from behind makes me gasp. Once I see who it belongs to, I spin in a circle and practically fall flat on my face.

"What are you doing in here?" I look around quickly, but no feet are under any of the stalls.

I relax a notch.

Eric runs a hand through his shock of red hair, unease on his face. "It's been nearly impossible to find you for a full week, Caoine. It's like you dropped off the face of the earth."

"Or I'm really good at hiding. Like right now. In the girls' bathroom. A place made for *girls*, not for *boys*. Which, last I checked, you *happen to be*."

He shrugs and leans against the wall. "Like I said, you're a hard one to find."

I rest my hip on the sink. "What are you doing in here, Eric? And why all the urgency to find me?"

"Isn't it obvious? Oliver, of course."

A pit falls to my stomach, and I stifle a swallow. "Oliver? What about him*?" Did something happen to him?*

Eric sucks in an impatient breath. "You've wrecked him, Caoine. You need to talk to the boy."

"What?" I flinch like I've been burned. "What are you talking about? We went on one date."

"You stopped talking to him for no reason. And he really likes you. You messed that boy up."

My jaw falls open and I splutter, but I can tell Eric isn't buying it.

He shakes his head. "Just tell me why."

"Why what?"

"Why you're ignoring him. Why the sudden change of heart? I mean, you had me fooled too, Caoine. I really thought you liked him."

I sigh and hide the way my hands shake. "I did—I . . . *do*."

"So what did he do that was so bad?"

Tears sting the backs of my eyes, and I fight an out-of-place laugh. "Nothing! Oliver did nothing at all."

Eric shakes his head again. "I'm sorry, Caoine. You've lost me."

Sorrow envelopes my whole body. "Oliver did nothing wrong, Eric. Really. In fact, he's the complete opposite of wrong. He's perfect. He's absolutely perfect. I mean, he's amazing and funny and kind and—"

"Totally hot. I get it. So why ignore him?"

"Because he's All. Those. Things." I give him a sad smile.

"He's too good for me, Eric. And no, I don't mean that in the self-deprecating way most teenage girls use as a cry for attention. I mean it for what it is. He *really* shouldn't be around me."

Eric drops his pack and crosses his arms. "Sorry. I'm still not buying it. What could any of that possibly mean?"

"It means what it means. Oliver shouldn't be around me, end of story."

"Why?"

"Because it's what's best for him."

"Why?"

"Because. I can't tell you. Just take my word for it. Hanging with me is bad for him."

"Why?"

"Because, Eric. It just is, okay?"

"Why?"

"Because I'm dangerous!" I flinch at my own outburst, heat flooding my face.

Eric doesn't move, not even when the bathroom door opens and a pair of junior girls stop dead in their tracks, mouths open.

"Give us a minute, okay? We're having a private conversation." Eric doesn't even look at the girls as he addresses them.

With an exaggerated eye roll, the girls turn and leave us to the silence of porcelain and air fresheners.

"Caoine. How on earth could you be dangerous?" His voice is soft. Kind.

I blink away moisture. "I just am, okay? Take my word for it." My nails dig into my palms. I hate the way my chin quivers.

He narrows his gaze. "I don't buy it. You're a teenage girl, Caoine. And, sorry to be a downer, but you don't come across as someone involved with drugs or gangs or anyone else that could actually cause Oliver any *real* harm. So I ask you again, *why*?"

"Because I like him too much. He's too wonderful for me to

ruin. Which is exactly what will happen if he sticks with me. Believe me, Oliver needs to stay as far away from me as possible."

Eric is quiet for a minute as his gaze drifts over my face. Then, "So that's it? You're giving up without even really trying?"

"I did try, Eric. And my suspicions were confirmed. I'm not a normal teenager, and I don't deserve a normal relationship."

His shoulders sag. "That's a shame, you know. Oliver likes you so much. You have no idea how he's been going out of his mind the last few days, missing you. I mean, you won't return his calls. You don't have a cell, so he can't text. He can't find you between classes or after school. It's like you're a ghost."

Blood rushes through my veins. The boy has no clue just how close he is to the truth. "We went on one date. He can't possibly—"

"Like you that much? Believe me when I say, he *does*. The boy is crazy about you. And the boy happens to be my best friend. And on the soccer team. Which, I might add, he's currently in danger of being kicked off of."

"He is? Because of me?"

"Well . . . yes . . . and no. Honestly? With the way he's sucking right now, I'm surprised Coach hasn't followed through on the threat to make him *not captain* anymore. I doubt he will, though. We need the players." Eric purses his lips. "But his mood is affecting the way he plays. And my guess is it's affecting his schoolwork, too."

Pause.

"Really, Caoine. Just talk to him. Even if you decide you want to stand your ground and stay away from him—which I think is nuts, by the way, considering how much you both like each other. But still. At least give him an explanation. He needs that. He needs closure. Or I might go insane." Eric gives me a small smile. "Seriously. The boy has become *boring*. I'd knock him out, but it seems overly cruel at the moment."

I laugh and swipe at a stray tear. Eric laughs with me.

My smile drops. "I'm afraid, Eric."

"Afraid of what? Of your crazy-dangerous side that might harm him?"

I sigh. "No. I'm afraid if I talk to him, I won't be strong enough to stay away. That we'll get back together."

He frowns. "Isn't that a good thing?"

I say nothing. Because of that fear. The fear of what the Unseelie prince might have planned for the town. Fear for Oliver, who could be too close when we all find out.

I fear for *him*. But most of all, I fear my next wail in the night might be for the boy I care so deeply about.

36

CAOINE

THE ROOM IS DARK, the scents of popcorn and old fabric the only things that stand out. I squeeze my eyes tight so they'll adjust to the lack of lighting but jump when the double doors close behind me. My eyes fly open. Now the room's brighter, a little less scary than a second ago.

A little.

With a slow inhale, I step around the partition and squint to find the aisle that leads through the auditorium and to the stage.

Mrs. Pearson, ninth-grade English teacher and head of the drama department, asked me to meet with one of her students during my off period so I could get the interview done. Apparently this dude wrote the entire fall play, so she's even letting him direct the thing. Impressive, I'll admit. She made it sound like kind of a big deal, anyway. Honestly, I don't care if I'm about to interview Luke Skywalker. I need to get this thing written. This incredibly boring article isn't going to write itself, but it will look great on a college application so . . . sigh.

I slowly pick my way down the aisle, my feet constantly feeling for anything I might trip over. The lights on the stage are set at half blast—not quite as strong as they would be on opening night but definitely not bright enough to light the remainder of the room. I stifle a grumble and finally find the stairs onto the stage.

I stop. Hairs on the back of my neck stand at attention. Why do I have the feeling I'm not alone? Inside my chest, my heart pounds like a runaway horse. With sweaty palms, I tighten my grip on my backpack. Really? It's bad enough I'm the new girl and have to write a crappy article for the crappy newspaper. But do I have to add "take a tour of the psycho-scary haunted theater" to my resume, too?

A second passes, and I gather courage to take a peek. By now my eyes have fully adjusted. I can make out the outline of every seat in the theater, including the partitions along the back and the exit doors at the end of each aisle.

Nothing. Not a soul in here. Well, except for the dude I'm interviewing. I hope.

Before another second passes, I race up the stage stairs, my heart in my throat, a scream an inch away from tumbling out. For whatever reason, I imagine the boogeyman on my heels, ready to grab my leg or yank the back of my shirt until I tumble backward. I don't stop running until I stand dead center stage.

I'm still alone.

Fantastic. Where is this guy again?

"Hello?" My voice is small and weak in the grand-ish theater. As grand as a high school theater can get, anyway.

Piles of props are scattered across the stage. I step over a mound of clothes and around stacked chairs. *This boy had seriously better be here.* With shaky hands, I grab my pack and fight to control my breathing.

The stage wings are just as dark as the main part of the theater, and my eyes scream as they attempt to adjust once again. Ropes hang beside the curtains, but all I can see is emptiness beyond. My feet insist on continuing my creep into the abyss, even though my brain has accepted that this will be the death of me. It's definitely over.

Where is he? And why am I wandering around in a deserted theater where a serial killer could be waiting for me?

"Hello?"

"Ah!" I yell in the absolutely most ridiculous way possible. Because, that's what I do.

I spin around so quick I almost fall, both hands on my chest. Sweat pours from my hairline, and that horse inside my chest has decided to break free and run away, along with my heart. At least he's safe from attack from a mass murderer.

A guy with light-brown skin and ash-colored dreadlocks looks panicked. "Uh, sorry. Didn't mean to frighten you." His voice is light, high-pitched, despite his oversized clothes and the nose ring. Why does this style scream a few decades ago?

I gasp for breath and manage to lean against a prop sofa that is — thankfully — close by. "No problem," I breathe.

"You knew I was here, right?"

"Yeah, yeah." I wave him away. "I just got spooked by —" *The imaginary ghosts and invisible murderers hiding between the seats.* I close my mouth before I spew something stupid. "I just couldn't find you."

He lifts a brow. "Well, I'm right here. Caoine, right?"

I nod, but things get awkward quick. Teenagers don't shake hands, and he hasn't offered his name. I shift from one foot to the other. "Erm. And you are . . . ?"

"Wyatt." His hands on are his hips, and he still hasn't moved.

Right. "So should we get started?" So I can leave this monstrosity of scariness?

"Sure." He points a thumb at the sofa that saved me from kissing the floor.

I waste no time pulling my pad and pen from my pack. "Tell me a little bit about the play."

Wyatt leans back in his seat, one arm looped behind the

sofa, his ankle resting on his other knee. The ultimate picture of relaxed. Or confident. I attempt to focus on his words and not his lackadaisical attitude.

"Well, the play is meant to show the audience one truth by depicting another story altogether. The setting preps the viewer for adventure before they're thrown right into an old-fashioned pirate tale that takes place on the eastern seaboard. Although the plot revolves around seven families of pirates, fighting over a specific piece of unclaimed land, the reality is, each of the families could easily procure the treasure if they only chose to work together."

Great. Why does this guy sound intellectual? "So this is a myth? Since it has an element of a lesson learned?" *Please don't sound dumb. Please don't sound dumb.*

"Yup. In fact, that was what I was hoping to achieve when I wrote the play. I want this to come across as a historic folk-tale, something that may have been passed down through the ages."

Just how long has he been working on this thing? I clear my throat. "So, uh . . . you wrote it? Like, by yourself?" He nods. *Ohmygosh. Don't sound like an idiot, Caoine!* "Erm, is it significant that it takes place on the sea? Wouldn't it have been easier to write a story that takes place on land? It seems like a lot of work to make all the set pieces."

He grabs a dreadlock and twists it. "Well, that's the challenge, now isn't it? How much fun would it be to create something easy? It's through the challenge that great art is produced."

Eep. Did I just insult him?

I plaster on a smile. "Of course."

"Besides, the ocean gave me the setting I needed to achieve my goal of incorporating fundamental truths of the psyche of man."

I blink. *Okay.*

His upper lip twitches as he waits for me to question him

on what that last statement means. Because, clearly, I have no choice but to question him, since it amounts to a large pile of dog poo, in my understanding.

I pretend to scribble a few notes. "And what would those truths be, exactly?"

"Why, the core of all human nature, Miss Roberts." His smile is condescending as he shifts forward, both elbows on his knees. "Every being on earth has struggled with dark versus light since the beginning of time. Every good story deals with it on some level. I incorporate the struggle between good and evil by a physical representation of the core evil that distracts us all."

"Evil?" I seriously try hard to keep the boredom from my voice. *So cliché.*

"Sure. It was easy to attribute the physical wanting of beauty through the mermaids and the lazy nature of the sailors who chose to give up a life of sailing for a life of drinking. And then there's the reoccurrence of the number seven displayed throughout each grouping of characters." His eyes lock with mine, and one corner of his mouth tilts up in a smirk.

My stomach drops right out of my body. Ice trickles along my fingers, and I fight to unfreeze myself. "Um, did you just say seven?"

He nods again, this time inclining his head to the side just slightly. "Yeah. See, that's what I meant when I said the physical representation of the core evil within us all. The Seven Deadly Sins. Are you familiar with them?"

Air refuses to penetrate my lungs, and my mouth goes dry. "I've . . . heard of them." A lot, lately.

"It was easy to create groupings of characters to represent each of the seven sins. I took it a step further by making each group contain a total of seven persons per sin. And of course there are the seven families fighting to find the treasure in the first place. I wanted the number to penetrate the audience's mind, even if they aren't conscious of it." He leans back, that lazy demeanor a mask he slips right back on.

My breath feels ragged, stifled within my chest, yet somehow I force myself to speak. "But why represent the number in so many different ways? Wouldn't just having seven sins do the trick?"

I'm only half listening as my brain attempts to contemplate what this could mean. There's zero chance our school drama being about the Seven Deadly Sins and the Unseelie prince using them to his advantage *aren't* related.

"Well, seven is a perfect number, isn't that right?"

I shake my head. "Perfect?"

"Yes. Biblically the number represents God. It has long been believed to show completeness and perfection. On another level, according to numerology, that is, the number seven represents the searcher of truth. Seven knows nothing is as it seems, that all is merely hidden beneath illusion."

I gasp. "What did you say?"

"Illusion, Caoine. The number seven is meant to uncover that which is hidden, to seek out truth."

The room spins around me, and I fight to keep hold of my pencil. There's no way this is coincidence. I get the feeling the Unseelie prince has more control of things within this school than I gave him credit for. And he's pulling the strings to create an illusion I may never know the truth behind.

37

CAOINE

IT WOULD BE SO MUCH EASIER if the unexpected could be expected. After I'm blindsided by a situation—any situation—I reflect on how I wish I'd done things differently. How I could have *not* come across like such a freak.

Like the time in eighth grade when Kevin Henderson passed me a note halfway through pre-algebra saying how big a crush Ben Lyles had on me. The way my cheeks turned hot and I actually allowed my eyes to lift from their refuge, to connect with those around me. That small smile, usually hidden beneath layers of distrust and doubt, actually showed itself to the tight circle of classmates who were in on the joke. Then the laughter from them all as it hit me that not a single word of the note was true. That I allowed myself to believe a lie. A silly lie from some silly junior high kids. Stupid me.

For weeks I went over and over how if I had only crumpled the note before I even read it, everything would've turned out all right. How it wouldn't have been so bad if I just didn't show that smile. If I just didn't allow my face to turn that shade of pink that told the tale I so long wanted to be true: I just wanted a boy—any boy—to notice I was alive.

So my brain has zero idea how to react to the fact that a

boy—not just any boy, one who noticed me weeks before—is now sitting on my front porch, waiting for my return from school. Like a lost puppy who's only joy is finding his beloved owner. How I stand before him like an idiot, jaw ajar, frozen in place.

I drop my backpack at my feet.

"Hey." Oliver climbs to his feet as if he's in pain.

His eyes dart from right to left before he shoves his hands in his pockets. He's unsure, nervous. I'm nervous. Terrified of what will come next from that boy's mouth.

I swallow and stay silent. I'm the worst of the worst.

"Where—?" He clears his throat. "Where've you been? Haven't, uh, seen you around?"

"Yeah." Because I'm not just an idiot, but I'm a complete and total jerk, too. *Say something, Cavine!*

His eyes are sad, and my heart skips five different unmistakable beats.

"I've missed you." He shifts on his feet.

Mentally I calculate how far the end of the driveway is from the street and how fast I might be able to run compared to the super-star soccer player. Not far, I surmise.

"I—I—" *Am a jerk. I'm sorry.*

"Do you think I'm the son of the Unseelie king?"

"What?" I blink and falter where I stand. Total opposite of where I thought this conversation was going.

He huffs a breath. "Is that why you've been ignoring me? Because you think I could be him? 'Cause if it is, then where's that crushed herbal stuff Aubree gave you? I'll rub it all over my body, promise. Please believe me. I have nothing to do with any of this."

"I—" This is crazy. "No." I shake my head like I've got a tick. "No. No way. I never thought you were him." Although, I never did rub that stuff on him. Maybe I should? I rub my palms against my jeans. "I just—wait. How do you even know about—?"

"Aubree. She told me everything."

My eyes bug out of my head. "She what?" So much for secrecy and all that jazz.

"She trusts me." Pause. "Unlike some others." His gaze is obsidian.

I flinch as if I've been stung. His words are fair, though. I swallow again, since saliva appears to be so hard to come by at the moment. "I—I—"

"What, Caoine? If you don't think I'm him, then what could possibly make you hate me all of a sudden?"

I'm frozen, shock rocking my body. "I don't *hate* you." So the opposite.

"Then why? Why have you been ignoring me?"

"Because—" *Because I want you to live and not die.* "It's not —*safe.*"

"What? Of course it's not safe. There's a mad faerie serial killer on the loose at the school. *No one's* safe."

"No. Yes! I know, it's just . . . I don't think you should be involved."

"Not involved? In case you haven't noticed, I'm all kinds of involved, Caoine. Even Aubree can see how deep I'm in this thing. There's no turning back for me. Why won't you trust me? Are you ashamed of me?"

"What?" My jaw does that dangly thing again. "No, why would you—?"

"I can help. I told you I *want* to help, Caoine."

"Yeah but . . ." I bite my lip and taste blood. "It's just, I don't think it's a great idea."

He narrows his eyes. "Is this about you? What . . . you don't think I'll want to stick around once I learn about all the crap in your life?"

Yes. "No." My chest squeezes like it's got a clamp around it.

Oliver puts his hands on his hips. "It is, isn't it? Even after I told you I'm all in? That I like you enough to handle anything that comes my way? You still don't believe me?"

My gaze is locked on my feet. "No. It's not that, it's just . . . you don't know everything about this. There's a lot you don't know."

"And you do?"

My eyes snap to his. His look is hard, challenging.

"I just didn't—"

"You didn't think I could handle it?" He steps toward me, and I'm like a block of ice. "After that night on the lake? You *still* don't trust me?"

"I trust you, Oliver." I do. So much more than I should.

"Then what? Why? You don't think I'll want to stick around once I find out who you really are? Because I will, Caoine. I have. I know exactly who you are. You're no different from me. We're both broken and hurting and stuck in a sucky life we can't do anything about. But you aren't the only one hurting, Caoine. I hurt, too. And I know you. I like you. I like you a lot."

"But—" Tears tremble on the edge of my eyelids.

"But what?" He steps closer now, inches from me. "I like you so much, Caoine. And I thought you liked me . . ."

"I do." Why is my voice so whiney?

"You do? Because it doesn't seem like it. I don't see how you could walk away from me if you like me all that much. I know I could never walk away from you like that. Not that easily."

A flaming-hot brand stabs me in the chest. "Who said it was *easy?*" There's fire in my voice now. "And I *do* like you. Probably too much. But I walked away because it's what's best."

"Best for who? You? *Me?* Is it best that we're both miserable?"

"No." He flinches at the strength in my voice. "I don't want you to be miserable. I never wanted that, Oliver. Can't you see?" The tears fall freely now. "I like you so, so much. I can't stop myself. But it's not right. It's not okay that you're near me."

"Why not?" His hands are on my arms now, his breath hot against my face. "Why, Caoine? You don't think I can handle a little danger?"

I squeeze my eyes shut and feel the hot wet on my cheeks. "No. It's not that." I open my eyes, look right at him. "This is real, Oliver. It's not a game. This is life and death. And when death calls you, I won't be able to stop it. I can't—I—"

His brow creases. "What's that supposed to mean?"

"I—" Sigh. "It's nothing." My hand finds his chest, and I lean toward him slightly.

"No, tell me, Caoine."

I shake my head. "My dad . . . he thinks I can use my curse. That it's a gift. That maybe the reason the faeries gave it to me is to stop death, not allow it to happen."

Oliver's face falls, and he looks around in wonder. "Is that possible?"

"I . . . don't know. We've tried for years to figure it out, and I don't think we ever will. But that's not what's important right now. Right now there's a killer at the school, and I've got to figure out who he is before he kills again. And I can't have you anywhere near me."

He starts to protest, but I place a finger over his lips. The tears grow stronger, and I hiccup to keep them at bay.

"I'm serious, Oliver. I like you too much, and I can't stand to see you in danger. You don't understand. I don't know what I'd do if anything happened to—" I hiccup again and gag on my spit. Because I'm slick like that.

He huffs and yanks me into an embrace, places a kiss on top of my head. "Thank God." He pulls in a shaky breath. "I was so scared, Caoine. So scared I'd done something wrong. That you were avoiding me for another reason." He pulls back, sets both his hands against my cheeks, our noses an inch apart. "I'm here, Caoine. You aren't getting rid of me, no matter how hard you try. I like you so much, and I'm going to be by your side every single day until we figure out who this dude is. And when that's over, I'm going to be here to help you figure out what your dad means about your gift."

My chin trembles, and a dribble of snot seeps from my nose. I'm a hot mess. I frantically grab at the edge of my sleeve to wipe way the offending fluid.

Oliver places a kiss on my forehead. "I'm not going anywhere, Caoine. So accept that and let me take you on another date."

I exhale, relax into his embrace. Then my eyes fly open, and I step back. "Aren't you . . . don't you have a game right now?"

He shrugs. "I begged off. Told Coach I hurt my ankle and had to see the doctor."

"But you—"

He gathers me into his arms. "But nothing, Caoine. You're more important than any soccer game. You're worth it."

And then, for the first time, he kisses me—really kisses me —on my front porch, as the sun sets and my heart tumbles to the next level of disbelief. His hands move along my back, and mine are in his hair, and the world around us slips away. Heat, soft lips, a buzzing sound that vibrates inside my head— nothing else registers for a full thirty seconds. That boy kisses me in a way that surpasses every idea I ever had about what a kiss could be.

My boyfriend kisses me, and all my worries disappear. For a moment, anyway.

He only stays a few more minutes before he heads to his car parked on the street, the one I somehow missed on my pathetic walk up the driveway. My heart swells, and my feet remain firmly planted as I watch the boy disappear with a little piece of my heart.

It's not until he's gone that a sudden chill washes down my back, one that has nothing to do with the dropping temperatures of the approaching night. I glance down the road to the left, then the right. The only thing I catch is the way the bushes alongside my house—just below my bedroom window—come to life for a split second.

I swallow, bending to pick up my backpack, and head toward the front door a little faster than normal. It's probably just a squirrel fighting for that last piece of food to store before winter settles in. This is what I tell myself so I can sleep, anyway.

38

CAOINE

FIVE DAYS. That's how long it's been since Oliver and I officially became a couple. Again. And the length of time in which my banshee beast has only predicted two deaths—again, why am I suddenly sleeping through the night? And neither of them have anything to do with the Seven Deadly Sins. To say Aubree is on edge is an understatement.

Seamus on the other hand . . .

"Wake up." Aubree nudges her faerie friend with her elbow.

We're in the school cafeteria, our final lunch before the beloved weekend. The table is filled with the usual crowd: Oliver and I, Aubree and Seamus, Eric, and Catherine. Since working on the paper with her, I've found she's super cool. And I think she might make a good match for Eric. I've been trying desperately to get them to talk. Easy for him, way difficult for her.

"Mmph, harrumph." Seamus pulls away from his friend and settles back in his spot, his head nestled neatly on top of his backpack. His cheese pizza, ignored.

I look the so-called lunch over. Yeah. I'd ignore that, too.

"So how'd you do on the AP bio test?" Oliver looks at Eric as he tosses a fry in his mouth.

My belly grumbles. *French fries.* I've already eaten half of his. It's far too selfish of me to steal another one, right? I pinch my lips together and try not to stare at the heavenly carb goodness.

"We had a test?" Eric looks up in surprise.

Oliver frowns. "The one we got back today? We took it on Monday."

"Oh. Is that the thing I shoved in my notebook without looking?" He cackles. "No clue. I don't like disappointment, therefore I don't look at little things . . . like grades." He gives me a wink and turns back to Oliver. "Speaking of which, you weren't such a disappointment on the field this week. Way to go, Caoine, for helping my man get his mojo back."

Pink blossoms beneath Oliver's dark skin. I duck my head to hide a smile. Things have gone well for Oliver and me this week. Very well.

"I scraped by with an A," my boyfriend says. He'd been hoping for a perfect grade but no such luck. "You might want to look over the test. I don't think she's grading on a curve this year."

Eric's face falls. "She's not? Oops. Not good."

I laugh as he scrambles in his backpack to find the mystery test grade.

"What about you, Caoine?" Aubree says. "How's the paper going?"

I roll my eyes and glance at Catherine, who returns the sentiment. "Slowly."

Catherine giggles and nods.

"The articles Jessica gives us have been less than stellar," I explain. "She's obsessed with unsolved mysteries. Boring ones. Cat, at least, has an interesting column she convinced Jessica to let her do. But the rest of us?"

I give her the thumbs down with a grimace. I'm still not

convinced she isn't trying to sabotage me, even though Oliver denies it with impressive loyalty. That guy only sees the good in people.

"True story." Catherine shrugs. "I feel for you, Caoine."

I smile at her. She lets me call her Cat, which apparently is something only her good friends get to do. Which doesn't include Jessica. I try to be careful not to call her that while working at the paper. It sort of feels like our dirty little secret. Like we're breaking a rule somehow.

"Oh well," I say. "I just need to get through the month. I'm hoping the holidays will promise more interesting prospects."

Cat snorts and raises her brow, which does nothing to help my self-confidence.

"How about you?" I ask Aubree.

Seamus starts a soft snore beside her, and she stabs him with her plastic fork to quiet him down. He doesn't.

"Well, I've been busy lately. With that *research* project, remember?" She gives me the eye, and my belly shrinks in on itself.

Oh, right. Her time has been spent trying to figure out what the hay Mr. Unseelie son is up to. Besides the fact she, Oliver, Seamus, and I continue to search for the culprit. Oliver totally isn't a faerie, as he so proudly showed me by rubbing a handful of the foxglove powder all over his hands and face and neck. I tried to get him to stop, but he really wanted to prove it. It made quite the mess to clean up, and I couldn't touch him for the rest of the day.

"Any movement in that area?" I bite my lip and lean an inch closer to Oliver.

"Oh crud," Eric says under his breath.

He's found his AP bio test and holds it like a viper ready to strike. His face reflects his grade, and none of us bother to ask how he did. Seamus begins snoring again.

"Not much." Aubree sighs. "But I'm working on it."

"What's this?" Cat asks. "What class do you have a project in?"

I glance away and steal another of Oliver's fries.

"Erm, history," Aubree says.

And I almost choke on that fry. Oliver pats me on the back like a good boyfriend.

"Nothing interesting," Aubree explains. "Something I'd rather not be doing, honestly." She looks around the lunchroom with indifference.

This is true. The best case scenario will be if this whole thing just goes away and my curse goes back to normal and people just die regular deaths again. The blood in my veins pumps a little harder, and Oliver's hand brushes mine. Ever since our little talk last Friday, he's been slightly overprotective when it comes to my feelings and faeries and impending death. Like he can read my thoughts or something.

"Do you think she'll let me retake it?" Eric's face is screwed up like a toddler about to throw a tantrum.

Oliver ignores him. "Maybe Caoine should take more time to help you with research." He gives me an eye that says we need to talk after school. "I've taken too much of your time lately, babe."

Aww. He called me babe. My insides go squishy, and my toes tingle at the way he grins at me.

I shake my head and force my thoughts back to the conversation. Except my thoughts can't be forced back to where they should be, because now I'm distracted by something else.

Something urgent.

Seamus continues to sleep on his backpack, a dribble of drool now accosting his schoolbooks. All would seem normal to the average person—a student asleep during lunch break, not uncommon in high school. If only it weren't for the pointy ears that poke out from under his hair. And not just regular pointy ears, but ones that are slowly but surely turning green, along with the rest of his face.

His faerie glamour must be fading now that he's unconscious! My heart smacks into a wall and stops.

"Ah!" I practically jump in my seat as I try to attract all the attention from the table at once.

Oliver startles beside me, and I successfully draw the gaze of everyone—save Seamus.

"Caoine?" Oliver blinks rapidly.

"I'm fine, I'm fine. Totally fine. Thought I saw—"

With my eyes I try to signal Aubree to look at Seamus. She doesn't get it.

"A spider!" I yell. I kick her under the table. Hard.

"Ow!" She yelps and grabs her leg.

Eric's eyes go wide, and Cat looks scared.

"What's going on?" Oliver asks.

"Nothing." I glare at Aubree so hard I think I might bore holes through her head.

She gets my drift and gags on her own spit.

"Ah!" I yell again and grab my ankle in the same fashion Aubree had.

She smacks Seamus so hard he falls from the table. But at least his glamour is back. His skin is normal color, his ears perfectly rounded. I exhale with relief.

"Caoine!" Oliver still hasn't given up trying to help.

"We're fine. I'm fine." I settle back in my seat and smooth my hair. "It was . . ."

"Fire ants," Aubree says matter-of-factly.

"Fire ants?" Eric asks.

"Yup. Fire ants." I stomp my foot to kill those pesky— invisible—fire ants.

Oliver jolts in surprise.

"But I thought you said it was a spider?" Cat cringes.

"It was. Both, I mean." My smile is pathetic.

Seamus wobbles a bit as he gathers his wits.

I catch Oliver's eye. "We're fine now. Really."

He nods, and the others shrug off the strange outburst. I

glance at Eric and Cat and try to surmise if they saw Seamus change. They go back to their conversation, and my heart rate returns to normal. That was too close.

One thing is for sure, Aubree and I need to find out who this Unseelie prince is. Now. I'm not sure how much longer this high school can take having so many faeries in one place.

39

CAOINE

"You should probably go." I'm snuggled nice and warm within the confines of Oliver's arms as we sit on the sofa.

Oliver frowns and places a kiss on my forehead. "Why so soon?"

I nuzzle my head another inch against his. "It's a school night."

"Um, no it's not. Friday night does not count as a school night."

Crap. He knows why I'm asking him to go. And I know, too. As much as it pains me to send him away, it must happen. It's already past nine, and my curse could kick in at any moment. *If* it decides to party tonight.

"Five more minutes?" he begs.

I totally relent. I'm such a softie.

With a small smile, I close my eyes and breathe in his scent. Spicy aftershave clashes with the floral aroma of his laundry detergent. But it tells me he's close, so that's all that matters. I relax. My living room is empty and silent, other than our gentle whispers. I've even got the curtains pulled shut and only a single lamp in the corner turned on to give us more privacy. Every molecule in my body is ecstatic over the fact Oliver came chasing after me and forced me to be his girlfriend and that I somehow gave in.

Oliver's fingers dig into my waist, and he gives a squeeze. I jump in place with a squeal.

"Hey, don't go falling asleep on me," he says.

Oh, right. My eyes are still closed. I open them only to find the smooth brown of his staring back. And those lashes! How on earth did he get blessed with such long eyelashes? And why haven't I ever noticed them before?

I sigh. He laughs.

"What?" I whine.

"You're cute." He kisses my temple again.

Great. Apparently I'm cute. Not what I was going for, but okay.

The coo-coo clock in the kitchen chimes half past nine. *Crud*. I attempt to pull away. "Okay, lover boy. Time for you to hit the road."

He groans and holds on to me with one hand, rubbing his eyes with the other. "Really? Is there no way I can stay just a little longer? If you go into your trance thingy, I can just cut out and head home."

My belly clenches, and I swallow. "I don't think that's a good idea."

Oliver sticks out his lower lip and rubs one hand along my back. "Please? Pretty please?"

Adrenaline pumps through my blood, and I yell at the squiggle in my stomach to stop its jumping. Everything about this boy makes me want him to stay forever. But my logical side says no. It's just not a good idea.

Still . . . "Well, maybe we can ask my dad what he thinks." That's the responsible thing to do, right? Let the dad make the decision? Because, let's be honest, I stink at decisions.

He shrugs and hops to his feet, then pulls me alongside him with too much force. I fall into him, and he easily catches me, his hands around my middle and his lips ready to catch mine. "Sounds like a plan."

Then he kisses me again and *wow*. The world continues to spin, even though he's holding me perfectly still. That boy and those lips. They are seriously going to make me faint someday.

"Where's your pops?"

I blink back to reality. "Oh, um, probably in his bedroom? He sometimes likes to read until my curse comes to life."

Oliver frowns at my use of the word *curse*. I know how he feels about it, but I refuse to call what I do anything other than that, despite what Aubree might think. It is not a *gift*, no matter how hard she or my dad try to convince me otherwise.

We head upstairs, and I knock on my dad's door. There's no noise from inside. I crinkle my brow at my boyfriend, and he raises his. Oliver nods with his chin that I should open the door. He's right.

I turn the handle and push my way in . . . and see why he didn't answer. He's passed out on the floor. And not just from exhaustion from work—since he doesn't actually do that anymore. Eight or ten beer bottles surround him, all empty. One is still in his hand. The stink of alcohol slaps me in the face, and I gag a little. My belly hits the floor, and heat rises on my cheeks. Not how I wanted my boyfriend to find my dad. *At. All.*

But Oliver's more concerned about my dad's welfare, so I shove aside my pride and help him lift my dad onto the bed.

"Here," Oliver says. "Get his feet up so he doesn't slip off the bed if he rolls over."

I do what he says, and my boyfriend settles my dad onto the pillows. He even grabs a blanket and covers my dad, all snug like a bug in a rug. My heart palpitates at his consideration. But I can't be truly happy at the moment. Not when my dad is stinking drunk, mourning the loss of his job and direction in life. This is a first for him. He's *never* allowed himself to get so drunk he might jeopardize helping me with my banshee song.

Oliver continues to make my dad comfortable while I pick up a few of the empty bottles. A note is stuck to the bottom of one of them.

A green note.

My chest squeezes as if all the air was suddenly sucked out of it.

I turn my back to Oliver and scan the words as quickly as I can.

Dearest Caoine,

Your father and I had a pleasant conversation, although he'll never remember it. I learned so much about you, more than I knew before. It makes me feel like our connection is even stronger, Caoine. So much stronger.

Sorry to leave such a mess, but you know how alcoholics are. It's a messy business, addiction.

This is just a friendly prod to remind you that I'm in control here. You may think you control what you do, or that one of your faerie friends will find how to stop what I have planned. But remember, I'll always be one step ahead of you, no matter how hard you try.

Consider my previous proposal. The only way to learn who you are —to truly take control of your gift—is to join me. Give me a chance and maybe you'll understand why I must do this thing you so badly hate. Maybe you'll grow to see its value.

My hope is that you'll join me, soon. Don't tarry, lovely. Or next time your father might drink himself to death.

Yours for always,

Your Prince

I blink away shock as I crumple the note between my fingers, demand my heart to slow its beating. My skin vibrates with fear, and the room tilts as I regain control of my senses.

"He's out for the night," Oliver says quietly from behind me.

I squeeze my eyes shut. *Get yourself under control, Caoine.* The note fits neatly in my pocket as I spin to confront my boyfriend. The one who *can't* know anything about what I just read.

Didn't the Unseelie prince tell me he'd hurt anyone I told? *He sneaked into my house and got my dad stinking drunk!* His next attack could be so much worse. I have no choice but to forget what I just read, push aside the terror that pulses inside my flesh.

I swallow, somehow manage to avoid eye contact with the one person I wish I could confide in right now. "What am I going to do if my curse wakes up?"

Oliver bites his lip. "What have you done in the past when your dad's been drunk?" Sadly, the boy knows my dad and his love of alcohol.

I shake my head. "He's never been this drunk before, especially not at night when my faerie-ness likes to wake. He's always been so responsible to put me first, to protect me." *Until the Unseelie jerk showed up!* My arms slink around my waist, and I shrink into myself. "What am I going to do if my banshee wants to sing?" *When* she wants to sing?

I have a hard time catching my breath. What will I do? I've never gone for my walk alone before. I have no idea what it'll be like to deal with the aftermath of *me*, once my wailing is done. The headache, the blackouts. The lying on the ground in a stupor. I see spots dance before my eyes and sway.

"Whoa." Oliver takes my hands to steady me. "I'll help you."

"What?" My jaw drops. "No. I—I can't let you. It's too weird."

"Weird? You're worried about weird? I'm more worried about my girlfriend getting hit by a car on some back road while she sleepwalks."

I bite my lip again. "I . . . I'm not sure—"

"Come on, Caoine. It's your only solution. I'm the one person who knows about you . . . well, one of them. I can help. I'll keep you safe." He steps closer and pulls me against his body. "Besides, I'm the one who wanted to stay a little longer, right? Now I'll get my wish."

"But . . . what about your parents? Won't they be expecting you?"

He shrugs. "I'll call and tell them I'm crashing at Eric's. It's not like it's the first time."

"But—" Nothing. I've got nothing. Oliver is absolutely, one hundred percent, unequivocally right. I need a protector when I sing. End of story.

"Caoine," he whispers. He leans close so we're nose to nose.

And my heart tumbles down a million steps once again, just like it does every time that boy is near. *Swoon.*

"Okay. But there are a few things I need to tell you so you'll know what to do once it happens." I look at my dad and sigh. "It never occurred to me someone other than my dad might ever have to be with me when I sing."

I lean my head against my boyfriend's chest, and he holds me.

It also never occurred to me that I might ever have another man in my life besides my dad. And maybe my dad feels the same way. Maybe his drinking has more to do with the fact he feels like he's being replaced than with anything else going on in our lives.

Maybe it wasn't so hard for the Unseelie prince to get him to drink one more beer. Maybe I'm the reason he's drunk and passed out.

40

CAOINE

"This is my cloak." I hold the bolt of silver fabric reverently between my fingers. "It may not look like much, but it's crazy important that you *not* forget this, okay?"

Oliver nods with a serious expression on his face. Every molecule in my body vibrates with the fear that something might go terribly wrong. We sit on my bed, our thighs touching, the heat from our bodies kissing.

"I'm usually aware the song is about to come, and I can grab this and slip it on. But just in case, do not let me leave the house without this in place. Including the hood." I flip up the soft material to reveal the ample section that hangs around my head like a cloud. "The hood needs to be in place *before* I sing."

"Got it. Is that it? I just follow you wherever you go?"

"Yep. Pretty much." I blow out a breath. "Generally, it's never too far. It might be as much as a couple miles, but I think you can handle a little exercise." I squeeze his knee to break the tension. It's fantastic he's passionate about helping me, but his hard exterior is making me feel numb inside. Is this still my boyfriend or a robot? He's totally in game mode.

He doesn't flinch. "What about traffic? Danger? What do I do if I can't stop you?"

"That's one of the main reasons you're coming. When I'm in my trance, I have no control over my body. So yes, if I'm in danger, please don't let me die." I shake my head and shove away the chills that cover my arms. "I won't fight you or anything, so if you grab me, I'll obey. I'm sort of like a limp rag doll, to be honest. Except I'm steady on my feet and I've got a destination in mind. If I can't go the route I want to and you redirect me, I'll naturally find another way to get there."

"Right." He exhales a little too heavily and rubs his hands together. Where's his confidence from earlier?

My heart picks up speed. "Oliver, you'll be fine. This isn't rocket science. I just need someone to be with me when I cross into Crazy Town."

"I don't want to screw this up." He swallows. "I know how important this is to you."

Important? I try not to snort. My curse has never held any importance in my life.

"Just remember to pull my hood off as soon as I'm done."

"How will I know when you're done?"

"Well, I'll be falling to the ground in exhaustion and no longer singing. Dead giveaway, promise." I stop myself from rolling my eyes. "Oh yeah, you'll need to help me home since I won't have much strength left. I mostly just need a shoulder to lean on."

He nods again. "Why the hood? Why does it need to be on during your song but off right after?"

"Well, I believe you already heard my *song* without the hood." I air quote the word *song*. "At the lake?"

He nods with a cringe.

"Yeah. It's basically a bunch of screeching without this thing. And I don't like the hood in place after I'm done singing because of the images I see."

"Images?"

I clear my throat. "Uh, yeah. Of the . . . death." I pause. "Soon after the song ends, pictures pop in my mind of the person who's about to die. How they'll die, et cetera. It's not pleasant. I mean, it's bad enough I have to predict their death, let alone watch it happen in my mind, over and over again. And it hurts. Like bad."

His shoulders release some tension. "Okay. I think I've got it. Make sure you have your cape before we leave—hood in place, follow where you lead but keep you from danger, then catch you when you're done so I can pull your hood off."

I smile. "Right. See? You've got this. No problem. You'll do just fine." Am I trying to convince him or me?

He sighs. "We'll see."

He looks nervously at the bedroom doorway, probably in the hopes my dad will wake up soon. Something I *don't* see happening until the break of dawn.

"Okay, so . . ." I glance at my bed. Awkward. My boyfriend and I are alone in my room, on my bed, with my dad totally unconscious across the hall. *Nice.* "Yeah. I have no idea what time my curse might wake me up. Sometimes it's in the middle of the night. We both might want to get some sleep."

I give him a sheepish grin, but his nod is just as serious as it's been since he volunteered for the job.

He holds up both hands. "Wait here." Then he runs out of my room.

I blink. *Where did my boyfriend just go?*

Two minutes later he races back in, quietly shuts my door, a large object tucked against his body.

"A guitar?" I'm on my feet. "Why did you just grab my dad's old guitar he never plays?" It sits on a stand in the corner of the living room, more for show than any other reason. The top half is covered in dust, and I scrunch my nose at the sight of a cobweb drifting from the neck.

Oliver takes my arm and seats me on my bed, properly. "Here. You sit here, and I'll sit—" He glances around my room and spots a small chest in the corner with boxes piled on top. "Here!"

He gingerly leans the guitar against the wall as he loads the boxes on the floor and pulls the chest into the center of the room. Then he picks up the guitar and takes a seat, a proud grin in place. His fingers strum the strings, and we both groan. Even someone as tone deaf as I am can tell it's way out of tune. Oliver chuckles and begins tuning.

"I didn't know you played a musical instrument." I bite my lip, my heart fluttering at the prospect of what I'm about to hear. *The callouses on his fingers!* I refrain from hitting myself on the head.

One corner of his mouth tilts up, displaying his single crooked tooth. "There are a lot of things you don't know about me."

"Oh really?" I lean back on my elbows, my eyebrows raised.

He laughs again. "It's no big deal, really. I started playing when I was ten. My brother won a guitar off his buddy in a bet, but he had no clue how to play. The thing sat in his closet for six months before I finally got the nerve to ask him if I could mess around on it. He told me I could have it, outright gave it to me."

His smile fades, and I see a memory in his eyes.

"That guitar is one of my favorite memories I have of my brother." His voice grows thick, and he clears his throat. "It only took a few lessons to realize I had an aptitude for it. I picked it up quickly and moved on to writing my own songs a few years ago."

My eyes go large. "You write songs? You're like, a real musician?"

Oliver shakes his head. "I don't know about that, but—" He clears his throat again. "I'd like to be." This part is so soft I barely hear it.

But I do.

"You want to be a musician? Why have I never known this about you?"

He shrugs, his gaze anywhere but on mine. "Because it's never going to happen, I guess. I mean, sure, I like to play and sing but . . . well, performing music isn't in my future."

"Why not?" I sit up, pull my knees close to my chest, my arms wrapped around them.

"My parents." He sniffs. "They've had their heart set on me being a doctor ever since I can remember, so . . . well, that's that, I guess."

"You're going to be a doctor just because your parents want you to? Even though you don't?"

He pauses, finally looks at me. "They lost their oldest son, Caoine. It's the least I can do, right? To make them happy? I mean, they didn't ask for any of this . . . none of us did." Swallow. "I just—need to do this. To honor their wishes, ya know?"

No. Not really. Suddenly my alcoholic dad doesn't seem so bad. Sure, he insists I go to school and protect my banshee curse, but at least he doesn't tell me what I can and can't like in life. I'd die without my poetry. And I haven't even thought of what I want for a career. I just always assumed I'd travel from town to town, singing my stupid song with my dad.

I lick my lips. "That's really kind of you, Oliver." Really kind. How is it possible someone so kind has chosen to be with me? I sigh. "Play me something?"

This brings a small smile to his lips.

And so he sings.

He sings a haunting melody I've never heard before. Words about love found—and lost. About pain, joy. Learning to wait. It's as if he's inside my mind, spilling my darkest secrets for all the world to hear. His melody circling and floating between each of my memories, convincing them to step outside, to blend into the universe the way a puff of smoke disappears.

His voice is smooth and deep, so different than what I would've imagined. The song continues, and his body sways with each beat, his fingers dancing from fret to fret, almost magical. Everything is so perfect, I expect to see his phone glowing beside him, with an admission he was just lip synching this entire time.

But he isn't. This is him. This is Oliver.

The song ends too soon, and we're both silent.

Finally, he nods. "Lie back and settle in."

I crinkle my brow.

"I'm singing you to sleep, silly." He gives me a crooked smile. "Get some sleep so you'll be ready when the time comes for your show to begin."

I open my mouth to protest but stick out my bottom lip instead. No snuggles?

He smiles. "I don't think I'll be falling asleep tonight, Caoine."

Right. I sigh. My heart beats a little slower knowing I'm not alone in this. I settle against my pillow and snuggle into the warmth. Now all we have to do is wait for the inevitable.

I close my eyes and listen as my boyfriend serenades me with his talent. His love.

Somehow I don't think I'll be falling asleep tonight, either.

41

CAOINE

THE DREAM BEGINS, even though I know it's not a dream. It's reality. But for me, it feels like a dream. A dream from which I cannot wake, not until my task is complete. Not until I've predicted another death in a world with so many already dying.

Oliver senses the minute I break from his arms. At some point in the night he moved to hold me while I sleep. Did I talk in my sleep? Make a noise that cautioned him to join me? My brain is too foggy to comprehend such thoughts. He's on his feet and has my cape even before I reach for it. I slip it over my head as he slides on his shoes.

Oliver tugs my hood in place, and somewhere inside, I'm grateful. The banshee side of me couldn't care less, since the cry will come either way. But the human side of me is definitely grateful.

The stairs appear before me, and I walk down them in the trance that holds me, somehow still aware of Oliver, an ever-present cloud of heat by my side. I blink, and I'm in the cool night air. Blink, at the end of the block. Blink, two streets away. The school comes into view. Why am I at the school? No one lives here.

Oliver is saying something, but all I hear is buzzing, the buzzing of the song begging to be set free. Desperate to roam the earth and find its victim. Eager to taste blood and pain and sorrow. My mouth opens, and I say something. Did I just speak to him? Or was that my song?

We're behind the school now, crossing the athletic fields, a mass of trees looming ahead. Where am I going? Who lives back here?

Twigs break beneath my bare feet as I crunch my way through the brush and foliage of the small patch of trees. Oliver's hand is on my arm, gentle but urging. I ignore it. My song will always ignore someone who wishes to stop me from my purpose. Is he worried?

I break free on the other side, past the trees, past the bushes and all things green and brown. A clearing sits here. I've heard the kids in my class talk about bonfires and parties thrown right at this very spot. But I've never been here.

A hill stands in my way. I attack it like every other obstacle I consume during my thirst for death.

Up, up, up.

At the top is a large flat rock, a sharp decline on the other side. It's wide and level up here, something that can't be seen from far below. Oliver puffs beside me from the exertion. I haven't even broken a sweat.

My mouth opens.

I sing.

But I don't understand. Who am I singing to? There's no one here. No movement, no noise. Nothing. Yet my lament continues, low and sorrowful, quite possibly the most beautiful I've ever sung in my entire life. Even the banshee side of me can appreciate the elegance my voice carries. Over and over, the same tones and syllables tumble from my lips. I close my eyes. How long have I been singing?

Then, a noise. I don't turn my head because the banshee would never allow that, not during my song. But there's a commotion to my right, a scream, an *umph*. That voice is male. More screams are muffled by a gurgling sound, a thing that reflects nothing of life. Oliver is no longer beside me. He's fighting. Who is he fighting? I can feel his fear, his anger, his desperation. Someone cries near me. A female wails like her lungs might explode if she keeps the anguish deep inside her another second.

My song ends. My vision goes black. I fall.

Oliver is there to catch me. How, I don't know, but he's there. He yanks my hood back just as images flit across my vision, a familiar face in front of my eyes.

"Oliver, what—?" I gasp.

But he can't hear me, not from the wails and cries and the thousand metal screws that rip across the chalkboard from the girl's grief. Pain slices across my neck as I lift my head, force my body to comply. What happened during my song? Who joined us?

Oliver's body shakes with something—rage? Agony? My gaze settles on the lump of people on the ground just twenty feet from where I lie.

Aubree.

Aubree is the girl screaming, the one crying with sorrowful keening. But she's not alone. In her arms lies another I recognize, the same face that flitted through my mind just seconds before.

My world stops spinning, and a surge of bile threatens to rise. A cry sticks in my throat. I convulse in the same misery as my friends.

Lying in Aubree's arms is Seamus's lifeless body.

My song of the banshee was meant for him.

42

CAOINE

SOMETIMES MY DAD talks about where he was when 9/11 happened. He talks about it in the same way I've heard old people tell their stories of when JFK died, too. Like it's this one moment in time, frozen forever in their minds. As if the world might stop spinning at any second. That one breath in the span of all eternity where the whole earth pauses to mourn.

For me, that moment is right now.

I sit on my bed, my back propped against the wall. Aubree is curled in the fetal position, tucked neatly on my lap. My purple comforter is soft beneath us, piles of pillows behind my back and around my ankles. Why do I have so many stupid pillows? A faint fragrance of lavender hangs in the air from when I ran my diffuser earlier. We lay in silence, my fingers stroking her hair, my cheeks stiff with dried tears. For now. Another flow will soon follow.

Aubree hasn't stopped crying since I woke from my trance. I have almost no memory of how Oliver got the two of us back to my house, but it happened, somehow. That was almost eight hours ago. None of us have slept a second since we lost our friend.

My chest squeezes as an image of Seamus flits through my

mind. I fight the urge to puke. Instead, I bite the inside of my cheek until it bleeds, squint my eyes closed to keep those ridiculous tears at bay.

How could this have happened?

Oliver sits in my oversized armchair, his elbows on his knees, head in his hands. He's been in this position for hours. Maybe he fell asleep?

My dad was awake when we stumbled in the door, well past midnight. Again, I'm thankful we had Oliver to explain the details. There was zero chance I was going to leave Aubree's side, and she wasn't ready to talk. I'm fortunate my dad knows what I am. I'll have no problem getting an excuse for missing school today. Neither will Aubree, with her faerie magic. Oliver on the other hand . . .

I look at him and sigh. Why is he even here? It's bad enough he's dating a banshee. Does he need to clean up my mess every time someone dies, too?

"Aubree, you okay?" Oliver's voice is muffled from his position.

He looks up with far too much effort. I gasp. His eyes are so red, weariness and pain chiseled across his face. I had no idea a teenage boy could feel such emotion, let alone feel it for someone else. I swallow and yearn to go to him, to hold him as I hold Aubree. When had he and Seamus become so close?

In my arms, she moves, rolls onto her back. She's stopped crying. Probably cried away all her tears. That's what my dad used to say whenever I'd cry that we were moving to another town, that I'd have to go to an all-new school. He'd tell me to cry it all out until I had no tears left in my body, then I'd feel better.

Somehow I don't think Aubree will ever run out of tears.

She wraps her arms around her middle and keeps her eyes closed. My lap is cold now that she's gone. Cold spills along my spine. I resist the urge to pull her back to me.

Finally she opens her eyes, her faerie magic gone for now.

Her sea foam-colored irises match her hair perfectly, her ears pointed and elegant. "We . . . we were just hanging out." Her voice is groggy, like she needs to cough but refuses to. She sniffs and continues, her gaze focused on the ceiling. "Seamus wanted to go see a movie, but I insisted on doing more research on the Unseelie prince. He was bored. He found an old copy of the school paper and was browsing through it when he came across that article you wrote about those missing animals."

I startle. Something I wrote was linked to Seamus's death?

"He got all excited. Said he remembered hearing something about a couple of dogs going missing just that day. The more he talked about it, the more convinced he was those pets were linked to the Unseelie prince, like, maybe they were disappearing because of him or something."

"I thought faeries were supposed to be kind to animals," Oliver says, brow pulled together.

Aubree still doesn't budge. She just continues to stare at that ceiling. "We are . . . the Summer fae, anyway. And usually the Unseelie wouldn't harm animals either but . . ."

She swallows.

"We figured the prince must be involved somehow. So we decided to visit the spot behind the school, to see if his theory was right. When we got to the field, we had to hide. The prince was in the process of opening the Unseelie Veil, although I don't know how he got it opened so easily. They normally can only be opened at certain times of the month, under certain conditions."

Oliver rubs his eyes. "The way to the Unseelie Court is behind the school?"

"Do you remember when Seamus and I told you of the Veils to the faerie worlds?" We nod, so she goes on. "That's where they converge. At that exact spot. Humans would never be able to see them, but anything supernatural would know they're there. Animals, too. That's what we figured out. The animals are disappearing because they keep falling through the Veils, drawn to the faerie magic on the other side."

"Did you see who the prince is?" I ask.

She shakes her head. "He is very powerful. He had a crazy glamour that made us forget his face as soon as we looked away. I remember saying his name out loud when we saw him. Seamus said it, too. But as soon as the prince slipped away, neither of us could remember him. Faeries can't usually glamour themselves so strongly against another faerie. This guy is more powerful than we thought."

I shiver. "Where did he go after you saw him?"

"Through the Unseelie Veil. We were waiting for him to return when we saw you and Oliver appear on the hill. We called to Oliver, tried to get his attention, but it was too late. The Unseelie prince came through the Veil and headed straight for you, Caoine. I think he was going to kill you. It was obvious he wanted *you*."

My throat clenches shut, and I fight for air. He was going to kill me while I was singing my song? Is that even possible? Was my song really for Seamus or for me?

"Seamus jumped from our hiding place and attacked the Unseelie prince. I tried to help but was too far behind. All it took was one blow from the Unseelie, and Seamus was gone." She gags and presses her lips together, a new stream of tears falling down her temples and onto my bedspread. "That was it. Oliver tried to jump in, to help, but . . . Seamus was gone."

I look at my boyfriend. "You did?"

His eyes show how ripped to shreds he is inside, destroyed. He gives me a short nod.

"Who is it? Did you know him?"

Oliver takes in a slow breath. "I do, yes. But like she said, as soon as I looked away, I forgot who he was. I honestly can't even begin to guess who it might be. I only know that I do know him."

My stomach drops to my feet, and my fingers dig into my

sheets. "Aubree, you need to be careful. If the prince knows who you are, then he's going to kill you. You're not safe."

"I'll be fine," she deadpans.

My heart stabs with pain at her negative tone. Will she ever recover from this?

"If the Unseelie wanted you or me dead, he would've done so. I think killing Seamus was a warning for us to stop meddling. I honestly think he knew who we were before last night." She pauses. "If he'd wanted us dead, we'd be dead. Oliver included. But he walked away, didn't he? Which means he wants us alive . . . for now."

My head spins, and I blink away spots. The Unseelie prince wants me alive. But why?

And will I be able to figure it out before he uses me for something worse than death?

43

CAOINE'S DREAM

TWIGS BREAK beneath my bare feet as I crunch my way through the brush and foliage of the small patch of trees. A hand is on my arm, gentle but urging. Who is with me? I can't see, my vision clouded. Focused. Determined.

I move past the trees, past bushes. I'm surrounded by green and brown. I stumble into a clearing. It's familiar. I've been here before. Why have I been here?

Warmth gathers along my right side. Whoever is holding my arm is still with me, hovers like a protective shield.

A hill stands in my way, but I attack it like every other obstacle I consume during my thirst for death.

Up, up, up.

At the top is a large flat rock, a sharp decline on the other side. It's wide and level up here. My feet move of their own accord. Yet these steps are laced with deja-vu. I've been here before.

No, not before.

I've been here now. This reality is also my past. How do I know this moment?

My mouth opens and I sing.

Who am I singing to?

Then, a noise.

I turn my head as my lament continues. Seamus stands before me, his eyes pleading, begging me to stop this, to put an end to my bloodlust. But I don't. I don't stop singing, and I don't stop walking.

His eyes widen. My hands snake around his throat, squeeze like a vice around muscle and bone. My body quivers with excitement, desire. I clench my fingers harder. Heat pulses across my chest, a joyful tumble within my belly.

I'm smiling. Why am I smiling?

Seamus's face turns a beautiful shade of blue, then a lovely lavender. His ears, those ears, those ridiculous faerie ears that tell the world he is something other than human, come to a point. Warn me not to trust him. Not to believe he could possibly be the good guy in all this.

After all, he is fae. And all fae are bad, aren't they? They killed my mother, turned me into a monster. Destined to murder and destroy, every single night of my life?

The fae are bad. The fae are evil. The fae deserve to die.

Fae deserve to die.

Deserve to die.

Die. Die. Die.

My grip goes tighter still.

I want you to die, Seamus! You must die!

A scream echoes to my left.

Sweat breaks along my brow as I lower his body to the ground, my fingers clutched around his neck like my life depends on it. Because it does. My life hangs in the balance of each and every fae that remains alive. Because my job is to kill. I must kill.

And who better to send to the afterworld than the very kind that ruined my life? Left me maternally orphaned?

Someone cries near me. And I don't care. Not even a little.

A female wails like her lungs might explode, and my insides rejoice.

My song ends. My vision goes clear.

Oliver and Aubree stare at me in disbelief.

My gaze drifts to Seamus, who lies dead on the ground, a broad smile plastered across my face.

44

CAOINE

WHEN I WAS eight years old, my dad moved us to northern Maryland. To a little brick house in a historic neighborhood, with Halloween parades and fireworks at Fourth of July, and kids. Lots of kids.

Natalie lived next door and was exactly my age. Even though I was weird looking and I never spoke, she was the only kid who wasn't mean to me. Not when she saw me walking to my dad's car, or when no one would sit near me on the bus. Just her. She seemed to know I was different but didn't blame me for my misfortune.

For a whole year she kept her distance, but not in the same way as other kids. Not in a cruel, unwanting fashion. She *wanted* to know me. Deep down I could sense it.

And then one day, she did. The first kid in my life who gave any indication she just might be a friend. Then the vans came. She invited me to her swing set on a Friday, and by Saturday, she'd moved away. Maybe that's why she finally allowed me to know her, even if only for a day. But I couldn't help thinking how odd it was, how out of place it felt to know when I sat on my front porch and watched the other kids play kickball in the streets, she wouldn't be there. That I would no longer see her though my window by accident, as she sat at her piano and practiced for her scheduled twenty minutes per day.

One day I woke up, and she was just gone.

Just like Aubree.

I don't know when she left, or where. She's just gone. I'd say she went back to Faerie if she wasn't the Seelie queen's daughter. I've got the distinct impression failure is not an option for a princess, even one as heartbroken as she.

I sit up in bed and stretch. Sunlight pours through my window, and guilt floods my core. It's a beautiful day. Cotton-ball clouds float against azure sky, and I swear I catch the scent of lilies in my stagnant bedroom. But that's impossible. It's October. Things are dying to make way for winter.

Dying.

Dying.

Seamus dying.

A knife stabs my heart, and I press my fists to my eye sockets, forcing hot tears back. My throat closes in a second, and I can't breathe. Can't breathe. Why? Why did Seamus die?

I mean, is this even real? How can he be dead when it's so beautiful outside?

How can he be dead?

Why am I not dead?

My body convulses with an agony I've never experienced before, my arms wrapped tightly around my knees, my face pressed against my skin's perspiration. And then there's the sound, that wailing. For the love, where is it coming from?

Wait. That's me.

That sound, the inhuman echo of anguish, of a person in never-ending torment, it's spilling from me. And I can't stop it. I can't stop the strange moans that tumble from my body like a wave that crashes against the sand over and over and over and over and—

Stop it.

I clench my fist, beat it against my thigh.

No. Stop.

I can't do this. I can't lose control, not now. Not when my curse is already spiraling downward. Not when Aubree's missing. Not when the prince is still alive.

Anger burns deep in my belly, and I swallow, open my eyes. Pull in a ragged breath. *Keep it together, Caoine.*

Hot tears continue to course down my cheeks, but I dig my nails into my palms, set my teeth together.

The prince. He's needs to pay for what he's done. For what he did to me, to Aubree.

To Seamus.

A chill spills down my back, and I shudder, my breathing even now. This is what I was meant to do. Even if Aubree is gone, I've still got a job to do.

No matter what, I need to stop the Unseelie prince, no matter the cost. I need to find out who he is, what he plans to do. I need to stop him, once and for all.

And then, maybe—just maybe—I'll be able to figure out a way to stop my curse. To end this hell I've lived for seventeen long years.

Once the Unseelie prince is out of the picture, I can finally take control of my life.

45

CAOINE

Dearest Caoine,

Please forgive me. I didn't want to kill Seamus. Please know this. But it was a necessary sacrifice. I had to get your attention, Caoine. Had to make you understand. Can't you see that?

I don't want to see you hurting. Your pain is my pain. Watching you hurt is the worst kind of torture. Which is why I'm begging you to see what I know. Your future can be different than the hell you're living, Caoine. Join me, and you will never hurt again.

End this ridiculous quest to stop me. Give in to your desires and allow me to help you. Do what you were created to do, and you will be without pain. I promise you will.

Sing. Sing your song. That is what you were meant to do, who you were created to be. Don't fight it. Leave the rest to me. I will come for you when the time is right.

Always yours,
Your Prince

I CRUMPLE my latest note and shove it into the pit of my locker, run a hand through my loose hair. *How can I survive this week now that my life is so changed, now that I've killed one of my own?* Tears prick the edge of my eyes, and I force my way to class.

No amount of apologies from that monster will ever make things right. They'll never bring Seamus back.

I'm ready to make the prince pay for what he's done.

46

CAOINE

"As a final reminder, students are not permitted access to the storage closets in the science wing labs. Any student caught without a teacher's permission will face suspension."

The weekly morning announcements have gone longer than usual. I stifle a yawn. Comfy in my first period seat, I pretend to actually care about what our principal relays to the student body, unlike the rest of the class. My eyes drift to the seat beside mine. Aubree is absent. Again.

This makes five days now, not including the weekend. My belly squeezes, and I blink away tears.

She's not over Seamus's death, not even close. If I'm going to be honest with myself, neither am I. But that girl? Yeah, she's known him for over a hundred years. I was lucky enough to have his friendship for six weeks. I can't imagine what she must be going through. Warmth crawls up my cheeks as another wave of emotion spills over my chest. *Keep it together, Caoine. No one else in the school knows he's dead yet.*

Suffering in silence stinks.

I close my eyes, and the familiar scent of clove tickles my nose, a memory of that fateful night less than a week ago. Aubree held Seamus's body for what felt like hours, even though it could've only been minutes. She rocked and moaned in mourning. Oliver and I sat in stunned silence beside her. Seamus had finally lost his glamour, and we were able to see him for the first time as he truly was. The way she must've known him her entire life. His pale-green skin was the most beautiful sight I've ever seen. A gaping hole oozed at his chest, caused by a powerful faerie blade. The fae are not easy to kill, usually only possible by a blade made by their own kind. An attack of one fae on another is unheard of. Horrific.

The ground around us appeared to swell, to foil like an unfelt earthquake, threatening to swallow us. Then he began to fade. Seamus's figure dimmed, flickered, the edges of his being turning to mist. As if he were evaporating into the earth. Aubree's fingers grasped at nothingness as he melted into the shadows, his angelic face dissolving into memory. And then he was gone. Vanished.

Aubree explained his spirit would travel back to the Seelie Realm and he would become one with nature again. Like he was before the King and Queen of the Seelie world called him —created him in the first place. My heart broke into a thousand pieces, ones Seamus carried with him through that Veil, even though I couldn't see him any longer. In all my years of lamenting and predicting, this is one loss I will never, ever recover from.

This I know deep in my heart.

"Caoine?" The voice startles me from my daydream.

I look up.

The teacher is looking at me, his brows taut. "Do you have any idea where Ms. Robeson is today?"

I shake my head. Because that's the truth. Aubree's missing, and I haven't seen her. Maybe she went back to the Seelie Realm to tell her mother what transpired.

"If you see her, tell her we all hope she feels better soon."

I nod. At least it's Friday. My plan is to spend the entire weekend tracking that girl—or faerie— down. Even if it means locating the Seelie Veil and crossing over myself. I'm part faerie, right? I can totally get away with crossing into the Summer Realm. I think.

The teacher begins his lecture on "The Lady of Shalott," but there's no possible chance I'll be able to pay attention today. Not even if it is my favorite poem by Tennyson. I growl under my breath and dig through my pack for the list of names. Before . . . *that* night, Aubree and I decided to expand our search of the Unseelie prince to the remaining underclassmen. Aubree has this crazy idea he might be hiding in a way we wouldn't expect, possibly even as a freshman. Which is just great. I know exactly zero freshman.

I glance at my backpack where my latest love note from the Unseelie prince resides. Should I even be doing this? Is it worth it, in the end? Seamus is gone, Aubree is missing. Oliver will always be in danger as long as he's connected to me. I can't do this alone. Can't fight this battle by myself.

So why am I? Maybe just doing what I've always done and allowing my curse to continue to control me is the better choice. Maybe I don't need a boyfriend or friends or anyone else in my life right now. Is it possible the Unseelie prince isn't such a bad guy? I mean, what do I even know of him?

"Hey." A whisper comes from my right.

I blink away my thoughts but ignore the voice. Whispers are never meant for me. Not for the girl with the weird eyes and pale skin.

"Hey." It comes again.

I glance up. Eric is nodding to the floor at my feet.

When did he get here?

"You dropped something."

A miniature stuffed narwhal lays sprawled on the floor, between my desk and his. I bite my lip. I forgot all about my plan from the previous weekend. On Sunday I spent a considerable amount of time pulling apart the seems of my beloved stuffed animal and pouring bits of the foxglove powder into its body. And I spent even more time sewing the poor dude back up. The plan was to stuff him as full of the flakes as I could get, then use him as a distraction for unsuspecting guys. I forgot all about my poor ocean-loving friend. He looks like he's been squished at the bottom of my pack. Which, now that I think about it, he has been.

"Oh, right." I bend to pick the creature up, preparing myself for the sting.

But not before Eric throws me a wicked grin and kindly bends to help. We smack heads with a *clonk*, and I grunt in pain.

"Caoine? Eric? Is there a problem?"

Eric laughs it off and flashes the teacher a smile, his cheeks red enough to match his hair. "Sorry, Mr. Stanley. She dropped something, and I was just helping her out."

Mr. Stanley eyes us like we're up to no good but continues with the lesson.

Eric throws me a quick grin and shrugs. He nods toward my prized animal, and I give him a nod in return. He's being kind, which shouldn't surprise me. He's Oliver's best friend. Oliver would do the same.

He reaches down and snags the animal. But before he can sit up, he winces and drops the stuffed pile of love right back at my feet. He shakes his hand as if it's been burned and squeezes his eyes against obvious pain.

My jaw falls.

The narwhal burned Eric just like it burned me. Which can mean only one thing.

Eric is fae.

Eric is the Unseelie prince.

47

CAOINE

I FIGHT TO BREATHE, to control my urge to puke as the overwhelming sense that my enemy has been right in front of my eyes this entire time slaps me in the face.

Eric is the Unseelie prince.

I gag, curl my fingers into my hands, squeeze as tightly as I possibly can.

Beside me, I can sense Eric shift in his seat, cross then uncross his legs. I won't look at him. I won't, I won't, I won't, I—

He drops his pen and purposely smacks my leg when he bends to pick it up. I stifle a yelp and glare at the boy.

His eyes are pleading. *Let me explain,* he mouths.

A shiver runs down my spine, and I turn away from him. *No thank you, Mr. Prince. I'd rather stay alive.*

I bounce my leg, watch the clock, tap my fingers on my legs —anything to make time move faster. But it doesn't. It goes. So. Very. Slow.

Eric is watching me. I can tell from my peripheral. Ugh. *Go away.*

I need him to go away. And I need to find Aubree. Like, right now.

No, seriously. I can't handle this another minute.

I shoot my hand straight in the air.

Mr. Stanley pauses midsentence, his brow pulled tight. "Is there a problem, Miss Roberts?"

"Can I go to the bathroom?" I say as I stand and start walking toward the door.

"Of course, you'll just need —"

But I don't hear the rest of what he says. I run. From the room, down the hall, around the corner, and into a deserted alcove.

I press my back against the cool slab of stone. My heart pounds like a freight train inside my chest, something I'd very much like to be on at this exact moment. A train could take me far from here. Away from Unseelie princes and scary fae that want to kill me. I lean my head against the wall and close my eyes. Inside my head I call out to Aubree. I can't breathe, can't see through the red invading my vision, can't feel my legs that have gone numb. I have to warn Aubree!

Then hands that don't belong to me find my arms, wrap around my shoulders, yank me through a door to my left —

And into the janitor's closet. I gag. Fantastic. *I'm* the one who's going to end up dead, apparently.

I scramble away from the dark shadow that looms before me and press my back against the wall. My fingers find the wooden end of a mop handle, and I whip it in front of me so fast, water splashes against the wall. All feeling has returned to every part of my body, and blood pounds inside my ears like a marching band drummer gone wild.

"Whoa," he says. "Take it easy, Caoine."

The overhead fluorescent light flips on. Eric's face comes into view.

I lash out with my mop handle along with a karate chop *hiya!* Because I'm all about those crazy ninja skills. And mops have been scientifically proven to be the best defense against attackers. Sigh.

He holds his hands in front of him and easily grabs the end of my stick. "Wait. Slow down, Caoine. Wait, wait! I'm not going to hurt you."

Muscles across my back and neck clench as I think of Seamus. "Yeah, right. I'm not falling for that one, faerie killer." I grip the handle tighter and try to jiggle it from his palm. It doesn't budge.

He rolls his eyes. "Look, you're overreacting."

"Puh!" I sputter. "No way. *You're* the Unseelie son. The prince sent to kill us all!" Okay, maybe that was a bit dramatic.

Eric blinks. Fast. "I'm the *what*? Why would you think that?"

"Because my narwhal burned you. I saw it. Don't deny it. You're fae and I can prove it!"

The boy shrugs, his slim shoulders more skeletal than muscle. "Yeah, so? So are you."

"Sooo?" I draw out the word like it might bite him. "So that means you have to be the prince. The Unseelie prince sent to enact . . . whatever evil plan you have planned." *Awesome, Caoine. Way to exude confidence.*

He scrubs long thin fingers through his shaggy red hair and raises his eyebrows. "I'm not sure how much you know about faeries, but there are more of us around than you realize. And no, that doesn't mean all fae have evil plans to take over the world."

He smirks, and I want to smack him with my stick, which he's given back.

Big mistake.

"Whatever, Eric. You've been hiding the fact you're fae all this time, so that means you're bad, which also means you're *him*. I know it."

He reaches out and gently disarms me for real this time. I stutter something unintelligible and frown. How did he do that so easily?

"Look, if I were him, don't you think I'd do a better job staying hidden?"

I point at him. "Ha! You know who I'm talking about! See? You're part of the plan!"

He groans. "Just because I know who you're talking about doesn't mean a thing. Are you ready to shut up so I can talk? I don't want to be in here any more than you do." He shifts uncomfortably and glances around the tiny closet. With effort, he pulls in a breath, then refocuses on me, his voice gentler. "Will you hear me out, or are you going to spend the entire class time accusing me of things you know absolutely nothing about?"

I press my lips together and cross my arms. Jerk. *I know plenty!* "You've had lots of opportunities to alert Aubree and me that you're fae, Eric. It's obvious you knew who we were. You have no other reason to lie to us."

"First off, okay, yes I'm fae." He tosses the mop to the side. "Secondly, are you even aware that fae can't lie?" I blink in surprise, but he continues. "And, yes, I know you're fae too. And I haven't been hiding. It's a simple glamour spell to keep me hidden from a certain person I've been trying to avoid. For the same reasons I'm guessing *you* don't want to be found by him, either. Am I right?" He scrunches his face like he smells something bad. "I shouldn't be here anyway."

I scowl. "Why not?"

Eric shrugs. "Look. It's obvious you know nothing about the Realms of Faerie, so let me be the first to clue you in: they're not all that great. Not like what humans are taught in their fairytale stories, anyway." He swallows and looks at his feet. "I'm no one important, okay? I shouldn't even be here. Crossing the Veil into the human world is something reserved for the powerful, those in royalty."

"And you're not?" I casually look him up and down.

In my flight, I missed the obvious. His ultra-white skin

sparkles under the unnatural light. Pointed ears poke from behind his hair. His eyes are a deep shade of plum, so intoxicating I have a difficult time separating my gaze from his. Yep. Definitely fae.

He shakes his head. "I was born a Wood Sprite. I never even knew who my father was. My mother is a Firre."

I frown, and he refrains from rolling his eyes. Almost.

"It's a type of Eladrin?"

I shake my head.

"Yeah, you've got a lot to learn. There are as many types of fae as there are colors in the spectrum." He grins that cocky grin. "It's okay. You've got time. Anyway, my mom, her type of fae are supposed to aid artists, help protect their work and all? Except there was an accident. An unforgivable one. She was banished by her people long before I came along. We've lived a transient life, always moving from one place to another, avoiding detection by those who might try to banish us from the Faerie Realm for good. To be honest, I'm a nobody and shouldn't even have access to this world." He looks around the closet like it's magical.

"So why are you, then? Here, I mean?"

"Well, as so often is the case, the woods have ears."

I cross my arms.

"The Unseelie king and the prince were in the woods one day. I heard their whole conversation. I overheard a little about what they have planned and *why* the Unseelie prince is here. The king sent him secretly because he knew the rest of the Unseelie Court would never approve of their plot. The king and the prince have gone rogue. Literally."

"Really?"

"Yes. Believe it or not, not everyone in the Winter Court is evil. We've just got a bad rep."

I sink into one hip and tilt my head. "That doesn't explain how you got here."

"That's a long story. But I can say it endangered many fae lives to find the spell that would allow me to cross. My mission here is more important than any student in this school can imagine—or any adult. I've been sent to find the Unseelie prince.

"I'm here to save you all."

48

CAOINE

THE SUN IS DANGEROUSLY close to dipping below the horizon. I glance out the window at the buttery yellows and robin-egg blues and peach hues as they blend together into an impression of a messy finger painting across the sky. I sigh. Nighttime comes far too soon, now that fall is in full swing. It's not even five o'clock yet, and already I'm exhausted.

I yawn.

Or maybe it's because one of my only friends in this world died less than a week ago. And my best friend is missing. And I've run across another fae—a fellow creature I didn't think existed a month ago, let alone *three*.

I lean back in my stiff metal chair and stretch.

"Done with your article yet?" Cat asks from the desk across from me.

"Um, sure." I tap the keys of the school-loaned laptop to wake it back up. A stark-white page with a single sentence stares back at me. *Right*. I'd much rather write poetry.

The overhead fluorescent light flickers. The compact room feels smaller somehow, closer. Quill and Pen huddle around one desk, which is how they always work. For siblings, they're incredibly intimate. Maybe that's a thing with twins? Adam fusses over photos he's laid out, and Jessica is her usual stalker-self, stepping between each of us, looking over shoulders, making comments. She's been stuck near Quill and Pen for the past twenty minutes, which is good for me, since writing isn't really a thing for me today.

I lean down and grab my backpack, then power down the laptop I'm using.

Catherine's eyes go wide. "Are you leaving?"

"I . . . I can't concentrate." Understatement. "I need to go home, detox a bit. I'll see you tomorrow." Maybe.

"Okay." She looks a little hurt, which makes me pause.

It's not like I can tell her what's been going on in my life. No one can know. About Seamus, Aubree, Eric. *Me.*

I refrain from sighing again. "We'll do lunch tomorrow?"

Cat's pale skin pinks as she smiles. "Sounds good."

I stand and turn—and run smack into Jessica. Great.

"Going somewhere?" Her arms are crossed, her talon-like fingers tapping against her sleeve, nails bright red and razor sharp. Dang, this girl would be perfect in the world of *Riverdale.*

"Erm." I clear my throat. "I'm hitting a spell of writer's block. I thought maybe a change of scenery might help?"

She narrows her eyes. "And by change of scenery, you mean you're going home?" My non-answer is answer enough for her. She puts both hands on her hips. "This thing is serious, Caoine. In case you haven't noticed, the entire team is working their butts off to get this issue ready for print tomorrow. Where's your dedication?"

"But—" I frown. "I mean, all my articles are turned in. I don't have anything left for tomorrow's issue."

She tilts her head, a perfectly coifed red curl spilling over one shoulder. "I don't see the one I gave you today finished yet."

"That's not due until next week—"

"Change of plans." She tosses her head. "I'm adding it to

the lineup. I want it written, edited, and ready for print by bedtime tonight. Feel free to email me the final copy."

"But—but—" *I have a date with Oliver tonight!*

"What? You had plans that are more important than the *Red and Black*?"

My belly flips, and the temperature increases by twenty degrees.

She knows.

She totally overheard my conversation with Cat about my date with Oliver and how he made reservations somewhere really special because he's crazy worried about me and just wants to help me relax. Jerksica is totally sabotaging my freaking love life now. Seriously?

Two can play this game.

I straighten my shoulders. "No problem. I'll just stay in tonight. I can have Oliver stay late and help me get this written. It always helps to have another set of eyes, right?" I flash her an innocent smile that quite possibly drips as much sarcasm as pumps through my blood.

Her glare turns icy, but she doesn't change her expression. "Get it done. It better not be late."

"Yes, ma'am." I salute her and imagine steam puffing from her nostrils.

She spins on her heels and heads back to Quill and Pen.

Well, now that that's taken care of . . . I roll my eyes and wave goodbye to Cat. She giggles quietly in reply. The door swings behind me with a slam, and I lean against it as I breathe in the sterile scent of the school hallway, eyes closed. Fantastic. How am I going to get this thing written while at some fancy-smancy restaurant? Argh.

I head down the dark hallway, the silence heavy against my ears. A few sports teams are still practicing, but none of the members grace the halls. The place is eerily empty. Like something out of a movie.

A chill tiptoes down my spine, and I walk a tad faster

toward the exit. Crap. *Forgot my coat!* I hesitate for a beat but don't stop. Nope. No way. There's zero need to hit my locker for that. I'll chance the cold and will run home if I have to.

I turn a corner to a hall that's even darker than the last. A door creaks to my left. I jump.

"Hello?" *What? Why did I just say that? This isn't a horror movie, Caoine. Don't ask stupid questions. Run!*

I speed walk across the scuffed white linoleum, sweat trickling along my back.

"Caoine."

I freeze, the air stalled in my chest. My name. That was definitely my name.

Slam! Another door closes from the hallway behind me.

The Unseelie prince. *He's here to get me!*

And I take off like a rocket. I sprint from one hall to the next, the exit growing smaller and farther away with each step. My muscles tense, a pounding inside my skull.

"Caoine." This time the voice is closer. Beside me.

Inside my head.

This totally can't be happening. No way this is real.

My breath is ragged. My backpack bounces against my back as I make a fool of myself, running between lockers and classrooms and shadows that want to kidnap me.

"Caoine."

There's the exit ahead. He won't get me.

"Caoine."

I see it. He can't get me.

"Caoine."

Just a little farther. I won't go down that easy!

"Caoine."

I slam my body against the metal bar of the front door.

"Caoine!"

I flip around, my back pressed to the glass as I release a pathetically high-pitched squeal.

"Caoine?" Aubree steps from the shadows, her eyes round.

"Are you all right?" Her hands are on my arms as she bends to look at me.

Aubree. *Aubree is here!*

My gaze darts around the halls, my staccato breathing still out of control. "I—I—"

"Is someone else here?"

"I don't know. I—" I pull in a lungful of cool air, concentrate on slowing my heart rate. "I'm just stressed, I guess."

"Come on." Aubree puts her arm around my shoulder and looks around the darkness before ushering me out the door. "I'll drive you home."

"Thanks." I rub my hands across my face and allow the cool night air to cling to my skin, a surprisingly welcome feeling. *At least I'm alive.* I shake my head. No, I won't think that way. "So you're back?"

She presses the remote to unlock her new cherry-red Ford Mustang, and it calls back with a beep. My belly squeezes. My dad would be downright jealous if he saw me in this thing.

"I'm back." Her voice is soft. Sad.

"I'm . . . glad."

Aubree glances back toward the school. "Yeah, I guess." She gives what could've been a chuckle a week ago and slips into the driver's seat.

I settle into the passenger leather seat, the strong plastic scent assaulting my senses. "Thanks, by the way."

"No problem. Now, you going to tell me why you were so freaked out?"

I huff. "It's . . . dumb." She raises a brow. "Well, since you've been gone, there've been some . . . developments." She stays silent but nods, so I go on. "We've got another ally, in the war against You-Know-Who." I bite my lip, look at my feet. The mat beneath them is so clean, cleaner than any car I've ever seen. *Man, this is a nice car.*

She starts the engine to warm us up, but we don't pull away yet. I tell her everything I know about Eric and our conversation earlier that day. She only nods. I breathe in the new car scent, watch as the sky goes black and the lights around the school parking lot flicker to life. Finally, I finish.

And she stays quiet.

"Well?"

She shrugs.

"That's all? I tell you Eric's fae, and it doesn't even faze you?"

"I'm not surprised, if that's what you mean." I flinch but she nods. "There're probably more in our school. Maybe hiding. Maybe playing. Probably totally unaware of what's happening with the Unseelie prince. Or us. My guess is they don't know how many other fae are here, just like we don't know about them." She pauses, looks over my white hair and odd-colored eyes. "Well, they've probably figured out you, but they're keeping their distance." She winces. "Banshees aren't faeries you mess around with."

My heart sags. "Thanks."

She shrugs again, despite my biting wit.

"By the way. Where. Have. You. Been?"

Her face falls, and her eyes glisten. She looks away. "I had some loose ends to tie up."

I swallow. Yuck. This conversation had to go in this direction, didn't it? "In Faerie?"

She nods. "I had to, uh, tell Seamus's remaining family members. About . . . *him*."

"Did you—did you have a funeral?"

Aubree bites her lip. "Fae don't do that, Caoine. We . . . we're one with nature. When we die, we go back to our natural state. Back to the earth. Fae die all the time. Everyday. For most of us, it's no big deal. Just part of nature."

My ears buzz. Why do I have to listen to this? I hate this.

"But Seamus, he—" She blinks quickly and looks out the window, toward the soccer field. "Things are different in Faerie. Like I said, for most fae, when they die, they just disappear. But the fae? We're different from humans. We have a hierarchy. Sort of like a class system . . . but *not.*" She sighs. "Because we live for so long, the fae can have a lot of children. Lots. Somewhere along the line, it became important for fae families to honor the firstborn. All other children are of the same significance except the one born first."

She pauses and draws in a slow breath, tears slipping down her pale cheeks.

"Seamus was firstborn, Caoine. His death means so much more than you could possibly know. It has . . . repercussions."

I gasp. Seamus was the oldest in his family? He was so sarcastic. Lazy, almost. Somehow I envisioned him being the youngest. *The trickster.* The avoider of responsibility. How did I miss this?

"I had to go back to, uh . . . take care of business." She wipes at her cheeks, but her lashes stay wet.

I stop and look at her—really look. She has no makeup on. Her outfit is plain, jeans and sneakers and a hoodie that probably cover a shirt just as plain as the rest of the ensemble. Her hair is brown, a single color, pulled back into a ponytail. I've never seen her like this.

"So . . ." I clear my throat. "What do we do now?"

"We pick up where we left off, I guess." Her voice is tiny, hidden.

I nod. "Well, I never really stopped. I mean, testing with the foxglove powder, anyway. Anthony Marino *isn't* fae, BTW." I scowl. It would be so much easier if it were him.

"Okay, so it sounds like we've got Eric now, so there's that. It's sort of weird, huh? That he's been on our team all this time and we didn't even know?" She licks her lips. "We move forward . . . with his help. We keep doing what we were doing with Sea—" Seamus's name catches in her throat.

The warm air from the heater is beginning to get a little too hot. Sweat pops along my brow, and I'm suddenly thankful I don't have that coat. I nibble the inside of my cheek, my heart pounding a whole lot louder than it was a minute ago.

My knee bounces against the door of her car. "Aubree?" My voice is so small, I think it might be swallowed by the dark night.

"Yeah?" she whispers.

"Are you sure you only left to work things out in Faerie? You sure you didn't leave because of me? Because you think it was my fault that he d—" I choke back a sob.

Her gaze settles on me, her jaw set. "No, Caoine. I don't think it was your fault. I don't think you killed Seamus."

Fae can't lie, right?

But what if they can? What if somehow, they can?

She puts the car in gear, and we drive toward my home. In silence. And I wish I could believe her. I wish I could believe she doesn't think I killed him.

The problem is, somehow I think I did. I killed my mom. I killed my friend. Maybe she's right. Banshee's aren't faeries you mess with. Because we kill people.

It's what I do.

49

CAOINE'S DREAM

THE DREAM COMES AGAIN. Like so many other nights, I face the same people, the same words. The same feeling of death.

I'm with my friends. Aubree, Oliver, Catherine, Eric. Even Jessica. Seamus is present, despite the fact my brain knows this cannot be. They stand shoulder to shoulder in a straight line facing me, their expressions blank. Like robots.

Or those without souls.

I shudder, a soft chill skimming across my skin. How can I be so cold inside a dream?

"Oliver," I say, because of all my friends, he's the one who will answer.

But he doesn't. Just like always. He stares straight ahead. Right at me. Right through me.

"Aubree! Cat?" With each name I call, I step in front of my school-mate but get no reaction. They are like stone.

Then a voice, gentle and calm at first, but gaining in urgency. In warning. "Blood of the innocent. Blood of sinners. Blood of the firstborn. Blood of greatness."

My heart squeezes tight, and I clench my fists until I feel pain. Should I feel pain inside a dream? I know what I'm about to see. Who I'm about to see.

I turn and face my mother. I know it's her because I've seen pictures. And also something deep inside my heart recognizes her, longs to hold her. To touch her. But she doesn't touch me, she won't. She repeats the phrase over and over. The same words, in the same order. This melancholy chant won't go away, refuses to go away, fights to stay inside my head.

The air around me grows thin, and I can't catch my breath. I sway on my feet, close my eyes, blink several times. "Mother. Why are you here? What does this mean?"

Her chanting grows louder, and I know what comes next. Even though I don't want to do it, the song inside me will not stay hidden forever. My mother's eyes widen, and a pulse inside me leaps, claws its way out of my throat, into my mouth. The song floods out of me. I can't stop it or control it. My friends begin to shake, convulse. Pain envelops their faces, yet still I sing in agony.

I'm killing my friends, but my song goes on. It will not stop, never stops.

"Blood of the innocent. Blood of sinners. Blood of the firstborn. Blood of greatness." The words are louder now.

Oliver flinches, drops to one knee. Aubree cries out.

"Blood of the innocent. Blood of sinners. Blood of the firstborn. Blood of greatness."

Blood powers through my veins, pounds inside my head.

Seamus is on his back, and Jessica's eyes are closed for good now.

"Blood of the innocent. Blood of sinners. Blood of the firstborn. Blood of greatness."

My song is stronger, more beautiful than ever. Sweat pours down my back, my knees go weak.

Catherine—sweet Cat—grabs her throat, choking, begging. Eric's face matches his hair.

"Blood of the innocent. Blood of sinners. Blood of the firstborn. Blood of greatness."

Heat rises from my feet through my core, across my chest, under my neck, and beneath my skin. Inside every molecule of my body.

I can't stop it. There's no way to stop it.

My friends are going to die!

"Save them, Caoine," my mother screams. "Use your song. Save them now, before it's too late!"

Thunder echoes in my ears, struggles to defeat the power of the song. My bones are cracking, breaking. Tears flow down my cheeks, my palms filled with blood from where my nails have etched away the skin, peeled it back like the fabric of my soul. Still the song goes on.

"Save them, Caoine!" She screams it again and again, yet I continue to sing.

I sing.

I sing.

I sing.

Sing.

Sing.

Sing.

Kill.

Kill.

Kill.

I murder my friends. Because that's what I do. No matter how hard I try, no matter all the good I try to do in this world, it will never be enough. I will never make up for the destruction I've brought. The terror I bring. I can't stop it. It's who I am. Because I'm a banshee.

And banshees kill people.

I kill people.

50

CAOINE

I WAKE from my dream with a jump.

Arms — strong arms — wrap around me.

"Hey," a voice says. "Whoa. You okay?" Oliver holds me, presses his lips to my forehead. "What's this about?"

We're seated on my sofa, the TV softly reverberating in the background. The welcome scent of cinnamon and nutmeg floats around me. My dad sings as he works in the kitchen. Is he baking something? He's not intoxicated yet, so anything's possible.

I sit up from my makeshift bed and rub my eyes. The curtains are pulled shut, but I can still see a sliver of sunlight as it creeps through the cracks of fabric. A lazy Saturday afternoon nap kidnapped me without warning. I didn't fight it when Oliver offered his lap as a pillow. I scrub my face once more, then settle into the comfort of my boyfriend's shoulder, his arms still my refuge. He smells like soap, which relaxes me for some reason.

"Caoine?" he asks again.

"A dream. It was just a dream. I'm fine." My heart rate speeds.

"Um, it doesn't sound like you're fine. At least not while you were asleep."

I frown and turn in his arms to look at him. "Did I say anything?"

He shakes his head. "No words. But I was wondering if you were in the middle of an MMA fight." The corner of his mouth cocks up. "I didn't mean to wake you, but I was worried you might get hurt or something."

"Inside my dream or outside?" My sarcasm doesn't make him laugh like I thought it would.

"Both." He takes my hand. "What was it about, anyway?"

I shrug. Like I'm *really* going to tell him I have dreams where I sing my song and kill all my friends. Including *him*. Ha! "It was about my mother."

Oliver sits an inch straighter. "Your mother? I thought you said she died when you were baby?"

I nod. "She did."

"But you still dream about her?"

"Yeah. I mean, I think it's her. She looks just like the picture my dad keeps on his nightstand. And she knows me."

"What does she say? What's the dream about?"

It's about death, Oliver. Everything about me has to do with death. I bite my lip and lie. "She just . . . she's trying to help, I think."

"How? Help with what?"

Ugh. The boy isn't going to drop this! "She tells me a poem. Chants it, actually. Over and over again. I don't know what it means, but it feels important when I'm there." I let go of his hands so he won't feel how sweaty mine are.

"And you've had this dream before?"

"Several times, yes."

He twists his face in thought. "Do you remember the words? To the poem, I mean."

I scrunch my brows and think. "Nope. They always disappear as soon as I wake up. I mean, I guess if I tried to write them down super quick once I woke—"

"What else happens? You said she wants to help you? How?"

I sigh. "Uh, well, near the end of the dream, she tells me to save them."

"Save who?"

You. I press my lips together and breathe. "Just people, I guess. She's talking about my curse, I know that much. She wants me to save people instead of killing them." I pick at a stray thread on my jeans. "Easier said than done." My sarcasm is back.

My boyfriend is silent for a moment, and my throat closes. Is it finally sinking in I'm a real honest-to-God murderer?

"Think she could be right?"

I do a double take. "About what?"

"About you saving people with your gift. I mean, your dad keeps saying it's possible. What if there's something you don't know?"

I shake my head. "No. Not possible. I can't possibly stop singing. I've tried. Like, a bunch of times. I think the dream is my subconscious repeating what my dad has told me over the years. He says that's what the faerie told him and my mom before she died, but I think somehow the wires got crossed. There's no way I can stop what I do. I think my brain is being unusually cruel and imagining both my parents ganging up on me."

He scowls, and my heart skips a beat at how incredibly adorable he is. "That's sadistic, don't you think?"

"Parents gang up on other teenagers. Why not mine? Doesn't matter that I only have one, right?"

He lifts one eyebrow. "Maybe." His tone sounds melancholy, like he might actually be buying into all this mumbo-jumbo Caoine-can-save-the-world crap. His gaze drifts to the TV. "Whoa." His eyes widen.

I glance at what he's gawking at and almost toss all the

cookies I've ever had the pleasure of eating all over the floor. *Really*.

The mayor of our town is dead.

Dead.

A scrolling bar moves along the bottom of the screen, and the news anchors for the local channel look like they've run a ten-minute mile to get in front of the camera. They're both talking animatedly, and a picture of the mayor is plastered in the upper right-hand corner of the screen. I swallow against blades that coat my throat.

This isn't good. Nothing about this is good. Mostly because it's a high-profile death that will certainly hijack the news channels for the next month. But more importantly because I could've told them his death was coming.

I predicted it the night before.

51

CAOINE

"Caoine?" Oliver says when I don't breathe for a full minute.

I blink, yank myself back to reality. Blink. Now my curse is killing local celebrities. *Is no one safe around me?*

"Caoine." He says it more as a statement this time, tension flooding from every muscle in his body.

"I'm fine." I shake my head. "I just . . . I sang my song in his neighborhood the other night." I wince like I've given myself a paper cut. Except this pain runs so much deeper.

"You're sure it was his?"

"I'm guessing." I shrug. "I mean, it's the gated one where all the richies in town live. I'm assuming he lives there too? I just feel bad I've now deprived the town of their only leader. Even if he was a turd." I scrub my hands over my eyes and face, remembering the tingle along the back of my neck from a few nights before.

The fact that he's a turd is true. Or, *was* a turd. His extreme narcissism, self-righteousness, and unwillingness to see any other person's point of view never made him a fan favorite. He only won the office on a technicality. He was the sort of jerk people only tolerated until the next election, hoping he wouldn't do too much damage, if his arrogance allowed it.

I stop and almost gag on my own intake of air. "Ohmy-gosh! *Pride*. The mayor totally represents pride, doesn't he? I mean, you couldn't find a more prideful man in the whole state, right? Erm, maybe the whole country."

Oliver stops and thinks, then nods. "You're right." He doesn't sound happy. "If we're looking for the fulfillment of the Seven Deadly Sins, then he would most certainly fill the pride slot."

"Great." I sigh and slump back against the sofa. "So now we know *that's* started up again. And apparently I've now moved on to killing our country's leaders. Awesome."

Oliver frowns. "Hey, you have no control over who's going to die and you know it. You aren't killing anyone."

I scowl. "I feel like I do, though. I don't know." I pick at the lint on my pants. "I just . . . ugh. I've never been this discontent with what I am before, ya know? I mean, I've lived with this thing for almost eighteen years, right? I should be used to things by now. But for whatever reason, being here—right here, in this town, with you, at this school—it's not right, Oliver. I feel like I'm failing. Like I learned nothing over the past dozen and half years and I somehow missed my one shot at actually becoming normal."

"Hey." My boyfriend's voice is firm, demanding. He circles his arms around me and pulls me close. "None of that is true and you know it. It's your brain trying to get you down. Just ignore those negative thoughts. You're part faerie, Caoine." He forces me to look at him. "You're not fully human, you shouldn't want to feel normal . . . whatever normal is. I mean, I'm not normal. Who really is?" He bites his lip. "Normal is overrated, by the way."

My heart skips as he runs a finger along the edge of my jaw.

"Seriously. You can't expect to feel something that isn't natural. Don't beat yourself up over it. It's not wrong that you're different, Caoine. It just *is*. Accept it and be who you are. Be human, but also embrace your faerie side. Because that's the part of you that predicts death, Caoine, not the human side. What you do is perfectly natural for faeries. Do you think a full faerie in your position would be obsessing so much over her job?"

I press my lips together and reluctantly shake my head.

"No. They wouldn't. They would do it because that's what they were born to do, not because they were cursed or because they're horrible or being punished. It's a gift you were given at birth, and gifts are meant to be used, Caoine, not hidden. Accept this is what you do, then rejoice in the moments you get to be a regular teenager with your friends and *adoring boyfriend*." He pops a kiss on the end of my nose. "It's sort of amazing. You get the best of both worlds."

I shift my gaze as I fight a smile. He's totally right. Every single word he said is perfect. All the words. Every single one of them. My entire life I had a bad attitude over something I have no control over. It's time I get over it and start living. I tilt my head back and return his show of affection by dropping a kiss on his chin.

He chuckles. "Now, I'm glad we've come to an agreement regarding your self-esteem issues, because I've got more news."

Oh great. What now? I lace my fingers through his but stay silent, my smile still in place.

"I think you need to get used to the fact I'm your new partner when it comes to your midnight jaunts. Because I've decided it's time to give your dad a much-needed break."

52

CAOINE

"Hey Sugar, wanna go to the dance with me?"

I do a double take at Eric, who sits across from me at our regular lunchroom table. The noise and chatter of my fellow students make it difficult to hear, so I just blink at him. Has he just asked me to the Halloween dance a week away? Who waits until a week out to ask someone to a dance? And why would he ask me, of all people?

Aubree rolls her eyes. "You might want to ask someone who isn't already taken?" Her cheeks pink, and she looks away.

Our normal group, which now includes a new dude from the soccer team, are squeezed tight at our little table that holds fewer people than we brought. I don't mind the fact my knees are pressed against Oliver's or that he has no choice but to rest his hand on the back of my chair. Weird fluttery things happen in my stomach, and I fight the urge to sit and stare at the amazing beauty of that man, even if he does look more average Joe than superstar. Mostly because it will send Aubree into a fit of gagging, but still . . .

Speaking of which, I swallow back a gag of my own and

glance around. *What is that smell?* I glance at Eric's bag at his feet, dirty soccer cleats peeking out. Yep. That's got to be it. Or is it the strange non-organic odor that drifts from the lunch line that has my stomach in a rumble? I resist the urge to crinkle my nose and concentrate on my sweet peppers and ranch.

"I'm serious," Eric says in a not-at-all serious tone. "I'd sort of like a date for once. No one likes the redheaded kid. I'm treated like a court jester." He presses his lips together, but it only makes his freckles bunch together.

I roll my eyes and bite my lip so I don't laugh. My gaze catches on something in the far corner of the cafeteria, a figure or shadow or *something*, lurking by the boys' bathroom. I squint to see who it is but am distracted by Aubree's snarky reply to Eric.

"I'm sorry, was that *not* what you were going for?" Aubree asks as she tosses a potato chip in her mouth.

Eric scowls in reply.

"Why would it matter what her answer is?" Oliver asks. "She's my girlfriend. Therefore, she's clearly going with me."

My jaw drops, and I turn slowly to face my love. "Excuse me? I'm *clearly* going with you? What am I, your property now?"

"Uh-oh." Aubree sits back with a grin. "I'm out of this fight. Good luck with that one, O."

All color drains from Oliver's face, and he stutters. "No, I didn't mean it like that. I was just saying—"

I cross my arms. "You were just getting all competitive with your buddy and your testosterone took over?"

He relaxes. "Yeah." Then his eyes go wide, and he jerks up again. "I mean, no. It's not a competition. I was just defending your honor."

I narrow my eyes at my boyfriend.

"Erm, does anyone else think this is getting awkward?" Cat quips from her end of the table.

Aubree and I burst out laughing. Oliver sighs in relief as he scratches the back of his neck.

Eric just looks perplexed. "Okay, then. Will you go with me if Oliver stiffs you?"

Aubree looks down at her lap.

Oliver shoots his best friend a glare. "Why would I stand up my girlfriend? I *like* her, see. I sort of want to keep her around."

"Then maybe next time you should let me speak for myself." I give Oliver an I-told-you-so grin and turn to Eric. "No, but thank you for the chivalrous offer, Eric. I'll be going with this guy, as long as he remembers Women's Suffrage was a *thing* about a hundred years ago." I point a thumb at Oliver and give him another playful look. I swear his ears turn pink.

Eric raises a brow at me, and I flare my nostrils to tell him to back down. *What is with him? Does this have something to do with the whole Unseelie prince thing?* Guilt floods my core. Oliver doesn't know his best friend is fae, and Eric asked me to keep it that way. Lying to my boyfriend is definitely at the bottom of my to-do list. My only hope is Eric will let me tell Oliver once this whole Unseelie mess is over and done with. I really need as little friction between Oliver and me as possible. Especially with Jessica in this world.

I sigh. "Why don't you take Cat?"

From the other end of the table, Cat's head shoots up, her cheeks bright red. "What? Oh, um . . . I don't know that I'll be going. I'm auditioning for the school play, so we might have rehearsal."

I open my mouth to tell her she's a spoilsport but freeze. *The school play?* I hadn't really thought about it since my interview with Wyatt. The whole getting-back-with-Oliver thing overshadowed it. I bite my lip. *Holy smokes!* How had I forgotten about this? *Wyatt.* Wyatt knows so much about the Seven Deadly Sins. And hadn't I felt a strange warning the day

I was in the auditorium? Why haven't we tested him with the powder yet?

I swivel my head and nail Aubree with my gaze. *We need to talk*, I mouth. Her brow pulls together, but I shake my head. This needs to be said with Eric present. With the way he's hunkered over his lunch, there's no way I can get the two of them alone right now. This will have to wait.

"Dude, is it true Coach is making us stay for double practice today?" New-guy-whose-name-I-still-don't-know asks the guys.

Eric and Oliver are both pulled into the conversation, and poor Cat gives Aubree and me a weak wave from her end of the table. She's caught in the Land of Men.

"Hey," Aubree whispers. "Eric say anything to you about you-know-what?"

I shake my head. "I told him about our theory of the mayor before math class. He didn't seem too concerned. Like, at all."

She glances at the boy in question out of the corner of her eye. Eric is deep in the middle of a heroic soccer story and the others are transfixed, so she goes on. "This makes me nervous. The whole deadly sin thing had stopped for so long, I was hoping we were wrong about that. That leaves only two sins for the killer to plot before his mission is complete. We're out of leads on how to stop this guy."

"I'm not so sure about that." I finger one of my peppers and purse my lips. "I've been thinking."

"Yeah?" Aubree blows at a stray piece of aqua-blue hair that's teasing her eye. The rest of it is pulled up in a loosey-goosey bun with a pair of chopsticks shoved through them for flair. She's outdone herself with her outfit today, complete with a one-piece long-sleeved jumpsuit, thick glittery belt, platform shoes and enough bangles for every student in school. Her makeup is straight out of a magazine too, with shimmer across her cheeks and thick blue eyeliner complemented by uber-long fake blue eyelashes.

How many hours must it take her to get ready in the morning? Oh wait, she's fae. She probably snaps her fingers or something. Lucky. At least she's visibly bouncing back after . . . Seamus. And weirdly eyeing Eric. What's up with that?

"Well, I keep having this dream," I continue. "It's the same every time. In it I see my mom."

"Your mom?" Aubree perks up.

"Yeah. She's chanting. Like repeating the same phrase over and over. Somehow I know it's important. Like it might actually mean something we should know."

"Okay, so what is it?"

I frown. "That's the thing. I don't remember. When I wake up, I forget what she said."

Aubree sighs and places a single manicured finger to the corner of her lip in contemplation. "Well, maybe I can help with that."

"You can?"

"Sure. I've got a few faerie tricks up my sleeve." She shrugs. "Actually, it's just an herb. Not real magic. But I'll give you some. It helps a person remember their dreams."

"Are dreams important to faeries?"

She nods. "Very. We take them very seriously. We believe they can hold truths our wakened minds can't see or don't want to accept." She pauses. "But what does this have to the do the Seven Deadly Sins?"

I take a deep breath. "I think the Unseelie prince's magic is strong. Very strong. I think the sins are only one part of what he has planned."

Eric says something funny that makes the guys laugh, pulling Aubree's attention away. I bite my lip, mull over what she's just told me.

I see movement to my left, in the same corner I noticed a shadow in just a few minutes ago. Except the shadow isn't a shadow anymore. It's a person. Or maybe a faerie. My belly drops.

Wyatt is standing in the corner, his backpack slung over one shoulder, staring right at me. He's been watching me this entire time.

53

CAOINE

"HE'S NOT GONNA SHOW, C." Aubree slumps against the cool brick of the school building. "He totally stood us up. Probably off doing something idiotic, like using his faerie magic to get free sodas from the vending machine."

We're huddled against the chill of the afternoon breeze, faded grass beneath our feet. And we're literally one of the last five students left since the final bell rang. The rest of the student body has made it to the safety of their homes or are tortured with sports or other extracurriculars.

Like Oliver, who says he won't be home until well after supper. Which means I won't see him until bedtime. Bummer. I sort of wanted to talk to him about this deadly sin stuff.

I sigh and slump alongside her. "He'll be here. Eric promised he'd meet us when the coast was clear so we could talk."

"When the coast was clear? What does that even mean? I mean, what? Is he like, FBI or something? Who the freak is he hiding from?"

"A psycho faerie serial killer who wants to see us all dead," I deadpan.

"Yeah, but really? I mean, how would the Unseelie prince

figure out who Eric is just because he sees us talking or hanging out together? It doesn't make any sense. We both have lots of friends."

I roll my eyes and give her a glare.

Aubree shrugs. "Okay, fine. *I* have lots of friends. You have . . . a *respectful* following."

I snort. "A respectful following? That's being generous." I don't mention how thankful I am for said *following,* considering I've never had a friend in my life—let alone a boyfriend. My heart does little trippy things as Oliver's face flashes through my mind, and I curl my hands into fists. Sometimes I think I might wake from some crazy dream and find myself single again. Not that I couldn't survive without him. But being a girlfriend is just so much fun.

She blows into her hands and rubs them together. "Why are we meeting him again? I forget already."

"To tell me how good looking I am?" Eric says from behind me.

Aubree and I both jump. How the freak did he sneak up on us so silently? You'd think Aubree would at least hear him, what with her superhero faerie hearing and all.

"Yes, that's exactly what I've been dying to tell you." Aubree looks away.

I'd almost believe her sarcasm if her cheeks weren't so pink.

"No," I say. "I have something big I need to tell you guys. I mean, I should've said something weeks ago, but honestly, it totally slipped my mind."

I don't mention the elephant in the room, which is that Seamus's death sort of put a damper on things.

I clear my throat. "So, uh, well, do either of you know Wyatt?"

Aubree shakes her head.

Eric nods. "Medium height? Senior? Crazy hair and nose ring?"

"Yeah. Well, I sort of interviewed him for the school paper, and guess what?" I don't give them a chance to answer. "The whole play—he wrote it, you know—well, it revolves around the Seven Deadly Sins."

"Wait, what?" Aubree pushes off from the building. "Are you serious?"

I cringe. "Sorry. I'm an idiot for not bringing this up sooner."

"Um, yeah you are." My jaw falls open, but she shrugs. "Said with all the love in the world, of course. But come on. Really? No way that's coincidence, right?"

"Chances are slim," Eric agrees. "You test him yet?"

I curl my upper lip. "Forgot. But we definitely need to do it."

"Duh." Aubree sighs. "Okay, one of you do it, since you both know what he looks like. I don't need to draw attention to myself by walking the halls screaming names of people I don't know."

"Aw, but you'd look so cute." Eric laughs.

She practically growls back at him.

"Okay, so besides testing Wyatt, what else do we need to do?"

"What do you mean?" Eric tosses his backpack down and crosses his arms, one hip slumped against the building along with his lanky frame.

By all appearances, the three of us look like we're up to no good. Which almost makes me wish we were being super rebellious. Loitering outside the school for no other reason than to talk seems so . . . lame.

I shrug it off. "Um, about the fact the killer—regardless whether it's Wyatt or not—has started his weird voodoo ritual thingy again?"

Eric frowns. "It's totally not voodoo. It's—"

I ignore him. "We've only got two sins left to go. And Halloween is only a week away. Weren't you the one who said that's the night he'll make his move? Whatever his move might be."

"Relax, we have a week to figure things out. Everything will be fine." Eric blows at a lock of red hair that's fallen over his eyes.

Aubree huffs. "Really? This is your attitude? What about a few days ago when you were all *the prince is here to release hell on earth*?" Her voice drops to a sad impression of a very feminine male. "Where's all that enthusiasm?"

Eric raises his brows. "First off, I totally don't sound like that—"

"Not the point." Aubree looks like she's about to spit nails.

Why's she suddenly so mad?

"And secondly, I am *all* about figuring this thing out. Let's hope this Wyatt guy is *him*, by the way." He has both hands on his hips now, and I don't miss the way Aubree's gaze drifts to his shirt that has gone taut across his chest. "But even so, like Caoine said, we know the night he's going to pull his crap, and we know what he's going to do. The plan is to show up and stop him. No problem."

I brighten. "It's that simple? Really?"

"No, dummy." Aubree all but snarls. "It's not."

I wince, but she doesn't see. Where is this coming from? She's never been so unkind before.

She turns back to Eric. "Faerie magic is way more complicated than that. The stuff this guy is doing is clearly *building* on itself. If we wait until the last possible moment, he could finish what he started anyway, and everything will be shot to H-E-double-hockey-sticks." She's breathing heavily, and I fear steam might shoot from her ears. "We need a plan, a *real* plan, to stop him *before* Halloween. We need to figure out exactly what he's doing."

Eric presses his lips together, and his nostrils flare. I cringe. This guy can look really scary when he wants to. "Like I said,

I've got it under control. We've got a week to create a plan. There's no use freaking out over—"

"Who's freaking out?" Aubree shouts. "Are you? Because it certainly doesn't look like it! You look like you're taking a stroll along the beach or something. Like nothing matters to you." Tears swim in her eyes, and her voice catches. "Do you even have anything to lose if the stupid door to the Seelie Realm is closed? No. You're *lucky* to be on this side of the Veil." She swallows and her voice drops. "Maybe that was what you wanted all along. You want the Unseelie prince to finish his plan so you can stay here. You certainly don't have anything waiting for you on the other side of the Veil."

He flinches like he's been punched.

"Aubree." I reach toward her.

She shrugs me off, bends to grab her bag. "I mean, do either of you even care that Seamus is dead?" She runs off without a glance at either of us.

I gasp for air. *What. Just. Happened?*

"Ummm . . ." Eric shifts as he watches my best friend retreat.

"I think she might still be having a tough time." I clear my throat and study my hands.

"They were close, huh?"

I nod. "The closest. Sort of like brother and sister, even though they weren't."

"Were they . . . ?" He tilts his head.

"No. It wasn't like that. There was never anything romantic between them. They were closer, almost." I turn to watch my friend leave, but she's already gone. "Like twins."

We stand in silence for a moment.

"Can I ask you something?" he finally says. I nod. "Are you sure she was in Faerie taking care of stuff associated with Seamus's death? When she disappeared last week?"

My jaw drops. "What's that supposed to mean?"

"It means, all this time we've been looking for a male—an

Unseelie *prince*. What if it's a trick? What if the king sent a female instead? Someone working for him. It would make a great cover, wouldn't it?"

"But I thought you said fae can't lie? How could she say that if it wasn't true?"

He shrugs. "The Fair Folk are tricksters. Especially the evil ones with plans for world domination. It's possible she minced her words to confuse you."

I lick my lips, cross my arms. "Aubree *isn't* an *Unseelie*, Eric. And she's definitely not working for the Unseelie king." *It's Wyatt. It's definitely Wyatt.*

He holds up his hands. "Okay, okay. Just had to ask. I mean, you know her better than I do. I just wanted to cover all our bases, right?"

I sigh. Sure. I guess.

He shifts, his gaze darting toward the parking lot. Awkward.

But not unreasonable, really. I mean, he's right. It could be her, *if* I didn't know her that well. But it definitely isn't. The Unseelie prince is *not* my best friend.

"Are you sure? About next week?" I whisper this as I stare at the spot where she disappeared. "You're sure we'll figure something out before then? That we won't miss our chance to stop this guy? This—" I pull in a ragged breath. "This *monster* who killed Seamus? Because this is about more than just him, ya know. The way my curse has been acting lately . . ." I exhale, lick my lips. "I'm terrified things might get even worse." I pause. "What if I lose total control and can never get it back again?" I peek at him.

Eric squints and gives me a serious nod. "We'll be prepared, Caoine. I promise."

Adrenaline surges though my belly, and my toes tingle. "Good. I want to catch the demon. I want to make him pay for what he did to Seamus." I look in the direction Aubree retreated. "I need my best friend back."

54

CAOINE

Hot coals burn the backs of my eyes as I blink away tears. My chest is stretched tight like a rubber band, a constant vice that won't let up. I shake my hands out, as if movement might actually make the pain that's invaded my stomach go away.

"Why?" I whisper.

Oliver's shoulders sag, his face melancholy.

We're seated on the front steps of my house, away from the prying ears of my father. The sun has almost sunk completely behind the trees across the street that hides my neighbor's house. A dog barks from somewhere down the road, and someone close by has decided to have a late-in-the-year barbecue before frigid temps set in for winter. My neighborhood is normal. Even though I'm not.

Even though my relationship with my boyfriend is most definitely not.

"I don't understand why you're obligated to attend a wedding of someone you don't even know, with an ex-girlfriend you broke up with six months ago." I'm trying desperately to keep the agony from my voice but sense I've already failed.

His lips work like he's got something to say, but nothing

comes out. His Adam's apple bobs as he swallows. I sigh. We've been through this at least three times already, but none of his answers satisfy any of my questions.

My boyfriend is leaving town, leaving me to attend a wedding with Jessica. Over the past thirty minutes I've heard excuses about how he committed to going back when he and Jessica were together, how he hadn't thought to tell her he wasn't going anymore, and how the cost of his meal and guest gift were worth more than the iPhone I didn't own. She was livid when he attempted to turn her down and as much as threatened to sue him if he forced her to show up without a date.

It's obviously true love. I roll my eyes. None of this adds up or makes me feel any better about the situation.

"Why can't I just come along?" I beg. I clench my nails into the skin of my palms. I sound crazy amounts of whiney.

When? When had I become *that* girl? Pleading for the affection of the school soccer star so she didn't have to mop the floor with the puddles of her tears? *Pathetic.*

"Cay, it doesn't work like that." His voice is tired, defeated.

"But it could." I stifle a whimper. "I just won't eat. And I wouldn't expect a gift, like, ever. I would just be there to . . . to —"

"To make sure nothing happens between Jessica and me?" A muscle along Oliver's jaw twitches. "Do you seriously not trust me?"

I crunch my teeth together. "It's not *you* I don't trust."

He huffs a breath and runs a hand through his hair. "I . . . I don't know what to say. I can't back out, Caoine. I'm just not *that* guy. I mean, do I want to go? Of course not. You know I'd rather spend the weekend with you. But I owe it to Jessica. It's my fault I didn't renege my RSVP. I can't put her in a tough spot like that."

I snort. "A tough spot? Right. The only thing she's worried about is her pride when she shows up dateless. She doesn't care about you, Oliver. She just wants eye candy on her arm so she can impress her family."

He brightens and turns to me. "Exactly. Which is why you shouldn't be worried. She doesn't care about me, and once this weekend is over, I won't have to do anything like this again."

My belly rebels, and I grind my teeth. The problem with my statement is it's partly false. Jessica *does* care about Oliver. I just can't tell him that. Not without looking more like a psycho girlfriend than I already do.

"It's just so unfair." I glance toward the road, as if hoping an emergency vehicle might show up and whisk me away from the drama of being a teen. "I just don't understand why you think you need to please everyone so much." My voice has no punch left to it. I'm losing this battle, and I'm not sure if I should be happy or sad about it.

He doesn't respond. Instead, Oliver slips his arm around my shoulders, and for the first time this evening, I don't push him away. I slide my eyes in his direction and catch the corner of his mouth as it tilts up. I flare my nose and squeeze my lips together to prevent that ever-present grin that lingers close by when my boyfriend is near.

Stupid boys. Why do I like him so?

"Fine. Go to the wedding with Jessica. See if you have a girlfriend when you get back." My pouting is incredibly unattractive.

He chuckles, pulls me close. "You won't wait for me?"

I lift my head an inch higher. "Maybe. Maybe not." I pause. "Maybe I'll go to the Halloween dance with Eric after all."

"Ouch." Oliver grabs his chest. "Running off with my best friend. That's cold, Cay."

"Not as cold as running off with your *ex-girlfriend.*" I lift a single eyebrow.

He winces but pulls me close once more. "I hear ya. And if there were any way I could get out of it, I would. Believe me.

Spending a weekend with that amount of awkward is not my idea of a fun time."

"At least you get your car ride to yourself." I tilt my head and give him *the look*. "You're making the two-hour drive alone, right? You promised?"

He nods. "Oh yeah. That's a definite. There's no way I could handle spending that amount of time locked inside the car with Jessica or her parents. And she says I'm in a hotel room all by myself, so I'm safe there, too. My plan is to duck out of the festivities early so I can get to bed early and be on the road first thing Sunday morning." He leans his head a few inches closer to mine. "With any luck, we'll be reunited before you and your dad get settled in front of the afternoon football game. Save me some chips and salsa?"

I cave. "Okay." My gaze drifts to his lips, and my heart skips around inside my chest.

"Good," he whispers. He leans another few inches closer. "I was hoping you'd say that."

He gives me a kiss that makes me forget all about Jessicas and weddings and my doubts before he turns to go home. I watch him as he jogs to the end of the driveway, to the spot where he's parked. He hops in his car and is gone. Somewhere close by, a cricket chirps. Why are the crickets out so early? It's barely even nighttime.

With a sigh, I twirl and head toward my house. Can this night get any worse? Just before I reach my doorstep, the bushes along the side of the house—the same ones that sit beneath my bedroom window—shake, just like they did last time.

An icy chill spills along my shoulders, down my spine. I swallow and command my feet not to jump out my shoes. I hightail it up the stairs and race inside my house. Whatever animal is living outside my house had better find a new place of residence. I seriously can't handle any more drama than what my life already has.

55

CAOINE

I FLOP onto the sofa with an *oomph*. My skin begins to warm. It's becoming far too cold outside to do silly things like fight with my boyfriend after the sun is gone and the witching hour approaches. Pressure lances my chest, and I close my eyes, sink into the soft cushions beneath me.

It's totally okay that Oliver is going to this, right? I mean, it's really okay. Why am I so afraid?

"Got a minute, honey?"

The voice pops out of nowhere, and I practically leap from my seat. Along with a ridiculous scream. Because I'm classy like that.

"Dad!" I glare at my father who stands above me, eyes wide.

He holds up a hand. "Sorry, hon. I didn't mean to spook you." He nods to the armchair to my left. "Mind if I . . . ?"

I crinkle my nose in a "why would I care" kind of look and sit up straighter. "We sit together all the time."

He licks his lips. "Yeah, but . . ." He clears his throat. "There's, uh, something I'd like to discuss, if you've got a moment?"

My belly lurches, then does about fifteen flips. *Awesome.*

Serious talk with boyfriend. Now serious talk with dad. My night really is getting worse.

I flash a feeble smile. "Sure. Bring it on, Pops."

My dad falls into the chair beside me, then leans forward so his elbows are on his knees, gaze intent on mine. "So I got a new job. Thought you should know."

"Dad! That's fantastic!" My jaw drops. Why is he making this out like it's a bad thing?

He nods but doesn't rejoice with the same energy I express. "I also wanted to talk to you about, uh . . ." He shifts in his seat. "About my, um, drinking."

My heart falls. *Crap. Here's the bad thing.* Heat floods my face, and I avoid his gaze. "I'm not sure what you—" I clasp my hands and squeeze my fingers together. I never said it out loud, never once mentioned he might have a problem. It was so much easier to just clean up after him.

"Caoine, I've got a drinking problem. Don't act like you haven't known your whole life." He pauses. "I know what I am . . . what I have been, all along. And it's not right. I'm not the kind of father you need—"

"You're a great dad." My gaze is back on his now, fire in my belly.

He huffs, scratches a hand through his hair. "Okay. Maybe I've done a decent job for what I've had to work with but . . . well, I haven't done my best. And I'm here to tell you I'm starting over. All that drinking, losing jobs . . . that all stops now. I—" He clears his throat again. "I've come to terms with a few things, stuff I think we need to discuss."

I swallow.

"It's about your mother."

My mother? I blink. This isn't anywhere near where I thought this conversation was going.

"All these years I've had this massive guilt, this idea I didn't do enough to keep her alive—"

I gasp. *He* didn't do enough?

"It's time you knew the truth about the night you were born."

My body goes still, and I have to will myself to breathe.

"When the faerie showed up to take your life, it was like . . . like your mother knew, like she was prepared or something." He stops and coughs. "She spoke to the faerie with authority, demanding she leave us alone."

His brow creases, and I'm suddenly aware of his age.

"Me? I could barely wrap my brain around the fact an honest-to-God faerie stood in my living room. But your mom . . . she was amazing."

He stops, a half-smile on his lips.

"She wasn't having any of it. She pointblank told her leave, that she wasn't to lay a finger on her child. The weird thing is, the faerie complied. I already told you it seemed like the faerie didn't want you to die. Well, she just accepted what your mother said like that."

He snaps his fingers.

"Then she whispered in your mother's ear. Her face looked pained, like it was the toughest choice she had to make. Your mother only nodded. She never did tell me what the fae said. Immediately after, the faerie explained the conditions. Because her faerie magic was being altered, there would be a price to pay. *You* would pay the price."

He closes his eyes and drops his head.

"She said your job would be simple, that you might enjoy it, even. That it wouldn't interfere with your life, and you would grow to be a normal human child." He looks at me. "I'm so sorry she was wrong."

Chills spill across my arms. *Was she, though?*

"Minutes later, the faerie disappeared, faded into nothingness. I assumed she went back to the Faerie Realm."

I suck in a breath but hold very still. *She disappeared?* She died. That means she died. Just like Seamus. *The fae gave her life for me?* Tears prick the backs of my eyes.

"I . . . I don't understand," I breathe. "How could that faerie turn me into what I am? Do faeries have the power to create new faeries? And what did mom know? Why wasn't she shocked to see a faerie like you were?"

He shakes his head. "Those are questions that may never be answered, sweetheart. All I know is, the faerie gave you a job, and that night, you started your banshee cry. I had no idea your mom wouldn't be around to answer my questions."

A blade of agony slides across my chest, but I swallow the pain.

My dad scratches a hand through his hair again. "When your mother died, I thought the faerie had lied, that something had gone wrong. Your mom wasn't supposed to die. It should've been *me*." My dad shoves his fists to his eyes, his voice muffled. "It was supposed to be me that saved you, not her." He breaks down.

The only sound between the two of us is his crying and the way I'm gasping for air.

Is this even possible? My dad thought all this time he was the one who killed my mom?

"But Dad," I finally choke. "It was . . . me. I mean, wasn't it? I thought I was the one who killed her."

He blinks, his sudden rush of emotion at a complete halt. "You?" His face twists in pain. "Why would you think that? You didn't kill her."

"I just thought . . ." I rub my eyes with the heels of my hands. "I mean, that's why you drink, right? Because you're mad at me? For killing mom?"

"Sweetheart, no!" He's on his knees now, my hands in his. "That's never been the case. I've always thought it was my fault she died, that I missed a choice somehow." He reaches up, one hand on my cheek, now wet with tears. "But I was wrong about that, too. I think I know now—I've finally figured it out."

He takes a deep breath but stays close to me. I squeeze his hand tight.

"That thing the faerie whispered to your mother?" he says. "I believe she asked permission. I think she told your mom there was an even bigger price, bigger than just you becoming part fae. She asked your mom if she'd be willing to give up her life for yours, and she accepted."

My dad sighs.

"I finally know, sweetheart. I figured it out. This thing was never about me or you. There was no way I could control what happened. Your mom made her choice. She decided that night to make the ultimate sacrifice." He rubs my hand. "We should be thankful for that, not sad. And I certainly shouldn't be drinking away my life, and yours, when she clearly gave us so much. Your mom died to save us both, Caoine."

Heat pours from my head to my toes, and I can't stop the tears. My dad envelopes me in a hug as my body is wracked with sobs, a wail most unbecoming of a banshee tumbling from deep inside me.

My mom died for me. She chose to die. It isn't my fault. It has never been my fault.

My dad doesn't hate me.

Minutes pass as we hold one another, as my dad allows me to cry on his shoulder while he silently sheds his own tears. We sit and we rock and we allow the hurt of our past to melt away.

My dad loves me. I know this now. He's not keeping a part of himself from me as punishment for something that happened the night of my birth. He's only been keeping that part away from himself.

But no more. Now we are one. Now maybe we can move on to whatever future our destiny holds for us.

In the shadows of the living room, my dad and I are healed. A relationship mended amidst the chaos of an impossible world.

56

CAOINE

"Caoine."

The voice floats around me, against me, through me.

"Caoine."

I can feel it as it penetrates my skin, begs to slip inside my body, to find the deepest parts of me.

"Caoine."

Like rain as it drips across my skin on a warm spring day.

"Caoine."

The scent of fresh lilacs, the ones that grew outside my childhood home.

That first taste of chocolate as it slides across my tongue.

The way my dad would hold me when I had a nightmare as a child.

The melody of my name as it spills from Oliver's mouth.

Oliver. Oliver. *Oliver?*

Then, images flash before my eyes, racing past, too fast to decipher or understand.

I grab my head in agony, squeeze my eyes shut. The pictures still fill my head, bleed across my vision.

A woman crosses the street and is hit by a car.

The woman parks in the garage but is hit by the same car on a different street.

That same woman takes the bus, departs, sees the car barreling toward a child and jumps into the street, pushing the child to safety but facing the car herself.

Burning hot coals scorch my belly, dive deep into the confines of my chest. I can't breathe, even though fresh air fills my lungs over and over again. Still I gasp, beg for life. But there is none.

Death. Death. Death.

Deathdeathdeathdeathdeathdeath.

It consumes me, cradles me in its arms, dares me to challenge it and warns me to obey.

Obey. Obey. Obey.

Why must I always obey?

I gag on a cry, plead with myself to wake from this nightmare. Knives stab my skin, flay the flesh from my bones. Pain, agony. It doesn't want me to feel, the dream doesn't want me to know. Makes me think I can *never understand.*

But I do. In this moment I know. *I understand.* I feel what I must do, what I *can* do.

"Caoine!" Hands are on my shoulders, on my back. Am I lying down?

I drag a lungful of air into my body, the one that is still alive. I'm not dead. I'm not hurt. Another cry rips from my parched throat. Oxygen sets my chest on fire, welcome and unwelcome.

Visions fill my sight. They won't go away. Refuse to go away. *Leave me alone!* My hands are clenched and something slick coats my fingers, a dull ache in my palms. *Go away!* My heart pounds in the cavernous hollow of my chest. *Let me be!*

"Caoine!"

I blink. The pictures are gone.

Oliver stands above me. Sweat drips along his brow as his jaw shivers. Chills accost my arms and legs. It's cold. So cold.

The scent of frost and midnight air and the sweet perfume of Oliver's breath spill over me.

I'm on the ground. The very frigid, nearly frozen ground. My upper body is in Oliver's arms. His face is panicked. Terrified.

"Oliver?" I whisper.

How did I get here? Why am I here?

"Caoine. You had me so worried."

Worried? But how did I . . . ? The soft edge of my cloak brushes my cheek, and I remember.

It must be late, past midnight. I fell into my trance, Oliver followed as he promised he would.

Before we went to sleep, we discussed it, agreed this would be the night. Tonight I would give it my best effort. I would keep my cloak's hood on after my song ended.

My dad believes there is something more to my curse. And Oliver echoes the sentiment. For whatever reason, my dad is convinced the answer to this mystery lives within the fabric of my cape.

Before I fell asleep, I decided I would leave my hood in place, test it once more. Find out if Oliver was able to find the answer my dad never could.

It was a great plan. But we failed. Again.

It didn't work. Nothing about the visions give any answers that make sense. None of it helps me see if the woman's death can be avoided or delayed. Except a little niggle behind my heart . . . a strange sensation I *have* figured something out. That something *had* made sense, for just a fleeting moment.

But not any longer. Whatever revelation presented itself is gone. Just a dream.

Once again we failed. *I failed.*

All I've accomplished is allowing myself excruciating pain when there was absolutely no need for it.

"Are you all right?" The warmth of his body calls to me, and I settle within his embrace another inch or two.

"Yeah. I'm good. Just help me—" I gasp in pain as I attempt to sit up.

His eyes open wide. "Stay still. You need to rest."

"Rest?" I gag. "Out here in the freaking freezing cold? No thank you, Love-of-Mine." I grit my teeth and force myself to a sitting position. "Take me home. I'll rest once I'm in bed."

His shoulders sag, and he lowers his gaze but helps me to my feet anyway. "Did you um"—he clears his throat—"see anything?"

I shake my head, heat filling my cheeks, that burning sensation returning to my chest. My swallow takes effort. The silent answer I give isn't a total lie. I saw lots of stuff. Just nothing of consequence. Nothing that will change the fact this woman will die. *Is destined to die.*

There's still nothing I can do to save her.

Tears sting the backs of my eyes, but I blink them away and struggle to my feet.

Oliver frowns, nods. Then we begin to walk home, hushed.

I lean against him as we walk, allow my disappointment to seep into the earth beneath us. To fade away as quickly as my dream.

At least now I know. My curse can't be stopped or changed in any way. My dad truly has been wrong all this time.

I will have to announce the arrival of death for the rest of my life. And there's nothing I can do to stop it.

THE UNSEELIE PRINCE

TIME IS RUNNING SHORT. I can count the number of days left before I will finally make my father happy. Before I will earn the love meant for me.

Yet Caoine continues to grow closer to the answer. To knowing the one thing that will take her away from me. That can stop me from what I must do.

This cannot happen. I've tried so hard, done whatever I could to make my father happy. And she still evades my advances.

Why?

Why can she not see how much I care for her? If only she'd listen, I could tell her. Could explain just how perfect we would be together. If only she'd give me the chance.

I stand in the exact spot where she sang her song. The one where she almost learned her true worth. Luckily for me the woman she lamented has truly been called to the other side. Her death, inevitable. Caoine and Oliver are long gone, but still I am here, drawing from the energy she left. Soaking in her essence. Filling my lungs with her scent.

Oliver.

The name leaves my mouth feeling dirty. Like I've eaten a

rotten egg, and there's not enough water in this world to wash away the foul taste.

He almost ruined everything I've worked so hard for. Almost convinced her to discover the truth behind her banshee song. But at least there was pain. The pain that will always be there when she attempts to use her gift for good.

I've made sure of this. A simple spell I cast months ago, assuring she can never keep that piece of fabric in place longer than need be. Not with the pain it causes. If she ever figures out she just needs to push through the pain, to allow it to wash over her a few seconds longer before it will disappear. She'll know she has a gift—answers to every question she's ever sought . . .

This I cannot allow. She can't see what she could *be* without me. *She needs me.*

I need her.

I close my eyes and breathe in, beg the night air to freeze my lungs, to chill the blood in my veins and bring me back to life. To bring my Winter nature back into my body.

Caoine must work with me, must help me set my people free. To release the Winter fae that have been slaves for far too long to that wretched Seelie Realm. That pathetic queen and all her rules. Her attitude that she deserves to control us all, to keep us in our place when all we want is to live our lives.

My spell will work. I will help my father complete his plan.

Caoine will belong to me.

I look back at the house Caoine sang to only moments ago. Take in the scene around me.

Only a few more days, then this will all be over. Caoine will know the truth.

And she will be mine.

"TELL me again what you plan to do while we're at the dance?" Aubree runs her fingers across her face, but somehow her perfectly applied makeup doesn't budge. Faerie magic, for sure.

Which is good since it's the main thing she's got going today. Her ensemble is uncharacteristically low key. Almost cringe worthy. I don't want to be the one to tell her the 1980s craze has passed and her sweatpants with leg warmers aren't quite doing it for her. At least her off-the-shoulder sweatshirt looks cute.

"I'll be hiding by the Veils, air horn in hand." Eric gives a goofy grin. He's seated in the spot Seamus normally took at the coffee shop. Aubree looks stressed.

It's officially the weekend. Friday. School over. Oliver gone. I bounce my knee in an attempt to distract myself. The next few days will be crazy depressing. Especially with Halloween so close. *When did I become so dependent on my boyfriend?*

The shop isn't too crowded, and I'm comforted by the familiar hiss of the espresso machine and the heavy scents of coffee and sweet syrup that hang in the air. Since when does the smell of coffee *not* make me sick? Someone started a fire in the fireplace, and I sink a little deeper into my chair, woozy. I could fall asleep. Which I might do, since that will help pass the time until Oliver comes back.

"Double shot dirty chai, almond milk!" the barista at the counter calls.

Aubree rolls her eyes and groans. "Seriously? They got it wrong *again*. Skim. Milk. I asked for skim milk!" She throws her hands in the air and marches over to the counter to fight with the barista.

I settle in my chair and watch the fire flicker. Eric is watching me. I should start a conversation while we wait for Aubree, but it still feels weird, talking to Eric about fae stuff. Especially while he's sitting in Seamus's chair. The only thing we've ever had in common is Oliver, who's now very gone. Would it be too awkward to talk soccer?

"I knew he'd fall for you, ya know."

I jump and turn to him. "What?"

"Oliver. I knew you two would get together."

Weird. Did he just read my mind? Can faeries even do that? I clear my throat. "Am I his type or something?"

Eric shakes his head. "You're fae."

I frown. "I don't follow."

"You're fae? Certain humans are more in tune with the fae than they realize. He pretty much cornered me the day I arrived at school. We've been best friends ever since. He took a liking to Seamus and Aubree fairly quickly, too. As soon as I saw you walk through the door, I knew he'd be drawn to you. Romantically."

I gesture toward Aubree. "What about—?"

"She's always had Seamus, even of they weren't together. Oliver is a gentleman. He'd never interfere with someone who appeared to be taken."

"Oh." I look at my hands and fight the warmth that fills my throat. What is Eric saying? Is this supposed to be a pep talk?

Because somehow it sounds like he's saying Oliver is only attracted to me because I'm part fae.

Eric continues to stare at me, his eyes taking in my hair, the slope of my neck.

I fight to swallow, but Aubree saves me from the weirdness by plopping back into her seat.

"Got it straightened out!" She places her coffee on the table beside her and looks at Eric. "I still don't get the air horn part."

"Huh?" He blinks rapidly.

"The air horn? What we were talking about before I left?"

"Oh, right." He shakes his head and eyes me like I might spill a secret or something.

I look back to the fire.

"Well, if the prince shows up early to the party, I need some way to let you know," he says.

I cringe. "Yeah, but I think what she's asking is, *what good will the air horn do*? I mean, say he does come before midnight. You blow the horn. We come running. Fine. But it will take us at least ten minutes to get to that area of the woods. You'd be dead by the time we got there."

Eric wrinkles his upper lip. "A little faith, ladies. You don't think I can take on the Unseelie prince?"

"Um . . ." I cross my legs and pretend something at the counter has caught my eye.

Aubree ducks her head and sips her coffee.

"Oh come on. I know a few things." Eric pretends to flex his muscles, and Aubree chokes.

She dabs her nose to keep the liquid from seeping out as she stifles a belly laugh. My own belly drops two inches. It's the first time I've seen her laugh—*really laugh*—since Seamus died. I blink away the mist in my eyes and join in laughing.

"No, really," Aubree says after she's caught her breath. "We're serious. We're worried about you. What if something bad happens?"

"Aw, how sweet. You're worried about me, Bree?"

Her ears elongate just slightly. I go stiff. Only Seamus ever called her that.

Eric leans toward her so his elbows are on his knees. "How about this? I promise to stay alive until you get there. Even if it means letting him slip through the Unseelie Veil and start whatever magical war he's come to start."

I snort. "No, you won't." I roll my eyes at his pouty face. "You were sent here for one reason, Eric. To stop the prince no matter the cost. You're perfectly willing to do whatever it takes to stop him. Don't try to deny it."

He sits back with a huff and scrubs a hand through his hair. "Fine. Yes. You got me." He stops and looks right at Aubree. "But I promise to do my best to stay alive as long as possible. Is that better?"

Pink spots appear on her cheeks, and she swallows. Instead of answering, she simply nods and takes another sip of coffee.

It's weird that we're talking about death. Not the kind of death I predict, but *real* death. The kind that touched Seamus. The kind that could affect Aubree or Eric or me or—I suck in a breath as an image of Oliver pops in my head. No. *Not an option.* There is zero way I'll let him anywhere near the Veils.

"So what about us?" I shake off the adrenaline that zips down my spine. "Why do we have to be at the dance again?"

"To throw him off." Eric nibbles his lip. "He knows who you are. That's our one disadvantage. He'll be watching you two. If he knows you're on to the fact the whole thing goes down on Halloween night, he'll be on guard when he gets to the Veils. I guarantee he's going to check the dance first to make sure you two are preoccupied." The corner of his mouth tilts up. "But our one advantage is *me*. I'll be there to stop him."

"Which is how exactly?" I ask.

"That's what we need to talk about next." Eric's smile beams brighter than the fire beside me. "Here's what we'll do to be sure the Unseelie prince doesn't have a chance to close that Veil."

59

CAOINE

I PACE my bedroom for the hundredth time in an hour. This is the first Saturday I've had to myself in weeks. Even if Oliver had to work, we always got to spend a morning or evening together.

And with Aubree off on her mysterious last-minute trip to Faerie, there's nothing to take my mind off the circus spinning inside my head. Even my poetry can't fill the empty hole that gapes from the center of my chest.

There are just no words. *No words.* Every single molecule in my body has become a jumping bean. I. Can. Not. Turn. Off. My. Brain.

Monday looms ahead like a storm cloud ready to unleash. *Two days.* Forty-eight hours until this whole thing will either be over or . . .

Or just beginning.

I squeeze my eyes shut and exhale. *Please don't be just beginning.*

I flop onto my bed and stare at the ceiling. Kick my legs back and forth. Twiddle a loose string on my bedspread. Then I hop up to throw some lavender oil in my diffuser to see if I can get these nerves of mine calmed.

It's Saturday. Crazy beautiful outside. *So what the freak am I doing inside?* Sun shines super bright through my window. Even the temps are unusually high for late fall. On the other side of the glass, it's a balmy sixty degrees. I should be outside, taking a walk, getting some exercise. *Doing anything other than this.* But I can't stop worrying. It's like the rational part of my brain has put up picket signs that say, "No way! We won't stay!"

I run a hand across my face as I curl against my pillow. This is seriously worse than a six-year-old waiting for Christmas.

Poetry. It's been days since I've written a thing. Maybe I just need to focus my creative energies.

I lean across my bed and take a swig of the herbal tea Aubree has been making me drink for the past week. It's supposed to nudge my memory about that dream I keep having, but nothing has happened so far. I grab my cerulean-colored notebook—adorned with a unicorn with a blue mane, of course—and a fluffy, jingly pen I got as a birthday present last year and hunker down to write.

At first nothing comes. My mind is blank. Blanker than blank. Like, as blank as the stupid piece of paper that stares back at me, blank.

Growl.

Okay, what to do? I saw a YouTube video once on ideas to get creative juices flowing. Maybe one of those techniques will help?

I close my eyes, put my pen to paper. *Empty your mind. Empty your mind.* My pen moves. My brain regurgitating what-ever is at the forefront, whatever words it decides to scrawl. *Don't think. Don't think. Just write.* I concentrate on *not* thinking, just allowing my hands to do the work.

Finally, I open my eyes.

The page is a complete mess.

Of course. None of the lines are even close to straight, and I'm not sure I can tell where one sentence ends and the next begins. But there are words, so there's that. I bite my lip in anticipation of what my subconscious mind came up with while my conscious mind pretended to sleep.

Blood of the innocent. Blood of sinners. Blood of the firstborn. Blood of greatness.

Wait, what?

Blood of the innocent. Blood of sinners. Blood of the firstborn. Blood of greatness.

Where have I heard that? Why is it familiar?

Blood of the innocent. Blood of sinners. Blood of the firstborn. Blood of greatness.

My throat closes.

The dream. My hands begin to shake. These were the words my mother said. I blink away spots. Is this real? Could my subconscious mind really remember something so specific from a dream? And what can they—?

The cell on my bedside stand buzzes. I jump three feet in the air.

I glance down. *Unknown Caller* appears, and I squeal with delight. *Oliver!* My poetry is completely forgotten.

As part of the agreement to go on this crazy wedding adventure with She-Who-Shall-Not-Be-Named, he left me his cell and grabbed his mom's old cell. Thus far things have worked splendidly, albeit, sporadically. Actually, he's only texted me once to let me know he arrived at the hotel the night before. But at least he was thinking of me!

And now he's sent another. Which means I'm on his mind once again. Relief floods my chest, and I close my eyes to breathe before checking to see what it says. The girly part of me knows it doesn't matter how short the message is or what it contains. Just the fact he sent me something means he misses me. Eep!

My fingers are swift as they glide over the screen, type in the passcode, pull the messaging app to life. I can't keep the grin from my face as my heart pounds and my toes begin to wiggle. An image flashes across the screen, and I realize it's a picture, not a text. But that's totally fine, too! A nice little selfie of my boyfriend showing me just how much he misses me works just as well as words.

The phone takes a stupid amount of time to load the image, and I bite my lip as I wait. But then that image appears, and it's no longer fuzzy. It becomes totally clear. I bite much harder into my lip than needed and don't stop until I taste blood. A metallic flavor registers in my brain, but I can't think on it.

I can't breathe or move or think or speak.

The picture is of Oliver. But it's also of someone else. Someone has taken a picture of them dancing at the wedding reception together, Jessica pressed tightly against his body, her head on his shoulder. Her hands are slipped nicely over his muscled shoulders, and he's gazing down at her with a smile on his face. Content.

They look perfect together. Happy and right and totally free from anything to do with death or faeries.

I can't believe I hadn't seen this before. The wedding was just an excuse, a chance for him to rekindle what he had with his ex-girlfriend. How could I have been so stupid? I mean, who the heck goes to a family wedding of an ex-flame? *No one, Caoine. That's who.*

Stupid, stupid, stupid. That's exactly what I am.

Of course Oliver would want to get back with her. Eric pretty much came out and told me, right? Oliver had only ever been attracted to me because I'm fae. Because my weird unspoken faerie powers somehow tricked him into thinking there might actually be a chance for us. But none of that had been real, apparently.

Had Eric told me this to try to spare my feelings? To help me get through the pain of a breakup? Because he knew this moment would come? I press my hands against my eyes and fight the tears.

The phone makes a clicking noise. Words have finally appeared.

We need to talk about us.

I shove my fist between my teeth and bite. Hard. He wants to have the breakup discussion. How did I not seen this coming? I squeeze my eyes shut as hot tears flow freely. Of course he wouldn't want me.

Jessica is the better choice, anyway. Her life is uncomplicated and couldn't possibly get him killed. Who knows? Maybe she put him up to it and he only stuck around long enough to learn as much about the school freak as he could. Enough to give Jerksica more fodder for whatever article she's going to write about me.

To expose me and my kind to the world.

My hands begin to shake. I'm going to be sick.

I'm such an idiot. How could I believe Oliver actually wanted to be with me?

Oliver and Jessica are meant to be together. And he's happy about it. He's truly happy.

I click the phone off and stare at the blank wall. It takes just a few seconds before the tears come, but when they do, they come in droves. I no longer worry about Monday or Unseelie things or anyone who might die. I spend the rest of the day crying into my pillow, mourning my own death. The death of my relationship with Oliver.

The realization that I'm a fool.

60

CAOINE

Dearest Caoine,

The end is near. You know it, I know it. Soon all will be revealed, and you can join me for good. The two of us will be unstoppable, together.

When we are one, you will have no need for Oliver in your life. You won't want a guy who only throws you away like trash. Why would you want to be with a fickle human when you aren't truly human to begin with? You think you know what you want, but that's only because you've been among humans for far too long. You are one of us.

You are like me.

Soon you will know what you were created for. You will know your true family. You won't need to be manipulated by Aubree or be made a fool of by Jessica. Or even used by Oliver. You will be you. You will be power.

Wait for me, Caoine. I promise you won't be disappointed. We were meant to be.

All my love,
Your Prince

I'M HIDING under the stairwell, the latest note crushed between my fingers.

Hiding from the Unseelie prince. Hiding from my ex-boyfriend.

With a sigh, I close my eyes. I have no clue if anyone saw me slip away, or if they even care. Besides the never-ending notes from the Unseelie prince, I still haven't spoken to Oliver. Or had to face him, thank God.

School is not the place I want to be on the Monday morning after my life got flipped upside down, but I have little choice. Policy says a student must be present the day of an event if they want to attend. And I *need* to attend the dance tonight. Even if it won't be with Oliver. My insides clench.

Oliver broke up with me, and the Unseelie prince wants to be my boyfriend. How backward can the world get right now?

The prince said I was just like him. What is that even supposed to mean? I'm far more like Aubree than him, that much I've already figured out. And wait for him? Wait for *what*? *Another death? A surprise party?* Because right now I'm not ardent to face either.

I glance at the phone. *Oliver's phone.* Two minutes until the final bell for the morning will ring. And I don't care. I pull a deep breath through my nose and immediately cringe. I forgot how moldy this tiny corner of the school smelled. My fingers shake as I run them through my hair, steel myself to step into the day.

Seeing Oliver will eventually be part of the package, considering I'm definitely going to see him around at some point. But I'm just not ready to face him. Not after Saturday. Not after those pictures. My vision goes blurry, and I close my eyes to steady myself.

No. The Unseelie prince is wrong. Oliver and I are good together. *Were* good together.

By Saturday evening, I received another picture, this one of Jessica kissing his cheek. He was smiling like he was the happiest guy on earth. It was obvious they were both in his hotel room. Then another came, this one of him on his back,

Jessica straddling his torso. Again, that cursed smile was plastered on his face like clown makeup. They were wrestling. Like boy-girl-about-to-get-it-on wrestling. Then the final blow, the humdinger of a pic that drove a steal blade right through my heart.

Jessica's tongue down his throat, his arms wrapped tightly around her as her hands pulled his shirt partway up his back. I can only imagine what happened after that one was taken.

My belly flips. Stupid boys. He didn't even show up to watch the Sunday afternoon football game with my dad, something that became habit.

This. This is why I never had a boyfriend!

I slump my shoulders and begin the trek down the hallway toward my first class. Why did I ever allow myself to be pulled into a relationship? Everything about them is just . . . *complicated.* Not to mention I'm not even fully human. I mean, do I even need to find true love? Will I crave companionship the same way a normal teenage girl would?

Why can't I just believe the Unseelie prince and forget Oliver altogether?

I take another deep breath and try to blink away the spots that float before me. The stinker part of the whole thing is that he *Never. Even. Called.* Never even bothered to contact me yesterday when he got back from his trip. I guess his idea of breaking up was with those ridiculous pictures but still . . . I had more faith in him than that. I really thought he'd at least call to explain what happened. But nothing. Nada. No word from the boy.

Students push against me as they rush to class, and the bell rings right as I slide through the door to my classroom. Aubree sits in her usual spot, head down. I grab the seat next to her and wait for her to acknowledge me.

I need to tell her about the note. It's time. I bet Aubree and I can take down this prince before he has a chance to hurt her, if he finds out I told. Seconds pass as I wait for her to turn to me.

She doesn't. Just keeps typing on her phone like nobody's business.

I sigh but she doesn't hear. The teacher starts his lecture. Crap. I really need to tell her about my crazy pen pal. I glare at her. Still nothing.

Am I stuck in some sort of vortex? How is this even possible? First my boyfriend ditches me, and now my best friend?

My best friend. My best friend?

The one who disappeared for almost a week? To the Faerie Realm? And then again this past weekend?

The conversation with Eric pops in my head, and my insides quiver. *All this time we've been looking for a male—an Unseelie prince. What if it's a trick? What if the king sent a female instead? Someone working for him? It would make a great cover, wouldn't it?*

Warmth pricks the backs of my eyes, but I blink it away. Heat fills my chest, my gut, while my feet and hands go cold.

This seriously can't be happening.

But what if it is? What if she found a way to lie to me? I mean, I think I can trust her, but should I? Maybe telling her about the note is the last thing I need to do right now.

She looks up, and I jump. Her face falls as she looks me over. *Where's Oliver?* she mouths.

I shake my head. I don't know.

No, she can't be working for the enemy. There's no way. Despite her less-than-attentive friendship at the moment, she still cares about me.

She frowns, then returns to typing frantically on her phone. I shift my gaze to the teacher and pray he doesn't see her indiscretion. She could so lose her phone for good if he catches her texting again. And although I'm totally miffed at her at the moment, my interest is peaked.

Who is she texting?

The class drags on like a tortoise in a race. I grind my teeth and attempt *not* to make permanent marks in the wood of my seat as I dig in my fingernails. Would it be more merciful if my heart gives out? The bell rings.

Aubree jumps from her seat and pulls me by the arm, even before the teacher is done giving instructions for homework. Oh, great. Guess she's given up the ignore-Caoine campaign.

Cool air slaps my face as we enter the hallway, a sterile scent that tells me the janitor mopped recently.

"Whoa, whoa!" I yell, retrieving my arm and rubbing my elbow. "What was that all about?"

She pushes me away from the traffic flooding from the classroom door and lowers her voice. "What was what about?" She crosses her arms, all business.

I raise my eyebrows. "The way you ignored me in there? Like, the whole class? And the way you're dragging me around by the ear?"

She sniffs and looks away. Dark bags hang below her eyes, and her Adam's apple bobs as she swallows. *Has she lost weight?*

"Seriously, what's with you?" I narrow my gaze at her.

Her jaw almost hits the floor. "What's that supposed to mean?"

"I mean . . ." I suck in a breath. Nothing about this is going to be easy. "You've been a little Jekyl and Hyde lately. And I get it, I really do." I pause, catch her gaze. "I miss him too, Aub." She looks away, her eyes glossy. "But really, sometimes you're fine. Like *more* than fine. Same old happy Aubree. Then the next minute you're Grumpy the dwarf. Or you're Miss Obsessive, like *right now*."

Wait. I'm being unfair. She has a right to be this way. Doesn't she? I step closer, as much sympathy as I can convey in my posture. "How can I help you, Aubree? What can I do for you?"

She sighs, her eyes still watery. "I . . . I don't . . . know." Swallow. "I—some days I just . . . want this to be over with, ya know? I want that stupid Unseelie prince to *pay* for what he did to Seamus. But then . . . then I think, what then? What will happen once that's done? Once he's paid for what he's done? It won't bring Seamus back, right?" She pauses, pulls in a steady breath before blowing it out again. "What will I do then?" A single tear drips down her cheek. "Who will I become?"

I've been punched in the gut.

Really and truly. Nothing could've prepared me for her words. Yet I totally get it. She's right. At least I have a purpose once this thing is over—to find a way to end my curse. But her? Seamus was like family. How will she go on?

"You—" I lick my lips. "We will get through this. And then you'll help me become . . . *unbanshee*, or whatever. And then? We'll figure it out. Okay? We can do this, Aub. I know we can. Together."

She nods, chokes on a sob, blinks away the remaining tears. "Okay." Her voice is still a whisper.

"I'm sorry I attacked you like that." I bite my lip. "It wasn't fair, and this is definitely not the place." I look around the hall and roll my eyes.

She laughs as she wipes a stray tear. "It's okay. You're a dork, but I forgive you."

I quickly give her a hug. "Okay, so tell me what that texting frenzy was about. What's going on?"

She huffs a breath. "Before I tell you, I need to tell you the bad news."

I lift my brows in panic.

"Wyatt's not the prince."

"He's not?"

"Nope." She shakes her head. "I had the chance to test him this morning. You said he's got weird-colored dreadlocks, right?"

I nod.

"Then I got the right guy. He was with a bunch of friends and one of them called his name. So I quick snagged that bottle

of lotion you laced with foxglove and squirted it on him. Good
thinking, by the way. Totally works."

I stifle a laugh. "You . . . squirted him?"

She tries to hide the fact that one side of her mouth wants
to tilt up. "Well, yeah. He wasn't happy, like, at all. But I didn't
care. Now we know."

"Yeah." I sigh in disappointment. Bummer. It would've
been so much easier just to look for him at the dance.

"Okay, next order of business," she continues. "You haven't
heard from Oliver at all? You're sure?"

"No, why?"

"What about yesterday? Did you see him when he got
back?"

My stomach drops through the floor once again, and my
hands go clammy. The words have trouble coming out, what
with the invisible sword stuck through my chest and all. "No."

Her jaw sags. "What do you mean, no? You haven't heard
from him since he left for the wedding?"

I gather my courage. "I wouldn't say that. I've *heard* from
him, just not in words." She gives me a *what* look, so I elaborate. "I got a couple of texts from him on Saturday." I pull up
the thread on Oliver's phone and hand it to her.

Her eyes go wide. The hallway around me spins, and I grab
the lockers to steady my equilibrium.

"What?" Aubree whisper-yells. "Is that really Oliver?"

I look to the side to hide the tears that beg to come out
again. "Yeah, well, pictures don't lie, right?" I sigh and grab
the phone from her. *Why am I still carrying the dumb thing around?*
But I know why. It's my pathetic excuse to keep an opening so
he might text back, that maybe he'll change his mind. That
maybe there's still hope . . .

"This totally doesn't make sense," she says, snapping me
out of my lofty dream.

"It does if he's been playing us the whole time." I shake my
head. "Playing *me*. We might want to be careful what Jerksica

prints in the school paper in the near future." Something I assume I'm no longer a part of. I swallow hard.

"I don't know. Something seems off. Doesn't sound like Oliver, but I guess we've got proof." She frowns. "Maybe it *was* all an act."

"Why does it matter where he is? Why do you want to know so badly?"

"Eric. He was asking. He said Oliver's been crazy strange since he got back. Moody, angry. He wanted to know your take on it." She glances at the phone. "Now I think we know why O is so off kilter."

My eyes pop. "Eric's his best friend. How far off the deep end did the boy fall this weekend?"

She shrugs and gives me a pitying look.

I scowl. "Is that who you were texting during class?" She nods. "Aubree! You could've gotten in trouble. Like *detention* trouble." I drag the word out. "Not been allowed to go to the dance tonight. It couldn't wait until lunch?"

She shakes her head. "Apparently not. He's been texting all morning. It sounds urgent. Something about new information he uncovered last night. He wants to see us ASAP. I told him we'd skip second to meet up with him."

The bell rings, and everyone in the hallway scatters.

I press my lips together. "I don't think that's going to be a problem, since we're already late." Nothing about school is appealing to me anymore, and the less chance I have of running into Oliver, the better.

She tucks a piece of pink hair behind her ear. "Awesome. I've got a few things to talk about, too."

Without another word, she leads us to our meeting spot. I've never been so happy for a distraction from this thing called *life*. Even if it does involve an Unseelie prince trying to destroy the world.

61

CAOINE

WE'RE in the janitor's closet. *Again.*

The scent of disinfectant is stuffed into every inch of the five-by-five space.

"Do you have a thing for cleaning or something?" I crinkle my nose as I eye the mop bucket.

Eric ignores me and holds up a book that looks oddly familiar. It's as long as his forearm and twice as thick as his palm, with pages that look like they could be a hundred years old. The front is embossed with a golden emblem of wings and maybe a snake? He flips it open, and the stench of mold invades the space.

Yep. That thing is definitely at least a hundred years old.

It's clear he's rather excited because his fae ears are out and his eyes have gone that shade of deep plum unique only to him. And his skin is now sparkling.

Aubree gasps. She's right beside him, leaning as close as possible to read the text. "This . . . this is it! *The Book of Judgment!* This is the sister copy to the book I have."

Eric's brows pull together. "You have a copy of this?"

"No, a *sister copy. The Book of Discernment.*" She stops and glances at me. "It's the reason Seamus went home so many weeks ago. He brought it back, thinking it would be important to the cause." Her gaze is melancholy as she returns it to Eric. "But neither of us could figure out which spell the Unseelie prince was using. I think that's because it's the first part. This is the second half." She leans down to glance at the spine. "Yeah. This has to be it. This is awesome, Eric. This means we might actually get some answers! I mean, look at what it says here."

I sigh. I couldn't read if I wanted to. All the letters are wonky and look like complete gibberish.

"A little help here?" I twist my head to the side to get a better look, but neither of them appear to care that I can't see.

The two are huddled like there's zero reason to have personal space. Which they should, since they've never seemed to get along before this, but, fae and all . . . I clear my throat.

"Oh!" Aubree jumps, and her cheeks go red. "Caoine, sorry. Yeah, see this here?" She points to a spot at the bottom of the page.

I cross my arms and blink. "You mean the strange faerie text I can't read?"

She opens her mouth, then closes it. "Right." She gives Eric a cringy grin.

"What is that thing, anyway?" I point at the monstrosity of the tome.

"It's pretty ancient, even for faerie years," Eric says.

I huff and give him a *no-duh* look.

He cradles the book like it's a baby. "It's been in my family for a long time, no clue how we got it. But I brought it along in case it came in handy."

I raise one eyebrow. "Let me guess . . . it's suddenly handy?"

Aubree squeaks and bounces on her toes. "So this section actually talks about magic. Like, deep faerie magic, not the typical stuff the Fair Folk can do." She's talking with her hands. "Seriously, I've never seen anything like it. I don't think my mom is even aware something like this exists."

I nod impatiently. "Yeah, yeah."

"Right, so this section goes into some serious detail about deep magic, the kind that takes like, years of practice? And guess what this spell is right here?"

"Bet you're gonna tell me," I say in a high-pitched voice to match hers.

"The Seven Deadly Sins." She looks at me pointedly.

I feel the blood drain from my face. "Wait, what?"

"Yeah, honestly?" Eric scratches his head. "I wasn't totally sold on the SDS thing when you first told me your suspicions."

SDS? I mouth to Aubree, and she mouths *Seven Deadly Sins* back.

"I mean, it made sense, yeah, but I'd never heard of any kind of magic like that until recently. So I did some digging. Turns out you two are totally right. I looked at the town records and noticed a pattern of deaths over the past twelve-ish months. There has absolutely been a pattern of the Seven Deadly Sins. And not just this one time. The cycle we're in right now is the *seventh* cycle."

"Seven of seven." Aubree gasps and covers her mouth.

Eric nods. "Exactly. The prince has taken this spell to the next level. Multiplying the required number makes the spell almost impossible to stop. A person representing each sin of the Seven Deadly Sins has died with a total of seven cycles. Seven times seven."

The room goes still as my memory is flooded with Wyatt's voice from a few short weeks ago.

"Seven is a perfect number. Biblically the number represents God. It has long been believed to show completeness and perfection. On another level, according to numerology, that is, the number seven represents the searcher of truth. Seven knows nothing is as it seems, that all is merely hidden beneath illusion."

"What did you say?"

"Illusion, Caoine. The number seven is meant to uncover that which is hidden, to seek out truth."

I blink. This is real. Eric has found the key to the Unseelie prince's magic.

"Forty-eight people have died," he continues. "We're down to the final sin in this last cycle. *Envy.*"

Aubree's brows pull tight. "Aren't there two left?"

He shakes his head. "Nope. Yesterday greed was taken care of. Some CEO of a local company was found dead in a hotel room. Turns out he'd been laundering money from the company for years and was about to be arrested by the feds. He committed suicide."

"Wait." I frown. "You found out all of that last night? How late were you up?"

"All night." He blinks at me like I should know this.

"Faeries don't sleep, Caoine. Didn't you know?" Aubree bites her lip.

My cheeks warm. "Erm, no. I love to sleep."

"Huh," is her only reply.

He nods at the book. "So I did more reading and found some interesting stuff in here. I couldn't wait to text Aubree, so we've been communicating pretty much nonstop since four a.m."

I glance at Aubree with a *what-what?* glance. She rolls her eyes and returns her attention to Eric, cheeks pink.

"This spell isn't complete, but it does give us a good idea of what to expect from the Unseelie prince."

"Meaning?" I ask.

"It talks about the SDS spell and gives the many purposes for it—one being to close a Veil for good." Aubree lifts her hands as if to say we already knew that. "But other components are optional, so the book doesn't go into much detail for those. I'll bet it's laid out better in *the Book of Discernment*, the companion book I have. Which is at home."

"Fan*tastic*." I frown. No immediate answers.

"Still, this is better than nothing." Eric is excited again, his uber-white skin sparkling even brighter. "I mean, this at least confirms what he's doing. Now we know for sure this is definitely what he wants, and he will definitely be doing the deed tonight. Aubree, maybe I can come home with you after school to compare books and work out details?"

"Wait, it gives instructions for Halloween?" I'm so confused.

"Not in so many words, exactly." Aubree shrugs. "But it supports our original thought. It says the spell must be performed on a night when the Veils are thin, which technically could apply to other nights as well. But Halloween works perfectly for what the prince needs to make this happen."

"And considering the cycles of the SDS have almost been completed seven times, we've got to assume tonight is the night." Eric looks optimistic.

A stone sinks to the pit of my stomach. Nothing about this makes me feel any better. "Okay, so what else do we know?"

"Well, one of the things the spell requires is a *sacrifice of great magnitude* from a *strong faerie.*" Aubree puts quotes around the words from the book.

"Which would be?" *Tell me again why I never learned how to read fae?*

"We're thinking the *great magnitude* thing is going to happen at the dance." Eric nods like this is a good thing.

"Excuse me?"

"The sacrifice. There won't be more of a *great magnitude* of people gathered tonight other than our very own senior Halloween dance. So . . ."

"You think princie-boy is going to make his move here? *Tonight?*"

Aubree nods.

Blood of the innocent. Blood of sinners. Blood of the firstborn. Blood of greatness.

My head spins as the words crash into my consciousness.

"Which leads to a change in plans." Eric wags his brow in my direction, and I'm yanked back to reality. "I'm staying back with you girls, at the dance." He holds up the book. "This pretty much guarantees the Unseelie prince will be at the dance until midnight. All we've got to do is spread out and figure out what he's up to, then put a stop to it. The *great magnitude* part, anyway. We'll have to figure out the rest of the spell after we stop the first part."

"Gee, that sounds easy." I avoid their gazes so they won't see me roll my eyes.

"Exactly!" Why does Aubree sound almost happy?

I attempt to keep my sigh to a minimum. "Fine. It will be *easy* finding the guy we haven't been able to find for the past six weeks. Whatever you say. What about the other part?"

"What other part?" Eric asks.

"The *strong faerie* part? We need to know who that is, don't we?"

Eric scrunches his brows. "It's you."

I blink as my heart drops out of my chest. "Huh?"

Aubree looks away, and her shoulders slump in a way that's not natural for her.

"You didn't figure that out? This whole thing revolves around *you*, Caoine. It's the reason the Unseelie prince has waited a year to enact his plan. He needed a fae strong enough to empower his spell. He needs more power than he can generate to close one Veil and open the other permanently. He only just figured out who you were a couple of weeks back, right? Now he knows for sure. Another reason why we're sure it'll be tonight. Everyone knows you're going to the dance with Oliver."

Bile crawls up my throat, but I swallow it, take a deep breath. "Okay, whoa." I wave my hands and shake my head again. "Back up. *I'm* the strong fae? I'm not even *full faerie!* I'm part human, for Pete's sake! How can I be the 'strong one'?" Now I'm air quoting. Ugh.

"So?" Eric looks truly perplexed. "You're a banshee. Do you think those are a dime a dozen?"

I shrug as my jaw drops open. *I don't actually know any other banshees. How would I know?* I pin Aubree with a look. "Is this why you said banshees aren't faeries to mess around with?"

She continues to avoid my gaze. *Is she blushing?*

Eric saves her from my inquisition. "Banshees are a rarity. There are almost none found in Faerie, since they're bound to earth. They're the loneliest of fae, always working alone, unable to hold long-term relationships. With other Fair Folk, anyway. Couple that with the fact you predicted Seamus's death—which is insane, BTW—and yeah, you don't mess with banshees. End of story."

I gasp. Aubree freezes out of the corner of my eye.

"What did you just say?" I whisper.

Eric looks uncomfortable now. "Um, Seamus?" He eyes Aubree with care. "You predicted his death, right?"

I nod.

"Well, that never happens."

"What do you mean, that never happens?"

"Exactly what I said. It doesn't happen. Banshees are sent to earth to predict *human* death. To help humans mourn the loss of their loved ones and help those who are about to move on to another life. There are very few times in history a banshee has predicted the death of a fellow faerie, and those were extreme circumstances. You've got to be a pretty powerful faerie to predict the death of another fae, Caoine."

"Why didn't you tell me?" I turn toward Aubree.

She shrugs but still avoids my gaze. A wash of guilt spreads down my spine, across my arms, touching my toes. *This is why she was absent for so long.* She was morning the death of Seamus, sure, but . . . she also didn't want to face me. *She does think I was the cause of his death.*

Because I'm a bigger monster than I thought I was. I killed Seamus.

My best friend is afraid of me, probably terrified I'll one day predict *her* death.

Pain stabs my belly, and I resist doubling over. Instead, I pull my chin up and set my jaw. "Fine. I'm the strong faerie he wants. Why would he think anyone at the dance would be a sacrifice to me?"

"Easy," Eric says. "You've never had a friend before you moved here, right? This is the first time you've ever made attachments . . . grown close to anybody. He wants to take away the first bit of peace you've ever had. He wants to destroy everything good that belongs to you.

"He's going to kill the entire senior class."

SIX HOURS. I have less than six hours until the dance. Just a few hours until the Unseelie prince will unleash—what? *Wrath? Vengeance?* And how will he do it? Poison in the punch bowl? How will he kill an entire group of people at once?

I duck my head as I go to my locker after the last bell of the day. Suddenly the past two months feel more like two years. Nothing about any of the other schools I attended or other classmates I had even register in my brain. It's like I've lived here my entire life, and every minute of it culminates in just a few short hours. My stomach is tied in more knots than a sailor might use.

And what of this nonsense that I might be some sort of special faerie? That's the one point I want to fight Eric on the most—

"Caoine!"

Someone yanks on my shoulder, and I spin around. I'm leaning against my locker, books in my arms—which I almost drop right on my feet. I foible to keep them together but lose my balance even more when I see who accosted me.

Auburn hair frames an all-too-familiar face, complete with full lips tilted in a frown, azure eyes narrowed in my direction.

"Have you seen Oliver?" Jessica demands.

"I—no, I—" My jaw falls.

"Where is he?" Her tone has drawn the attention of at least twenty people around us.

I avert my gaze to her feet. "Why would I know? Go ask Eric." *Isn't he with you?* The blood in my veins begins to boil, and I curse the heat invading my face and neck.

"Just checking." She lowers her voice. She lifts her chin and looks down the hallway like nothing I say could possibly be important. "I mean, of course he would find me first and all . . . I just can't figure out why he hasn't." Her pout becomes even poutier.

My eyes raise to hers. "You haven't heard from him?"

She clears her throat and pinches her lips. "Well, no." Her stance looks unsure. "I mean, I saw him yesterday when we got back in town, after the wedding and all." Now her lips hold a smirk. "I'm just curious why I haven't seen him in school today. Or why he hasn't texted me."

Is it possible? Can it be that Oliver regrets getting back together with Jessica? That maybe his skip today isn't as much to avoid me as it is to avoid her? My heart rate picks up massive amounts of speed. "I could text him if you—"

"No!" she practically shouts, then clears her throat again. "No. That won't be necessary." Pause. "Under the circumstances, it's probably best if you don't." Her smug smile is back. "Considering how awkward it might make things."

The same heat has now invaded my chest, threatens to jump right out and uppercut Jerksica's perfect chin. I pull in a slow breath. *Fine.* We'll see how it plays out. Maybe he is having second thoughts, or maybe he just realizes what an idiot he is for getting back together with a crazy girl.

"Sorry I can't help," I say, even though I'm *so* not sorry.

She makes a face like she smells something rotten. "Yes, well. If you see him, tell him to call me right away."

Sure. I'll get right on that. "M'kay." My smile is as fake as I can muster.

Jessica sniffs and struts away. I finally exhale, and my heart rate considers the possibility of slowing down.

Well, that's that, then. My first encounter with enemy number one is out of the way, and I didn't melt down or cry like a toddler in the middle of the hallway. *Yay me.* I deserve a freaking medal.

I lower my head and get back to my locker. Is it possible after this is all over, I'll be able to stop my banshee curse? That maybe I can be a normal teenager for the first time in my life? One who can date any guy she chooses, not just the ones who take pity on her?

Oliver's face flashes in my mind, and pain pricks my core as I blink away tears.

I bite my lip and glance back to watch Jessica walk away. Will I see Oliver before Jessica does? And will he even show up to the dance tonight?

I swallow. What scares me more, though, is whether we'll be alive before this night is over, or if the prince will claim us all as victims to add to his list of names.

63

CAOINE

THE VIBRATION of a bass line echoes through my core and pounds against my eardrums. Music so loud it could split an atom bounces off the high ceiling of the school gym. The lights are low, and multiple disco balls hang from the rafters, scattering reflections across the floor, along sweaty bodies, into the depths of my soul.

I swallow and feel for the wall behind me. The senior class Halloween dance is definitely the last place I want to be right now. *Happy Birthday to me.*

Costumed bodies press against one another, bump, grind. I honestly don't understand how so many teenagers can be this touchy-feely without the interference of an adult. My fake wings dig into my back, and I stand another inch straighter. I glance at my bare legs, at the way my lime skirt hits my upper thigh, the remainder of my dress basically a glorified leotard with sequins. Maybe this costume wasn't the best choice for tonight. One thing I have going for me—glitter. I've literally covered every millimeter of my skin with the stuff.

"A faerie, Caoine?" Aubree sidles up beside me where I keep the wall from falling down. "How very . . . cliché." She raises her brows.

I roll my eyes with a laugh. "And dressing as the devil isn't?"

She shrugs, her pointy horns jiggling from the motion. If I thought my costume was revealing, hers is much more so, especially with her height. Dressed in a full-body fire-engine red leo, she shifts and the entire thing sparkles, a long tail peeking out from the back. In her hand is a pitchfork. No lie. A bona fide pitchfork with the words *"Who's your baddie?"* on the handle. She glances around the room.

"So what are we looking for exactly?"

"No clue." I clench my hands and focus on breathing.

She watches the crowd as they dance. "The Unseelie prince is somewhere in here. We've got to figure out who he is or what he's doing, *soon*. We don't have much time left."

I glance at the clock that hangs behind the basketball net, a black iron grid protecting it from stray balls. *Ten forty-five.* "Where's Eric, anyway?"

"Said he wanted to do a perimeter check."

I fan myself and scrunch my nose. "Well, he'd better get back quick. It's so stinking hot in here. When can we leave?" I'm suddenly thankful for the lack of costume I'd just been questioning.

Two teachers who are clearly not even a little bit concerned with the exotic dancing going on walk by and settle at the door just to our left.

"I just found it open again," the woman with glasses says. "That's the second time this week. Not to mention how many other times it's been broken into over the past month. We need to find out who it is and why they're taking items from the science department storage closet."

"Has it always been ingredients for experiments?" the dark-haired teacher asks.

"Yes, always. You'd think they'd try to nick something of value to resell. But powders and liquids? What could they possibly need with those?"

The other woman shrugs, and they move into the hallway, their conversation fading. "I still say it has to do with some sort of drug activity . . ."

Aubree frowns.

"Ladies . . ." Eric appears out of the shadows, and I barely contain my squeal of fright.

I smack his arm. "Eric! Stop doing that! How is it you can sneak up on everyone so quietly?"

He chuckles. "Call it part of my faerie charm."

He gives me a wink. I flare my nostrils in response.

"Hey, don't hate. I'm here, aren't I?" He leans a few inches closer. "Looks like I got to take you to the dance, after all."

His breath is warm on my neck, and his smile isn't the normal happy-go-lucky jokester expression he usually wears.

My own smile drops as I flinch and glance at Aubree. I get the feeling she'd rather he said that line to her.

"I'm kidding." He socks my arm this time.

Oh. *Right.*

Still, I take a step back, survey him carefully. Old, ratty clothes. Dirt spread across his hands and neck. And a large — albeit fake — knife in his hand. Something sits on his head I can't quite make out. "And what are you supposed to be?"

"Oh." He pulls a mask from his head over his face.

"Ew." Aubree crinkles her nose. "Jason Vorhees? Really, Eric? Aren't there more recent horror icons you could've mimicked?"

He pulls the mask back up. "Hey, did you girls hear what those teachers just said?"

"Yeah, about the science closet?" I say. "So strange, right?"

Eric exhales. "I've got a suspicion I'm hoping *isn't* right. It has to do with household chemicals and things you can make in a basement with the right YouTube videos."

"Wait . . . you don't mean — " Aubree's face falls.

He nods and looks at me. "Now that I think about it, I heard the principle ranting in her office a few weeks back.

About the same exact issue. Except she named what was taken." His eyes darken. "Separately, the items are just regular things you'd find in a science lab. Together, though . . ."

"Boom?" Aubree whispers.

He nods again.

My jaw drops. "You think the Unseelie prince built a *bomb*?"

Eric steps closer and waves for us to be quiet. He lowers his voice. "It's possible. Think about it. It makes perfect sense. A *sacrifice of great magnitude*? How else would he take out so many people at the same time?"

My heart races like it's headed to Neverland. "Well, we need to tell someone!" I whisper-yell. "A teacher, or maybe we just call the police?"

Aubree shakes her head. "No, Caoine. That won't work. We can't let the prince know we're on to him. We need to make it look like we have no clue what he's about to do."

All feeling leaves my hands and toes, my eyes wide. "So what do you propose we do? *Die?*"

Eric glances around the room. "It's got to be somewhere in here. He'll want to be sure as many people are, uh, hit, as possible. So it must be close."

"Great. Very reassuring." I huff and my eyes throw daggers at Aubree. Why isn't she more upset about this?

"We split up," Eric says. "Each of us takes a corner, and we'll meet in the far one. Not many places he could've hidden it, right? I'm guessing no one's noticed it because the lights are so low and no one knows to look for it. It's possible some unfortunate soul is sitting right on top of it."

I blink in horror. "Fine. Let's go. I don't want to be in this building any longer than I need to be." And I'm not ready for *anyone* to die, let alone multitudes.

"Cool." Eric begins to pull his mask in place but stops to say one more thing. "Oh, and if you find it? Do me a favor. Don't touch it."

64

CAOINE

Oliver still isn't at the dance.

As I peruse the outside of the room, checking beneath tables and chairs and peeking up at windowsills, I still can't spot him. I haven't seen him all night. My skin grows cold. But *why?*

Did he decide to skip the dance so he wouldn't see me? Maybe to sneak off with Jessica for a snog-fest? Or maybe my earlier assumption was correct. He changed his mind about her and is afraid to face us both?

And *why* can't I get over this? Why can't I just accept my life will remain the way it always has? *Alone. Safe.* It's always been safer for me to be alone. That's what I've always believed. And isn't it better he's not here? When a bomb could go off at any moment and turn the entire senior class into nothingness?

My chest tightens, and I close my eyes. *Breathe. We'll find it.*

I shuffle behind a table and hear whispers from a group of three girls at the next table over. Out of the corner of my eye, I glance at them. They're all looking at me, smug smiles hidden somewhere beneath their Wonder Woman and Black Widow and Scarlet Witch costumes. *Oh, how original.* The three Queen

Bees decided to dress as superheroes. Nice. At least some things haven't changed from school to school.

The bracelet that dangles from my wrist clinks together, and on a whim, I unhook it and allow it to fall to the ground. I drop to my knees to pretend to look for it. Partly to search for the freaking scary bomb that just might kill us all and partly to get out of sight of the Mean Girl squad. A quick check underneath the table produces nothing unusual—again.

And this completes the end of my side of the wall and corner of the room. I have no choice but to head to the spot where Eric told us to meet.

With a sigh, I come to my feet, refastening the bracelet.

And then my heart stops.

Jessica is standing ten feet away. Dressed as a sexy vampire. Ironic, considering the way she sucks the life out of all that is good and holy. She doesn't look happy. A glass of punch sloshes in her hand. *Have they spiked the punch bowl?* Every five seconds she glances at her phone as if expecting a text. She looks my way, and our eyes meet. Crap. *Look away, look away, look away!* She frowns and disappears into the crowd.

Wait, what? I was so sure she was about to attack me again.

I run after her into the throng of people as they dance—if you can call it that. I fight through and have to divert myself from some guys who try to sandwich me, twice. Do they not see my wings? How would that even work? The entire time I'm looking for her, my mind is racing.

She's not here with Oliver? If he didn't come with her, then where could he be? And why would she bother to come to the dance alone?

I break free to the other side of the dance floor, but I've lost her. *Crud!* Then a flash of black to my left, which disappears into the hallway. I take two steps.

"Caoine!" Aubree all but jumps me before I can make it to the door.

"Guh—" is all I have time to get out before she grabs my arm and yanks. Really. Hard.

"Come on! I have something important to show you!"

"But—but—" I glance over my shoulder at the door Jerksica went through, but I don't see her anymore.

"There's no time. I found something. *Big.*"

I'm being pulled through those same bodies again, between those same guys who have a strange interest in my fairie wings . . . and what lies beneath. Gross.

"What about Eric?"

"There's no time. I haven't seen him since he left to search. But this is crazy important."

"Yeah, you said that." I try not to roll my eyes as we slip from the dance floor and into the shadows along the back wall of the gymnasium. "Okay, what's the big deal?"

She forcefully pulls me to my knees.

"Ouch!"

"Sorry." She totally doesn't look sorry. "Here, look." Aubree slides a black cloth off a large square object lodged between the wall and the bleachers.

All feeling leaves my hands and feet. "That's a—"

"Bomb, yeah." Her voice is so calm.

Why is her voice so freaking calm? "But—but—" I gag on my words.

"Relax, Jiminy Cricket. It won't go off."

"What?" I blink rapidly in confusion.

Aubree's brows are pulled together. "Something's not right."

"What do you mean?"

"Well, it's a bomb, but what I don't get is, why build a bomb you don't intend on setting it off?"

"Huh?"

"Look at the wires. None of them are properly connected. And there's no countdown device. I don't even see how it could be detonated in the first place. This thing isn't even dangerous."

"It's not?" My heart slows a tad, but my head still spins from the surge of adrenaline. "Why would the Unseelie prince go through all the trouble of stealing from the science closet just to build a bomb he'll never use?"

"I think it might be a decoy." Aubree's face has gone white, and I can see her fighting rising panic.

My stomach plummets. "What do you mean?"

"Meaning, this isn't how he's going to kill anyone. The whole thing was just one big rabbit chase." She pauses. "For us."

I fall back onto my butt like I've been sucker punched. A rabbit chase? For me?

"Of course," I whisper, tears swimming in my eyes. "He did this to throw us off so we wouldn't stop his real plan. He did it to keep us away." I slam my fist into the floor. "And we fell right into his trap!"

"You fell into a trap, little Caoine?" A slurred voice says from behind me.

I jump to my feet and spin around. *Jessica.*

"That's easy for you to do. You're predictable. You're easy to trick."

She's got a new glass of punch, cheeks pink, clearly unsteady. Images of my alcoholic father flit through my head. It doesn't take a genius to know this girl is drunk. Stinking drunk.

"Not now, Jessica. I've got more important things on my mind." I attempt to push past her but only succeed in making her slosh more of her drink onto the floor.

Aubree slowly stands but stays in her spot, her arms crossed uncomfortably across her chest.

"Oh, whatever, Caoine," Jessica sneers. "Go ahead and gloat, will ya? You won. Okay? There. I said it. You won. Are you happy now?"

I throw my hands up in disbelief. *Is this really happening right now?* "Seriously Jessica? I have no idea what you're talking about, nor do I care. I really don't have ti—"

"Oh shut up." For the first time since I've known her, Jessica actually loses her cool. "You can stop the purity act, Caoine. I know. All about you and Oliver."

"What?" I glance at Aubree, but she's still frozen.

"Look, I get it. I thought I could break you two up, but it didn't work. Fine. But you don't need to pretend like you aren't together."

My jaw drops.

She steps closer, eyes narrowed. "I tried my best, Caoine. Those pictures? Ha! I thought they were genius! Really, I did. My cousin assured me they'd be foolproof. That you'd never be able to tell. All that time Oliver was curled up all alone in his hotel room, and I assumed you were actually buying my little cheating-boyfriend act. But I guess not. I guess you saw right through it, didn't you? I stole his stupid cell for no reason."

"What?" My mouth is still open in the most annoying way. But I can't get it to close. Just like I can't find any other words to say.

She shakes her head. "Just stop pretending, okay? I get it. You two are together. You don't need to hide your romance from me. You're not hurting anyone but yourselves."

Aubree finally speaks. "So you and Oliver didn't get back together at the wedding?"

Jessica turns to her, surprised to find we aren't alone. "Of course not. Oliver hasn't been mine for a while. I know that." She turns and gives me a faltering smile. "But I had to try, right? I had to give it One. Last. Try."

"But I don't understand," I say. "Why would you think we're back together? I mean, I haven't seen him since he got back from the wedding."

"Oh, haven't you?" She furrows her brow like she's trying

to remember something. "Funny. I just saw him, outside. You don't need to lie anymore, Caoine."

"You did?" I practically shout in her face.

She winces. "Yes, of course. He was with Eric . . . sitting in Eric's car. Actually, sleeping in Eric's car, to be exact. It looked like they were about to go somewhere."

"Eric?" Aubree says quietly from the corner.

"Anyway, enjoy your dance, Caoine. Just figured I'd officially congratulate you before I finish off that stupid punch bowl." She saunters off, not at all in a straight line.

I swallow, blink, think, agonize at the new information she's given me. "Aubree?" I say very, very softly. "Who's idea was it the *sacrifice of great multitude* would be the senior class?"

"Eric's," she squeaks.

Previous conversations come flooding back to me all at once. "And the night Seamus died? Did you ever tell Eric outright that I sang my song? That my banshee actually sang before Seamus died?"

"No." Her voice is still a whisper.

The room tilts, and ghostly images dance across my vision. It's no longer hot in here, but cold. Very, very cold. My entire body is covered in chills.

"Caoine?" Her voice is hoarse now. "Remember how I said *the Book of Discernment* had been in my family for generations? A *royal* family? Didn't Eric say the same thing about his copy? That it had been in his family?" She swallows. "How much did he tell you about them?"

It's my turn to shake my head. *Only royalty can come through the Veils.* I lean against a nearby table. Aubree and I make eye contact.

She knows.

I know.

Neither of us want to say it out loud.

"And how is the prince going to make a *sacrifice of great magnitude?*" Aubree asks with a shaky voice.

Blood of the innocent. Blood of sinners. Blood of the firstborn. Blood of greatness.

Greatness. Great magnitude.

My heart bursts into a million pieces, a million different fragments. So many tiny pieces, there is no possible way I will ever be able to put it together again. Just like Humpty Dumpty and his stupid shell.

I am fractured.

I am broken.

I.

Am.

Nothing.

I know what the Unseelie prince has planned. And it most definitely is a sacrifice of *great magnitude* meant only for me.

Only for me.

Only for me.

He knows who I am, and *he knows me*. He knows my deep, dark secrets even if I'm not willing to admit them to myself. No matter how hard I try, I can't fool my heart into believing I'm not in love with Oliver. And I can't fool the prince, either.

Eric.

Eric is the Unseelie prince.

Eric has Oliver.

"I know what he's going to do," I whisper. My vision goes blurry, and something warm and wet trickles down my cheeks. "He's taken Oliver. He's going to sacrifice Oliver."

65

CAOINE

MY LEGS BURN like they're on fire. Flames lick up my thighs; hot coals simmer along the base of each calf. I try to breathe, but there is no air. No air. Noairnoairnoairnoairnoair.

I blink away tears and plead with my heart to stop beating through my skin, soaking me with grief and shame and conviction times a thousand. It's time I faced the truth.

I love him. I love Oliver as I've never loved another human being, ever.

And I can't lose him now. I. Can. Not.

Aubree sprints beside me, although I'm definitely in the lead. Raw emotion pushes me forward, demands I not give up. That I ignore the way every molecule in my body wants to explode, to punish me for missing the most obvious thing ever. How could I assume Oliver was avoiding me? He's the strongest person I know. Of course he would've been at school. Even if it was to break up with me. I'm such an idiot.

"It's not too late! We'll get there in time, Caoine," Aubree yells between pants.

We're headed to the woods behind the school. As soon as the puzzle fell into place, I fled, pounded across the soccer field toward that nice even line of green.

"Caoine!" A voice echoes from the sidelines, and I stop mid-run, spin on my heel.

"Dad?" I squint at the figure racing toward me. My dad. My dad is totally running like a marathon runner right at me. "Dad, what are you doing here?"

He gasps and bends at the waist, one hand on his knee, the other holding a lump of cloth.

Only it's not any old cloth. It's my cloak.

My cloak!

How did I forget my banshee song? In the flurry of activity and my quest to stop the prince, I forgot my banshee scream could come out at any second. My heart pounds against my chest as if to punish me for stupidity. What if I screamed during the dance? Inside the building?

A chill runs along my arms, and I gladly take the proffered gift. "Thanks, Dad. But you didn't need to bring it all the way out here." Lie. He totally did.

He simply nods and tries to catch his breath. Our conversation from the day before floods my mind. I told him about my experiment a few nights before, how I tried to keep my hood up, how his idea still didn't work. How there was just no way for this stupid cloak to change the way my curse worked.

"Where're you headed?" he asks.

"Oh, um . . ." I clear my throat. "I—we—"

"There's a party," Aubree chimes in. "On the hill behind the trees. A few of the seniors wanted to make the night memorable." She gives my dad a wobbly grin.

"Yeah, a party." I swallow. "No worries. No underage drinking, I promise."

"You're going to a party?" He does a terrible job hiding his shock.

"I'm making friends. That's what you wanted, right?"

"Yeah, but . . . why are you in such a hurry?"

"I—we're late. I'll explain later, okay? Thanks for bringing this. You're a life saver!"

I throw a kiss on his cheek and begin to take off, but he grabs my arm. "Wait, Caoine. About your cloak . . . we need to talk."

"I can't right now, Dad. Can we talk later?" I eye Aubree, who's practically bouncing on her toes. Oliver could freaking be dead at this point!

"Caoine, you need to know, I think I understand now. How your gift works."

My curse? That's what this was about? "Dad, really. You can tell me later tonight. But I've got to get up there or—" My mouth flaps open, my panicked gaze on Aubree.

"They're waiting on her," she says. "Everyone's waiting for Caoine. We've got to run, Mr. Roberts. It was nice seeing you!"

I leave my dad behind.

A pang of emotion tugs at my heart, but I immediately squash it. I have no idea how this whole thing will go down. That might have been the last time he sees his daughter alive. I grit my teeth. That *so* is not happening.

I'll get through this, then I'll talk to him. First thing.

He yells what I assume is a goodbye. I don't know, and I can't think about that at the moment. All the emotion of the last few minutes rushes back into my chest like a tidal wave. Fear, confusion, determination. Anger.

We're not too late. We will save Oliver. He will be just fine.

I blink away tears, bite the inside of my cheek until I taste blood.

I'm real. This is real. I'm going to save Oliver. I will. I will. Everything will be just fine. He can't be dead yet.

HE'S NOT DEAD.

We break through the edge of the tree line, and I hurdle a small bush to keep momentum. Thick emotion closes my throat, and I fight the vomit that floats along the back of my throat. This is not the time to lose my supper. A branch pops out of nowhere and *thwaps* me on the forehead. Heat rages across my skin, blood trickles along my temple.

Please don't do something stupid like turn an ankle!

"Caoine," Aubree stutters. "Slow down."

No. No way. I'm not going to stop. Not ever. I will run until I wrap my fingers around that stupid freaking Eric's throat and squeeze as tightly as I can. How dare he mess with my boyfriend? How dare he mess with me!

My wing snags on a branch, and a distinct tearing noise fills the deadly quiet of the night. A forceful tug yanks along one shoulder, but I don't stop. I lost a wing. Big deal. So I'm a wingless faerie. What else is new?

"Caoine!" Aubree finally catches me, one hand on my arm.

I'm shaking and convulsing and on the edge of a nuclear meltdown. "Aubree, let me go!" I don't bother to keep my voice low.

She presses one hand across my mouth and leans close, eyes frantically looking around. "Will you shut up? We need to slow down. The clearing is just ahead. If we can give an element of surprise, it might work in our favor."

"I don't care. He's got Oliver. He could be hurting him right now—"

"Shh! No, he won't. Oliver's alive."

"How do you know that?" My voice is finally low enough not to attract the attention of every woodland creature.

"Because he needs Oliver for the spell. The one that needs to happen when the Veils are thinnest. That won't happen until exactly midnight. We've got some time yet."

I stop. My breaths come in gasps, but at least I'm standing still. "I'm listening."

Aubree steps back. "Okay. Since we've got some time, let's plan this thing out. He probably doesn't think we're coming, right? Not yet anyway. I'm guessing he thinks that decoy will take a bit more time than it did. And he has no way of knowing we've figured out he has Oliver. Plus, I have a plan."

For the first time since inside the building I look at her, like really look at her. She's just as flushed as I am. Her horns are completely gone, along with her tail. And her tights have rips all along the legs. Her gaze is soft. Melancholy.

Hopeful.

"I figured we needed a backup plan, just in case things didn't go our way," she says. "I prepared for it this weekend." She bites her lip. "And I sort of didn't tell anyone, not even Eric." A breeze flutters her hair, and she pushes it aside. "I don't know why, but somehow I knew—I had a feeling I needed to keep this part secret. That this was meant only for me. Until now."

"What is it?"

She glances to the side, her look unsure. Scared. "I can't tell you. Not yet. If Eric questions you, I don't want you to have any information that might give it away. Otherwise, it might not work."

Really? We're doing the secret thing again? Ugh. "Fine. When do we get in there?"

She clears her throat and glances around warily once more. "That's the thing, see. Part of the plan is . . . well, I'm not going into the clearing. Not yet."

"I don't understand."

"It's you, Caoine. You're the one Eric wants. You're the one who has to face him. Alone. You're going into that clearing all by yourself."

66

CAOINE

I STEP through a set of trees. Moonlight bathes the grass before me, not a cloud in the night sky. The air drops ten degrees. My bare legs and arms scream in protest as I move forward, heart pounding in my chest.

Everything is silent. Not a creature moves or calls or even breathes. A sharp scent of moss attacks my senses as I climb the short hill. My hands go numb, but my armpits choose this moment to overdo the sweat thing. *Fantastic.*

At the top are two figures. The first is hunched over, on his knees, a cloth tied around his mouth, hands tied in front of him. Moonlight reflects off his dark skin. *Oliver!* I gasp and stop mid-step. We make eye contact. Guilt floods my core.

I never told him. Never clued him in to the fact his best friend is a faerie. A psycho faerie far more dangerous than I ever was. I bite my cheek.

I step forward. Only a few more steps until I reach my mark, the exact spot where I'm supposed to stop. Aubree was very specific about where to stop. Her words echo inside my head. *Don't step past the spot where the double rocks sit side by side. If you do, I won't be able to save you from danger.* Yeah. Whatever that means.

Chills cover every inch of my skin, and I swear the air becomes so thin, it's impossible to breathe. I close my eyes, gather my courage —

"Happy birthday, Caoine," a deep voice says. "Figured out my little trick, did you?"

My eyes fly open. "Eric." The word falls from my mouth like lead.

His pasty-white skin glitters from the natural light. Plum-colored eyes almost glow in the night, focused on me. Sharp ears poke out from under this hair, a red muted to an almost brown. Is this his natural color or has he given up only part of his glamour?

He chuckles. "Finally getting your memory back?" He clucks his tongue and crosses his arms. "Too bad you couldn't remember a little sooner. In fact, you don't even remember all the times I used that little trick on you."

I frown but stay silent.

"I thought I royally screwed up, that one night weeks ago, when you were singing outside the house of that adulterer. You saw me hiding in the bushes. But in your trance you couldn't quite comprehend what you saw, I guess. Luckily your dad didn't spot me, and I was able to toss that memory charm your way before school the next day. It's good for me my little spell worked, huh? And on the faeries, too." He looks around. "Where's our one remaining friend?"

My fists curl tight at his unspoken reference to Seamus's death. "Let Oliver go, Eric. Stop messing around. This has nothing to do with him." My voice is ragged. Every part of me just wants to leap into that clearing and take him down. But Aubree told me to wait.

I have to wait.

"Oh, I'm not messing around, sister. I'm pretty sure you know exactly what I have planned tonight, and let me reassure you, there will be no stopping what I want to do."

"I don't understand." My voice is small. Too small. "You said faeries can't lie. You lied, Eric!"

He flinches in mock surprise. *"Moi?* Whatever do you mean, Caoine?" His voice goes icy. "I never lied. Told a few half-truths, maybe. Spoke of myself in the third person, sure. But lying? Not a chance, love."

Oliver tries to talk through his gag, but Eric slaps the back of his head.

I grind my teeth so hard I think they're going to crack. "The cycle's not complete, Eric. You said so yourself. There's still one sin left—envy. Oliver may be my *great sacrifice*, but no one's here to fill the seventh sin."

Eric chuckles. Actually, honest-to-God gives an evil chuckle. Like from a movie. I vomit a little in my mouth but keep a stoic face.

"What? You don't think envy is represented here, Caoine?" His eyes suddenly flash. "Envy is *me*, Caoine. Me!"

I narrow my eyes but stay silent.

And there's that stupid chuckle again. *Why can't he decide if he's happy or angry?*

"The envy comes from *me*. Because of *you*." He sucks in a breath. "Why couldn't you just *see*, Caoine? See how much I like you? I gave you a chance. More than one. What's so wrong with me? What does this idiot have that I don't?"

He looks at me with puppy-dog eyes and—*is that a tear in the corner of one?*

"Please, Caoine. You have to see. This was always about you. You and me. Can't you see that?"

I nibble my lip. Something is off. This isn't right. "You're lying. You're not the final sin. The spell wouldn't work that way. You're just trying to play the sympathy card. There's no way you're the final sin in the cycle."

His jaw hardens, nostrils flared. "Fine. Don't believe me. But you also can't be that stupid, Caoine." He practically spits my name. "I mean, give me a break. Have you not seen how envious Oliver is of his brother? How he would do anything to take his *dead* brother's place?" Eric tilts his head and looks down at the friend he betrayed. "If only he could get the love he wanted from mommy and daddy. Life would be so much better, wouldn't it?"

Oliver struggles once more beneath the ropes, curses muffled behind the gag. Eric's fist crashes against the side of his head, forcing Oliver to blink several times.

"Eric! Enough!" My heart pounds so loudly I can hear nothing else.

He stops, glances me over, his expression blank now. Unreadable. "I'm actually impressed you came for this pathetic excuse of a boyfriend. After all those naughty pictures you got on his phone this weekend . . ."

"How did you know about—?"

"You think that was an accident? Come on! You have no idea how easy it was to convince Jessica that Oliver still had feelings for her. That all she had to do was manipulate things until everything fell into place. And she was more than happy when I suggested she toss a few doctored photos your way, just for the brag factor. You see, sweet Ollie here never cheated on you. Let's be honest, he couldn't. He doesn't have the guts for it. He's pathetic."

I narrow my eyes. "You put her up to that?"

"Of course!"

"Why?" A knot forms in my throat, and I can't swallow around it.

"Why?" He steps toward me, anger in his voice. "Because, Caoine, even I could tell your true feelings for him. Everyone could! It just made this whole thing all the sweeter to watch your heart get broken twice. Once when you lost him to Jessica, the other when you watch him die."

I blink back tears and dig my nails deeper into my palms.

"Aw, come on, Caoine. Don't you have any last words for Oliver here? A little, *I love you? I'll think of you always?* No?"

Oliver freezes, and our gazes meet.

Heat rises throughout my entire body. "Shut up, Eric. It's too late anyway. I'm here. I won't let you finish the spell."

"The spell?" He reaches behind him and pulls a knife longer than my forearm from somewhere. Where was he hiding that?

I fight to keep my eyes from going as round as the moon above.

"You mean, the one where I complete the final sin in the cycle *and* kill the one you love, making this spell ten times stronger than it would have been? Um, yeah. I think I will, actually." He holds the blade along Oliver's throat, jerking his head back with the other hand.

I gasp.

"Oh, don't worry, mutt. You've got a few more minutes to see his lovely face. I won't be pulling this knife along his jugular until the stroke of midnight. That's when those Veils will be the thinnest, after all."

I squint behind him and finally see the faint outline of two rectangles, one on either side. A soft pulse vibrates from each, and all the vegetation on the opposite side of them is blurred.

"But I am going to do it right here, right in this spot. Oliver's blood will need to flow fast and free into the earth at my feet. Feeding it. Embracing it." Eric closes his eyes with a grin. "Giving his very essence as a sacrifice to our worlds." He opens them again and looks at Oliver. "Thanks for that, by the way. You really are my best friend."

Anger flares in my belly. "How could you? He's always been loyal to you!"

He laughs. "You think I care about that? I'm the son of the Unseelie king! What would I care about human loyalty?"

"Fairies can feel," I whisper. "I know they can. Even about humans."

He sucks in a quick breath, his grip on the knife a little

tighter. It trembles and drops a few inches from its spot on Oliver's throat. I relax a notch.

"I know fairies can feel, *Caoine*." His nostrils flare. "I feel." He pauses, but I don't speak. "I feel, Caoine. I care. I care very much about . . . some."

This is good. He's talking. Distraction is good.

"Who? Who could you possibly care about?" I ask.

Eric visibly clenches his jaw. "My father, first and fore-most." He stops and shakes his head. "Do you even know, Caoine? Can you possibly *know* what I've been through to get here?" He's yelling now. "My mother was a nobody! A pathetic servant at the palace. Nothing going for her . . . until she caught my father's eye. He alone cared for her, nurtured her. But then she got pregnant, and he had no choice but to banish her, to force her to leave the kingdom so the queen wouldn't find out.

"But she didn't. She hid in the woods. With me. Carved out a life for the two of us, as deplorable as it might have been."

Eric closes his eyes and holds the blade against his fore-head, a dangerous grin in place. "See, my childhood was the *worst*, Caoine. Literally. The. Worst." His eyes fly open. "You think you had it bad? Try having to hide from every faerie *ever*! The only companion I ever had was my mother. My pitiful mother!" He composes himself. "But I only needed time, isn't that right, Caoine? Just a little time to figure out who I was. Who I *am*."

He smiles at me, that ridiculous blade once again inches from Oliver's dark skin.

"Who are you, really?" My voice shakes.

"Why, the Unseelie prince, of course." He almost chuckles. "A few years ago my father came to find me. He found out my mother's transgression, and when he learned he had a son, he was elated. He was overjoyed to welcome me into his family. Me. An Unseelie prince!"

"Why would he want to find you when he sent your mother—?"

"Because he loves me!" Eric explodes.

I flinch. He swallows.

"I mean, he still couldn't bring me to the castle to be with his other sons, since the queen would just kill me. But he came for me. Isn't that enough? Don't you see he cares for me?" Eric looks like a child now, his question for me real.

"That's not the way I heard it," a voice says from the darkness.

Aubree steps from the shadows, shoulders straight, a triumphant look in place.

Eric flashes me a look. "I thought you cared enough about me to come alone."

67

CAOINE

I BLINK. Why would I care about Eric?

His gaze diverts to Aubree. Her skin reflects a bluish hue in the moonlight, her eyes matching their intensity, an unnatural cerulean. Her face is serene. She walks to the opposite side of the circle, flanking me. A breeze picks up, and suddenly all that angered heat I felt toward the Unseelie prince is blown away. Ice forms at my core, and I corner him with my gaze.

Two are stronger than one.

I glance down to be sure I haven't crossed whatever imaginary line Aubree warned me about.

"Are you sure Daddy really cares for you so much, Eric?" Aubree's voice is like iron. "Why wouldn't he just ask one of his other sons? Oh, that's right. He did. None of them agreed with his little plan."

Eric's face melts into pure hatred.

Aubree turns to me. "Raghnall tried to do this once before, isn't that right, Eric?" She glances at him. "But his first attempt failed. Colossally. All because of those pesky Laws of Necessity." Eric growls under his breath, but she ignores him. "It's one reason he so badly needs you to be part of the spell."

"Me?" I look between her and Eric. His jaw is flexing overtime.

She nods. "I wasn't sure until just now, when he revealed who he really was. But now I know for sure. Caoine is the result of Raghnall's failure, isn't she, Eric?"

I gasp.

"*King* Raghnall." Eric oozes evil. "Be careful how you tread, insignificant one."

She laughs. "I'm the insignificant one? What about you?"

"My father *chose* me!"

"Did he though? Or did all of his other sons just refuse to do the deed because of how badly it failed before? None of them wanted to be a part of the plan this time around, huh? In fact, no one in the *kingdom* would go along with his plan to open the Unseelie Veil. So he had no choice but to find you. He knew you'd be willing to help him. He used you."

"You don't know what you're talking about. Shut up!"

"Don't I, though?" Aubree has lost her smug smile and has joined the yelling match. "Tell her, Eric! Tell her what you did to your mother. How you abandoned her, betrayed her, just to please a man who never loved you."

"He loves me!" Eric is pointing the knife in her direction now. Oliver groans as Eric digs his fingers into his neck.

"You betrayed the only person who ever loved you for a false love. Isn't that right?"

"I know love!" he explodes. "I love her!"

My vision goes dark before it refocuses on the sight before me. Eric is pointing at me. He's looking at me.

He loves me?

Visions of words on green paper, a tidy script, declaring words of affirmation, sift through my mind. He loves me. Thunder pounds my eardrums. How can he love me?

His face crumbles, and the moonlight glints against the wet of his eyes. "Don't you see, Caoine? Can't you see? I was hoping you'd remember me. That you'd know me from all the other schools."

"Other schools?" My voice is small. So small.

"I've been there for you, Caoine. Always. I'm the one who's always been by your side. Not him." He points dangerously close to Oliver's neck with the blade. "Although, I had to change my appearance so you wouldn't get suspicious. But I always thought you knew it was me. That you knew how much I cared."

"What are you talking about?" Somehow my voice is steady.

"My father asked me to trail you a few years back. He needed you to be part of the spell, so he wanted to track you until the time was right. And I did. I tracked you perfectly. I did everything he asked me to do."

"Until you fell in love with her?" Aubree says. "That was never part of the plan, though, was it?"

His brows yank together, and he snarls. "What does that matter, common faerie? It didn't affect my mission. If anything, it made my job even more meaningful." He looks at me now, his face soft. "To know I would wake up each day and get to see Caoine. My love."

The air around me clings to my skin, and I pull my gaze from his. How is this even possible? How could he have fallen in love with me?

"Don't you see, Caoine? We belong together. You and me. Destiny brought us together." He smiles. "There's still time. You don't need to stop me. We can do this together. There's darkness in you, I can feel it. You're just like me. If you join me, it will make the magic so much stronger than it ever could have been. My father will be so proud—"

"Join you?" I step back. "Why would I join you? You're about to kill my boyfriend!"

His gaze goes hard. "Be honest, Caoine. You never cared for him, am I right? Dating Oliver has always been a decoy to hide what you are, so the other students wouldn't know you were a banshee."

"No, Eric. I care about Oliver. I always have. I—"

"No! No! No!" He holds the knife against his head and drops Oliver to the ground. He paces back and forth as he clenches and unclenches his free hand. "That's not true, Caoine! You love me! I know you do. I've seen signs. There have been signs, all along. I've seen them." He stops and points at me. "You're going to join me. It will happen. Destiny says so!"

"Why?" I counter. "Why are you so sure destiny demands that we be together?"

"Because of who you are! Your birth." He shakes his head. "I mean, don't you even know what happened the night of your birth? Didn't your dad ever tell you?"

I lower my gaze, search my memory for anything that might solve this puzzle.

"You were supposed to die," he continues. "It was one of the Seven Deadly Sins. You were the final sin needed for my father's spell to work the first time around." His neck goes red and he scowls. "Until that stupid faerie took pity on you. She listened . . . the stupid faerie actually *listened* to your parents' pleas! What an idiot! She spared your life, and in so doing, she broke the spell, stopping Father's plan to open the Veil."

"So that's why Caoine is so powerful?" Aubree asks in astonishment.

"Which is why you needed to be here tonight." He points at me with that knife again. "Why the sacrifice must be from *you*. *I* will complete what my father couldn't before. *I* will finally earn the love I deserve. Nothing is going to stop me."

"Even though I don't love you?" I say.

He makes a face like I've slapped him. "But will you come with me? We can still do this. We can be good together."

"No one is going with you. And Oliver isn't going to die

tonight." I look to Aubree and pray she has that something special up her sleeve.

She nods. Then lifts her hands in front of her, chanting softly. Eric's eyes go wide, and he loses his grip on the knife so he has to bend to retrieve it. The wind picks up around us, and the gates behind Eric begin to glow. Whatever she's doing is working.

I blink and glance between Aubree and Eric. This is magic. Real faerie magic! Eric says something, but it's lost in the hum of the chant, in the crash of leaves tossed around by the raging wind that envelops us.

Aubree raises her hands high above her head, her voice rising. She shouts the last few words as she looks to the heavens. I'm ready to see our enemy drop dead in his spot.

Boom!

A bomb goes off in front of me, a flash so bright I'm blinded. The sound is so loud it shatters my eardrums, leaves my head buzzing, heat dripping from my ears. I'm thrown at least ten feet, landing on my back, the wind knocked from me. My head hits the ground with a crack. I see black spots.

And I hear nothing. Buzzing, groaning. *Is that me?* I blink and blink and blink. Finally things come into focus. But there's still no sound.

Aubree lies thirty feet to my right, in the same position I'm in, except it looks like she blacked out completely. She doesn't move. I swivel my head left and am met with vertigo that makes me want to vomit. In fact, I do vomit. My body can't stop the flow as it heaves up and out and onto the ground beside me. I wretch until there's nothing left, then I wretch once more. My head pounds. I wipe my mouth and look toward Eric, who's still standing as if nothing happened. His mouth moves. I hear nothing.

I climb to my feet, walk toward him. High-pitched ringing fills my ears. I put one foot in front of the other in agonizing pain. Why does my thigh hurt? What happened to my shoulder? I don't look. I might vomit again if I see blood. The ringing is louder. So loud.

I reach the spot I was told not to cross . . .

And I run into an invisible wall. Literally. It's like I'm trying to walk through glass. Nothing I do works. I'm stuck outside the circle. Panic rockets through my core, and my gaze finds Oliver. The ringing in my ears clashes like a cymbal, and I can suddenly hear again, although muffled. Soft.

Eric begins to laugh. A deep, anger-causing belly laugh. I drag my eyes from my boyfriend to my nemesis, promise myself I'll be the one to kill him.

"What? You thought I wouldn't know about your stupid plan?" He sounds like he's underwater, but I can still hear him. "You two are more dense than I thought. You tried to trick me? I don't think so! I'm the Unseelie prince. *The. One.* The one who will save *my* world, who will claim my place beside my father on the throne. Something none of my pathetic half-brothers have *ever* been able to do."

I stick a finger in one ear and wiggle. Why does my head feel like it's stuffed with cotton? "What did you do to Aubree's spell?" And why are my words slurring?

Eric snorts. "You didn't see the little runes she carved into the earth? Go ahead, look. They're all around. In a complete circle every few feet."

I look at the ground and finally see what I've been missing this entire time. Sure enough, circles are every few feet. The spots are missing grass and have some sort of symbol carved deep with a strange ink. The grass around each one looks like it was maneuvered to cover the circles, to keep them hidden. The one thing each symbol has in common is a large crack through each of them.

"See what I did, Caoine?" Eric asks. "See how I stopped you? I broke the seals! I turned her magic around so it will be used against you." Eric runs a finger along the outside of his blade with a large smile in place. "Let me spell it out for you, kid. Your little friend?" He points to Aubree with his blade. "She thought she could trap me. She used an entrapment spell to try to keep me and my magic inside this bubble. I wouldn't be able to leave the circle, and none of my magic would be able to leave, either. The only problem for you is, once I broke the seals, the magic reverses itself." He shrugs as if apologetic, even though his smile is wider than ever. "So that means neither of you can cross into my circle, and none of your magic can, either. But me? I can do whatever I want." He walks through the back of the circle to prove his point.

My heart drops to my feet. This is bad. This is very bad. Aubree's idea was a good one, but this makes things exponentially worse!

I glance in her direction. She's finally beginning to stir.

Eric looks at his watch. "Oh look. Just a few more minutes till midnight. Caoine, aren't you forgetting to do something?"

He turns his left wrist so I can see it. A tattoo is there, a dark symbol I've never seen on Eric's wrist before, probably glamoured away from prying human eyes.

The symbol is familiar. *Slavery*. His pointy teeth reflect in the moonlight as he runs his fingers across the symbol. A chill washes along my neck, makes me lightheaded.

And just like that, I have the urge to scream.

Eric.

Eric's been controlling my song in connection with the Seven Deadly Sins this entire time.

Not me.

Heat builds inside my chest, threatens to erupt, to split my body in two. The world around me swims through my tears.

Then my dad comes running from the trees.

68

CAOINE

Pressure builds inside my chest, crawls toward my throat, rips at my flesh, begging to be released. I circle my arms around my waist to hold it in, anything to keep my inner banshee from flying free.

"Dad," I breathe, barely able to speak.

He runs toward me, panic in his eyes. He knows I'm about to explode, about to let my song loose for the world to hear. I glance at the ground around me. Where did I drop my cloak? I had it in my hand until I saw Eric, but everything after that is a blur.

I swallow back my banshee scream. "How did you—?"

He shakes his head as if telling me to shut up and presses something soft into my hand. "You dropped this a dozen feet back."

With a sigh, I cling to the fabric against my chest. "But how did you find me?"

"I knew there was something off with the way you were acting. Since when have you ever been excited to go to a party?"

I squeeze my eyes shut but nod.

"I followed you."

"You followed me?" The urge to scream is painful now, red flashing lights behind my eyes. My fingers tremble as I tie the cape in place, so he reaches out to help me. "Dad, you can't be here. It isn't safe—"

"Yeah, got that," he whispers. His gaze flickers over my shoulder toward Eric. "But this is more important. I remembered something the faerie said, the night you were born. About your cloak."

"What do you—?"

But I can't finish. My song is ready to come out, and the pressure is too much for me to contain any longer. With nimble hands, my dad flips the hood in place just before my mouth opens and I fall headfirst into my song.

The melody flows free and smooth from my lips, and I delight in the way it echoes against the trees and back again. I'm vaguely aware of those around me. I can feel the way the faeries watch in awe, how Oliver has gone so still I'm not even sure if he's alive anymore. The way my dad stands calmly by my side, as he's done for me for so many years. Always faithful. True love for an ungrateful daughter.

Sound vibrates from my chest, swirls in the air around me, mixes with the scents of pine and winter and night. All the heat floods from my body, the cold like a winter blanket wrapped so tightly around me I can barely breathe. My song is short tonight. Probably because there will only be one death. And the boy is kneeling right in front of me, only minutes left in life.

I finish singing and reach up to pull my hood down. But my dad stops me.

Every ounce of energy leaves me, and I collapse into his arms. "N-no—" I need my hood off. I can't take the pain of seeing the many ways Oliver will die. *Not tonight.*

"Leave it." My dad's voice floats around me, even though I can't quite focus on where he is yet.

Oliver's face flashes behind my eyelids, and I gasp. "No!"

I'm struggling but have no idea just how much of a fight I'm giving my dad.

His face is close to mine, touching my cheek and ear. "Leave it, Caoine. You can do this. I believe in you."

"It hurts!" I scream just as another stab of pain slices my skull in half.

"Don't fight it, baby. Stop fighting it and think about something happy. Think of the happiest time of your life. Embrace your gift. Be who you are. You can do this, hon."

It's the desperation in my dad's voice that actually makes me stop. *Be who you are.* The agony is rippling across my torso now, my legs. But I stop fighting. I go limp, allow my curse to do whatever it will do. Maybe I'll be the one to die in place of Oliver tonight?

Be who you are.

As soon as I relax—fully give myself to my curse—I see his face. Oliver. Laughing with Eric, concentrating in study hall, looking at me the night of our first date. His face is all I see. Being with Oliver is the happiest I've been in my entire life. I'm thinking my happy thought.

But also, I'm not.

This is the vision. This is what the cloak wants me to see. What my curse demands I see.

The vision blurs into the face of now—swollen left eye from where Eric has punched him, gag in his mouth. Eric's knife sets against Oliver throat and he pulls.

Nooooo!

A sea of red flows from his neck and over his chest, his eyes wide and lifeless. I want to vomit again. I fight to relax, to remain calm. *Where is that other vision?*

Another image takes over. This time Oliver is in the same position, but Eric hasn't pulled the knife yet. Oliver is still alive. Eric says something—I think he's speaking to me. His eyes go wide. He hesitates. My dad jumps into view, and they both disappear into the Unseelie gate at his back.

I gasp as air returns to my lungs, as the visions fade into the ether. I haven't been in pain. Not for the last minute or two, anyway. Somewhere in my acceptance of the images, the pain stopped.

"Did you see it?" my dad whispers so only I can hear.

I yank my hood back and sit up, his arms still around me. Once more, panic slams into my chest.

He was right. My dad was right all along. I needed to leave my hood on. I had the right idea the night I tied myself to the bed—relax, think happy thoughts. But I'd forgotten my cloak. *My hood.* They need to work together for me to see an alternate future.

"Did you see any visions? That will save Oliver?" he asks again. "It worked, didn't it, Caoine? We finally figured it out. We know how your gift works." He pauses. "Tell me what to do so we can end this."

I blink. Then I shake my head. How does he know? How does he know there's a choice? I lick my lips and look at him.

My dad is asking me to choose between the boy I love and him, the only parent I've ever known. *My dad.*

He must see the fear in my eyes. His face grows solemn, then peaceful. "It's me, isn't it? I'm the only one who can save Oliver."

"No!" I grab his arms. I will not allow him to do this. *This isn't possible. There has to be another way. There must be.*

I swallow and cram the tears that threaten back inside. My gaze connects with Eric's as heat blooms deep inside my belly.

No. I cannot let this happen. I will not. No one has to die tonight. I won't allow it.

"See anything interesting?" Eric taunts. His knife scrapes against Oliver's neck, and I see a speck of red.

My stomach twists, but my boyfriend stays still, not even a flinch.

I need to bluff, to gain some time. "I saw enough. Enough

to know I'm not going to allow you to follow through with this, Eric. It's over. You've lost."

He snorts and looks around. "Um, excuse me? Have you been drinking faerie wine? You're the one who's lost, Caoine. You're trapped outside the circle. None of you can come in to stop me. And I'm here, waiting to execute your boyfriend. What about this don't you understand?"

Blood pounds in my ears, and I clench my teeth. "I will stop you, Eric. I won't let you win this time."

Eric cocks his head to the side with a pouty face. "Sore loser, are we? Don't worry, sweetheart. Give it a few more minutes, and all this will be over. Like a bad nightmare."

His eyes glint with the last words, and I lunge forward, fists balled. He throws his head back with a laugh. The fury inside me is almost too much to contain.

Fire rages throughout every single limb. I want to kill him. "If you hurt Oliver—"

"I'm sorry. Like this?" Eric slams the blunt end of the knife against Oliver's head, knocking him down.

My boyfriend grunts but rights himself just as quickly.

"Oliver! Eric, I'm going to—"

"What?" he teases. "What're you going to do, little song girl?" His gaze is as sharp as his knife. "I gave you a chance to join me, Caoine. It's not too late, you know."

"Caoine, the vision," my dad whispers from beside me.

The vision.

I feel as if I've been punched square in the stomach. All the air leaves my body, and I sag, my gaze no longer connected with Eric's. Instead it rests on my dad, those eyes I've been avoiding ever since my last vision.

That vision.

I saw something different. Something other than Oliver dying. He was right. All this time, he was right about me, about my gift. I can change things. I can save lives. Nothing is finite. Not all the deaths I predict are set in stone.

I'm not who I thought I was. I've never been that person. I've simply *chosen* to be her.

My breaths come in huffs now, ragged, unsteady. The world around me tilts, and I lock my knees to regain my balance.

Tears fill his eyes, and he nods. "I always knew this day would come, Caoine. Please let me do this."

"Dad, no!" My cheeks are warm and wet, and my heart feels like it's breaking into pieces.

"Tell me what to do, baby. I'll do it."

I shake my head again as I choke on the cry I fight to contain. "I can't let you. Not you, Daddy. It can't be you!" I look back to the Unseelie prince. "You're wrong, Eric."

He raises his eyebrows. "I'm sorry? Did you just say I'm wrong? Wrong about what? Every single thing I've said would happen has come true. What's so wrong about that?"

"About me." I lift my chin an inch higher. "Those things you said about me, you were wrong."

He narrows his eyes but stays silent.

"I'm not darkness, Eric. I never have been. I am light. I am good. I know that now." A new kind of heat fills my core, shoots down to my fingertips. "All this time I thought I was bad, thought I couldn't change my destiny. But I see now, my destiny is what I make it. I've always had a choice, Eric. A choice to be dark or light. We all have dark and light within us, Eric. It's what we decide to do with it that makes us who we are."

Eric snorts again.

"It's a choice, Eric. Maybe I won't be able to save everyone, maybe my gift isn't perfect, but it's good enough for me. Even if I can save one life, it will be good enough. I chose to be light, Eric. And you can, too. All you've got to do is put down that knife and end this madness."

He scowls now, anger rippling along his shoulders and chest. "That's easy for you to say! You're not the son of the

Unseelie king. You don't know what kind of pressure I have on my shoulders, what's expected of me. If I fail, he'll never welcome me into the family. I'll never be a prince!"

"You're right, I don't know that kind of pressure. But just because you're a prince doesn't mean you have to do what you father says. You can make your own choice, Eric. You can choose light."

"No! That's impossible. That has never been an option."

"Choosing light is always an option, Eric. Just like choosing to love. Do you really love me, Eric?"

His face crumples as he glances toward the moon. His jaw sets. "It's too late, Caoine. The spell has already been enacted." He exhales slowly, regains his composure. "I think it's time for you to sing once more, just for old time's sake." He rubs the small tattoo on his wrist.

My dad tilts his head and gives me a melancholy smile. "Let me do this, Caoine. Please."

And then I feel the overwhelming urge to open my mouth, to allow the song I've hated for so many years to spill from within, to flood the ground and soak the earth and bleed its way to Oliver. I want to sing. Again. Why is he doing this to me?

I clench my teeth together, even though I know it won't do any good. "Daddy," I whine. *No.*

"Go on, Caoine," Eric shouts. "Sing your song. You know you want to."

"No," my dad breathes. "No." His voice is stronger now.

My heart skips a beat. I know this scene. I've seen it before.

The song pushes, crushes against my chest, demands to be set free.

I fight.

And fight. And fight. And fight.

My fingers twitch to grab my dad, to stop him from what

he's about to do. But Oliver's life hangs in the balance. What choice do I make?

The scream slams into my vocal box like a freight train. I hit the ground, on my hands and knees, eyes squeezed shut as I fight the song.

"The spell can't be completed unless you sing just one more time." Eric's grin is savage.

My dad bends low, his words in my ear. "I love you, Caoine. Everything I've ever done was for this moment. I've never regretted a single moment of my life. Your mother made the choice years ago, even though she knew she was going to die. She asked me to guide you, to help you find your way. And you have, Caoine. You know who you are now. Make me proud, baby. Use your gift for good." He looks toward Eric, who still stands with a smug smile. "It's time I joined your mother in the afterlife." My dad smiles. "I've missed her so much."

"Daddy," I beg again, my jaw tight. My cheeks are hot with tears.

He gently kisses my forehead. Then he's running. Racing into the circle, past the faerie magic meant to stop faeries, unable to hold humans. He runs right to Eric.

The boy with the knife.

Eric lets go of Oliver a second too late. My dad's fist connects with the Unseelie prince's jaw. But an old man isn't a challenge for someone as strong as the Unseelie king's son. Eric grabs my dad by the neck; my dad's hands press against Eric's chest. The faerie pushes against my dad, backs him up step after step after step.

Exactly as I saw it happen in my vision.

No! I want to scream, to cry out. To beg my dad to retreat. But I can't, not without my song breaking loose. I can't let my song break loose or the spell will be complete.

But it's too late. I know that now. My dad has made his choice, and I've made mine.

To embrace the light side of me means to allow my visions to come true.

I must allow my vision to come true.

Eric's knife comes down, deep inside my dad's chest.

My dad's eyes go wide for a split second.

Then they gently settle on mine. A thousand memories of a thousand stolen moments flash through my vision all at once. Hugs and kisses, laughter and tears. Daddy-daughter dates and moments cleaning up his empty beer cans. But every single one of them screams that he loves me. And I love him.

He gives a slight nod, the only sign he's ready to accept the fate he chose. Then he grabs Eric's shirt with both hands. Eric struggles to get away, but the momentum of my dad falling backward is too much. Both of them fall through the open gate into the Unseelie Realm.

69

CAOINE

SILENCE. All movement and sound have ceased. The moon still shines bright overhead; the air that clings to my skin is still just as frigid. Otherwise, there is nothing. Not a single animal makes a peep. Even the wind has given up her rage against the powers of good and evil. All is still.

I blink and breathe. *Is this a dream?*

The spots where the two rectangles hung are now empty. Void. All that remain are trees and grass and all the things that had been there before the battle for the Faerie Realms began.

"Caoine?" Aubree says softly.

I gasp and look at her. That's my name. *I'm Caoine.* I look back to the spot where my dad disappeared. He's gone.

Gone forever.

My fingers tremble as I reach up, feel moisture on my face. That's right. I've been crying. Crying because I just lost my dad. How can this be? How could he be standing beside me one second and gone the next? A dam breaks inside me, and the fragile shell of my soul cracks in two.

Arms—warm, solid arms are around me. I lean into Aubree's embrace and don't bother to stop the flow of emotion that falls from my eyes, the sobs that wrack my shoulders.

My dad sacrificed himself for me. For Oliver.

Oliver!

I pull in a sharp breath and jump up, pushing away from Aubree.

"Caoine?"

My legs wobble as I scramble to my feet. "Oliver."

He's unconscious. He must've been too close to the gates when the whole thing went down. I'm on the ground beside him in seconds, my fingers at his neck to check his pulse. I exhale in relief. He's alive!

His eyes flutter as he groans, but I'm already working on the gag. He coughs like a baby with croup once I do get it off. I pat his back as he struggles to his knees, still hunched over. He doesn't need to ask me for help with the rope around his wrists. As soon as he's free, he bends them and rubs his hands, a wince on his face.

"Oliver?" My voice is soft.

He closes and opens his eyes slowly, as if in a spell. *Oh no.* What if Eric somehow took his memories? My heart stammers over hidden rocks inside my chest, and an icy spike stabs my gut once more. Did my dad sacrifice himself just for me to lose the one I love in the end anyway?

Oliver looks at me. Blinks. Then, "Caoine?"

My shoulders sag in relief, and new tears flood my face. He's okay. I tackle him with a hug that sends him tumbling backward once more. This time he isn't frowning, though. His hands are on my waist, and his lips are on mine before I even have to ask.

He pulls back. "I don't understand. How am I alive? I thought your song was for me?"

I open my mouth, but a stone lodges in my throat, threatens to choke me. "That was only one possibility," I finally say.

"What? But how?"

"Yes, do tell, Caoine. What just happened?" Aubree stands above us, frowning.

I swallow and clear my throat, shake my head. "I'm not positive. I think my dad may have had a better understanding of my gift than I do." Another wave of pain slams my chest. "He always told me my curse wasn't a curse at all, but a gift. A thing I can use to help others."

"Yeah, silly." Aubree gives me a sad smile. "I've been trying to tell you that, too."

I nod. "He said the faerie who made me this way said I was a protector. I never understood what she meant, since all I ever do is predict death. But he never lost faith. He always believed there was more to my cur—um, *gift*, than we knew." I lick my lips. "I never wanted to keep my cloak's hood in place after my song because I would see images, visions of more death. And it hurt. But he had an idea that finally clicked in place tonight, I guess."

Aubree's eyes are sad, but she offers me a small smile.

"He told me to keep my hood up this time," I continue. "To relax and accept my gift. Not to fight it. And the pain went away. It didn't hurt anymore." I'm astonished to hear my own words come out of my mouth. "I've left it on before, but the images I saw always ended in the person's death. I didn't understand how to prevent it. But I think I know now. I understand."

"How?" Oliver asks.

I nibble my lip. "Well, this time, I saw you die, that much is true." I reach out and take his hand to remind myself he's really alive. "But then, right after it, I saw an image of my dad and Eric falling through the gate, exactly as it happened. A different ending to what could be."

"So it was your dad's choice to take Oliver's place? He changed the vision?" Aubree's eyes are wide with wonder.

I shake my head. "No, he didn't change it. He only took one

possibility. Oliver's death wasn't imminent. He could've died, but his time here on earth wasn't necessarily finished. The other vision I had, the last time I kept my hood up, was of a woman who kept dying over and over again. It was her time to pass on to the afterlife." I press my lips together. "I believe some of my visions are finite. There will be nothing I can do to stop that person's death. But others—" I bite my lip again. "I think I'm meant to help save people, to stop unnecessary deaths."

"So when you sing your song, you'll be able to see if that person is able to be saved?" Oliver asks. I nod. He runs a hand along my cheek. "Then you really are a protector, Caoine. You do have a gift."

My face warms, and my insides war over whether I should be crying over the loss of my dad or the fact I hold the man I love in my arms.

"Well, I guess two good things came out of tonight, then," Aubree says. "We stopped the Unseelie prince from finishing his spell—"

"And I found my gift." I lean against Oliver and sigh. "I finally found my gift."

70

CAOINE

OLIVER'S ARMS wrap around my body and pull me against his chest as we sit on the dock. He's brought me to the same lake we went to the night he found out who I truly was. *Who I am.*

It looks different during the day, with the sun so bright overhead. A gentle breeze laps the water along the sandy shore and against the wooden posts of the docks. Clouds are reflected in the serene gray-blue of the water. It almost tricks my mind into thinking it's summer.

Life has almost returned to normal. The new normal.

A normal without my dad.

A normal of living alone. Sort of.

Aubree agreed to move in with me so I wouldn't have to deal with a house all by myself. Having officially turned eighteen, I don't need to worry about social services, and with Aubree's faerie magic, our bills somehow magically get paid. Another plus of being less than human, I guess.

Goose pimples pop all over my skin as a sudden gust of wind tosses my hair and makes my jacket flap open. *Or not.* I shiver and pull it closed. These quiet, stolen moments won't be spent here much longer. The threat of winter is firmly upon us.

My heart sinks a little knowing I'll need to wait until spring to appreciate the beauty of this place again.

"What are you thinking?" he asks.

I sigh. "Nothing." *Everything.*

He places a gentle kiss along my neck then rests his chin on my shoulder as we both watch a lonely bird skim the top of the water. He's probably the last of his kind, ready to head south. I run my fingers along Oliver's hands, his skin. His warmth radiates heat through my body.

"What about you?" I ask. "What are you thinking?"

He pauses, clears his throat. "Um, well, I'm wondering how long it will take for me to hear back."

I look at him quizzically.

"From Boston School of Music."

I blink, push against his chest. "You didn't!"

He laughs. "I did. I applied last week. I'm going to pursue a career in music."

I gasp, then throw my arms around his neck. "Oliver! I'm so happy for you. I can't believe this. This is amazing!" I freeze, my gaze on his. "But what about—I mean, what about your parents?"

Oliver licks his lips, nods. "They weren't super happy. Worried about how I'm going to support myself, of course. Totally understandable, actually. I mean, I get it." He scratches the back of his neck. "Being a musician is hard. Crazy hard. But—" He bites his lip. "I can't imagine doing anything else. They said they'd support me no matter what I do. It's time I start living my life for me, not other people."

I close my eyes, lean my forehead against his. "I'm so happy for you. You've got a gift, Oliver. You really do."

"Speaking of which. Did you see the news?"

"Mm." I did, but I don't mind letting him tell me again.

"Three car pileup on the highway this morning, no casualties."

I close my eyes and smile.

"Everyone walked away with minor injuries. Thanks to you."

My lips find his for a moment before I pull back and look at him. "No. You're the one who told them."

He nuzzles my nose with his. "And you're the one who saw the vision."

This is true. Over the past two weeks, we've managed to save five lives. Five whole lives that would've been lost had I insisted on pulling off my hood, as I've done for so many years.

Yet, for those who died, I sang their lament with peace. Welcoming them into the afterlife that awaits. Because even though their time on earth is done, there is still something more for them, something beautiful. It's not my fault they must leave their home, but it is my privilege to usher them into something greater.

What matters now is we're saving lives. Like this morning. If Oliver hadn't caught up with the mother of the teenage boy who was going to die and warned her to be sure he had his seatbelt on, then the boy would've joined the throng of others gone from our earth. True, not everyone was convinced when we told them of their predicted death, but for whatever reason, they all listened. So far. The threat of death will do that to a person, I guess.

"Another one saved," Oliver says.

"Are you keeping tally?"

He chuckles. "Maybe I should. Then it would be even more proof for you down the road if you ever doubt your abilities."

And one more reason my dad's death was not in vain. Renewed pain washes across my chest, and I blink back tears. The past few weeks have been hard without him. So much harder than I thought they would ever be. Some days I wasn't sure I'd make it through. But I have, with the help of Oliver and my friends. My dad will forever be in my heart. I'm not sure I'll ever truly get over his death. But his sacrifice has meaning. I see it in every life saved and will continue to do so until I die.

I swallow back emotion and take peace in the fact his sacrifice is a gift to a fallen world.

I turn to him. "What about you? Do you have any doubts about dating a banshee?" I give him a coy smile he kisses away.

"Not even a single one." He rests his forehead against mine. "I'll be here by your side forever, Caoine. Until the day you sing your song to me and I know the inevitable is coming. Then I'll hold you in my arms until I'm gone."

I force myself to breathe. "I don't deserve you."

He shakes his head. "No, Caoine. The world doesn't deserve one as good as you. Always remember that."

I nod. *Always remember.*

My life was never a curse, but a gift, one to help save others and make the world a better place. I know this now, thanks to my first real friends and a dad who gave me so much more than just his life.

"Always remember," I whisper before he places one more kiss on my lips.

I'll always remember. I am banshee. I am blessed. I am protector.

THE END

Do not miss

Lament

Book Two of the Banshee Song Series.

Coming Soon from L2L2 Publishing.

ACKNOWLEDGMENTS

I SEE YOU, Reader. I appreciate you. Thank you for taking this journey with Caoine and me. Singing has always been a part of my life. When I thought about writing a book about a girl who sings, all I could think was, "But will anyone read it?" And you did. For that, I am forever grateful. Thank you.

For my husband, Tim. Going on that trip to China was the best decision I ever made. You have made the past two decades more amazing than my wildest dreams. Thank you for being my Oliver. Thank you for your patience, love, and for being my cheerleader even before I realized I needed one.

My beautiful Gabrielle. You were my inspiration for Caoine. She became all the strength I see in you. Gracie, my love. This story was born while we bonded watching *Teen Wolf*. You will forever be engrained within these words. Scarlett, sweetheart. Thank you from the bottom of my heart for spending so much time with those Barbies so Mommy could write. Now let's snuggle.

Mom and Wayne, Dad and Judy. Thank you for your support throughout the years. Dad, you instilled the love of storytelling within me. The countless hours we've spent talking and creating stories will remain with me always. For that, I am grateful. There's always another story to write!

Paige. You are the best big sister, ever. Your excitement over everything I write is contagious and beautiful. Love you.

My agents at Hartline Literary. Cyle. Thank you for taking a chance on me and helping this clueless girl manage the world of getting published. And for cheering me on to pitch, pitch, pitch! Tessa, my sounding board. Thank you for all of your encouraging words and walking beside me on this adventure. I can't wait for the next one to begin!

Michele, Jebraun, and the whole L2L2 Team! Thank you for all of your patience as this newbie stumbled her way through the publishing process. *covers eyes* I am so thankful to call L2L2 family. Michele, I'm ready to visit Paris whenever you are! Jeb, your excitement over *Keen* made me want to read my own book!

My beta readers, a.k.a. Superheroes with Red Pens! Jill, Kelly, Ora, Brandy. Your input made this book happen. Thank you for your honesty. Thank you for your love. I can never repay you.

Jill. There are no words. You are my heartbeat in the north. You have my back, you pick me up when I'm a puddle, you are my biggest cheerleader. Thank you.

Brandy. Again, where do I find the words? We have read every YA novel written and spent a million hours discussing them. You didn't laugh when I asked you to read my zombie books, ten years ago. You've supported every crazy idea I've had for a story ever since. You can always be the first to read my books. Robert and Ellie, too. *wink*

My amazing critique groups. The Scribes. Keep a Thursday night open for me, I'm headed your way! The Armorers. You've supported me with all my writing. You guys rock!

My Street Team, the Caffeinated Readers. Thank you for your unending support. You took a chance on me, even before this baby was in print. *blows kisses* See you all at the coffee shop for a celebration latte!

Katie Phillips. My personal genius. Your coaching was invaluable for getting this book into print. *hugs* I'm still planning that trip to Kansas.

Allen Arnold. After hearing you speak at my very first writer's conference, I knew I wanted to stay on course with what God had laid on my heart. Your obedience in writing The Story of With changed the way I write. Your faithful encouragement and fellowship help me love the way I write. Thank you for listening to our Lord and doing what you do.

My Savior. My Jesus. The greatest storyteller of all time. Nothing I create is ever created without you. I am forever grateful for the path you've set me on. Proverbs 3:5-6.

Journey into the night and find your song, Reader.

~Laura

CAOINE'S SONG

Music has always been a big part of my life, so when it came time to write Caoine's story, it felt natural to put a strong focus on her song and how it would feel to hear such beauty. Thankfully, I'm surrounded by talented friends who can bring my crazy dreams to life! Special thanks to Delany Callahan-Bird for capturing Caoine's heart and soul in song!

Scan the QR Code to hear Caoine's song. ("'Caoine's Fan Song" written and performed by Delany Callahan-Bird.)

ABOUT THE AUTHOR

LAURA L. ZIMMERMAN lives in a suburb of Charlotte, North Carolina with her husband, three daughters, and three furbaby felines. As a child, she became convinced she was a mermaid, which she still believes to this day. Being a mythological creature, she caught the traveling bug at an early age and spent two-and-a-half years with a missionary organization roaming the world.

During her travels she met her Mr. Darcy, and they married soon after. Recently, she and her family moved across the country twice in a ridiculously short amount of time, but she's happy to report she plans to stay put for a good number of years, thank you very much.

Laura is currently a stay-at-home mom and home educator by day, drinker of coffee by night. Besides writing, she's passionate about loving Jesus, fangirling over anything *Star Wars*, and singing loudly. An avid reader, she often has overdue library fines and a TBR pile as tall as Trump Tower.

Her favorite form of writing is flash fiction, which is evident from the number of stories she's produced on her blog and contests she's entered—and even judged! You can catch her in a bookstore, coffee shop, or local movie theater, most likely shoveling popcorn in her mouth.

This is her debut novel.

Laura loves to hear from her readers! Follow her on social media, check out her website, or drop her a line to let her know what you thought of Keen. *Happy reading!*

———

www.LauraLZimmerman.Wordpress.com
Facebook: @AuthorLLZimmerman
Twitter: @LauraLZimm
Instagram: @LauraLZimmAuthor

REVIEWS

Did you know reviews can skyrocket a book's career? Instead of fizzling into nothing, a book will be suggested by Amazon, shared by Goodreads, or showcased by Barnes & Noble. Plus, authors treasure reviews! (And read them over and over and over . . .)

If you enjoyed this book, would you consider leaving a review on:

- Amazon
- Barnes & Noble
- Goodreads

. . . or perhaps even your personal blog? Thank you so much!

~The L2L2 Publishing Team

More from L2L2 Publishing

If you enjoyed this book, you may also enjoy:

Leah spends her days scrubbing floors, polishing silver, and meekly curtsying to nobility. Nothing distinguishes her from the other commoners serving at the palace, except her red hair. And her secret friendship with Rafe, the Crown Prince of Imperia. But Leah's safe, ordinary world begins to splinter. Rafe's parents announce his betrothal to a foreign princess, and she unearths a plot to overthrow the royal family. When she reports it without proof, her life shatters completely when the queen banishes her for treason. Harbored by an unusual group of nuns, Leah must secure Rafe's safety before it's too late. But her quest reveals a villain far more sinister than an ambitious nobleman with his eye on the throne. Can a common maidservant summon the courage to fight for her dearest friend?

Jocelyn plunges into the ocean near Calcutta, India, thrown overboard by a man claiming it's the only way to save her life. As she sinks, the transformation begins, and the ocean welcomes her back into its embrace. Jocelyn drifts in a world she'd forgotten only to find she's hunted by a deadly force from the ancient city of Thessa, the reason she was hidden in the world above. But she cannot get Aidan out of her head. Was what they shared real? Or was it a fantasy brought on by her unconscious need to seduce a human? Both Aidan and Jocelyn begin a desperate and dangerous journey to discover the truth . . . and hopefully each other. But will their love be enough?

More from L2L2 Publishing

If you enjoyed this book, you may also enjoy:

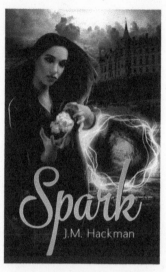

Brenna James wants three things for her sixteenth birthday: to find her history notes before the test, to have her mother return from her business trip, and to stop creating fire with her bare hands. Yeah, that's so not happening. Unfortunately. When Brenna learns her mother is missing in an alternate reality called Linneah, she travels through a portal to find her. Against her will. Who knew portals even existed? But Brenna's arrival in Linneah begins the fulfillment of an ancient prophecy, including a royal murder and the theft of Linneah's most powerful relic: the Sacred Veil. Hold up. Can everything just slow down for a sec? Left with no other choice, Brenna and her new friend Baldwin pursue the thief into the dangerous woods of Silvastamen. When they spy an army marching toward Linneah, Brenna is horrified. Can she find the veil, save her mother, and warn Linneah in time?

More from L2L2 Publishing

If you enjoyed this book, you may also enjoy:

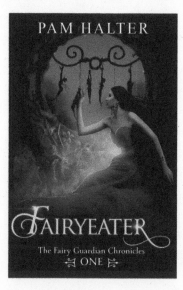

All fifteen-year-old Akeela has ever wanted is a family that will love her. But the only mother she has ever known is the old hag, Krezma, who berates her night and day. Why did the old woman even take her in?
But Krezma knows her charge is no ordinary child. She can see auras and can communicate with fairies. And the birthmark on her palm reveals a secret Krezma must hold close for the child's safety. A secret that the witch, Tzmet, hunts for night and day, drying and eating fairies for the power they contain. When Akeela discovers her fate lies in being the next Fairy Guardian, all hope for an ordinary life dissipates like a dream. She must protect the fairies from the witch—and an even darker power that threatens them all.

More from L2L2 Publishing

If you enjoyed this book, you may also enjoy:

Ro remembers the castle before. Before the gates closed. Before silence overtook the kingdom. Before the castle disappeared. Now it shimmers to life one night a year, seen by her alone. Once a lady, now a huntress, Ro does what it takes to survive, just like the rest of the kingdom plunged into despair never before known. But a beast has overtaken the castle; a beast that killed the prince and holds the castle and kingdom captive in his cruel power. A beast Ro has been hired to kill. Thankful the mystery of the prince's disappearance has been solved, furious the magical creature has killed her hero, Ro eagerly accepts the job to end him. But things are not as they seem. Trapped in the castle, a prisoner alongside the beast, Ro wonders what she should fear most: the beast, the magic that holds them both captive, or the one who hired her to kill the beast.

WHERE WILL WE TAKE YOU NEXT?

Enjoy *Common,*
Sink into *Drifting,*
Discover *Spark,*
Devour *Fairyeater,*
and Delight in *Kill the Beast.*

All at
www.love2readlove2writepublishing.com/bookstore
or your local or online retailer.

Happy Reading!
~The L2L2 Publishing Team

ABOUT L2L2 PUBLISHING

Love2ReadLove2Write Publishing, LLC is a small traditional press, dedicated to clean or Christian speculative fiction.

Speculative genres include but are not limited to: Fantasy, Science Fiction, Fairy Tales, Magical Realism, Time Travel, Spiritual Warfare, Alternate History, Chillers (such as vampires, zombies, werewolves, or light horror), Superhero Fiction, Steampunk, Supernatural, Paranormal, etc., or a mixture of any of the previous.

We seek stunning tales masterfully told, and we strive to create an exquisite publishing experience for our authors and to produce quality fiction for our readers.

Keen is at the heart of what we publish: a riveting tale with speculative elements that will delight our readers.

Visit www.L2L2Publishing.com to view our submissions guidelines, find our other titles, or learn more about us.

Happy Reading!

~The L2L2 Publishing Team